Anthony Capella is based in London and Oxford [...] novel. He writes regular travel pieces for the *Sun[...]* researches exotic foods.

Visit his website at www.anthonycapella.com

Praise for *The Wedding Officer*

'This is one of those delicious, unashamedly feel-good stories that begs to be read in the sun – preferably an Italian sun, as the book makes you long to be there, sipping at a beaker full of the warm south'
The Times

'Full of the same colour and verve as Capella's *The Food of Love*, this story also blends romance with gourmet delights'
Good Housekeeping

'*The Wedding Officer* resembles a cross between *Captain Corelli's Mandolin* and *Chocolat*, while remaining a charming and powerful fiction in its own right'
Michael Arditti

'This gently erotic book is so precisely of our time. The construction is simple but elegant and the writing sensitive . . . You are gracefully transported from page to page when you should be madly licking fingers and scrabbling to turn them . . . Capella's lightness of touch also conjures comedy set-ups with the delightful anticipation and resolution of any Marx brother classic . . . Brilliantly carries off a sentimental ruse worthy of any fifties Hollywood caper'
Sunday Express

'Food, Italy and romance are Anthony Capella's trademark topics. He combines all three deliciously in *The Wedding Officer*'
InStyle

'An enjoyable caper'
Mirror

'The descriptions of food are so mouth-watering, they may send you to the fridge in search of goodies! . . . An irresistible combination of love, humour and delicious food'
Yours

ALSO BY ANTHONY CAPELLA

The Food of Love
The Wedding Officer
The Various Flavours of Coffee

THE
EMPRESS
OF
ICE CREAM

Anthony Capella

McArthur & Company
Toronto

First published in Canada in 2010 by
McArthur & Company
322 King Street West, Suite 402
Toronto, Ontario
M5V 1J2
www.mcarthur-co.com

Library and Archives Canada Cataloguing in Publication

Capella, Anthony
    The empress of ice cream / Anthony Capella.

ISBN 978-1-55278-875-2

    1. Kéroualle, Louise-Renée de, Duchess of Portsmouth and Aubigny, 1649-1734—Fiction. 2. Charles II, King of England, 1630-1685—Fiction. 3. Louis XIV, King of France, 1638-1715—Fiction. I. Title.

PR6103.A64E47 2010   823'.92   C2010-903985-8

Cover photograph © Trevellion/Rebecca Parker
Cover illustration © Sarah Coleman
Cover design LBBG – Sam Combes
Typeset in Galliard by M Rules
Printed in Canada by Webcom

10 9 8 7 6 5 4 3 2 1

Let be be finale of seem.
The only emperor is the emperor of ice cream.

Wallace Stevens, 'The Emperor of Ice Cream'

For Louise Denne BCBA

Editor's Note

For many decades the sheaf of seventeenth-century papers discovered in the Great Library at Ditchley Park, which subsequently came to be known as the Ditchley Bundle, remained largely ignored by scholars. Like many texts of that turbulent period it was written in code, one apparently even more impenetrable than that employed by Samuel Pepys. It was not until the sale of the Bundle, along with dozens of other old manuscripts, to America in the late 1990s that an archivist – actually a bright young intern from Wellesley – wondered what might happen if the source material were written not in English but in French, and the hitherto private journal of Louise de Keroualle, mistress to King Charles II, was revealed to the world.

It seems that at some point during her time in England Louise began to write in her native tongue an encrypted account of her life at the English court. Whether this was to alleviate homesickness, as an insurance policy in case of arrest, or, as has most recently been suggested, as a kind of substitute for the confession she could no longer make to a priest – being by now, of course, in a state of unrepentant mortal sin – we cannot know. Nor do such speculations arise naturally from the manuscript itself, which in places reads more like a modern political strategy document or manifesto for a united Europe than a memoir; and which, despite her ostensible position in the royal household, actually contains far less in the way of salacious detail than, for example, Pepys' diary does. In making these extracts I have concentrated on Louise's personal experiences of the court and her circle, rather than on her involvement in the grand intrigues and plots that preoccupied much of Europe at the time, which are already ably described elsewhere.

Carlo Demirco's treatise – if that is not too grand a word for the preface to a practical book of recipes – needs far less introduction. Food historians have long been fascinated by the history of ice cream and, in particular, by the fact that the first recorded mention of it anywhere in the world comes in England, on the menu of a ceremonial feast given by King Charles II for the Knights of the Garter in 1671 – the same year, incidentally, that Louise became his mistress. Carlo Demirco is not the only person who can claim to be ice cream's progenitor – one must also consider rival accounts such as Lucian Audiger's *La Maison Réglée*, published in Paris in 1692 – but it is the only one which explains all the known circumstances, such as the fact that at the Garter Feast the royal confectioner served only a single bowl of ice cream, for the king's table alone; and which contains recipes to back up his assertions: recipes, moreover, many of which are still in use today.

Demirco's book – first printed in 1678, translated into five languages by the end of the century, republished during the great ice cream craze of the Georgian era as *The Book of Ices*, and only forgotten once modern refrigeration methods finally made his techniques outdated – may seem an odd companion piece to the secret, encrypted memoir of a royal courtesan, particularly one as generally unpopular as Louise, whom both the public of her own day and modern historians alike tend to view as an unprincipled representative of a particularly avaricious age. Perhaps the publication, finally, of these parts of her journal may go some way to presenting her in a different light. Intriguingly, there is good evidence that the two documents – the recipes and the diary – once lay side by side together in the Bundle during its long sojourn in the library cupboard: the kitchen stains which adorn the pages of *The Book of Ices* suggest that, at some stage in the intervening three hundred years, the Bundle was discovered and only Demirco's volume removed, being subsequently put to a use of which its author would surely have approved.

PART ONE

Carlo

To chill wine: take a block of ice or snow well pressed; split it and crack it and crush it to powder, as fine as you like; place it in a silver bucket, and push your flagon deep within.

The Book of Ices

It is the custom, in such writings as I now embark on, to begin by describing the circumstances of the author's birth, and thus by what genuine authority he may claim to address the reader (his position in life, what he has achieved, and so forth, naturally being determined by his place in society).

Alas! I can make no such claim, my birth being humble and my upbringing mean.

I was, I believe, no more than seven or eight years old when the Persian, Ahmad, took me from my family. All I can now recall of the island where my parents lived was how the groves of almond trees turned white in the spring, like the snow on top of the great volcano which looked down on them, and the greenness of the sea on which my father fished. This same sea brought us ships such as the one on which Ahmad had come, seeking a child to take into his employ. Seeing my father and I mending nets together, he spoke to my parents of the great life that I would follow, of the grandeurs of Florence and the marvellous court in which I would be placed. From that day on I found myself in the service of a cruel and capricious master. Not Ahmad – although he was stern, he was no worse than many others. No, the master who treated me so harshly was ice itself.

Once we had arrived in Florence, one of my first tasks was to transport the heavy blocks from the ice house in the Boboli Gardens to the palace kitchens. The first time I did this, the curiosity of playing with the frozen slabs – of seeing how they slid away from me like eels, how I could sit astride them and ride them like trolley-carts down the grassy parts of the slope, or shoot them at the kitchen wall from a distance and watch them shatter into dozens of jewel-like shards – enchanted me so much that, in a state of childish enthusiasm, I neglected my other duties.

When Ahmad found me in the courtyard, surrounded by dozens of ruined, glittering ice blocks, he did not at first show the displeasure which my ill discipline warranted. 'Come with me,' he said. He took me to the ice house, ushered me in, and locked the door.

Inside, in contrast to the heat of Florence, it was as cold as the temperature at which water becomes ice. I was wearing only a thin hose and shirt, together with the blue apron all apprentices wore. After a few minutes I began to shake. The cold felt like a flame, or a knife that was being dragged through my skin. After half an hour I was shivering with so much violence I drew blood from my own tongue.

Not long after that, I felt the shivering stop. At last I am getting used to it, I thought. A great tiredness was seeping through me. I was, I realised, drifting off to sleep. I could still feel the searing cold, but my body was no longer capable of fighting it. I felt my defences crumbling; felt it entering the innermost recesses of my flesh. It was not exhaustion I experienced now so much as an inner numbness, as if my limbs themselves were hardening, one by one, turning me into a statue, as cold and lifeless as the *David* of Florence itself. I tried to cry out, but my scream was somehow also frozen within me, and I found I could not so much as open my mouth.

The next thing I remember I was being carried into the kitchens. I woke up looking into my master's dark eyes, before the Persian dropped me unceremoniously to the floor.

4

'You won't do that again,' he said as he turned to go.

I never again played with the ice. But something else had changed too. It was not just that I no longer trusted my master. The cold I had felt never seemed to completely leave my body, so that there was always a sliver or two of ice deep within my bones, and – perhaps – even within my soul.

A few days after my incarceration in the ice house, the middle finger of my right hand began to turn black. Ahmad inspected it without remark, then summoned two of his brothers to hold my arm down on a block of ice while he amputated the finger at the knuckle with a cleaver. Warm blood spurted onto the ice, turning to pink crystals as it froze.

'It won't affect your work,' he said when I stopped screaming.

Each night, as tired as a dog and half frozen to death, I crawled into the palace kitchen to sleep next to one of the big, open fireplaces on which meat was roasted *alla brace*, over embers. The kitchen workers grew used to me, and no longer chased me out with brooms and knives. I began to watch the cooks as they went about their work; observing how they pureed fruits to intensify their flavours; how they extracted the perfumes of violets and orange flowers to flavour creams and liqueurs; how they made a verjuice from grapes and quinces to set the lighter fruits. But when I tried to suggest to Ahmad that these techniques could be of use in our own work, my master was scornful.

'We are engineers, not cooks,' he liked to say. 'Cooking is women's business. We know the secrets of ice.'

Indeed, these were ancient secrets, a body of knowledge which had been passed down from father to son within a few Persian families, suppliers of sherbets to the court of Shah 'Abbas in Ishfahan. Some of this knowledge was contained in stained leather-bound notebooks, their pages covered in diagrams and spidery Arabic writing. But most was kept only in Ahmad's head, in a set of rules and maxims he followed as blindly as any ignorant country priest reciting a Latin liturgy he does not truly understand.

'To five measures of crushed ice, add three measures of saltpetre,' he would intone.

'Why?' I would say.

'Why what?'

'Why must the ice be crushed? And what difference does saltpetre make?'

'What does it matter? Now stir the mixture clockwise, twenty-seven times.'

'Perhaps the humour of saltpetre is heat, and the humour of ice is cold, and so adding the one to the other means that—'

'And perhaps I may beat you with the paddle, if you do not use it to stir the ice.'

I had been working for the Persian almost two years before I dared to ask what the ices we made tasted like.

'Taste? What does the taste matter to you, child?' Ahmad said scornfully.

I knew that I had to be careful how I answered if I was to avoid yet another beating. 'Sir, I have seen how the cooks try their dishes as they make them. I think I will understand better how to make these ices if I know how they are meant to taste.'

We were making an ice flavoured with a syrup of the small sweet oranges that some call china oranges, and some mandarins. The syrup was thickened further with orange pulp, and scented with the aromatic oils extracted from the rind, before being poured over a pile of grated ice. 'Very well,' Ahmad said, gesturing at the pot with a shrug. 'Try some, if that is what you wish.' Before he could change his mind I took a spoon, scooped out a little of the confection, and put it to my lips.

Ice crystals cracked and crunched against my teeth. I felt them dissolving on my tongue – a cold, sparkling sensation as they shrivelled away to nothing – then the syrup ran down my throat, cold and thick and sugary. The taste swelled in my mouth like the sudden ripening of the orange fruit itself. I gasped with pleasure: then, a moment later, a terrible pain shot up inside my head as the cold gripped my throat, choking me, and I spluttered.

Ahmad's lip curled with amusement. 'Now, perhaps, you understand that it is not a dish for children. Or for the general populace, there being no nourishment in it. We are here to entertain, boy, not to feed. We are like singers, or actors, or painters, makers of fine meaningless baubles for the wealthy and the great: that is to say, kings, courtiers, cardinals and their courtesans. No one but them will ever be able to waste so much expense on something that melts to nothing on their lips even faster than a song melts on the evening air.'

But, once I had got over the initial strangeness, I found that the taste was one I could not forget. It had not simply been that extraordinary flavour of sweet, concentrated oranges; it was the ice itself, its cold, frozen grittiness, calling to me. From then on, without Ahmad knowing, I made sure I tasted every confection we made. And I never again spluttered when I felt the coldness grip my throat.

One night I found the whole kitchen smelling dark and pungent, as if livers were being cooked in a sauce of fortified wine; but this smell had a richness to it that was like no offal I had ever known. It was coming from a small saucepan on the range, where something thick and brown spat like hot lava as the cook stirred it with a wooden spoon. 'Xocalatl,' the cook said, as he poured the contents of the pan into a small cup for the Grand Duke's nightcap: then, seeing my incomprehension, he offered me the end of the spoon to taste.

That is another memory I have never forgotten, one of a different kind: a heat that filled my mouth and coated my palate, leaving it full of the same rich taste for hours afterwards; bitter and thick, yet strangely warming, like the very opposite of ice.

Carlo

To make a sorbet of apricots: stone and scald twelve apricots in season, and pass them through a sieve: take six ounces of soft moscado sugar, and beat the mixture with a little cream of lemonade. Simmer altogether, then put it in the freezing pot and work it very fine.

The Book of Ices

It was my great good fortune that there was among the Medici princesses at this time a lady called Cosima de' Medici, who never married. Instead she dedicated her life, and the considerable portion of Medici wealth entailed on her, to good works, of which just one was to establish a kind of schoolhouse for urchins, orphans and the children of her servants, under the tutelage of two or three great men of learning. I was fortunate enough to join this group, my master being too fearful of his own position to pretend that he was anything other than delighted with the plan. I cannot now imagine what those eminent thinkers and scholars thought about having to teach the rudiments of book learning to a collection of *ragazzi* like us, but such is the power of wealth that three times a week we all trooped into the great *biblioteca* above the Canons' Cloister and parsed our first letters from the priceless manuscripts it contained. Princessa Cosima was criticised for this scheme, I believe, most particularly by churchmen, for it was said that nothing but ill would come of spreading learning outside the Church, or of confusing poor ignorant children such as ourselves about our place in the natural order of things. But my education was not only of benefit to me in the matter of book learning. I did not purposefully study those around me and try to copy their manners, but just as a child will learn to speak the language of his parents simply by hearing it, so growing up in that court I acquired without realising it something of the manners and easy demeanour of a gentleman. I believe, too, that it was being tutored in Latin from such an early age that was responsible for my fluency with languages – a skill that has been almost as useful to me as my abilities with ice.

As the years passed, I gradually came to despise my master. For all that he took great care to ensure that I remained in mortal fear of him, he was a man in fear himself; and what he was principally afraid of was that someone would steal his secrets. He often told the story of the famous cook, *chef d'équipe* to a great nobleman, who was so proud of his creations that he decided to write his recipes down and publish them in a book. The book was a great success, widely copied and republished (with, of course, no further payment to the author); meanwhile, other cooks seized on the recipes and improved them, or simply served the dishes as if they were their own. The result was that the chef was dismissed, his position taken by a younger rival, and he died famous but destitute. It was, Ahmad said, an illustration of the folly of seeking acclaim instead of riches in this world.

I sometimes wondered why Ahmad was prepared to share his own knowledge so readily with me; but I soon decided that, so far as he was concerned, I was simply a workhorse, a creature incapable of reason. He taught me what he knew, not because he wanted to share his secrets, but because he wanted to share the labour. And so I learnt the difference between the four kinds of ice that could be made: *cordiale* or liquors, into which crushed snow was stirred to chill them; *granite*, shavings of frozen water over which were poured syrups made from rosewater or oranges; *sorbetti*, more complex water ices, in which it was the syrups themselves that were frozen, the mixture paddled as it hardened so that the fragments lay in the pot like a glittering mound of sapphires; and finally sherbets, the most difficult of all, made with milk that had been infused with mastic or cardamom, so that they resembled snow that had refrozen overnight. I learned how to construct chilled obelisks of jelly; how to use silversmiths' moulds to cast fantastic frozen plates and bowls, and how to carve the ice into extravagant table decorations. I mastered the spectacular entertainments of the great engineer Buontalenti, who had constructed fountains, tables, and even whole grottos out of ice. But I knew that if I so much as breathed a word of these techniques to anyone else, Ahmad would have me blinded and my tongue put out with one of the red-hot irons we used to carve ice sculptures. He hinted, too, that there were still secrets that I was not yet privy to: special ingredients and gums described in the notebooks which he was keeping to himself, to ensure that I would always know less than he did.

And yet the learning, I noticed, was all one way. As I have said, I often observed the cooks around us as they worked, and it sometimes seemed to me that the confections they came up with would make good syrups with which to flavour our ices. A summer *dolci* of lemon froth and dessert wine, for example, or slices of musk melon whose natural sweetness was offset with a sprinkling of ground ginger – these, surely, were tastes which would provide us with welcome variety. But if I suggested we try such a thing, even as an experiment, Ahmad would look at me as if I were mad.

'It is not one of the four flavours. If you don't believe me, look in the book.'

He was taunting me, of course: he knew I could not read the Arabic in his notebooks. Nor did I need to read them to know the handful of flavours – rosewater, orange, mastic and cardamom – which were all that the ancient vellum pages permitted.

It seemed to me, too, that if our ices had a drawback, it was that shooting pain which had gripped my throat as I crunched the orange-scented crystals between my teeth. It appeared to come from the action of biting down on the ice, and was thus presumably impossible to eradicate. We tried to make the crystals as small as possible, grating the ice from the blocks with a kind of chainmail gauntlet until they were as tiny as chips of salt or sugar: but once you went below a certain size the ice would melt away to water, and all that you had in your goblet or glass after that was a kind of orange- or rosewater-flavoured slush. I longed to make an ice that was as smooth and thick and soft as that chocolate the cook had offered me to taste; an ice that contained the cold of ice, without its harshness.

One day Ahmad was away from the kitchens with a toothache. He left me with strict instructions as to how I was to occupy my time, but evidently the tooth-pulling was more painful than he had anticipated, since he failed to return when he had said he would. At last I saw my chance.

Apricots were in season just then. The cooks served them to the Medici peeled and quartered, with the juice of melons and some cream. Taking a bowl that had already been prepared for the Grand Duke's table, I mashed it up, tipped the mixture into the *sabotiere*, the freezing pot, and waited eagerly for it to congeal, stirring it in the usual way.

It was not a success. The mixture froze, certainly, but the different parts had frozen in different ways – that is to say, there were rock-hard pieces of apricot, and crystals of frozen melon juice, but the cream had turned powdery, like curdled egg, and far from combining, the various elements appeared to have become more separate. When I tried to eat a spoonful of this granular mixture, the different parts did not even melt in the same way on my tongue, so that it was like chewing frozen gravel. But even so, there was something about the freshness of the fruit, and the sweetness of the melon juice, that was a refreshing change from the heavily perfumed flavours Ahmad insisted on.

A better solution, I realised, would be to make a simple apricot cordial or syrup and then freeze it – a *sorbetto*, in fact. The smoothness would have to wait for another time: it was the flavour of the fruit that was important here. I went to get another

11

dish of apricots, and witnessed a violent altercation between the cook who had prepared the previous one and a servant he was accusing of having stolen it. It was not the time to try to filch another. Besides, Ahmad might return at any moment, and I had to clean all the utensils before he realised what I had been up to.

And so I began a period in which I lived a double life. With Ahmad, during the day, I was a servant, following his instructions dutifully and without complaint. But by night I was a kind of alchemist, the kitchen my laboratory as I experimented with different combinations of flavour and ingredient. Nothing was too outlandish or ridiculous for me to try. I froze soft cheeses, *digestifs*, vegetable juices and even soups. I made ices from wine, from *pesto Genovese*, from almond milk, from crushed fennel, and from every different kind of cream. I experimented wildly, blindly, without method or purpose, hoping to chance on something – some method, some key – which I was sure existed somewhere: something that could unlock the deepest, frozen secrets of ice. It was as if the ice itself was calling to me, enticing me on: and, although I cannot claim that I ever truly got to the bottom of what would or would not work, just as a painter by practising at his palette will gain an understanding of what colours he must mix to achieve a given effect, so I gradually became more fluent in the language of tastes. Ahmad, I am sure, noted my increasing confidence, but doubtless put it down to the fact that I was becoming older in years.

There were other changes too. I was aware that I was becoming a man, from the fire igniting in my veins; and a reasonably good-looking man at that, from the admiring glances I received from the girls who worked in the kitchens, not to mention the ribald comments passed by their older, married colleagues. Then there was Emilia Grandinetti ... Like me, she was fifteen. Apprenticed to one of the seamstresses who made dresses for the court, she was the sweetest thing I had ever seen. Her skin was the colour of butter when it was heated in a pan: her teeth, and the whites of her eyes, were as clear and bright as snow in that dark, laughing face. Soon the glances between the two of us became smiles; flirtations became conversations; laughter turned to love. *I am the luckiest prince in all Florence*, I thought proudly. We spent stolen hours sitting on the roof of the palace where no one could see us, dizzy with love, holding hands and talking about our dreams.

'I'm going to be the greatest confectioner in the world,' I told her.

'Really? And how will you do that?' she teased.

'I'm going to make ices in a thousand flavours. The smoothest, richest ices that have ever been made.'

But when I told her I would make an ice especially for her and smuggle it out of the kitchen, she shook her head.

'I don't want to get you into trouble.'

I asked her about her hopes for the future too, but these were all about me: she wanted us to be together, to have a family; perhaps, if we were very fortunate, to see our children one day become servants of the Medici in their turn.

Marriage was forbidden to apprentices, but those who had their master's permission might become betrothed, and an apprentices' betrothal was considered almost the same as a marriage, if not quite in the eyes of God, then certainly in the eyes of those immediately below Him. So I waited for the most auspicious moment, and broached the matter with Ahmad.

We were working on a magnificent ice sculpture of a soaring eagle, the centrepiece of a table of iced jellies. I did most of the carving now, my hands wrapped in rags against the cold. Not only was my touch surer than my master's, and my eye truer, but I could bear the work for longer – almost as if the cold that had claimed my finger had at the same time numbed the rest of me against its effects. Or perhaps, I thought, as I polished the ice until

13

the sculpture seemed to glow from within, my master was simply getting old and lazy. I knew that on this occasion at least Ahmad was pleased with my work: when I had finished the Persian gave a nod and a grudging, 'Not bad.'

'Master, I have been thinking . . .' I began.

'Yes? What is it?'

'There is a girl I have become attached to. I was wondering if I could have your permission to become betrothed to her.'

Ahmad busied himself wiping down the table on which we had been working. 'What makes you think my permission will make any difference?'

'Those are the apprentices' rules, sir,' I reminded him. 'I may not marry without my master's consent.'

Ahmad shot me an amused glance. 'You see yourself as my apprentice, do you?'

'Of course,' I answered, surprised. 'What else?' For one delirious moment I wondered if he was about to say that he considered me no apprentice but his equal; perhaps even, one day, his partner.

'An apprenticeship is purchased,' he said briefly. 'Your parents were poor.'

'I don't understand. So poor that they could not afford to buy me an apprenticeship?'

'Poorer even than that. So poor that they were happy to sell you. You are no apprentice, boy, and never will be. You are my possession, and you will not be at liberty in your lifetime to become betrothed to any girl, let alone to marry.' He threw the handful of soaked rags to one side. 'Now take these outside and rinse them.'

It was the sliver of ice in my heart that saved me. But for that, I might have killed the Persian there and then, and to hell with the consequences.

Not to marry. That was bad enough, but if I was not at liberty to marry it also meant that I was not at liberty to become a craftsman in my own right. I would be Ahmad's chattel until the day I died. I would never get the opportunity to create anything of my own: I would go to my grave still churning out the four flavours of his damned notebooks. My life would have been wasted, my flesh and blood melting into the grave as surely as a block of ice left on a table melts away to water. At the thought of it a mute, terrible fury throbbed in my veins. But like a bulb in frozen ground I waited, my anger contained, until an opportunity presented itself.

The opportunity was a Frenchman called Lucian Audiger. I never discovered how he found me: presumably he bribed someone for information about the Persian ice makers and was told about an Italian youth who might be a weak link. Amassing information, truly, was Audiger's great skill, although he himself believed that he was driven only by a burning desire to become a great confectioner. That was why he had travelled – first to Spain, where he learnt the art of making seed waters such as pine-kernel, coriander, pistachio and anis; then to Holland, where he studied distillation, both of flowers and fruits; and from there to Germany, where he mastered the skill of making syrups. It was inevitable that he would eventually come to Italy, where both the Hapsburgs in Naples and the Medici in Florence were famous for mixing snow and ice into their wines and desserts.

He came to me in the middle of the night and shook me awake. The person who had brought him through the warren of service rooms slipped away, unseen, and by the time I was fully awake Audiger was already talking of Paris, of the glorious court that the young Louis XIV was constructing, the new palaces at Marly and Versailles; wealth to dwarf even the Medici's, and a city filled with fashionable men and women eager for new delights. Coffee and chocolate houses were opening all over Paris: those who could make iced drinks and chilled confections would never starve, and as a partnership – two young men who between us could create every kind of confection or novelty – we would surely enter the service of the king himself . . . By this time I was barely listening. I had heard all I needed to hear. If you were going to run away from the court of the Medici with a Persian's trade secrets in your head, you needed just two things: a patron at least the equal of the Medici, so that they could not simply demand your return, and for it to be somewhere a long, long way from the reach of a Persian's dagger.

'I have two conditions,' I said, when Audiger finally paused for breath.

'Name them.'

'Never to call anyone master. And twenty-four hours to convince Emilia to come too.'

'Done,' Audiger said, holding out his hand. 'I'll meet you by the Porta San Miniato at midnight tomorrow.'

As early as was respectable, the next morning I found Emilia outside the seamstresses' room. Drawing her aside, I told her of my plan.

'But . . .' she said. Her voice faltered. 'If you run away, you'll be caught. And then you'll be put in prison. Hanged, even.'

'It's the only way, now. Don't you see? There's nothing for us here. If we leave, at least we have a chance.'

She glanced around. 'I can't talk now. My mistress . . .'

'Emilia!' I hissed. 'I have to know. Are you coming or not?'

'I – I—' she said, glancing nervously at the door, and in that moment I saw that she was too afraid.

I said desperately, 'Look, I understand, *caro*. You loved me because you thought it was allowed. Now that you know it might get you into trouble, you're frightened. But this is the only opportunity either of us is going to get. I have to take it. The question is, will you come?'

'I will always love you,' she whispered.

I felt a great heaviness descending on me. 'That means no.'

'Please, Carlo. It's too risky—'

That night I was waiting by the Porta San Miniato long before the church bells struck midnight. By my side was a chest containing a sizeable haul of Ahmad's ice-making equipment.

We stopped the *diligence*, the high-speed mail coach drawn by six horses that went from Rome to Paris in long, non-stop stages. It did not usually take passengers; once again, Audiger seemed to have both the confidence and the money to bribe his way on board.

As we travelled north I looked out of the window. I had never before been further than Pisa, and I was thinking with an ache in my heart how each mile we covered was taking me further from Emilia.

'I have been thinking,' Audiger said.

I dragged my attention back inside the carriage. 'Yes?'

'Before we get to Paris we must get you some proper clothes.' The Frenchman indicated his own fashionable garb. 'It is important we do not look like tradesmen. At the French court, appearances are everything.'

I shrugged. 'Very well.'

'And we must think how best to approach the king. I know one of his valets: we can bribe our way into the royal presence, but it will be a waste of time unless we can present the king with a gift – something special, something which will make him talk about us to all the men and women of his court.'

'Very well.' I yawned. Now that the tension of our escape was behind us, I felt exhausted. 'We will make him an ice.'

Audiger shook his head. 'More special even than that.'

'I'll think on it.' It amazed me, this ability Audiger had to worry, not just about the next twenty-four hours, but about events that would not happen for days or weeks yet.

'There's something else.' Audiger hesitated. 'You said you would not have any man as your master. That is fair enough. But I think, nevertheless, that you should address me as your master when we are with others.'

I was fully awake now. 'Why?'

'It is simply that I am older than you. People will expect me to be in charge. And besides, I already have a certain reputation in Paris. It will seem strange if I turn up with an Italian ragamuffin in tow and treat him as an equal. Not that you are a ragamuffin, of course,' he said quickly. 'But that is how people may see it.'

Once again it was only the sliver of ice in my heart that made me restrain my anger. 'I said I would have no master.'

'And you will not have one. We will split our profits between us, that is completely understood. I will not *be* your master; it is simply that you will *call* me master. You see the distinction, do you not?'

A little reluctantly, I nodded. 'Very well.'

'Good.' Audiger looked out of the window. 'But what to give the king,' he said, almost to himself. 'Now *that* is a worry.'

It was only as I drifted off to sleep that I realised that Audiger had misunderstood what I had said, back in Florence. He had thought I said I would have no master; but what I had actually said was that I would *call* no man master; I was quite sure of it. And yet here I was, agreeing to do just that. But perhaps Audiger had forgotten the exact words of our agreement.

'Could one make an ice from peas?'

I jolted awake. The *diligence* had stopped, but only so the drivers could relieve themselves. Audiger stood by the side of the road, just beyond the open door, pissing into the field beyond.

'What?'

'I said, could one make an ice from peas?' Audiger called over his shoulder. 'Look, I am watering some right now.'

I looked out of the carriage. In the brilliant, flat light of a full moon I saw a field of peas, their plump green pods swinging in the breeze. The aroma of fresh legumes was, mercifully, more powerful than that of my companion's piss.

18

'The king has a strange passion for vegetables of all kinds,' Audiger said. 'Especially for peas. Each year his courtiers compete to bring him the first crop from their estates – it is the sort of contest he enjoys. And these are weeks earlier than any peas in France. I am wondering if we could make an ice from them.'

'But if you want to give the king peas, why not simply pick him some?'

'They will be withered long before we reach Paris. Even the *diligence* takes a fortnight.'

'But you could freeze them.'

Audiger's head appeared at the carriage door. 'What?'

'Freeze them,' I repeated. 'Preserve them in ice.'

Audiger stared at me. 'Such a thing is possible?'

'It is not just possible: it is simple. The Persians have long known that ice preserves fruit from corruption. Peas are surely no different.'

'Yes? Brilliant! What would you need? Ice?' Audiger gazed around the moonlit field. 'But of course, we have no ice,' he said dejectedly. 'A couple of ice makers, with no ice.'

'Audiger – where are we headed?'

The Frenchman looked nonplussed. 'Paris?'

'Via the Alps,' I reminded him. 'And although I have never been there, even I know that the Alps are—'

'Full of ice! Stuffed with ice! Ice and snow everywhere you look! Yes!' Audiger tossed his hat into the air, then caught it again. 'But first we have to get our peas to the Alps,' he said, more glumly.

'How long before the coach gets there?'

'Two days, perhaps three.'

'My chest of equipment will still be cold; the pewter buckets and so on came straight from the Boboli ice house. If we put the peas in there . . .'

'Yes! Yes!' Audiger threw his hat up once more. 'Of course!

With my vision, Demirco, and your expertise, we shall be the king's confectioners in no time!'

Two days later, in an inn high on the mountain pass that led to France, Audiger watched me prepare the peas.

'Packed snow is even colder than ice, and lasts longer,' I explained. 'Why, I do not know. But I intend to find out, one day.'

Audiger was staring at the *sabotiere* like a man awaiting a conjuring trick. Very well, I thought: I will show you some magic.

'Now I add saltpetre to the snow. That makes it much, much colder. Again, I do not know why exactly.'

'Go on,' Audiger breathed.

'Then I put the peas into the inner pot, like so.' I poured the peas in and placed the lid on top.

'Now what?'

'Now we leave them. It is no different from leaving a cake in the oven – if you open the door too often to check it, the heat will escape and the cake will never get baked. Only in our case, it is the cold which must be kept safe.'

Audiger pulled out a pocket watch. 'How long?'

'The length of time between matins and mass, according to the bells of Santa Maria.'

'What?'

'Say half an hour.'

Audiger spent the next thirty minutes pacing up and down. When we finally opened the *sabotiere* he looked inside and drew in his breath.

The peas had drawn together into a ball, a silvery-green cluster flecked with ice. Audiger reached in and pulled it out. 'Remarkable!' he breathed.

'Careful,' I warned. 'Your hands will warm them, and they will not taste so fresh if they have to be frozen a second time.'

'They're stuck!' Peas were dotted on Audiger's fingers, clinging to his skin like burrs on cloth mittens. He tried to flick them off, but they would not budge.

'Here, let me.' I pulled the frozen peas off one by one. They did not stick to my fingers as they did to Audiger's, I noticed. 'We should put them away now. And we must take a chest of pressed snow with us in the coach, so that we can keep them like this.'

Carlo

To make a ratafia of green walnuts: take your walnuts, not quite ripe; chop them into quarters, husks and all, then infuse them for a month in a gallon of aqua vitae, with a lemon and some leaves of the sweet lime bush. This cordial in France is known as *liqueur de noix*, and freezes pleasingly, though not hard.

The Book of Ices

In Paris we had to move quickly to get an audience with the king before our peas unfroze. Luckily Monsieur Bontemps, the king's valet, proved just as corruptible as Audiger had predicted, and within a few days we were shown into the presence of Louis XIV, his brother and several other members of the nobility. Audiger was so greatly in awe of them he could hardly speak. Fortunately our gift required little introduction, and Audiger's stammering oratory was soon ignored as the aristocrats crowded round the box of peas, trying them.

The king asked his valet to take what was left to the controller of the mouth to have them divided: one part for the queen, one for the queen mother, one for the cardinal, and the last one for himself. 'As for these intrepid gentlemen, Bontemps,' he said, gesturing at us, 'please reward them for their trouble.'

I looked at Audiger. This was the point at which he should, according to our plan, have uttered the speech he had prepared. But my companion, unusually for him, seemed to be struck dumb, and was now staring at the king with an expression of wide-eyed adoration.

'If it may please Your Majesty,' I said with a bow, 'we wish no reward, save only the privilege to make ices and other chilled confections, for the royal pleasure.'

Louis raised his eyebrows. 'Ices?'

Audiger found his voice. 'My assistant, sir, was lately at the court of the Medici, and is greatly accomplished in this art.'

The king's gaze scrutinised my face. 'What is your name, signor?'

'Demirco, sir.'

'And how old are you?'

'Eighteen,' I lied.

'Hmm. A good age – the same age at which I took on the government of France. I look forward to trying your confections. Cardinal Mazarin has long had the services of an Italian *limonadier*, and on several occasions I have had cause to admire his handiwork. His name is Morelli – perhaps you are acquainted with him?'

I shook my head. 'No, sir.'

'He is a most inventive man. But perhaps –' I felt the king scrutinising me even more closely – 'you will prove his equal. I certainly hope so. It would give me great pleasure to outdo the cardinal at table.'

I had a glimpse then into the character of this king. Rivalry – that was what drove him. Everything he did, or had, or patronised, must be the best, and any courtier or statesman who offered him anything – even so insubstantial a morsel as a flavoured ice – was only stoking Louis's insatiable appetite to outdo him.

I bowed again. 'I shall try, Your Majesty.'

Beside me, Audiger added, 'A task, sir, which would certainly be easier if we were able to establish a guild – a guild of confectioners – with a royal patent, and a council, and a right of issuing masterships—'

'Yes, yes. Make an ice and send it to me this evening at dinner time. If I find it acceptable, the honour is yours.' The king swept out, followed by the rest.

Audiger stared at the empty doorway, then caught at my sleeve. 'Tonight!' he hissed. 'We must send him an ice tonight!'

'It is no matter,' I said confidently. 'Get me green walnuts from the market, then find a cordial shop and buy some *liqueur de noix*. The liquor maker will have done most of the hard work for us.' I had no intention, now that I had finally got to France, of restricting myself to Ahmad's four flavours ever again.

It was the beginning of a remarkable period. In Florence I had been less than a servant: here in Paris, I was almost a courtier. Audiger arranged for me to be dressed in the style of a dancing teacher or a painter of portraits, my frock coat resplendent with twenty-four never-used buttons, my white breeches tight enough to show off my calves, my hat three-cornered, my wig – the first I had ever owned – long and liberally powdered with chalk. The latter itched abominably. After I had worn it for a week I realised that I was either going to have to shave my head, as Audiger did, or get rid of the wig. I got rid of the wig. But the rest of my clothes, I thought, suited me rather well, and when I caught sight of myself in one of the full-length mirrors with which the king's new salons were panelled, I could not help being impressed.

The two of us were given a cellar at the king's country residence of Marly, and in Paris we took premises in Saint-Germain-de-Pres, convenient for the Louvre. The labour I had been obliged to do in Florence, dragging blocks of ice from the ice house to the palace, here was done by others – Paris already had a thriving trade in ice and pressed snow to cool the nobility's wine, and good quality supplies could be obtained all year round. Even the work of chipping and grating was done by apprentices, of whom Audiger engaged no less than four.

But it was at the king's new palace of Versailles that we spent most of our time. Audiger had not been lying when he spoke of its magnificence. Although the building work was by no means finished – indeed, it was not finished all the time I was there: as soon as one project was complete, Louis immediately embarked on another, his ambition always outstripping his architects' abilities to fulfil it – the old house had already been enveloped in a grand new *façade*, the symmetrical, regular windows grander than anything I had come across even in Florence, at that time widely regarded as the most beautiful city in the world. Versailles – or 'the new palace', as it was usually referred to – had the elegant proportions of the Uffizi or the Pitti, yet it was surrounded by open parkland, like a country estate; it was the size of a castle, yet was entirely, confidently, without fortifications of any kind; it fulfilled the functions of a court, yet contained no mean little offices or functionaries' chambers, only gorgeous salons and sumptuous galleries. In short, it was a completely new kind of palace, and in it Louis carried out a completely new kind of government – one in which no distinction was made between matters of state and matters of fashion; where ministers were respected for the urbanity of their address or the elegance of their clothes as much as for the wisdom of their counsel; and where everything, from the length of a fingernail to matters of war, revolved around the impeccable person of the king himself: his moods, his manners, and above all, his tastes.

For Louis was a gourmet – some said, a glutton. Over three hundred people worked in his kitchens, which occupied a whole building adjacent to the palace, and sixty of those prepared nothing but desserts. There was a team of nine who made macaroons, plump meringue-like biscuits filled with brightly coloured pastes of pistachio, liquorice, blackcurrant, or almond. There were confectioners who specialised in subtleties of spun sugar, or who made confits from sugared seeds, or who prepared orgeat, a paste of scalded almonds, orange blossom and coriander of which the king was especially fond. I made sure to spend time in the kitchens of these specialists, ostensibly to warm hands frozen from working ice, but actually to see how they worked. Soon, to the king's great satisfaction, I was producing ices of a kind that had never been made before – chilled cordials flavoured with orgeat, or milk ices sandwiched between layers of meringue that looked like macaroons, or *sorbetti* that could be held in the hand within a little lattice goblet made of spun sugar, so that they did not drip on your fine court clothes as they melted.

There was no one now to tell me what I could not do: indeed, it soon became clear that novelty was an essential part of the service that Audiger and I provided. Every time the king hosted a collation, or picnic, one table would be set aside for us to fill. Around a centrepiece of carved ice, or a clockwork fountain of fruit cordial, we would arrange a *tableau* of jellies, sorbets, sherbets, chilled liqueurs, perfumed waters, fruits encased in ice, and other frozen delights. And then – perhaps a few hours later, perhaps the following week, depending on the whim of the court, which was to say, the whim of His Most Christian Majesty – we would do it all again, *with not a single repetition of a recipe or flavour*. If an ice of candied flowers was one of the dishes we offered on a Tuesday, at least a fortnight would pass before it graced the king's table again. If slices of peach fashioned into the shape of the sun's rays and flavoured with galingale dazzled the court on a Wednesday, then at least another Wednesday would go by before it shone for a second time. An *eau glacée* of cubebs and long pepper, or a sorbet of musk melon cordial sharpened with cassia, might divert the courtiers and their ladies today, but tomorrow it would no longer be a novelty, and the day after that it would bore them.

After I had been at the court a few months, I was summoned to the king's presence. At first I assumed I was to take him an ice: but when I asked how many guests he had with him, I was told there was only one, and that on this occasion no ices were required. I immediately concluded that my last offering – a milk sherbet flavoured with grains of paradise – had in some way been unacceptable. My heart thudding, certain that I was about to be disgraced, I followed the footman through the endless corridors to the presence chamber.

26

I found the king in conversation with a man whose court coat was dusted with green lichen, his white stockings and the linen buckles of his shoes splashed with mud. But the king was conversing with him as easily as with any courtier I had ever seen.

'Ah, Demirco!' Louis exclaimed. I saw that he was holding in his hand a small fruit knife and a pear. 'Have you met Monsieur la Quintinie?'

I had heard of the man, a lawyer by training, who supervised the king's vegetable gardens, but I had not yet met him. We bowed to each other.

'Smell this,' the king instructed, passing me a slice of the pear from his own hand. 'Go on – smell it!'

I sniffed deeply, allowing the pear's aroma to fill my nostrils. It was very good, with a fresh, floral perfume which put me in mind of Muscat grapes. The crescent-shaped slice which the king had cut from the fruit revealed that the skin was rough, almost warty, and tinged with a blush of red like an apple; but the flesh was white and crisp, like a block of marble before it is carved.

'Now try it,' he instructed.

I slipped the slice of pear into my mouth. The fragrance became liquid, filling my palate: the flesh crunched beneath my teeth, releasing more of those wonderful juices.

'Sir, that is magnificent,' I said truthfully, when I had swallowed.

He nodded. 'A new variety. Monsieur la Quintinie's gardeners have been nurturing it for three years, and this is the first time it has fruited.' He was silent a moment. 'Truly God is the greatest cook of all, and we can only honour his recipes with as much humility as we can muster.'

'Indeed, sir,' I said, unsure where this was leading.

'Perfection is simplicity, Demirco.'

I bowed my agreement.

'You have a great fondness for snuff and spices and so on, and that is all very well. But the productions of the potager, plain and unadorned, teach us the glory of God. Could you capture such flavours in an ice?'

'I believe so, Your Majesty,' I said cautiously. 'Whether it would retain the aroma that, for example, this pear has, I am not sure. But I would be honoured to try.'

The king spread his hands to indicate the two of us. 'La Quintinie and Demirco. Talk to each other. I look forward to tasting the fruits of your pollination.'

And so I learnt the virtue of simplicity, and sent to the king iced *sorbetti* of whatever fruit was most recently in season, adorned with nothing except a little sugar. I discovered that, although the process of freezing might indeed rob fruit of some of its scent, it also had the effect of concentrating the flavour, capturing its essence in a few sweet crystals on the end of a spoon. This was before la Quintinie had completed the vast *potager du roi*, the largest in Europe, which Louis himself considered the most beautiful part of his estate. But the orchards, kitchen gardens and glasshouses he already had at his disposal were producing extraordinary results. Louis loved pears, for example, more than any other fruit, and so la Quintinie set himself to growing the best varieties in France, as well as creating new ones for the king's pleasure. Globular, round, pendant, slender; green, yellow, russet, red; rough-skinned or smooth; with fancy names such as Bon Chretien d'Hiver, Petit Blanquet, Sucrée Verte, or the king's absolute favourite, the sweet, highly perfumed Rousselet de Reims – he grew them all, and I was given the precious fruits to do with as I pleased. Once, when I sent the king a simple wooden board containing nothing but half-a-dozen sorbets, each made from a different variety of pear, culminating in a bright pink *sanguinello* or blood pear which had been gently roasted so as to caramelise its flesh, he was so delighted that court business was put aside, Audiger and I were summoned into the royal presence, and the whole court was made to give us an ovation for our achievements. On another occasion I made him a bowl of cherries which, when examined closely, turned out to be twenty individual cherry cream ices which I had frozen one by one in a mould; while my mandarin sorbets – each one served inside the skin of a recently picked mandarin, the peel apparently unbroken, like a toy ship inside a bottle – were a wonder that the court discussed for days.

Sometimes the king hosted great *divertissements* for up to a thousand guests, when theatres and grottos almost as large as the palace itself were constructed out of papier mâché for the pre-mieres of specially commissioned masques and *comédies-ballets*. The fact that these elaborate buildings were to be destroyed after a single night's entertainment was simply another aspect of their magnificence. On these occasions we would create never-to-be-repeated ices in honour of a special guest, in the same way that a chef might name a new sauce after the patron who inspired it. Audiger took seriously the king's implicit command to outdo Cardinal Mazarin's *limonadier*, and even bribed servants in the households of the other great nobles to tell us what their confec-tioners were up to. It was a happy day, indeed, when we heard that the famous Signor Morelli had been reduced to copying our own idea of a bitter redcurrant sherbet served on a glistening silver spoon which, when placed in the mouth, turned out to be made of sugar.

For Audiger, though, our success was always mingled with frus-tration. The foundation of the guild – his great dream – was bogged down in bureaucracy, and at each step required another bribe to ease it on its way. The king's steward, Monsieur le Tellier, saw no difficulty, but referred the matter to the Privy Council. The Council could not consider it without a report from the prin-cipal clerk. The principal clerk referred the issue to the chancellor. The chancellor would only become involved if the measure was sponsored by some nobleman. The nobleman Audiger chose, unfortunately, turned out to be sleeping with a lady who was not his wife: hardly an unusual occurrence, but his wife happened to be the granddaughter of the chancellor . . . And so it went on, around and around, with no one eager to grant the patent which would create the guild until every last opportunity for profit, advancement, intrigue and corruption had been wrung from its passage.

'But why do you care?' I said at last, when Audiger was ranting yet again about the latest setback. 'Why is a guild so important, if we are making the ices we want to?'

'Have you understood nothing?' Audiger demanded. He strode abruptly to where I was pouring clove-scented milk into a pewter mould. 'Who do you think pays for this equipment?' he said furiously. 'For your clothes? Your fine hat? These premises? Who feeds our apprentices? Who pays our bribes? Who buys these expensive ingredients you use so liberally?' He dug his fingers into a box of cloves and flung the whole handful into the air. 'Do you never even ask yourself such things?'

I stared at him, dumbfounded, as the cloves pattered to the floor. What he had said was absolutely true. I never so much as considered the financial aspect of what we did. It was the one freedom which the slave shares with the gentleman; not to care about money.

'But . . . does the king not reward us?'

Audiger laughed scornfully. 'Sometimes. But never on time, and never enough. He knows that the coin in which he pays us is patronage, not gold. I've laid out nearly a thousand *livres* already on this venture – everything I had. And unless we get the guild – unless we have other men paying us for the right to join; unless we can charge people to take on their sons as apprentices, and then sell them the right to become masters in their turn – I'll be bankrupt within six months.'

'Audiger, I am so sorry. I had no idea. You are quite right – I have been thoughtless.'

'Well,' Audiger said, his temper vanishing as quickly as it had come, 'it does not matter. I have let you concentrate on the ices, rather than on business, since that is clearly where your true skill lies. But if I am a little quarrelsome sometimes, now you know why. If we fail at this, I lose everything.'

It was a small argument, soon forgotten. But it had an important consequence. From then on, I started to take an interest in the financial aspect of our enterprise. I began to understand the curious economics of our trade, in which it was not the ingredients that were costly, or the ice itself, but the accoutrements that went with it: our court clothes, our uniformed staff, the beautiful goblets and gold spoons with which a king or noble might enjoy our work. Ahmad had been right about this, at least: it was our *expertise* that made us worth the exorbitant sums we charged, just as a singer is paid for the beauty of his voice, or a painter for his skill rather than the cost of his paint. And that, of course, was why we must always keep our knowledge secret: once it was shared by others, it would no longer have any value. With this in mind I persuaded Audiger that we should charge even more for our creations. The king encouraged extravagance in his courtiers: if Louis praised a sorbet, or an ice made with some fashionable new ingredient such as jasmine, mulberry or mint, then sooner or later every courtier worthy of the name would have to grit his teeth and pay through his nose, in order that he might have the pleasure, eventually, of agreeing with the king that, yes, it was indeed very fine. By following this plan we gradually accumulated wealth as well as privilege, our coats even richer, our buttons pearl instead of horn – although that did not stop Audiger from hankering after his guild, even so.

But if Audiger had his own private frustration, I also had mine. In Florence I had always imagined that, once I was free to combine flavours and textures as I wished, I would eventually come across a substance which, when frozen, had the smooth richness of cream or melted chocolate, so that my confections would dissolve

31

sweetly and quickly on the tongue, like chantilly cream or the paste in the centre of a macaroon, without the telltale crunch of frozen ice. But, although I tried freezing each of those mixtures, and a dozen others besides, the answer always eluded me. There simply seemed to be no way to produce an ice that was truly smooth.

There was one thing, though, at which I did become more proficient. Where the Medici had tended to strictness in moral matters, as befitted Europe's bankers, the court of Louis XIV was more sophisticated. The French nobility married for financial and political reasons: their ardour they reserved for their affairs. Even at the lower levels of the court, no one saw any reason not to indulge in *liaisons*. A talented young Italian – who, if I may say so, looked rather fine in a three-cornered hat – was not going to be ignored for very long.

One day I was preparing iced cordials for the king's guests when a lady of the court paused to watch me at work.

'You are the one who is my countryman,' she said in Italian.

I glanced up, surprised at hearing my native tongue. She was short, plump-faced and dark-eyed, and the expression in her eyes was one of lazy mischief.

'I grew up in Rome,' she explained. 'My uncle brought me to Paris to find a husband.'

'And did you?' I said boldly.

She nodded. 'Several, as it happens. One of my own, and some who already belonged to others.' She glanced over at where the king stood, surrounded by a group of courtiers.

Now I realised who I was talking to. Even I had heard of Olympe de Soissons, the Italian beauty who counted the king himself among her conquests. She and her four sisters were known as the Mazarinettes, after their uncle, the powerful Cardinal Mazarin.

'What are you making?' she asked, watching me strain the liquid through a muslin.

'A cordial. Muscat pears and ginger, with a little—'

'Make one for me,' she interrupted. 'But not that one. I never like to have what everyone else is having.' She wandered off to join the others, but as she did so she gave me a brief, bold, backward glance.

When I had distributed the ginger cordials I made something else, and took it to her.

'What is it?' she asked prettily.

'A chilled tisane of green tea leaves from China, with essence of lime and some seeds,' I said with a bow.

Nodding, she took a sip. It was a recipe I had been working on for a few days, something a little out of the ordinary, using the newest and most fashionable of ingredients. The taste started with a sharp, clean punch of lime, followed by a little rush of smoky green tea leaves. Then there was a suggestion of jasmine, and a faint, warm aftertaste of spicy cardamom.

'Interesting,' was all she said. And then, as I turned away, 'And surprisingly refreshing. Thank you.'

The next day I was ordered to prepare enough cordial to make five gallons.

'Five gallons?' I repeated to the footman who brought the order. 'Are you sure? That would be enough for the whole court.'

'This is for Madame la Comptesse alone. She desires the one you made her yesterday. Take the ingredients direct to her apartments.'

It was easy to get lost in the sprawling palace, and several times I had to ask directions from one of the periwigged footmen who were standing on duty along the endless corridors. Eventually I found the right door. It was opened by a maid, who ushered me inside. Even by the standards of Versailles, the apartment was sumptuous. Wallpapers of red silk were in turn covered with works of art, the centrepiece of which was a painting of Olympe herself, wearing little more than a few velvet drapes.

33

The maid showed me into an antechamber containing a bath and a row of steaming ewers. There was nothing else except a screen made of embroidered silk, a chair, and a chaise longue upholstered in red velvet, on which had been placed a pile of thick linen towels.

'Madame, the confectioner is here,' the maid said, curtseying to the empty room.

'Thank you, Cecile.'

Olympe's head appeared over the top of the screen. She was unpinning her hair with one hand, shaking out the elaborate curls. 'Your cordial was so delicious, I decided I would like to bathe in it,' she said simply. 'Would you prepare it for me, please?'

I did as I was bidden. Rather than fill the bath with tea leaves and pieces of lime I set the muslin bags containing the ingredients directly in the water, and allowed them to steep. The water was quite hot – I would have altered the proportions slightly if I had known; the warmth would bring out more of the flavour of the tea leaves, whereas ice favoured the lime . . .

'Is it ready?' her voice called.

'It should infuse a little longer.'

'Then I shall infuse with it.' Olympe stepped from behind the screen. She was in her *déshabillé* – a chignon of gossamer-thin lace, loosely tied at the front, hardly reaching the knee. If she noticed my reaction, she gave no sign of it.

'Madame,' I said, bowing my head and preparing to withdraw.

'Wait,' she commanded imperiously, putting one leg into the bath to test the temperature. 'I may wish to alter the amounts, and besides, I like to speak Italian when I bathe. Sit in the chair and talk to me.'

I went to the chair and sat down, a little awkwardly. The screen, I now realised, had been positioned so that from where I was sitting it obscured a little – a very little – of the bath; although not, it transpired, the glimpse of Olympe's naked back as she disrobed and settled into the water with a sigh.

'What is your name?' she asked in Italian.

'Demirco, madame.'

'I know that. I meant your other name.'

'Carlo.'

There was a long pause, during which I heard a series of quiet splashes as Olympe spooned the water over herself with her hands. The aroma of lime, green tea and jasmine wafted over me. For my own part, I stayed very still.

Eventually she said, 'I find I do not want to talk after all, Carlo. Today it seems I am as tongue-tied as you are. You may come and join me.'

'Madame?'

'Join me,' she repeated. 'In the bath.'

Later she said, 'So. Was that as pleasant as you hoped?'

'Indeed. But you need more lime.'

'I need more lovemaking.' Like a cat she stretched voluptuously, as easy under my gaze as if we were both still fully clothed. We were on the chaise longue now: I had soon realised that, like the bath and the screen, it had not been placed there by accident.

I reached for her.

'Wait,' she said, putting a hand on my chest. 'That was quite good, for a first attempt. But the next time, you need to go more slowly. And to be a little more inventive.'

'Inventive!' I repeated, stung.

She laughed. 'Don't be offended. I've done this rather more than you, that's all, and like any other skill it is something you have to practise. Besides, there are fashions in lovemaking just as in anything else, and national specialities as well. The French are rather good at this; almost as good as they are at making pastries and desserts.'

'What can a Frenchman know that an Italian doesn't?' I said curtly.

She smiled. 'That's what I'm about to show you.'

When she had done showing me, and I was finally taking my leave, she added, 'Next time, when you come, you must bring some ices, and I will show you a use for those as well that perhaps has not occurred to you.'

Audiger was furious. 'You were seen leaving her apartment. Do you want to get us both banished from the court?'

'They're all doing it,' I said. 'Why shouldn't I?'

Audiger threw up his hands. 'Because their positions are secure, and ours is not.'

'I don't care,' I said. 'I'm not going to stop visiting her just in case somebody objects. I can't live like that.'

'Then you're a fool,' Audiger said shortly. 'A court is no place to fall in love.'

'Who said anything about love?' I said it without thought, as any young man might, but I also knew that it was true: the sliver of ice was too deeply embedded in me for that.

'Very well,' Audiger said reluctantly. 'But be careful not to lose your heart. Or you might end up losing another part of you as well – your head, which unlike that other organ cannot be mended.'

I nodded. I had known that Audiger would not be able to forbid me this. The balance between us had changed during these years at court. I had everything I wanted now – wealth, position, my bodily appetites sated by one of the greatest lovers of the age, the patronage of the most powerful king in Europe.

The next time I visited Olympe I strode confidently to her door, bearing a tray on which were arranged four glass goblets containing sorbets. Each was a different colour, and a different flavour: persimmon, pistachio, white peach, and golden honey. There were no spoons.

I raised my hand to knock, but as I did so a footman appeared as if from nowhere and inserted himself between me and the wood.

'Madame la Comptesse is not to be disturbed.'

I indicated the ices. 'I have brought her these.'

'And I will see that she gets them,' he said, deftly removing the tray. I did not protest. I recognised the man now: he was one of the king's personal servants. As I walked away I heard the door open as he slipped inside with the ices.

I waited nearby. Sure enough, after half an hour or so I saw the king walking away from Olympe's rooms, down the vast staircase that led to his own apartments. He was tugging at a shirt cuff, as if the garment had only recently been put on.

I went to retrieve the tray. Olympe was in her bath, but her maid said she would talk to me.

'The king was impressed with your ices today,' Olympe said without preamble when she saw me. 'Indeed, they were just the refreshment he required. It's rare these days he manages a second bout of lovemaking: he's pleased with himself, and that means he's pleased with me. Thank you.'

I stared at her, taken aback by her matter-of-fact tone. 'You are his lover still? But I thought—'

'That he lay in the arms of Madame de la Valliere? He does – mostly. But there are times when she is indisposed, or when he is disposed to variety. Or sometimes he flirts with a new lady-in-waiting and finds himself rebuffed: then he brings his wounded vanity to me to be restored. There are many reasons why a man may choose to lie with a woman, and not all of them are straight-forward. At the moment the king finds that he has a certain nostalgia for my company.'

'Then – you will not want me to come back?' I said, my own vanity a little pricked.

Olympe laughed. 'Not at all. With you, Carlo, the arrangement is completely straightforward, and therein lies its charm. I am tired today, and I hope that the king may return to me tomorrow, but

come back in a few days' time and we will see how things stand –'
she cast a mischievous look at my breeches – 'as it were. But in any
case, it isn't fair that I keep you all to myself.'

'What do you mean?'

'Simply that you lack experience. No, don't look crestfallen –
we were all in the same boat once, and besides, for someone like
you the problem is easily addressed. The palace is full of women
who would be happy to be your tutors in this.'

'It is?' I said, astounded.

'Of course. Why do you think Madame de Corneil sends for
your cordials every evening? Why do you think Madame
Rossoulet is always inviting you to cards? And why do you think
I made it my business to seduce you before any of them?'

'You mean . . . you were proving a point?'

Olympe smiled. 'Amongst other things.' She spooned water
over herself.

'And you would not be jealous if I slept with other women?'

'Jealousy is for the common people,' she said matter-of-factly.
'The people whose crumbs of pleasure are so few and so infre-
quent that they must squabble over them like beggars fighting
over a crust of bread. Here at the court, where we are surfeited
with the possibility of pleasant sensations, we can afford to be
rather more discerning.' She glanced at me, amused. 'But if you
are sensible, you will allow me to guide you in this. Just as your
choice of a cologne or your appreciation of a *sarabande* speaks
volumes about whether you are a true connoisseur, so your choice
of lovers will indicate to those around you whether you are a
person of refined tastes or an imposter.'

'An imposter?' I said uneasily. I was, I suppose, still a little fearful that I might betray my origins by a false step.

She nodded. 'No one but a brute, for example, would ever
seduce a servant. To lie with someone coarse, however willing
they are, is to risk coarsening yourself. And whatever happens, you
must never allow yourself to get carried away. Love is all very well,

38

but just as hunger does not excuse bad manners at table, so passion does not excuse behaving like an oaf in bed. An excess of emotion in a love affair is just as ugly as an excess of rosemary in a dish, or an excess of violence in a piece of music. It is possible – indeed, it is necessary – to display elegance in one's *amours*, just as in the rest of one's affairs.'

She spoke all this in a light, indolent voice, as if the subject were one which she had considered on so many occasions previously that there was nothing more to say on the matter. It was the way they spoke around the court, particularly the women: I had heard it described as *préciosité*, and the women who cultivated it in the salons and drawing rooms of fashionable Paris were known as *les précieuses*. But the glint of mischief in her eyes indicated that this was a project that she actually took very seriously indeed.

I bowed ironically. 'I would be most grateful for any instruction you can give me in this matter, madame.'

'Good,' she said. 'Then that's settled. Bring me an ice in two days' time, and in the meantime I will give some thought as to who your next conquest should be.'

And so began the next stage of my education. Just as in Florence I had experimented with different flavours and techniques of ice, so here in Versailles I sampled the different tastes and flavours of love. Olympe was right: I soon discovered that there were many women at court who were only too pleased to be my accompanists. I discovered something else as well, which was that I liked women, and that they generally liked me in return. That may sound a curious statement, but it was by no means self-evident: many of the court's most renowned lovers seemed almost weary of their affairs, as if falling in love were a duty as arduous and as inevitable as attending yet another ball or dance. Occasionally Olympe had to caution me against overenthusiasm – 'If you go around with a grin on your face like that people will think you are a simpleton' – but in general she treated me with an amused indulgence; and for my part, I soon learned how to present to the world that air of amused, lofty cynicism that was the great fashion of the age.

I found, too, that if a woman needed to be wooed, I had the perfect means at my disposal. There was nothing so persuasive, it seemed, as announcing that I was trying to perfect a new flavour or combination of ices, so far untasted, and that I needed the help of the lady in question to sample my work and give me her opinion. There was a certain skill, and a pleasure, too, in matching the sorbet to the woman: the younger, more innocent types – not that there was any such thing as true innocence, in that court – could be tempted with more sophisticated tastes, while older women preferred the innocence and youth of simple flavours.

As I became more accomplished, so I became even more inventive, both in the ices I made for the king and those I produced for my lovers. I still produced the single-fruit sorbets of which the king was so fond, of course. But once I had plucked every fruit that existed in nature, I proceeded to create new, imaginary orchards and potagers of my own, wherein grew such extravagances as a tree that was half lemon and half lime, or a bush that fruited with rye bread, or a plant whose pollen was the eggs of the Aquitaine sturgeon fish. Even the flowerbeds gave up their blossoms for sorbets of scented geranium leaf or lavender, or lent their aromas to perfumed *granites* of lemon balm, violet or rose. That these tastes could exist at all, let alone locked within the frozen crystals of my *eaux glacées*, never ceased to amaze the king's guests: my star rose ever higher, and my name became known even beyond the confines of the court.

And then one day I took a dish of strawberry ice flavoured with white pepper to the king, and although I did not realise it at first, my life was changed completely.

Carlo

To make a strawberry ice: take thirty fat berries with
plenty of scent, slice them and dice them and pass them
through a sieve: add one cup of sugar, and a pint of thick
cow's milk: mix it well, and stir it as you freeze. It needs
nothing more, but you can dress it with some mint or
white pepper as you please.

The Book of Ices

The ice would not set, and the king was waiting.

Despite the cold in the subterranean pantry, I was sweating.
Grasping the wooden bucket between my knees, I poured the
mixture of sugar, cream and crushed strawberries back into the
sabotiere, the inner container made of pewter, and began to work
the paddle one more time.

Beside me, Audiger was getting flustered. 'You need to go
more slowly, perhaps. But hurry, hurry.'

I did not bother to point out that it was difficult to do both
those things at once. 'The ice isn't cold enough. I need more saltpetre.'

'Ice is ice, surely. It has only one temperature, the temperature
of freezing. This has been established by many authorities. Galen
says—'

'It's over there,' I interrupted. 'Two measures.'

Going to the chests which contained our supplies, Audiger
scooped up a quantity of yellowish crystals and brought them
over. 'Here.'

I stopped paddling so that he could add them to the mixture.
Carefully, he poured the saltpetre into the outer part of the

bucket. As he did so, a footman in royal livery put his head inside the pantry door.

'The desserts are going to the king,' he announced.

Audiger rounded on him. 'Two minutes!' he exclaimed. 'Just two more minutes! His Majesty has suggested that today he would like a strawberry ice, and a strawberry ice he shall have.' Out of habit, he stood between the footman and our apparatus, blocking the man's view.

Between my legs I felt the bucket – finally! – grow colder as the saltpetre did its work. My paddle slowed, meeting a greater resistance. I slowed my own rhythm to match. This was hard labour, the hardest part, but, such was my relief, I could feel the ache easing from my shoulders.

If you are too eager, the paddle itself may heat the mixture, I heard Ahmad's voice say in my head. *Heed your hand, not your eye. When it feels like sand, it is almost ready.*

'It's ready,' I said. There was no time, today, for niceties. When the king expressed a sudden desire for a particular flavour, even the ice was expected to do as it was told.

'At last.' Audiger rearranged his wig and brushed cellar dust from his court clothes. Pulling on a pair of white gloves, he looked around. 'Where's the platter?'

I indicated with my head. 'On the shelf.'

The platter was also made of ice, cast in a mould and polished until it looked like crystal. It was already piled high with more crushed ice in readiness.

I inspected the contents of my bucket one last time. The mixture was now as dense and granular as raw honey. Clots and veins of crushed strawberry had spread through the cream. I put my finger in to taste it.

'What are you doing?' Audiger cried. 'There's little enough for the king's guests as it is.'

I did not reply. I tasted every ice we made, but Audiger was not to know that. I considered, then nodded. 'It's good.'

Taking a spoon that had been sharpened on one side, I laid a scoop of pale pink cream ice on the platter. Then I added another, and another. Soon the dish resembled a frozen sea, the curves and rolls of the ice shavings helping to disguise the fact that there was actually very little of it. 'Now go,' I said.

'Some cinnamon?' Audiger said anxiously. 'Gold leaf? Nutmeg?'

'Perhaps a little white pepper.'

'Pepper? On strawberries? Are you mad?'

'Just a pinch. Trust me.'

Audiger sighed. 'Some pepper, then. And some saffron. His Most Christian Majesty will expect nothing less.' Before I could stop him he had thrown a large handful of saffron threads over the dish.

'He'll like it all the more if it tastes as it should,' I muttered. Under the pretext of garnishing it with some frozen mint leaves I managed to brush off most of the priceless saffron with the back of my hand. 'Go,' I repeated, handing the dish to him.

Audiger went up the pantry steps with the platter held cere-moniously in front of him, his back ramrod straight, as if he were already in the presence of the king. I followed. Outside, the sun-light and the heat of the afternoon was like a blow after the icy dankness of the pantry. I saw how the strawberry ice bloomed with a faint silvery rime in the warm air, and I remembered the taste – that brief fingertip taste: sugar, milk and strawberries, con-centrated by the mechanism of the ice into a tiny blossoming of flavour.

Yes, I thought. It's good. A dish fit for a king.

This was what Audiger would never understand: that ices were not simply a novelty, a way of demonstrating man's ingenious mastery over the natural order of things. They were a completely new way of combining tastes and flavours, only ever as good as the recipes that you created for them.

The footman who had chivvied us held out his hands for the

platter. Audiger ignored him. For a moment the two of them locked eyes, then the footman simply turned so that he was walking in front of Audiger. A second footman fell in behind, and another behind him, while a fourth and fifth unfolded elaborate parasols to shade the ice from the sun. In command of this platoon was a craggy-faced, periwigged *maître d'hôtel*, bearing as a mark of his seniority a long silver baton. He rapped out a command, and together they all set off at a brisk trot through the rose garden.

The effort of keeping in step meant that, despite the fact they were jogging, the procession of footmen actually went little faster than I did, walking behind them. In any case, I knew where they were headed. At the edge of the rose garden, where the hedges opened out to an ornamental lake, thirty or forty courtiers and their ladies were promenading in their finery. Tables were set out under the shade of a cedar tree. Behind these, in rows four abreast, stood a small army of servants, sweating under their short wigs. To one side, a group of musicians played. In the middle, where the throng of courtiers was densest, I could just make out the dark, luxuriant wig of the king himself.

The trotting servants followed the zigzagging paths down through the formal gardens. I simply walked across the lawn, rejoining them as they skirted the lake. The procession slowed to a more dignified pace as it threaded its way through the outer circles of the party, a few courtiers turning curiously to inspect the platter as it passed. Many, I knew, had not yet had the opportunity to try this passion of the monarch's for themselves. And given how little of it there was, and how large the party, most would not get the chance today. Louis would already have singled out those who were to be honoured with a taste.

As we approached, the king turned. 'Ah! My strawberry ice!' he exclaimed.

Audiger stopped and went down on one knee – a little awkwardly, because of the platter in his hands. Louis waved him forward. 'And now you will see if I am not right, My Lord Duke. It is a most remarkable confection.' The words were addressed to the man at his shoulder. He was dressed in a somewhat similar fashion to the servants, but I knew that he was actually an Englishman, an important visitor, here to negotiate a treaty between the two countries. It amused Louis to have his servants wear the fashions of foreign courts. It was a way of reminding visitors how much wealthier and more magnificent his court was than theirs.

On the other side of the visitor was Madame, as she was called: Henrietta d'Angleterre, the sister of the English king. She was married to Louis's brother, but was also a favourite – it was said – of Louis himself.

'Yes, George, it may give you sustenance enough to contemplate joining us in a game of *paille maille*,' she was saying. 'I know that you know how to play: I am told my brother has introduced it to your country, and that the court plays every day.'

'Indeed,' the English lord said with an easy smile. 'Like so many French fashions, there is quite a craze for it in London just now. His Majesty has established a playing ground beyond Whitehall, which the people are already calling Pall Mall.' He inspected the dish of strawberry ice, a little doubtfully. 'He has built an ice house in St James's Park, too – another idea he brought back from his exile here, I believe, although his cooks have not yet thought of putting ice in their desserts.'

'This is rather more than an iced dessert,' Louis said. 'Try some, and you will see what I mean.' The king held out his hand. For a moment I saw panic in Audiger's eyes as he realised that not only had he not brought any bowls or spoons, but that with both hands holding the platter, he was unable to serve the king. But I was ahead of him. Having picked up half a dozen blue-and-white porcelain bowls as I passed the tables at the rear, I was able to fill one with strawberry ice and present it with a bow.

'Demirco here comes from Florence,' the king said as he took it. 'He is one of only a handful of men in Europe who know how to prepare this confection. What are you giving us this time, signor?'

'A sherbet of strawberries, sir, just as you requested, with a little creamed milk and white pepper.'

I saw Audiger's jaw tighten. With the Frenchman holding the platter as I served from it, not to mention discussing recipes with the king, it looked for all the world as if it were Audiger who was the former apprentice and I the master.

'Your Majesty?' It was the king's new physician, a man called Félix, edging forward.

'What is it, Félix?'

The doctor coughed. 'The day is particularly warm, sir, and the ladies . . . Even those who are not already of a delicate disposition have been warmed considerably by playing *paille maille*. In the circumstances, I caution against it.'

'Against the ice?' The king looked surprised.

Félix nodded firmly. 'On this particular point medical authorities are agreed. The consumption of ice on such a hot day can bring on a number of maladies. Even seizures. The English gentleman, perhaps, but for the ladies and yourself . . .'

'You mean that you are happy to kill our honoured guest the Duke of Buckingham, but not ourselves?' the king exclaimed. 'My God, Félix, we will make a diplomat of you yet.' Those around him laughed, but – I noticed – no one touched their ice. An uneasy silence fell on the assembled court.

It was an *impasse*. Already the shavings were starting to melt in the sun. I knew it was useless to argue with this fool of a doctor: it would simply embarrass the king in front of his guest. I tasted something in my mouth, and realised I had bitten my own cheek with the effort of keeping my courtier's smile fixed to my face.

Then a voice – a cool, female voice – said from behind the king, 'Perhaps I might try it for you, Your Majesty.'

It was a woman who had spoken – a girl, rather, for she was

even younger than Madame; perhaps eighteen or nineteen years old, and wearing a dress that looked like one of Madame's cast-offs, which made her seem younger still. There was something childish, too, in the set of her face: she was pretty, but with her overlarge lips and the dusting of freckles on either side of her nose, it was the rather severe, unformed prettiness of adolescence. The mass of unruly black ringlets that tumbled around her neck, *au naturel,* was more like a man's wig than the pinned elaborate coiffures the other ladies wore, and her skin was unusually pale, as pale as milk ice. But it was her eyes you could not help noticing: they were green, and one of them had a slight slowness to it, as if that eye had to think for a moment before it followed the other.

She turned to the doctor. 'That is the basis of the New Method, is it not? Hypothesis, investigation, and only then deduction?'

The physician nodded reluctantly.

'Well, then,' she said, 'I shall be your investigation, and if I die you can make your deductions accordingly.'

'Bravo, *la belle Bretonne*!' the king exclaimed. 'But what if you do have a fit, my dear? Your parents would never forgive me.'

'It is a risk I am honoured to take on your behalf, sir.' There was a sardonic note in her voice, as if to say, *But this is silly non-sense, and we know it.* 'Besides,' she added, deftly taking the bowl which Madame was holding, 'There is so little to be had. This way I ensure that despite my lowly station I get to taste this marvel that I have heard so much about.' She raised the spoon to her lips.

This was a moment I always enjoyed – the moment someone tried one of my ices for the very first time. It was best if they had no idea what they were about to eat, of course, so that it came as a complete surprise, but I found that even when people thought they knew what to expect they could never quite imagine in advance what the sensation would be like. Sometimes, if the person was foolish, they would start, and drop the bowl: ladies, in particular, would cry out in alarm, raising the hand still holding the spoon to their mouth, as if afraid they might hiccup or splutter or spit. Then, a moment later, the shock would turn to amazement, and amazement to delight. That was when the first spoonful had just melted in their mouths, and the sweet, intense taste – if I had done my work properly – immediately prompted them to take another, and then another, until the accumulation of so much cold suddenly numbed the palate, icy pains shooting around the inside of the head, and they gasped in a different way, gulping in warm air to take away the frost that now gripped their throat. But that, too, only lasted a few moments; then came the final tussle between caution and greed, as the desire to have another mouthful did battle with the wish to avoid another chill, until the whole bowl had been devoured, and every last sweet melting morsel licked off the spoon with which it had been served.

This girl did not shriek or splutter. But her eyes opened very wide, her expression for one brief moment startled, before she recovered herself.

'Well?' the king demanded.

There was a smear of milky whiteness on her upper lip. After a moment her tongue flicked out and licked it away. She addressed the king but her eyes – even the one that was not slow – stayed on me a fraction longer than they might have done, and just for a moment there was something in them – a flicker of something, instantly suppressed – that I recognised.

I had seen that look on a woman's face twice before: once on Emilia's, and once on Olympe's.

'I would say,' she remarked, 'that it is as cool and sweet as a lover's kiss on a warm summer's day – except, of course, that a girl like myself has no idea what such a thing might taste like.'

Some amongst them laughed at the impudence of her wit. The king clapped his hands. 'Félix, you have your answer – you are being overcautious, as usual. And *la belle Bretonne* has captured your share of the strawberry ice, so there will be none for you.'

48

'I should not want any, sir,' the doctor said sourly. 'A poor physician I would be, if I at least did not follow my own advice.'

The ladies and gentlemen of the court were clustering around Audiger and me now, their eagerness only increased by the fact that there would not be enough for everybody. Within moments all the strawberry ice had gone. Laughter and gasps of astonishment filled the air. Women were standing stock-still in amazement, their cheeks bulging around that first startling mouthful: men were laughing at their ladies, and then making faces no less nonplussed themselves. Some were trying to pretend that this was nothing so very remarkable or new to them – they spooned the ice into their mouths nonchalantly, a cynical little smile playing on their lips: but these, of course, were precisely the ones whose throats became chilled most quickly, and who were thus caught out by the head pains. I saw one fine courtier recoil as if he had been shot in the back, his eyes boggling. The sophisticated smile on the face of another turned to a chuckle of childish joy, while a third was actually singing with amazement.

'Well? What do you think?' the king was asking them eagerly, and they were all pressing forward in their rush to tell him that it was the most remarkable thing they had ever tasted, that surely no other court was so blessed with wonders as the court of France. He nodded, pleased; then, indicating Audiger and myself, he cried, 'The Great Demirco! Audiger! Master confectioners of France!' The court applauded, clapping with gloved hands; the two of us acknowledging their acclaim with gracious bows to left and right.

Such was the nature of a picnic at the court of Louis XIV.

'And milord Buckingham?' the king said, turning to the Englishman. 'What do you think?'

'Most refreshing,' the visitor replied, replacing the spoon in his empty bowl. 'I am sure my own king would be obliged to know how it is done.'

'Unfortunately, that is impossible. Demirco and his colleagues are very careful to protect the secrets of their art. And there are some things even a monarch cannot command.'

'I am sure that Your Majesty can command anything he wishes,' the Englishman said dryly.

'Are we talking now about a strawberry ice – or the harbour at Dieppe?' Laughter. I had the impression that even the bits of this exchange I thought I understood were actually part of some other conversation entirely, like a game of *paille maille* in which the important hoops were the ones set eight feet above the ground.

'Besides, you English have a somewhat peculiar taste in desserts. You are overly fond of pancakes, I believe,' the king was saying, to more laughter. I could follow this much, at least: pancakes were a Dutch dish, and it was against the Dutch that the French were now plotting, the second-greatest power in Europe moving against the greatest, intent on stealing the land that the Hollanders had stolen from the sea. Or something like that. I heard the political talk as it swirled around the labyrinth of kitchens and pantries underneath Versailles, but I paid it little heed.

'What do you say then, Demirco?' To my surprise, the king was looking directly at me. 'Shall we make King Charles of England an ice, something so fine that it will turn him away from pancakes for ever? A dish perhaps, that reminds him of France, and of his many years in exile here enjoying our hospitality, so that he does not forget old friends in the excitement of feasting once again on English pies and pottage?' He said 'pies and pottage' in a droll accent: once again his courtiers laughed and clapped their hands.

'Of course, sir,' I said, unsure whether Louis was joking now or not. 'If it would please Your Majesty. But would it not melt long before he could eat it?'

'Perhaps,' the king said, shrugging, and I wondered if I had somehow said the wrong thing.

Suddenly, Audiger found his voice. 'Sir, I would be honoured to make an ice worthy for Your Majesty to present to the English king.'

50

I looked at him, perplexed. What did he mean? Surely he did not think that he could create a better ice than I could? But evidently he did – he was glaring coldly at me: this, it seemed, was to be his revenge on me for monopolising the king's attention.

'Ah! Signor Demirco, it seems you have been challenged,' Louis said gleefully. 'Will you accept?'

I bowed. 'Of course.'

'Good! And we will have Procopio as well, and – oh, what is that other confectioner's name? Signor Morelli. You shall each do your best work, and milord Buckingham, perhaps you would do us the honour of judging of our little contest before you leave.'

'Gladly. But what shall be the prize?'

Louis thought for a moment. 'These people are always pressing me for a guild of their own. Let us say that the one who creates the best ice shall have the presidency of it.'

Out of the corner of my eye I saw Audiger stiffen. Were I not in the royal presence, I would certainly have sighed. Nothing good could possibly come of this.

'So this is how you repay me,' Audiger hissed as we walked back up the hill towards the palace.

'What do you mean?'

'Your condescension to me in front of the king. And as for that Breton girl – the jade, she must have planned it all.'

'The dark one? But surely she did us a service? If it hadn't been for her, no one would have eaten the ice at all.'

'She was working on Madame's orders, you can be sure of it.'

'Why, who is she?'

Audiger waved the question away. 'One of Madame's ladies-in-waiting. Aside from that, a person of no great importance. But if I had not been there to rescue the king's honour and accept the challenge . . .'

'What!'

'If *I* had not been there,' Audiger repeated, 'the king would have found himself embarrassed in front of his English guest. For that alone, surely, he will declare that I am the winner.'

'What will you make him?'

Audiger assumed a sneering expression. 'I do not know yet, and I will not tell you when I do. Something magnificent. Perhaps something that symbolises the brilliance of the sun.'

Of course, I thought with a sigh: the sun. It was every courtier's answer. Personally, if I were the king, I would have tired by now of sun-embossed snuffboxes, sun-decorated mirrors, sun-shaped jewels, sun-embellished paintings, sun furniture . . . But Louis never seemed to mind. Perhaps there was a value in having a simple symbol associated with your name, just as back in Florence the three balls of the Medici were on every palace and church.

'Perhaps you should serve an ice that has already melted,' I suggested. 'You know, to symbolise the king's dazzling sun-like warmth.'

'One day,' Audiger said grimly, 'that tongue of yours is going to get you into trouble. And I suspect that day may be sooner than you think.'

In that, as it turned out, he was quite wrong. It was not my tongue which got me into trouble that day but my eyes, when they alighted on a certain dark-haired, green-eyed lady-in-waiting. But of her I said no more to Audiger. There was no point in alerting him to my interest.

Carlo

You must stir your sorbet with a fork as you freeze it, to
soften the crystals and break up the ice.

The Book of Ices

A few days later I found myself walking in the rose garden, deep
in thought. I was thinking about the king's competition, and what
I might devise for it, but I was also thinking about my future.

It seemed that my partnership with Audiger, for so long uneasy,
was finally turning to rivalry, with the presidency of the guild as
the prize. I regretted it – if Audiger had not rescued me from the
Medici court, who knows how long I might have had to endure
there – but one could not go on being grateful for ever. And, if I
was honest, I was shocked that the Frenchman thought he could
beat me at the creation of an ice. I had always assumed – no,
knew – that when it came to this part of our work, my supremacy
was clear.

Louis's words to the Englishman had signalled that he only saw
the need for one ice cream maker: I would simply have to make
sure that it was me. There was no choice. I would win that competition, and Audiger would have to cede to me.

There was a place I sometimes went to be alone, when I
wanted to escape the constant ebb and flow of people around the
court: a small thicket of medlar trees where the low branches
made a sort of hidden bench. I directed my footsteps there now,
only to discover I was not alone after all. A woman was sitting,
reading, in the exact same spot where I had intended to sit myself.

Only as I came nearer did I see who it was. It was the girl with
the green eyes, the one who had tasted my ice. I was pleased: I

had not expected to have the opportunity to speak with her so soon.

'Madame,' I said, bowing. 'Good day.'

'Mademoiselle,' she corrected, glancing up briefly. 'My name is Mademoiselle Louise de Keroualle.'

'My apologies, mademoiselle. And I am—'

'The Great Demirco, the maker of ices,' she said laconically. 'Yes, I know.'

I bowed again, and waited for her to say something else, but she had already returned to her reading.

'I should thank you, mademoiselle, for tasting my ice the other day,' I observed. 'Had you not done so, I am sure that idiot doctor would have persuaded the king not to eat it.'

'Well, I have not suffered any fits as yet,' she said. She turned another page. 'Although your confection did have certain unwelcome side effects.'

'In what way?'

'Only that the whole court has been talking of nothing but ices ever since. It has been quite impossible to get anything done. I have had to come out here to escape from you, and read my book in peace. And yet now here you are, in person.'

All this was said quite matter-of-factly, and for a moment I wondered if my presence really was unwelcome to her. But then I remembered the eagerness with which she had devoured my strawberry ice, and resolved to proceed.

'And what do you do here at court, mademoiselle? This is not usually a place in which people read books.'

'If you must know, I am waiting,' she said, after a moment's pause.

'For whom?'

'For my husband.'

'And have you been waiting long?'

'Around three years. You see, I have no husband.'

Slightly baffled by this nonsense, I said, 'I would have thought that a young woman as beautiful as yourself would have no short-age of suitors.'

Nor did she react to this sally in either of the two ways I had been anticipating; that is to say, she did not blush prettily, as I might have expected her to do if she welcomed my interest; but neither did she turn up her nose, as she might have done to show that she was not receptive. Instead, she simply sighed, as if this were a conversation she had had too many times before.

'Do you mean to flirt with me? Please do not, Signor Demirco. Did they not tell you? I am much too poor to be worth flirting with.'

'Whatever do you mean?'

'Just that no one told my parents the price of a good husband nowadays is, oh, almost a dozen sets of fine clothes, and a house in town, and a hunting estate, and your accounts with tradesmen settled, and your losses at cards made good.' She spoke lightly, but it seemed to me that there was now a flash of anger in her eyes. 'So they mortgaged their last remaining lands and bought their oldest daughter a place at court, in the hope that the excellence of her wit might cause some wealthy courtier to forget the poverty of her relations, never realising their error.'

'I am sorry to hear it.'

'Don't pity me, signor. In any case, my time here is hardly wasted. While I am waiting, I can be Madame Henrietta's lady-in-waiting.'

Unsure if this was more irony, I said nothing.

'Oh, Madame is a great person,' she said with sudden passion. 'She's not one of these simpering court beauties, content to sit around embroidering cushions and plotting assignations.' She had closed her book, although I noticed that she left her thumb in it to keep her place. I glanced down, and got another surprise: it was not a romance she was reading, but Descartes' *Principles of Philosophy*. 'She is working for a great diplomatic prize – an alliance between her brother the king of England and her . . .' she hesitated. 'Her protector, the king of France. As you yourself witnessed yesterday.'

I shook my head. 'I witnessed only some courtiers being idle, a game of *paille maille,* and some dancing.'

'Dancing *is* diplomacy, in this court. And throwing dust in the eyes of the English, although amusing, is not always as easy as Madame makes it look.'

'"Dust?"'

'Forgive me,' she said suddenly. 'I am touching on matters I should not.' She got to her feet. 'You would do me the greatest service, signor, if you would forget that we ever had this conversation.'

'Forget what?' I said, puzzled. 'You have said nothing – nothing of any consequence, that is.'

She was already walking away, but she paused. Once again the lazy eye seemed to rest on me a little longer than the other.

'I'm glad you think so,' she said, mockingly. 'For my part, I thought I was exposing the very secrets of my soul.'

As she turned the corner into the rose garden, on an impulse I called after her, 'Perhaps we'll meet again.'

She did not stop, but her voice floated back to me. 'If we both keep looking for places to be alone, Signor Demirco, you may be sure of it.'

'Forget this,' she had said, but – rather to my surprise – I found that I could not. It was not her appearance, or not that alone. The French court was full of beautiful women; indeed, by their standards she hardly *was* a beauty; that lazy eye, almost a squint, must surely count against her on that score; no, it was something else, something in her manner.

It Italian they have a word, *stizzoso,* which means someone who is prickly, discontented, angry even; like a porcupine or hedgehog. Amongst those polished, languid court women of Versailles I had come across very few hedgehogs. But Louise de Keroualle was one.

56

'Perhaps we will meet again' – how clumsy I had been, but she had not rebuffed me altogether. 'You may be sure of it . . .'

Well, I had been back to the medlar trees half a dozen times since then, but she had not been there.

Olympe waited until our lovemaking was done, and the two of us were lying head-to-toe on the big four-poster bed in her apartments, before saying, 'You were distracted today.'

I turned and kissed her plump calf. 'Never.'

'Who is she?'

'What do you mean? There's no one but you.'

'Liar.' Olympe kicked me away and sat up, propping herself on one arm. 'Tell me. I much prefer intrigues to compliments, if the truth be known. Perhaps I can help you seduce her, whoever she is.'

'There's a girl . . .' I said reluctantly.

'Well, of course. Who? Come on, tell me.'

'Louise de Keroualle. I don't know why, but I find her rather intriguing.'

'Oh, *her*.' Olympe lay back down again. 'Forget her. You can't have her. Nobody can.'

'Why not?'

'Because she's not married, of course.' Seeing my look of incomprehension, she explained, 'One can tolerate infidelity in a wife or a mistress – indeed, it's to be expected, in a place like this. But a potential fiancée – particularly one as poverty-stricken as poor little Louise de Keroualle – has only her virginity to recommend her. Sadly, she's much *too* poor for anyone at this court even to think of marrying her. And so she will remain a virgin for ever, unless her parents realise their mistake and place her in a less demanding marketplace.'

'You make her sound like something for sale.'

'Of course. We women are all for sale. It is simply that some of us prefer to handle the negotiations ourselves. Or to loan ourselves out occasionally.' She stretched luxuriously. 'In any case, she's quite wrong for you. She disapproves of anyone having fun.'

'She disapproves of you, you mean?'

'Can you imagine,' Olympe said, not answering me directly, 'what a person like that would be like in bed? The only interest would be in seeing if you could get her there in the first place. After that –' she made a dismissive shrug – 'boredom.'

'She probably thinks bed is for reading books.'

Olympe laughed. 'I found a book I would quite like us to read,' she said teasingly. 'Aretino's *Postures*. The court is going mad for it. It shows twenty-seven variations of position, and there are at least four we have not tried yet.'

I glanced at her naked body. 'When shall I see you next?'

'Like this? That rather depends on whether you intend to do anything about the de Keroualle girl.'

'You said I couldn't have her.'

'You can't.' She swung her short, voluptuous legs off the bed and went towards the anteroom, where her bath was waiting. 'But I don't think that's going to stop you from trying, is it?'

I did not see Louise de Keroualle again for almost a week. The days were even hotter now, and there was a constant stream of requests coming down from the ladies and gentlemen of the court for iced cordials and cooling liquors, not to mention the king's competition to think about . . . I did not see her, but I found my thoughts returning to her, and the king's competition received less attention than it should have done as a result.

I was in the ice pantry, overseeing the making of a batch of sorbets, when a woman's voice said, 'Excuse me.'

It was her. She was wearing a simple short-sleeved dress of brown linen. But I saw the way the cold of the pantry had brought goose-skin to her forearms and the delicate flesh below her throat, and quite suddenly I could imagine just what it would be like to step forward, to take those velvety forearms between my hands, and rub them until the bumps had gone . . .

'Mademoiselle de Keroualle,' I said. 'To what do I owe this pleasure?'

Perhaps I spoke a little too enthusiastically: at any rate, it seemed to me that she eyed me somewhat warily.

'If this is really a pleasure, signor, then perhaps you are too easily pleased.'

I was not to be dissuaded by the rattling of her quills. 'If you dissect so innocent a pleasantry, perhaps you are too easily offended.'

'Perhaps,' she said with a sigh. 'Anyway, Madame has sent me. She would like a glass of iced chicory water.'

'Certainly – I will make it myself. But it will take a few minutes.'

'I can wait.' She leaned against one of the stone shelves that ran against the wall, folding her arms across her chest to keep warm, as I began to assemble the things I would need. Occasionally I glanced at her, hoping that my smiles might encourage her to reciprocate, but she simply looked around, as if curious about her surroundings.

At the back of the pantry stood a great stack of ice blocks, ready to be crushed, carved, or smashed. 'How beautiful they are,' she said quietly.

'Beautiful?' I had not thought of them that way. To me they were simply bricks, raw materials waiting to be used, but they *were* beautiful in a way, I now saw, each slab as individual as porphyry or marble; some clear as crystal, some opaque, some containing within their centres suspended cores and whorls of frozen whiteness, like water that turns cloudy as it is stirred. The stack was as low and as wide as a table, and in the dim light of the pantry it gave off a kind of cold, silvery glow.

'So pure,' she said. 'And so remarkable, here in the middle of summer.'

'These come by cart direct from the king's own caves at Besançon. There is no finer ice in Paris.' I glanced at her arms, at the fine hairs that once again had risen along her forearms. 'You're cold. Here, let me rub—'

'Thank you,' she said quickly, moving away. 'But there is no need, really. Like you, I am used to the cold.'

'Oh? Why's that?' Pulling on a grating glove – a gauntlet of thick leather covered with a lattice of chainmail – I began to shave ice into a bowl with a hard, rhythmic motion.

'Where I come from – the Bay of Brest – the winters are very severe.' She was silent for a moment, as if remembering. 'Even the sea fills with ice. Sometimes a fog comes in from the German Sea and freezes everything, every tree and blade of grass, and they become coated with tiny crystals, like a white fur.'

I nodded. 'I have heard of such a thing, though I have never seen it.'

'If you are warm, or rich, or young, it is rather wonderful,' she said. Her eyes had a faraway look in them as they followed the rhythmic motion of my hand across the ice. 'But if you are poor, or old, or hungry, it can be terrifying. Every year, when the earth could be dug again, we buried dozens of people killed by the bad weather. My family were better off than most, of course. We always had enough for a fire in the great hall – a fire of wood, that is, not sea coal. But in the nursery, or the sleeping quarters – there we had no heat at all. We used to look forward to snow, because that was a sign the weather was getting warmer. If you woke up and the grate was full of snow, you would pull on your clothes and run outside to dance and make snowmen.' Her eyes softened at a memory. 'Or throw snowballs at your brothers, of course. But that was before I was sent to court.'

I had a sudden image of this proud young woman dancing in the snow, spinning with glee, her dark hair glistening with fat wet flakes which turned to sequins as they melted.

'In Florence, it rarely snowed,' I said. 'Once or twice a year, perhaps.' The ice was ready to use. I hesitated. 'I must ask you to turn your back now. This part of the process is secret.'

She raised her eyebrows. 'You think I might steal your methods? And set up as a confectioner on my own account?'

'Of course not. But unfortunately there can be no exceptions. The king himself insists on it.'

She shrugged and turned her back. I added a scoop of saltpetre to the ice, then took a long-necked flagon, a *cantimplora,* into which I poured the cordial water. Pushing the vessel deep into the ice mixture, I rotated it, cooling the contents to just this side of freezing.

'I suppose the mystery is all part of the performance,' she commented to the wall. 'Like a conjuror, you have to make it seem more difficult than it really is.'

For a moment I allowed my eyes to rest unobserved on her back – the curve of her spine, the set of her hips, the way she stood; a little awkward, a colt rather than a horse. 'On the contrary. We protect only what we must.'

I spooned the remainder of the ice into a goblet and poured the chilled cordial over it. It was a fine colour, I thought, holding it up to the light to admire it: pale brown, almost golden, the ice glinting in its depths. 'You can turn round now.'

She did so. 'Is there any more?' she asked.

'Is this not enough?'

'She will want to know that I have tasted it.'

'Why?'

'She worries about poison.'

'Poison!'

Once more her gaze lingered on my face, as if wondering how much to tell me. She said seriously, 'You would not laugh if you knew the risks she takes. Her own husband . . .' She shuddered. 'Well, never mind. But she will certainly ask if I have tasted this.'

There was a little cordial left in the flagon, so I poured it into another glass. '*Prego,*' I said, handing it to her. A thought suddenly occurred to me. 'Was that why you ate her strawberry ice?

It wasn't to please me, or to confound that idiot doctor, after all. You were making sure it wasn't poisoned.'

She swallowed the cordial off in one draught, her eyes on mine, the slow one following the other. 'Very good,' she said, handing back the empty glass, and I could not be sure now if she was referring to the cordial or my reasoning. She picked up the other glass and placed it on a tray.

'And when you said it was as delicious as a lover's kiss on a warm summer's day . . .'

She smiled. 'That is the sort of nonsense the court likes to hear, don't you find?'

I grunted.

'Oh, don't be offended,' she said. 'The ice was perfectly pleasant, as it happens. We both have our secrets, signor. It's just that mine are a little more serious.'

'How can a woman's secrets be serious! The secrets of which dressmaker to use, or who has bested who at cards!'

'I'm sure you are right.' She carried the tray two-handed to the door, and stopped. 'And now I find I am such a feeble example of my sex that I can't even open this heavy door without the use of my hands.'

Sighing, I went and pulled the door open for her.

'I am much obliged,' she said with mock courtliness. 'By the way, signor, it was a pleasure talking to you. And you should know that, unlike you, I am not so easily pleased.'

I could not talk to Audiger. So I went to see Olympe.

'I know you told me not to come back until I was done with her,' I said, striding into her apartment. 'But I need your advice.'

As I told her what had happened I realised how ridiculous it sounded – a few glances, some spiky remarks, a conversation about a snow fight with her brothers. But Olympe heard me out, nodding from time to time.

'Well, that *is* interesting,' she said when I had finished.

'You think she likes me, then?' I said eagerly.

'Oh, I didn't mean your grand passion, amusing though that is. No, I meant Madame Henrietta d'Angleterre's flirtation with grand politics. Which is, as Louise rightly observed, a very serious matter indeed.'

'What are you talking about?'

She sighed. 'The problem with you, Carlo, is that you think this entire court exists only to eat your ices. Actually, it is a war machine, the greatest in Europe, and a dropped handkerchief here can lead to the burning of whole cities in Spain or Flanders.'

'But what does that have to do with Louise de Keroualle?'

'The king wants the English to be his allies in a war against the Dutch,' Olympe said, as if to an idiot. 'The English themselves are of no great account, of course, but they have a great deal of coast-line, and it must be denied to our enemies.'

'I know all this. That's why the English visitor is here. To draw up a treaty.'

Olympe shook her head. 'The real treaty was signed in secret three weeks ago.'

'I don't understand. How?'

'When Madame Henrietta went to visit Charles at Dover to celebrate his birthday, she took with her a treaty drawn up by her and signed by Louis – who also happens to be her lover,' she explained. 'Did he seduce her simply to enlist her help?' Olympe's shrug suggested that she thought it quite possible. 'Anyway, the treaty says that Charles will commit England to war with the Dutch, in exchange for a pension from Louis – a pension so generous that Charles will no longer have to bow his knee to the English Parliament that restored him.'

'That is hardly unreasonable, surely? A parliament should have no right to meddle in a king's affairs.'

'Of course. But I hear that the treaty also commits Charles to becoming a Catholic. And if the English king is Catholic, his country must be too. Effectively it is a treaty which, if it were known about, commits Charles to a conflict with his own people. Hence the need to draw up another version, one more fit for public consumption, with no mention of pensions or religion.'

'So the English duke—'

'Is, much to Louis's amusement, here to negotiate terms which have, in fact, already been settled. But of course, he must have no inkling of it – he must believe that he has, by dint of his own charm and hard bargaining, managed to secure exactly what he was ordered to hold out for. He will take the *traité simulé* back to England; their Parliament will ratify it, and no one will be any the wiser. *That* is what Louise meant when she let slip that remark about throwing dust in the eyes of the English.'

I nodded, although it seemed extraordinary to me, the complex lies within lies that made up French diplomacy.

'This plan, it is well known, has been Madame Henrietta's great preoccupation ever since her brother regained his throne,' Olympe went on. 'But there have been numerous obstacles – not least from those here at court who oppose an alliance with Protestants and regicides. Madame has suffered unexplained fits before, and the doctors believe it was poison.'

'I had no idea.'

'Of course you didn't. These are subtle, secret matters.' Olympe leaned forward, her eyes shining. 'But if little Louise de Keroualle, at her tender age, has become Madame's confidential agent, she must be rather more than the simple child I took her for.'

I thought back to that sardonic voice; the clever, lazy gaze. 'She is certainly no simpleton.'

Olympe nodded. 'Which, in turn, may a problem for *me*.'

'For you! Why?'

'Because I hope that the king will one day return to my own bed on a more permanent basis, of course,' she said simply. 'He took his present mistress from among Madame's ladies-in-waiting; I must take care that he does not do it again. Perhaps it is time for pretty, clever Mademoiselle de Keroualle to go back to Brittany.'

Her gaze shifted back to me. 'As for your little problem, that is easily settled.'

'It is?'

Olympe got up and moved towards the bedroom. 'I know I said we would not do this for the time being, but I find intrigues strangely arousing. Come: your cure awaits.'

Afterwards she said, 'So . . . Do you think your little virgin would really have been as much fun as that?'

I laughed. 'You are quite right, as ever. She is much too dull for me. I shan't give her another thought.'

'Don't be too hasty,' she said.

Something in her tone alerted me. 'Olympe, what are you scheming now?'

'I have had an idea,' she admitted. 'Rather a delicious one – I have all my best ideas while making love. It's very simple. Instead of seducing her, why don't you marry her?'

'Marry Louise!'

'Yes. It's perfect, isn't it? After all, you have to marry sometime, and it should be to someone who advances your interests. You have money – new money, admittedly, but someone in her position can't be too choosy, and time is running out; she must be at least twenty by now. But her family is a good one, and the king clearly likes her: by taking her as your wife, you would consolidate your own position.'

I was silent for a moment. 'And afterwards?'

She shrugged. 'As soon as she's pregnant, you set her up in a house somewhere suitably removed. It needn't affect your other arrangements.' She put her hand on my arm, stroking it idly. 'It might even make them easier. There are plenty of women who would rather have an affair with a married man than a single one. You would have the best of both worlds.'

'And it suits your interests too, by removing Louise de Keroualle from court.'

'Of course,' she said simply. 'I wouldn't have suggested it otherwise.'

I thought about it. It was true that I should marry soon: true, too, that my wealth, and the royal warrant, meant that I could hope to marry someone with connections. I had already risen further than I had ever thought possible; but with the right sort of wife, and, I hoped, the presidency of the guild, there was no reason why I should not go even further.

'Well, I will consider it,' I said. Olympe only smiled enigmatically.

Carlo

To make snow: take a pottle of thick cream, and the whites of eight eggs, and beat them all together with a spoon. Then take a stick, and cut the end four square: scent your mixture with some essence of bergamot or rosewater, and beat it hard until it rises.

The Book of Ices

In Florence, Ahmad sometimes told stories as we worked. The stories were about many things, but they were always, in some way, about ice.

One tale concerned our employers and a man who had worked for them a hundred and fifty years earlier. The story went that one winter it snowed in Florence. The children of Piero de' Medici tried to make a snowman, but being children, and unpractised, their efforts were unsuccessful. So Piero summoned one of his late father's artists and ordered him to carve them a snowman.

The young man tried to explain that working in the medium of snow was not a fitting use of his talents. Piero di Medici told him to be sure to be finished by morning.

All that frozen night, by the light of the moon, the artist sculpted the snow as if it were a block of the finest Cararra marble, his hands wrapped in soaked, freezing rags against the cold.

In the morning the Medici princes ran out to the courtyard to see what he had done. It was, a contemporary wrote, undoubtedly the most beautiful snowman that anyone had ever seen. But the day brought milder weather, and with the milder weather came rain. Soon there was nothing left of Michelangelo's first sculpture except a withered stalagmite of ice, like the stump of a decayed tooth, the only white thing left in the courtyard.

At this point Ahmad would pause. 'Some people take this story to illustrate the transience of beauty and the tyranny of time, boy. I take it to mean something else. Two things, in fact. First, when a Medici tells you to jump, you ask how high. And the second . . .' His eyes rested thoughtfully on my eager gaze. 'And the second is, always keep your ice away from rain.'

I made Louise de Keroualle a snowman.

It was probably not as spectacular as Michelangelo's, but then, Michelangelo's had not been edible.

First I had to make my snow. Milk and sugar, flavoured with rosewater, mixed with the white of eggs and beaten with a plaited whisk. Only when the froth was so light it floated off the whisk did I chill it, turning it to flakes of the purest, most delicate snow.

From this I fashioned two balls for the body and the head, adding a hat of crisp caramel and a smile of candied orange. The eyes were dried sultanas, the nose a cherry that had been preserved in liqueur. In one hand the snowman held a broom made of rosemary, while on his chest he bore a single slice of candied strawberry for a heart.

And, finally, I made it snow.

This was a feat, supposedly invented by the great Buontalenti, that even Ahmad had rarely attempted. When a fine mist of rosewater was sprayed over a mixture of ice and saltpetre, the droplets turned to crystals so light they neither rose nor fell, but floated in the air like specks of glittering gold leaf.

It did not take long for Louise to visit me – every day now there was another order for an iced chicory water to aid Madame's digestion, and either Louise or one of the other ladies-in-waiting would come to collect it. I waited until she came with her usual request, and said gruffly, 'I have prepared that one already.'

Her eyebrows rose as she looked around. 'I can't see it.'

'In there.' I indicated with my head the door she should go through.

She looked suspicious, but said nothing as she went. I heard her gasp, and then there was silence.

I stayed where I was. I suddenly realised that I had no idea whether she was going to like it or not.

Then something cold and wet smashed into the side of my head. I whipped round. I caught a glimpse of laughing, gleeful eyes before a second snowball, launched from her other hand, hit me in the neck.

'Signor Demirco – are you coming or not?' she demanded. 'I can't possibly have a snowball fight on my own.'

I followed her. The gust of air as I entered the second pantry made the snow billow and eddy around me, glittering in the light of a beeswax candle.

She turned, her hands already laden, and hurled another snowball, but she was too soon, and it disintegrated harmlessly on my coat. Then – I could not help it – I had taken two paces and she was in my arms; and her lips – her cool, pale lips – tasted of rose-water and sugar, dusted with flakes of frost like some soft, fragrant pollen.

For a long moment I kissed her, and she kissed me back – I was sure of it – her mouth warm against my own. And then, with a sudden gasp, she pulled away from me, horror written across her face.

'What are you doing?' she cried.

'Wait,' I said. 'Louise, let me explain. I want—'

But she was already gone. Through the open door I felt warm air sweeping in, like seawater breaking over a sandbank, and all around me I saw my snow melting back into water, like fool's gold.

I tried to write her a letter, but the sheet of paper was a field of pristine snow that I only ruined by covering it with my pen marks.

So I sent her the snowman instead, on a platter born by two foot-men, directed to Louise de Keroualle in the apartments of Madame Henrietta, Duchess of Orleans.

It was returned to me an hour later, unaccepted, half-melted from its trip around the palace.

I went to see her, but I was not admitted. So I lingered near the garden where the medlar trees were, hoping for a glimpse of her.

At last I caught sight of her going in the direction of the groves. She had something in her hands – a shawl, it looked like.

'Louise!' I called.

For a moment she turned her head, and I thought she hesi-tated, but then she hurried on again. I lost sight of her behind a hedge, and broke into a run to catch her up. The gardens in this part of Versailles were like a maze; a series of interconnected courtyards and lawns, each one hidden from the next. She was not in the next garden, but through a gap in the hedge I glimpsed the billowing of her gown.

Finally, rounding a corner by a fountain, I saw her. 'Louise!' I called again, but now I saw that she was joining a small group. Amongst them was her mistress, Madame Henrietta, sitting on a stone bench. Even at this distance I could see how frail and bowed she looked. Beside her stood the king, along with Buckingham and two of the king's ministers.

'Really, it is nothing,' Madame was saying weakly as Louise put the shawl around her shoulders. 'Just a little faintness, Your Majesty.'

'The air is rather chilly,' Buckingham offered. 'Perhaps you would prefer we move indoors?'

The king had seen me. 'Signor Demirco. Who do you seek?'

I realised I was standing there gawping foolishly. 'Your Majesty – that is, I wondered if Madame la Comptesse would like a cordial. I know she takes iced chicory sometimes, for her diges-tion.'

Louis looked at Madame enquiringly.

'Perhaps later,' she said faintly. 'You might send one to my rooms.'

'Signor Demirco?' the king called as I retreated.

'Your Majesty?'

'How do you fare with the ice for the English king? We are hoping for something marvellous, you know.'

I bowed again. 'I have not thought of anything suitable yet, sir.'

A look of mild surprise crossed the king's face. 'Well, do not leave it too long.' He turned back to the others, and as I walked away, my ears burning, I caught the words 'Italian – unreliable – but inventive: you will see, milord Duke, you will see.'

I waited until they were all walking back towards the palace. The king was pointing to either side, no doubt explaining to the Englishman his plans to extend the already magnificent grounds still further. Louise walked a little way behind. Seizing my chance, I caught her up.

'I need to talk to you.'

She glanced at the king. 'Don't you think you have offended him enough already for one day?'

I looked at where the king's hand traced imaginary fountains in the air. 'I told him I have not yet made his ice. How is that offensive?'

'You implied in front of a foreign visitor that chasing after a lady-in-waiting takes precedence over a royal command. The slight may be a small one, but you can be sure he will remember it – if he chooses to.'

'I was not chasing after you.'

'I am glad to hear it. Clearly you had some other pressing reason for running in my direction.'

'I came to tell you that I love you.'

She stopped dead. Then, her face set, she strode on towards the palace. 'Don't mock me.'

'Louise, I'm not joking. My feelings for you are entirely genuine.'

'Olympe de Soissons has thrown you out, has she?' She saw my look of surprise. 'Oh, did you think no one knew about that? This is the court, signor. Secrets are all people have to talk about.'

I made a gesture. 'She means nothing to me. A diversion, that's all.'

'Whereas I, of course, would be so much more.' She spoke sardonically, but she slowed her pace a little. 'Please understand: I do not mean to be abrupt with your feelings. But when I first came to court I made a foolish mistake. I allowed my name to be associated with that of a man – a person of noble birth, as it happens, but he had been mixed up in some scandalous affairs. Nobody criticised *him* for that, of course: but they saw me with him, and assumed that I was behaving as those other women had, and my reputation became tainted. If it had not been for Madame, I should have had to leave court in disgrace. I won't make that mistake again.'

'Nor would I want you to. I mean to marry you, Louise.'

She stopped again, her eyes wide.

'I have the king's favour: my position here is secure,' I went on quickly. 'And you would be an asset to me: you understand the ways of the court—' I halted, brought up short by the look in her eyes.

'*What?*' she said incredulously.

'I want to marry you,' I repeated.

For a moment she looked at me as if I was quite mad.

'I am Louise Renee de Penacöet, Dame de Keroualle, the eldest daughter of the oldest family of Brittany,' she said slowly and deliberately. 'Our lineage goes back to before the crusades.'

'So? You told me yourself that your parents sent you to court to find a husband—'

'They sent me here to find a *duke*. Or at the very least, a duke's younger brother.' She shook her head, as if she could not quite

72

believe that this was happening. 'Please understand this, signor: I have nothing against you personally. If you were of a noble family, I am sure that my father would overlook the fact that you are a frivolous, pleasure-seeking Italian libertine who spends his time doing nothing more worthwhile than producing titbits for greedy courtiers – when you are not seducing ladies-in-waiting, that is. But unless you are actually a Medici or a Mazarin, I'm afraid he is unlikely to take quite so broad a view.'

Angry now, I said 'I don't know who my parents were. Only that they were poor, and left me to make my own way in the world.'

She sighed, and it seemed to me that she spoke a little less acerbically. 'Well, I am sorry for it. But you know, being free to make your own way can be a blessing.'

I caught her meaning. 'So you do not actually want to marry a nobleman—'

'I have no choice,' she said flatly. 'I do not necessarily share my parents' obsession with breeding and nobility. But they are my parents, and I must accede to their wishes. It is my duty.'

'No marriage then,' I said stubbornly. 'Very well. But that does not mean—'

'Oh, no,' she interrupted. 'Do not for one moment think that I am like your friend Olympe.'

'I didn't mean to suggest you were,' I muttered.

But Louise was staring at me as if she had just been struck by a thought. 'Did *she* put you up to this?'

The answer must have been written on my face, because she added, 'Of course. How lovely. This is her idea of a joke, isn't it.'

'No,' I protested.

'Really? Teasing me about my predicament is just the sort of thing she finds amusing.' She smiled thinly. 'It pays me back for what I think of her and her kind, I suppose. Well, you may congratulate yourself, signor. By nightfall this merriment of yours will be all round the court.'

'Wait,' I called after her as she turned away. 'Wait. Louise – I was not joking. That is, it may have been Olympe's idea, but—'

I was too late. She was already hurrying back to the house. But not before I had seen that there were tears in those green eyes.

I returned to the palace. Where, almost immediately, I encountered Olympe. She had clearly been watching from one of the windows that overlooked the gardens.

'Well?' she asked.

'She said no,' I said curtly.

'Really?' Olympe's face was the picture of innocence. 'Any particular reason?'

'She said marriage with an Italian confectioner of no particular birth was unthinkable.'

Olympe nodded seriously, but there was a gleam of amusement deep in her eyes. 'Did she mention her noble lineage, by any chance? The oldest family in Brittany? Did she mention –' her eyes grew round – 'the Crusades?'

'She did,' I said. 'She also asked if it was you who put me up to this. Our association is widely known, it seems.'

Olympe's eyes had closed and her shoulders were shaking. 'Priceless!' she managed to gasp. 'Priceless!'

'I am glad you're amused.'

'Oh, Carlo, don't be like that,' she said, wiping her eyes. 'You have to see the funny side – she must have been *furious*; it serves her right for being such a virtuous little *prudefemme*.'

I laughed, but a little mirthlessly; although there could be no doubt that Louise de Keroualle had shown herself to be overly proud, and quite lacking in that sense of frivolity which so enlivened our time at court, I could not help feeling that I had not emerged terribly well from this episode myself. 'It seems I have been your dupe,' I said shortly.

Olympe smiled. 'You have duped yourself. *I* have done you a

74

favour. You were in danger of letting your emotions get in the way of your pleasures. Sometimes it is necessary to step back a little.'

'Of course,' I said. 'Thank you.'

There was no point in arguing further with Olympe; and she was right, of course: I *had* allowed my feelings to cloud my judgement. But I could not help reflecting on how very different I would be feeling now if Louise's answer to my proposal had been 'yes'.

Louise

On that fateful day I was a little late returning to Madame's apartments. There had been an incident with the one of the king's
confectioners, a thing of no consequence in itself but a little upset-
ting, as these things sometimes are. It was annoying, though, in
that it made me late, and I found as I hurried up the steps to
Madame's apartment that I was a little out of breath.

Then, as I entered the apartment, I saw that noble lady crying,
and all thoughts of the confectioner were instantly banished from
my mind.

'What is it, Madame?' I asked.

She started when she saw me. 'Just a vile letter.' For a moment
I thought she would say nothing more, then she added, 'From my
husband.'

I kept my voice level. 'I trust Monsieur le Compte is well?'

Madame smiled wanly. 'Well enough to tell me that I am a trai-
tor and a whore; that more rumours have reached him concerning
myself and a certain person at court, and that I am to leave here
immediately and go to him in Milan, so that he can once again
attempt to get an heir on me.' She spoke lightly, but of course I
heard the distress in her voice.

I should now describe this paragon, chiefly for the pleasure of
doing so, rather than from any need to fix her in my mind (for her
portrait is as well known here in England as in France, and in any
case there is still not a day that passes when I do not think of her).
She was of slight build – so slight that her clothes almost fell off
her. Only I and a very few others knew the extent of the padding
under her court dresses, or how her skin was now so pale that in
places you could see the blue veins far beneath the surface. But
when you looked at her you did not notice her frailty, so radiant

was her expression, so intense the goodness in her eyes; and when she spoke of her great concern – the plan to unite her two dearest friends, her brother Charles and her protector Louis, in a political alliance which would form the basis for a great Europe-wide empire of peace and prosperity – her eyes seemed to burn with conviction; a conviction which, together with her many amiable qualities and her charm, had been instrumental in the considerable success of her diplomacy so far. But she was certainly in no state to bear anyone an heir, even if her husband had been able to leave off buggering his own male lovers for long enough to get one on her.

'And? Will you go?' I asked.

'How can I? The *traité simulé* has not yet been signed. Until it is, the *traité secrete* is not secure; and with it, my brother's throne.' She lifted another envelope. 'There is a letter from him, as well.'

'From King Charles? May I see?'

'Of course.' Madame smiled at my enthusiasm. 'In fact, you may read it aloud. A draft of sweet cordial to take away the bitter taste of my husband's words.' She handed it to me.

Aware that my English was not as pure as Madame's, I read slowly. '*My sweetest Minette . . .*'

'Minette! He thinks I am still a child,' Madame commented, but there was a smile on her face.

'*First I must chastise you, for in your last letter you have once again addressed me as Your Majesty, not once but half a dozen times. Do not treat me with such ceremony, or address me with so many Majesties, as between you and me there should be nothing but affection . . .*' I paused. 'He writes so kindly.'

'He is the kindest man in the world,' Madame said simply.

'He certainly seemed so last month, at Dover.' The signing of the treaty, the *traité secrete* as we called it, had been done under the pretence of celebrating Charles's birthday. For two weeks the royal party, of which I was honoured to be a part, had sailed, picnicked, gone to plays and attended dances. When Madame's ship finally took us away, Charles ordered his own yacht to pursue us almost to the coast of France so that he could embrace his sister one last time, the tears streaming from his eyes.

Madame smiled again at the memory. 'I think they were the happiest weeks of my life.'

'How different the two letters are,' I said neutrally.

'It is difficult for my husband,' Madame said. She could not bear to speak ill of anyone for long, not even him. She put a hand to her stomach, wincing.

'Are you quite well?' I asked.

'A little indisposed. Would you get me some iced chicory? Abbé Bossuet will be here soon, and I fear he may linger. He wants to discuss the arrangements for my brother's conversion.'

'I thought the timing of that had not been settled.'

Madame smiled. 'My brother is a kind and charming man, but he is so often surrounded by those making demands upon him that he has a tendency to put things off. I fear that if I do not hold him to his promise immediately, he may allow it to slip his mind.' This remark, incidentally, was typical of her. She had an ability to believe the best of people, but also to see their weaknesses quite clearly, and to make arrangements accordingly.

'Of course. And would you like me to draft a reply to your husband? Something polite that commits you to nothing?'

'Thank you.'

I went to Madame's closet – the little room she used as a study – and found writing implements. I sent a maid for the chicory water. It would be best, I decided, if I could keep out of the Italian confectioner's way, at least for a few days, until this infatuation of his had passed. It was not the first time men had announced themselves in love with me, and I supposed it would not be the last, but for all the agonies they avowed I had noticed that they generally found someone to console themselves with after a week or two. Sometimes I felt sorry for these men, if they were sincere; or angry, if they were not; but I rarely felt any personal guilt, having long ago come to the realisation that it was my face and figure, those accidents of my birth, that were the cause of these ardent protestations, rather than anything I myself might have done – just as it was another accident of birth, that of being born into a once-great but now impoverished family, that seemed to have condemned me to a life of spinsterhood. Not that I particularly wanted to find myself at the beck and call of a husband, of course, but whilst I did not have one I was without any kind of status whatsoever, a figure of derision at court, my entire life dependent on the whims of others.

So I resolved to give no further thought to Signor Demirco. Even so, I could not help glancing out of the window for a glimpse of him bringing the iced chicory water to Madame: I found myself surprised, and a little disappointed, when it was delivered by one of the palace footmen instead.

There were so many letters to write – letters of thanks to the French ambassador in England; letters to the nobles who had been our hosts at various castles around Dover; everything possible that could be done to leave a favourable impression of our visit, so that an alliance with France – the Great Affair, as we had dubbed it – would, when it was finally made public, garner the support it needed. I heard the murmur of voices as the abbé arrived, but did not go to join them. Madame would call if she needed me, and the correspondence was more pressing.

More murmurs, as others paid their visits too. I looked at the little clock on the bureau, a present to his sister from the English king. It was almost time for cards, Madame's only vice.

Suddenly a man's voice shouted – shouted in horror. I heard a crash, and what sounded like furniture being moved. I rushed back into the salon.

The abbé was laying Madame down on a divan that had been hastily cleared of cushions. Playing cards littered the floor, and a basset table was lying on its side. Several court ladies were standing in the centre of the room, looking for all the world like frightened sheep.

Seeing me, the abbé shouted, 'Fetch a physician, girl. Hurry. It must be poison, or a fit – she drank from that cordial just before she collapsed.'

My eyes went to the flagon of iced chicory water. 'Poison?' I repeated stupidly.

'A physician, quickly,' he repeated. 'She will have to be purged.'

'I will send a footman. It will be quicker.' I went to the door, and ordered the man standing outside to go and find the doctor. Then I turned back to the room. The abbé was saying prayers over Madame.

'We need to loosen her clothing,' I said, interrupting him. 'Help me lift her.'

There were more gasps from the women as the two of us pulled Madame's limp form forward so that I could undo her stays. As soon as they were loosened she coughed, expelling a clot of brownish matter into her lap, and cried out in pain. It looked as if she were trying to pull her legs up into a ball. Her breathing was shallow, and the skin of her neck was clammy with sweat. I could see, too, that her lower belly was protruding strangely, almost as if she were with child, although I could swear that it had not been so swollen a few hours before. She was clearly in agony. If the doctor gave her a purgative, the effort of vomiting would surely kill her.

I heard one of the women repeat, 'Poison! We might all have died.'

Another said, 'The physician warned us not to take iced drinks—'

I reached for the chicory water. 'She has not been poisoned. Nor could a little ice have done this. Look.' Barely thinking of the possible consequences, I put the glass to my lips and drank from it. The women gasped in unison – an effect that would have been comical had it not been for the circumstances.

I put down the empty glass. 'If I collapse, you may purge Madame along with me. If not, it is something else.'

The physician hurried into the room. 'Where is she?'

I showed him. He knelt by Madame's side, taking in the situation, then pressed gently on her stomach. Madame screamed – a hideous, pitiful sound.

I said, 'She has been ill for months, with vomiting and fevers. She drank some chicory water but I am sure it was because she had already felt the fit coming on – she says it eases her pains.'

The physician stood up. 'We should make her comfortable,' he said uneasily.

'What do you mean, comfortable? What are you going to do?' I demanded.

'There is nothing I can do.' The doctor looked helplessly at the abbé. 'Father, your prayers are going to be of more use now than my medicine.'

The abbé got on his knees beside the couch. 'Do you believe in God?' he asked Madame quietly. They were the opening words of the *viaticum*, the last rites.

Madame's eyes opened. 'With all my heart,' she whispered.

'Wait!' I said desperately. 'There must be something you can do.'

'Louise.' It was Madame, whispering my name with an effort. I too sank to my knees beside her.

'It will be. . .' Madame closed her eyes as a series of violent spasms convulsed her fragile body. 'I am prepared. But you must make sure . . . my brother . . .'

I touched her wrist, gently. Even that was greasy and cold with sweat. 'I will make sure of the treaty. I promise.'

'Make sure he dies a Catholic.' Her eyes opened again, briefly, fixing urgently on me, as if to make sure I understood that this was what mattered the most. 'Make sure of it.'

They were the last entire words she ever spoke.

*

81

She died an endless hour later, in agony – such agony. As was the custom, the whole court gathered to watch her die. Whilst those closest to her wept, those at the back of the room – principally her husband's homosexual favourites, who had never liked her – carried on their gossiping and intriguing as casually as if they were watching a performance at the ballet. Only when the king himself appeared, coming to kneel by his sister-in-law's bedside, did the atmosphere become more dignified, those same courtiers who a few minutes earlier had been joking and laughing now vying with each other to weep as piteously as their monarch.

After her body had been carried away Louis, his eyes bleak, summoned me to his private apartments.

'Was it poison?' he wanted to know.

'Your Majesty, I believe not. I myself drank from the glass of chicory water afterwards, and suffered no ill effects.'

'Well, the doctors may be able to tell us more tomorrow.' He sighed. 'Thank you, Louise.'

Despite what I had said, the rumours refused to go away. It was common knowledge that Madame had feared poison, and that her husband and she were at odds. Those who knew that she had been involved in diplomatic work against the Dutch were even more inclined to believe foul play.

For my own part, her death devastated me. Not only had I lost the woman I idolised – the kindest, cleverest, sweetest person in the world – but I had also lost my employer, my protector, and my place at court. The project we had worked so hard on was in ruins too, for the rumours soon reached the English court: word of Charles's terrible grief, and his own suspicions, came back to us the same way. Nor did it help when Abbé Bossuet, who preached her funeral oration, described her as 'murdered'.

Carlo

To make a sorbet of pears: take twelve pears, peeled and
sliced, so ripe that the slices slip around in your hands.
Make a pulp, and sieve it fine; simmer with the juice of
one lemon and a cup of sugar, then freeze, stirring in the
usual way. If you add crème anglaise you will have a cream
ice instead of a *sorbetto*.

The Book of Ices

After the episode with Louise I shut myself away for a few days.
For some reason I felt myself a little consumed by that obstinate
dullness of the soul which physicians call melancholy.

I spent the time busying myself with the long-overdue task of
making an ice for the English visitor. I had neglected this process
appallingly. It was said that the English delegation would be leaving within the week: the king might demand to judge the contest
at any moment.

Listlessly, I began to assemble ingredients. What was required?
Something showy, obviously: something which demonstrated my
mastery of my art, and the splendour of the French court.

The corridors of Versailles were decorated with elaborate paintings: every candelabra was held aloft by golden cherubs. I began
to carve a cherub out of ice, holding up a frozen platter on which
I would place – what? A horn of plenty, perhaps: a cornucopia,
dispensing fruits. During my time at the court I had already made
wooden moulds which allowed me to construct ices in the shapes
of cherries, pears and apples. Now I added a musk melon, a perfectly pink peach, and a bunch of golden, translucent grapes,
dusted with powdered bakers' sugar to represent the fine pale

bloom of a vine. The whole thing was garlanded with vine leaves made of biscuit and sugar-work.

When it was done I looked at it, and I hated it.

It was magnificent and meaningless – a platter of pointless pomp, an exercise in empty display and grandiloquence that I could have done in my sleep. Even Audiger could have done it.

I heard Louise de Keroualle's voice in my head. *A frivolous, pleasure-seeking libertine who spends his time doing nothing more worthwhile than producing titbits for greedy courtiers . . .*

It was not true, and I would prove it.

Picking up the cherub and its platter, I dashed it to the floor. Ice shattered around my feet; imitation fruits rolled to the furthest extremes of my pantry. Those within reach I stamped on with my boots, crushing them, and kicked the pieces away. Then I began to pace up and down.

I spent a whole day and a night thinking, reaching for ingredients only to put them away again. I knew what I did not want to make; but as to what I *did* want, that was rather harder.

I looked over at my blocks of ice. *How beautiful they are.* No, I thought: they are not beautiful, they are implacable. They will forgive nothing.

What was the simplest, the most ridiculously straightforward ice I could make to please the king?

Pears. Louis loved pears.

So – I would make a pear ice. But this would be the best pear ice I, or anyone else, had ever made.

I used only Rousselet de Reims, the king's favourite variety, perfectly ripe that month. First I roasted them whole with a little thyme and some sweet wine, very gently, to sweeten the flesh. Then I pureed them with the zest of a lemon and a small amount of verjuice.

I added some salt, too. Salt, lemon, verjuice – these were additions which would be unnoticeable in the finished ice, but which

I knew would magnify the pears' flavour when it burst off the spoon and into the mouth. I had my sorbet – or at least, the beginnings of it.

Then, in a moment of inspiration, I added some *crème anglaise*.

I was thinking initially only of how I could make it more English, of course. But as soon as I tasted it I realised that the smooth, warm richness of the custard, flecked with specks of black vanilla, was the perfect accompaniment to the fragrant sharpness of the fruit.

I stepped back, amazed. I saw immediately what I had done: I had created a *combination*, an alliance of flavours, in which the whole was greater than the sum of its parts. Together, the French pear and the English custard were one dish, better than either on its own. Frozen together in a kind of cream ice, they would symbolise the special relationship between the two countries, united in one indivisible whole. And – best of all – it was simple; so simple that even a fool like myself could not fail to grasp the message.

Impatiently, I waited for the mixture to freeze, stirring it every half hour as usual. Each time I took the lid off the *sabotiere*, and worked the paddle around the sides of the pewter bucket, I noticed how fine and pale the flakes of frozen cream ice were. And they felt different, too. Instead of the grainy, sandy feel of crushed ice, there was only a smooth, luxurious firmness, as if I were stirring a rich, heavy paste.

Finally, it was done. In my impatience I did not even put it into a bowl, but tried some straight from the bucket.

It was extraordinary. Not just the taste, but the texture. Somehow, I had made an ice so thick, so creamy and so soft it was as if a macaroon was dissolving in my mouth. No granules of ice, no graininess: just the oily, smooth slipperiness of cream coating my tongue as it melted, leaving the sweet sharpness of pear and the warm richness of *crème anglaise*.

At last I had made an ice such as Ahmad could only dream of.

The only thing perplexing me was that I could not, immediately, see what I had done to make this ice so different. No matter: that could be sorted at a later time. For now, I just wanted to try my ice out on someone. It needed a worthy setting, of course: I had been keeping back a goblet of priceless Venetian glass, encrusted with flecks of gold, for just such an occasion. I reached for it – then hesitated. Once again, the key to making this special was simplicity, not extravagance.

I made two little coronets, royal crowns, out of brandy-snap, and filled each one with my pear-and-*crème-anglaise* cream ice.

Then I carried it outside. At first, there seemed to be no one about. But from the gardens I heard the sound of murmuring courtiers. Perhaps, I thought, Louis might even be with them.

Hurrying towards the source, I rounded a hedge. I was in luck: there was the king.

'Your Majesty,' I cried.

As I advanced towards Louis I became aware that people were turning to look at me. The murmuring died away. Too late I realised that, today, all their finery – their hats and canes and frock coats, and even the plumes in their hats – were black, as black as sloes. Someone had died. But who?

It was too late to stop, too late to go back, but my footsteps slowed. And then the king himself turned around, his eyes hollow, and took in the sight of me coming towards him, bearing a dish with an ice on it.

'Your Majesty,' I called again, and bowed. 'I have made your ice, and it is wonderful.'

The king had taken a step back, and the courtiers on either side of me were shrinking back too. 'Ice!' I heard someone say. And there was the doctor again, the idiot who had warned the king that eating ices might be dangerous. He was speaking urgently to one of the footmen, pointing to me as he did so.

'Would Your Majesty not like to taste a little?' I said, puzzled. And then two sergeants-at-arms had hurried forward, and I found myself being led away.

Louise

'What will you do, child?' the king asked gently.

I kept my head bowed and my hands laced in my lap. 'Whatever Your Majesty commands.'

The king looked at his principal minister, Lionne. It was the presence of the latter at this discussion which was both intriguing and disturbing me. That the king wished to talk to me about my future was certainly not unexpected. I knew I had no place at court now that Madame had been buried. There were only three options that I could see: I would be sent back to Brittany to endure the disappointment of my parents; I would be offered to some other well-placed lady at court – possibly even to someone like Olympe de Soissons, although heaven knew my parents would consider that a slight as well – or, if I was very lucky indeed, the king might choose me a husband himself, as a gesture of remembrance to Madame's wishes.

Of the three, none appealed greatly. Not even the third, although it was the whole reason I had been sent to court in the first place.

'I expect you are wanting to go home now, to your family,' the king suggested. 'Your parents must miss you.'

I kept my voice even. 'My parents, sir, more than anyone, are aware of the great honour you do them by keeping me at court.'

'Yes.' The king cleared his throat. 'Certain aspects of this life suit you, it seems. Madame spoke to me several times of your keen grasp of diplomatic issues.'

Lionne added, 'Her foreign connections were of the greatest importance to us. I believe you are aware that she corresponded with her brother.'

'Indeed, sir,' I said demurely. 'I helped Madame draft some of the letters.' Again the two men exchanged glances.

I now suspected that my earlier assessment of this interview might have been too hasty. If they were going to send me home, they would have said so by now. Indeed, I had the sense that they had begun this conversation without having, themselves, a clear view of what its outcome would be – that they were, in fact, sounding me out, and that there was some scheme or intrigue they had in mind for which I might be suitable, but which they were still unsure of.

The king said thoughtfully, 'And if there were some way to continue with her work – to further the cause of the alliance between ourselves and England – would you wish to be involved with that?'

At this, my heart jumped into my throat – for naturally there was nothing I wanted more. 'Most definitely, sir.'

'Even if it meant postponing – temporarily, of course – the prospect of marriage?' He smiled. 'I am sure a young woman as beautiful as yourself cannot be short of suitors. Would you mind asking them to wait for – what? A year? Perhaps eighteen months?'

So perhaps that explained their hesitancy – the necessarily delicate nature of this bargain. The king was offering – in his subtle, elliptical way – to find me a husband in a year or so, if I would dedicate myself to continuing Madame's work in the meantime. Well, of course that was a proposal I was eager to accept. I bowed my head. 'I am Your Majesty's humble servant.'

'Good.' The king got to his feet. 'I will leave Lionne to give you all the details. But remember this, my dear: the work you do for us in the coming months may be more valuable to France than a thousand warships.'

It seemed to me, at the time, that this was a remarkable suggestion for a king to make to a mere lady-in-waiting, and for a time I could scarcely believe my good fortune. It was many months, years even, before I understood how carefully they had played me.

PART TWO

'Must we abandon the Great Affair? It is to be feared that the grief of the King of England, which is deeper than can be imagined, and the malevolent talk and the rumours of our adversaries, will spoil everything.'

Colbert de Croissy, French ambassador in London, to Lionne, French Secretary of State, July, 1670

PART TWO

Carlo

A simple lemon cream is the noblest of ices, and may be easily assembled when others are uncertain.

The Book of Ices

This, then, was the land to which I had been exiled: a low bank of grey mud that gradually split apart and became the two sides of an estuary. On the silvery mudflats, pocked with the crests left by seagulls' feet, a few ramshackle farms stood out against the horizon. Except for some scrawny pigs, they seemed abandoned. The people must have been indoors, sheltering from the freezing rain: I would have done the same, but the boat had been put to use recently carrying animal dung, and my court-accustomed palate was still too refined to bear the stench below decks. Besides, I was fascinated by this country – fascinated and also appalled: by its drab meanness, its dullness, the way it lifted itself out of the grey water reluctantly, by slow degrees, so different from the dazzling crags and welcoming harbours of Italy or France.

At last, as the estuary narrowed and became a river mouth, there were settlements of some kind, docks. I shielded my eyes with my hand. The buildings were the same dreary brown as the mud, the roofs covered in some kind of dark straw. *I have come to a country without colours*, I thought, and it was not only the cold that made me shiver.

I recalled the occasion on which I had received my orders; from the great Lionne himself, in his vast office in the Louvre.

'We are currently engaged in a diplomatic operation of no little delicacy, which may affect the whole course of our military campaign. I am pleased to tell you that, despite your recent disgrace,

91

you are in the fortunate position of being able to be of service to His Most Christian Majesty in this matter . . .'

I was not being given a choice, that much had been clear. Always, beneath the surface, lay the unspoken threat. Madame's death remained a mystery, despite the doctors' best efforts, and rumours of poison or medical incompetence still swirled around the court.

'It is reported that the English monarch, King Charles, is prostrate with grief. When he heard the news about his sister he locked himself in his closet. For three days no one was allowed to enter, not even his physicians.'

Lionne paused. 'Our own king, of course, grieves too. But appropriately. Louis would never allow himself to become so unmanned.'

I had nodded my assent, still unsure where this was leading. If only I had listened when those around me discussed the finer points of these political issues.

Lionne came around his desk and began to pace to the window and back. 'In the case of the English king, it would appear that grief has actually unseated his reason. This formerly pleasure-loving, France-inclining prince has somehow got it in his head that his beloved sister was murdered by her husband, and that we are hiding it from him. He has dismissed his tailor, cast off his mistress, and plunged his whole court into the deepest mourning. Instead of parties and pageants, he now devotes himself solely to government and the interests of his country. Instead of allowing his generals to prepare for the glories of war, he havers, and talks of making economies instead. He walks great distances through the countryside, quite alone, and falls into conversation with his subjects, who tell him frankly that they are not happy with his policies to date: instead of rebuking them for their presumption, he shows every sign of agreeing.'

Lionne shrugged his shoulders eloquently at the folly of foreign kings. 'And so the merry monarch has become the sovereign of sorrows. And France, of all countries, suffers for it.'

Going back to his desk, he regarded me over the steeple of his hands. 'His Most Christian Majesty has decided, therefore, that he will give his English cousin a gift. Something to restore the royal spirits, as a token of the esteem in which he holds their continuing alliance.'

Ah yes, the alliance. If Louis wanted to persuade Charles that their treaty must outlive Madame's death, then the gift would clearly have to be a very special one indeed.

'His Most Christian Majesty has decided to give King Charles . . . an ice.' A frosty smile touched Lionne's eyes. 'That is where you come in, of course.'

I said hesitantly, 'Naturally, I would be honoured to assist His Majesty in this project. But the secrets of my profession are closely protected. If I were to allow them to be given to an English cook, would not my fellow confectioners accuse me of betraying their livelihoods?'

'It seems they may do so already. There is a master confectioner in Florence, I understand, who believes himself slighted by a servant boy.' Lionne lifted a document from the table in front of him and gave me an enquiring look. I said nothing, but my heart sank. Somehow, I knew, Audiger had a hand in this.

'In any case, we are not suggesting that you give away your knowledge. Far from it. It is the very fact that these methods remain secret that makes His Majesty's gift so generous.'

The minister fixed me with his lofty gaze. 'In order to give King Charles the ice, we must give him the ice maker. Do you see?'

I stared at him. Even in my most despairing moments, I had not imagined anything like this. 'I am being sent away? Banished?'

'Let us say, loaned. His Most Christian Majesty is in the fortunate position of having two skilled confectioners. It is only reasonable that he offer one of them to his ally across the Channel.'

'But . . . for how long must I be gone?'

Lionne shrugged. 'Your task is to make the King of England merry again. Once he is merry, he will become once more the friend of France.'

Because he will need your gold to pay for his pleasures, I thought, recalling what Olympe had said.

'He will declare war against the Dutch. Then we will make our own move. The war itself will be swiftly won, and you can return to Versailles.'

I said nothing. Even I could see that it was unlikely to be quite so simple. And even if it was, by the time I returned Audiger would be well established in Paris as the president of the Confectioners' Guild.

Lionne added casually, 'And from time to time there may be certain other duties . . . Messages from the Breton girl, which you will pass back to us. Observations of her, and him, and various others whom we shall point out to you in the English court.'

'The Breton girl?'

'Did I not mention? It has been suggested to King Charles that it might ease his grief if he were to employ, as an act of charity, one of his sister's ladies-in-waiting as an attendant to his own queen. That honour has been given to the Breton girl, de Keroualle. Yes? What is it?' The minister's shrewd gaze was searching my face.

I sighed. 'Nothing.'

Satisfied, he went on, 'It should be easy enough. You will move amongst them, hidden in plain sight, the purveyor of pleasures and trifles. What could be more natural?'

The little ship was beating upriver now, riding the last surge of the tide. The deck, despite the driving rain, had become quite crowded. More passengers had boarded at Gravesend, and even those travelling from France had come up from below, eager for a glimpse of familiar landmarks, chattering excitedly to each other in that guttural language that always put me in mind of the baying of hounds.

Louise was not on board. We had travelled together as far as Dieppe in a borrowed coach and a strained silence. Once I asked her what was wrong, and she turned her tear-streaked face to me incredulously.

'My mistress is dead, I am being sent to the most barbarous, heretical country in Europe, everything I have worked for these last two years hangs in the balance, and you ask me what is *wrong*?'

After that I stayed silent, and when we reached Dieppe I took myself off to buy the supplies I would need. I had been lucky to find this ship: most of the captains I spoke to spat laconically as soon as England was mentioned.

Now, as the deck filled with people, I found myself standing next to a man who said he was a wool merchant, but who stood in the posture of a soldier, his hand on his hip near where his sword would be. He was friendly enough, though, and had taken to identifying the sights as we passed each one.

'The Isle of Dogs.' He pointed to yet another expanse of marsh. 'And over here, Greenwich Palace.' I made out a series of ruined buildings amongst the trees. 'It does not look so very much, now,' he admitted. 'Like all the royal palaces it was much abused in – that is, during recent times.'

'During the Commonwealth, you mean?'

The man gave me a sideways look. 'Aye.'

'And what are those?' I pointed to some tall white poles, like ships' masts, festooned with coloured ribbons.

'Those are maypoles, reintroduced by the king's command, so that the common folk can join in the revels.'

'I don't see anyone revelling.'

He shrugged. 'Some of his subjects have not yet reconciled themselves to the king's return from exile. They will come round eventually.'

Now a building I guessed must be the Tower of London came into view on our right, a squat white castle surrounded by fortifications and bristling with armed soldiers. But my attention was drawn to what lay beyond it: a vast meadow of desecration, nearly a mile long and half a mile deep, strewn with rubble and cinder-heaps and weeds. New buildings were going up, but they stood cheek-by-jowl with the blackened skeletons of older ones, gutted by fire. My companion eyed it all curiously, remarking on some changes here and there, but otherwise made no comment. It was, clearly, nothing new to him.

I remembered the words of another of those who had briefed me, a minor intelligencer to whom Lionne had tossed me once our business was complete. *Of course they have been punished for their heresies: punished by God, with civil war, plague and fire. Perhaps they have learnt their lesson now. Perhaps not.* The man waved his hand dismissively. *Oh, you will find them industrious enough – they believe in hard work, these Protestants: religiously, one might almost say, although what glory there can possibly be, to God or anyone else, in rebuilding that muddy puddle of plague-infested ooze remains to be seen . . .*

Plague-infested. I did not fear fire, but London's infamous pestilence was a different matter. Automatically I crossed myself, then wished I had not. My companion's eyes had gone to my chest, following the gesture, and although he said nothing he looked suddenly thoughtful. Ah well: it could hardly be a secret that an Italian, lately come from France, might be a Catholic. Or perhaps the man had noticed my missing finger. But it seemed to me that from then on he watched me rather more warily.

The Great Bridge was ahead of us now. Made of stone and lined with houses, it was larger than any in Paris or Florence. Constrained by massive mill wheels on either side, the river rushed through the central arch as if through a giant spout, and although a few wherries from upstream nonchalantly shot the rapids, to the accompaniment of shouts and yells from their

96

passengers, it was clearly going to be impossible for our own boat to go any farther.

As the crew tied up at a nearby jetty, my companion nudged me and pointed upwards. 'See that?'

At one end of the bridge a necessary-house jutted over the water. Squinting up through the rain, I saw a row of half-a-dozen wooden privy seats into which were plopped, like eggs in an egg-stand, one pair of male and two pairs of female buttocks. But it was not that lewd display to which the man was referring. Above one of the arches was a row of iron spikes, topped with what looked like rotting cabbages. Only some strands of hair, and a glint of white teeth from one, showed that they were not cabbages at all.

'Papists,' the man said pointedly.

Well, perhaps that was true, although I had been told in Paris that one of the heads on display in London was that of Cromwell himself, the Great Usurper, severed from his disinterred body after his death. The others, I guessed, had not been so fortunate. Perhaps as a consequence of their recent troubles, the penalty for treason or heresy in England was far worse than mere execution. I could imagine it all too easily – not the pain, for that would be literally unthinkable, but the horror: seeing your own guts pulled from your stomach like silks from a mountebank's purse, then casually burnt before your eyes, the rain spitting and steaming as it met your innards, the last meal you ever had spilling and recooking as your intestines ruptured on the brazier. And that was before they had begun to saw you into pieces . . .

This time I managed to refrain from crossing myself, although my right hand twitched involuntarily. My companion noticed it and laughed. But he was not laughing maliciously, I saw: rather, having caused me this discomfort, he was laughing to show it had been done in jest. I had been warned of their strange sense of humour.

'Where are you headed, friend?' the man asked, clapping me on the shoulder as we walked up the narrow gangway.

'I am to lodge in Vauxhall, and present myself at court.'

'Court, is it?' the man said, clearly impressed. 'I did wonder. There's a few of your kind up there.' He nodded. 'In that case, we can share transport. I'm going towards Vauxhall myself.'

'Thank you,' I answered politely. 'But I will need to wait for my luggage.' We were on dry land now, my legs a little unsteady after the crossing – not that it *was* very dry, this land: the clinging, shit-coloured clay mingled with the rain to make a greasy mess underfoot.

'No matter. I'll wait with you. The rain may ease.'

It was a good twenty minutes before my chests were brought up from the hold. As the last one was heaved onto the quayside the man touched my arm.

'You'll want to make them pay for that. Those fools have soaked your baggage.'

'It isn't important,' I said quickly.

'Not important! Look at it!' It was true: water was dripping from one corner of the chest. 'You should check the contents,' the man insisted. He called to a porter. 'You, there: open that chest.'

'Really, it does not matter. Besides, it's locked.'

'Why? What's in it, that must be kept locked but cannot be damaged by water?' he demanded. His directness was unnerving, almost offensive. But that, I was quickly learning, was another of their characteristics.

I hesitated. 'It contains my tools. But they are mostly pewter, so a little water is not worth worrying about.' I paid the sailors a penny to carry the chests up to the street. 'Now I must find a cart.' Again, I saw the man – the soldier, as I was by now quite certain he was – looking at me curiously. Perhaps he was wondering how a foreigner knew that a cart would be faster than a boat. But my orders were to stay at the bridge as short a time as possible.

We loaded the chests onto a cart and set off. Where the fire had not taken hold the streets were narrow, with barely enough room

98

for the cart to pass between the buildings. Each storey was larger than the one beneath, so that what small measure of space existed at ground level had disappeared by the second or third floor, making the streets almost like tunnels. I was grateful for the rain now; at least it kept the muck, both horse and human, moving along the gutter that ran down the middle of each street – where it was not blocked, that is. Taking a handkerchief from my sleeve, I dabbed a few drops of rosewater on it and held it to my nose. I saw my companion smile, but he said nothing.

As we made our way slowly through the streets we passed several groups of men dressed in dark clothes, who, as they greeted one another, took each other's hands and held them briefly between their own. It was like the exchange of some secret sign; yet this was done openly, in public.

'It's called shaking hands,' my companion said, seeing me turn my head to watch. 'It's the custom among the hotter sort of dissenter when they meet. They refuse to bow to any man, since they say all are created equal.'

'In France that would be considered seditionary talk.'

'It's different here. The Commonwealth shook everything up. Things will return to the way they were, but it will take time.' The man suddenly looked amused. 'There was one dissenter who refused to take off his hat when he met the king. Know what happened?' I shook my head, and he continued, 'His Majesty took off his own hat instead.'

'Why did he do that?'

'As he said to the dissenter, it was the custom that one of them should be bareheaded, so now custom was satisfied. Good old Rowley.'

'"Rowley?"'

'Oh – the king's stallion, but it's what people call the king as well.'

'Why?'

'It's affectionate. You know, a nickname.' He chuckled. 'I

suppose it's because he's like his horse, you see, at least in certain respects.'

I was baffled. So men who had died in their beds were dug up and beheaded, but crude and treasonable remarks about the king were a source of amusement. And the king himself, it seemed, was forced to shrug off an impertinence which in France or Italy would cause a man to be sent to the gallows.

A barbaric and backward country, Lionne's intelligencer had concluded with a shudder. *Quite literally: they cannot even keep the same calendar as the rest of Christendom. And although in their calendar, as you will discover, they are only ten days behind us, in every other respect you will find it more like decades.*

I finally shook my companion off at the inn where I was staying. The Englishman's eyes followed the final chest as it was heaved indoors, still dripping, but he said nothing except a curt, 'Farewell, then,' before nodding and turning back to the street. I had been composing an insincere but elaborate speech of thanks for his help, as courtesy demanded; once again I was uncertain whether this brusqueness was intended as an insult or was simply another strange custom.

My rooms were adequate, however, the walls lined with wooden panels that did not seem to conceal any spyholes. Reassured, I turned my attention to the chests. The one that had been dripping felt cold to the touch – a bad sign. Pulling the coverings from the bed, I wrapped it up as best I could. I did not dare open it: the room was warm and I would simply make the problem worse. I turned to the next one and opened it, then rocked back on my heels, dismayed.

When I had sealed it, the contents had been in the form of yellowish crystals. Now there was just a powdery, congealed lump. I touched my finger to it. Damp. The other chest, the leaking one, must have been stored above it in the ship's hold. I had no idea whether saltpetre could be dried and the crystals re-extracted: I suspected not.

Well, it should not be an insurmountable problem. Presumably in London, as in Paris and Florence, they must have piss-pot men who collected the contents of people's chamberpots every morning in order to extract the precious saltpetre. I had seen an apothecary's shop a little further down the street: they should know where I could get hold of some. I washed with hot water brought up by the servant, then went downstairs and told the landlady I was going out.

As I walked towards the shop my attention was caught by a group of young men. They were swaggering down the road four abreast, a formation which, together with the fact that they were swaying widely from side to side, meant that they took up most of the available room. In contrast to the others I had seen on the streets, these were dressed in a manner which would have seemed ostentatious even in France, with petticoat breeches trimmed with yards of lace that hung low on their hips, muffs hanging from their swordbelts, linen shirts that billowed from under fancy doublets, more linen peeping from undone flies, and waistcoats edged in gold and silver thread. They were clearly drunk: one put his arm around his neighbour's shoulders, but the action unbalanced both of them, sending them staggering into the wall.

At the same time, a sedan-chair appeared behind them, evidently a person of quality being carried through the muck by two servants. Whoever he was, he was in a hurry, and the chair quickly overtook the group of young swells, the servants simply passing through a gap in the line without a glance to left or right. Then there was a roar from one of the young men – it sounded like 'Hippopotamus!' – and an answering shout from his companions. As one they charged at the sedan, upending it, so that the person inside fell sprawling into the road. He was, as I had surmised, a gentleman, of middling years, quite rotund, and his shriek of outrage as he rolled into the muck and filth would, I am sure, have been considerably louder had he not been winded by his fall; while

101

for their part the bucks were laughing so uproariously they could barely keep their balance.

'Oafs,' the man spluttered, still sprawling on his back; instantly one of the young men had drawn his sword and was standing over him threateningly.

'Yes?' he sneered. 'Is that insolence I hear?'

I was surprised at this, both because it was clearly the young men who were at fault here, and because they made no attempt to address the older man, who as I have said was a respectable personage, with the politeness due to someone of his standing. And I was even more surprised by the older man's reaction. Picking his wig out of the filth where it had fallen, he said meekly, 'I am sorry, Your Graces. I spoke in the heat of the moment.'

The rake who had drawn his sword now made several passes through the air, as if disappointed that the man had not given him cause to quarrel further. Then he turned, sheathed his weapon, and stumbled after his fellows.

What a curious country, I thought, watching the man climb back into the sedan under the impassive gaze of his servants. It was as if no one knew their own position – or perhaps, in the aftermath of a civil war, they knew it all too keenly. As an outsider, I would clearly have to be careful.

I entered the shop and pulled the door to behind me. 'Yes? Can I help you?' the apothecary said, looking up from the scales on which he was weighing a piece of ambergris.

'I wish to purchase some saltpetre. About two pounds by weight.'

The man blinked. 'It's not something we keep in such quantities. I could enquire from the armoury at Woolwich if you wished. But it will be expensive.'

'I understand. But I have to have it. I'll be at the Red Lion: send word there.' I went back to the door. The young bucks seemed to have gone, so I stepped outside. At the far end of the street was a market. I had nothing else to do, so I thought I might as well go and see what fruits, if any, were in season here.

It was more than an hour before I returned to the inn. The market, in fact, had been a pleasant surprise. Despite the lateness of the month, there was an abundance of small sweet apricots, and almonds and pistachios from Turkey, as well as some big, fat nuts I had not seen before which the stallholders called cobs or filberts. Of cheeses there was a good variety, and so many spices and herbs that even I was not familiar with them all. The English, it appeared, made up for in trading prowess what they lacked in natural resources.

It seemed to me that there were a surprising number of people about as I entered the inn, a basket of plums under my arm. Some of them were staring at me in that frank way the English had, but there was something else now too, a kind of shiftiness in their eyes. Feeling somewhat uncomfortable, I headed for the stairs.

'That's him!'

Suddenly a group of men rushed me from above, weapons drawn. Sword tips and musket barrels were jabbing at my face. I started, dropping my plums and almost toppling backwards in my alarm: as I did so I realised that there were more armed men below me, so that it was only by an effort I avoided falling onto their blades. Beyond them I saw the anxious face of the apothecary.

'Saltpetre,' he was crying to those who had come to see what the commotion was. 'Enough to blow up a house, he wanted. And a foreigner. Dressed like Guido Fawkes.'

'You did well, Isaiah Wentworth,' another man said. 'You have prevented a papist plot, for sure.'

'He has chests in his room,' the inn's landlord added. 'Chests of weapons. I heard them rattling as they were carried up.'

I was so startled I hardly knew how to respond, and fear was robbing me of my English. 'No weapons,' I said, raising my hands to show I was unarmed. 'No plot.'

The man who had congratulated the apothecary stepped forward. 'We should search his room.'

I was pushed upstairs and made to unlock my chests. As I opened each one, a dozen heads craned forward to examine the contents. My court clothes were pulled out and strewn across the floor – I saw my fine French handkerchiefs vanish into one man's pocket when no one else was looking. At the sight of my moulds there was a moment's puzzled silence before someone suggested that they must be for making explosives.

'And here's another,' a voice cried, discovering the last chest under its heap of bedclothes. 'Hidden. This will be the papist's powder.'

'Have a care, Obadiah. It may be dangerous.'

As the man called Obadiah put his hands to the lid he suddenly pulled back. 'Od's nails, it's cold,' he exclaimed.

'Cold?'

'As ice.'

Gingerly, he eased up the lid. Some stepped back; others pushed forward to look.

Nestled in the chest, within a stout cedar lining, were six silvery blocks, each the size of a bible. At one end there was a further compartment filled with thick-skinned lemons; at the other, a similar amount of blackcurrants, their dark skins frosted with rime. One of the men dug his hand in, then pulled it out as if he had been stung.

'What is it?' the landlord asked, puzzled. 'Treasure? Sorcery?'

A voice came from the door. 'Both, of a sort. It is ice.'

They all turned, myself included. In the doorway, perfectly calm, stood the man I had met on the boat.

He advanced into the room. 'This is no Guido Fawkes. He has not come to blow you up; he has come to make a pudding for the king. What is more, he is here on the personal authority of Lord Arlington. Unless any of you wish to incur my master's displeasure, I suggest you close that chest before it melts.' He nodded to me.

'I don't believe we have been formally introduced. Captain Robert Cassell, sir, pleased to make your acquaintance. I will post a guard here, so that your effects are not disturbed again, and then my master would like a word.'

A little later Cassell escorted me into a timber-framed building on the edge of the fire-scarred plain. It was a dispatch office of some sort: men came and went hurriedly, carrying letters and bags of documents. We were shown into a small room where a man dressed in black sat at a desk. To one side sat a second man – a courtier, to judge from the length of his wig. Across the bridge of his nose, somewhat incongruously, was a leather patch, such as soldiers wore to cover wounds that would not heal.

'Signor Demirco, welcome. My name is Sir Joseph Walsingham, and this is my Lord Arlington,' the man in black said courteously. My incomprehension must have been obvious, because he raised his eyebrows. 'I see our names are not familiar to you. Evidently you are even less prepared than we imagined. You make, if I may say so, a somewhat sorry spy.'

'I am no spy,' I said fearfully.

'Of course you are, and a good thing too,' he said easily. 'Where would we spymasters be, were it not for our spies? I must confess, though: I am curious as to why Lionne chose you for this particular task. These iced confections of yours must be remarkable indeed.'

'My services are simply a token of the great esteem—'

'Yes, yes. We can forget all that: I have to be in Whitehall in forty minutes.' It was Arlington who had spoken. His voice was high and fluting, and he enunciated each word with elaborate clarity. 'Understand, Demirco: in the matter of the Breton girl, our interests and the interests of France coincide. Those of us who fought in the last civil war have no wish to see that particular darkness envelop us again.'

'I don't understand,' I said. 'What do a lady-in-waiting and a confectioner have to do with civil wars?'

The two Englishmen exchanged glances. 'The Breton girl is no lady-in-waiting,' Arlington said bluntly. 'She is, God willing, the king's next mistress, and the future chancellor of his bedchamber. It is through her that we will govern a weak-willed monarch, and through him, an even weaker nation.'

My surprise must have shown on my face, because I saw that they were looking at me curiously. 'I think you are mistaken,' I heard myself say. 'I know this girl. She is famous for her virtue. Her family are expecting her to make a good marriage, to a noble family—'

Arlington waved the objection aside. 'She will do her duty. They all do, in the end. Now, sir: what do you need to make an iced dessert?'

Louise

'The Duke of Buckingham has taken with him Mlle. de Keroualle, who was attached to her late Highness; she is a beautiful girl, and it is thought that the plan is to make her mistress to the King of Great Britain; for it is said the ladies have great influence over the mind of the King of England . . .'

The Marquis de Saint-Maurice, Ambassador of Savoy, to Duke Charles Emmanuel II, 19 September, 1670

It had been a shock, at first, to discover that the king was sending me to England. But when I considered it further I began to see the reasoning behind it. If we wanted to hold King Charles to the terms of the treaty, then to insert someone into the English court whose presence would remind him of his obligations made perfect sense.

It was another remark Lionne made which puzzled me more.

'After all, we are already aware of the English king's regard for you, thanks to the matter of the jewel box,' he said idly.

'The jewel box, my lord?'

'Yes. Did you not know? Apparently at Dover, when Charles asked his sister for a gift by which to remember her, she sent you to get her jewel box. Do you recall the occasion?' I nodded. It was their custom to exchange gemstones in this way, as keepsakes. 'Later, when they were alone, Charles told her that the jewel he really admired was the one who had fetched the box.'

At this I found myself a little disconcerted, partly because

Madame had never mentioned this conversation to me when discussing her adored brother, and partly because of the frankness of Lionne's smile. 'I am sure His Majesty meant no more than to be gallant,' I said. 'And once I am in the queen's train, he will no doubt be a little more guarded with his gallantries.'

'No doubt.' Lionne consulted a calendar on his desk. 'Anyway, you leave tomorrow.'

'Tomorrow!'

'You travel with the confectioner as far as Dieppe, where the Duke of Buckingham keeps his yacht. The duke will meet you there and escort you across the Channel. There is no time to waste. We must have the English king's declaration against the Dutch before we make our move, and every week's delay is costing us money.'

I left Paris next morning, having spent the night packing. I had few gowns of my own, but I had been told to take whatever I needed from Madame's wardrobe. It felt strange, at first, to be trying on the clothes which I had so recently seen her wearing, but it was not the first time I had worn her cast-offs, and I knew that if I did not take them they would only go to the other ladies-in-waiting. There was no time to visit my dear parents; I wrote to Brest to explain what had happened, reassuring them that if all went well I would be back in France within a year, and that I hoped in the meantime to have earned the king's gratitude.

But at Dieppe, there was no sign of Buckingham. His yacht was in the harbour, but the crew did not know when their master might be expected. Thankfully, I had just enough money to take a room at an inn.

Two days stretched into three, then four. I passed the time walking beside the sea, feeling the salty air on my face, just as I used to before I came to court.

Then, on the fifth day, a note was sent up. *The Duke of Buckingham requests the pleasure of your company.*

I found the Englishman lounging across an easy chair beside the fire in his rooms. I curtsied. 'My Lord Duke,' I said in English, 'This is a great pleasure.' I had already decided that recriminations or barbed rebukes were of no use: better to ignore the fact that he had left me there without word, than make an enemy.

'Call me George,' he said easily. 'After all, we are about to get better acquainted.'

His servant placed the supper dishes on the table and made himself scarce. We had not even eaten when Buckingham came round behind me and—

Since I am writing this for no one but myself, I shall say it plainly: he slid his hands under my dress.

I jumped to my feet. 'My lord, what are you doing?'

Unperturbed, he laughed at me. 'I can hardly vouch for a mare unless I've sat on her myself. Just as you took it upon yourself to taste Madame's food, so I have assigned myself the role of tasting the king's women.'

I tried to keep my voice even, although I am not sure I succeeded. 'I do not think you would insult one of your own countrywomen this way.'

'Insult?' He leaned closer, and I saw that his eyes were glassy with drink. 'It's me who's been insulted, you French jade.'

'I don't understand.'

'This so-called treaty I've been sent here to negotiate. The Treaty of Paris – or should that be, the Treaty of Dover?'

So he knew. This was bad news indeed. 'I am ignorant of such matters. I was Madame's lady-in-waiting, nothing more—'

His lip curled. 'Don't play that game with me. You've been sent to ensnare him. Women are his weakness, everyone knows that.'

I shook my head, unable to speak.

'Well, it's no great matter. Even if you'd got to court, you'd not have lasted. He likes them with a bit more fire between their legs. You're a cold bitch, anyone can see that.'

He spoke so calmly that it was hard to believe what I was hearing. 'When you are done with this outrage—' I began.

'Oh, I am done,' he said brusquely. 'As you are. Go back to whatever French bordello Lionne found you in. I'll not be taking you to England. We have whores aplenty of our own.'

For a moment we stared at each other – me horrified, him contemptuous. What could I do? There was nothing that could undo the things he had said, no apology that could excuse his behaviour. With as much dignity as I could summon, I turned and hurried from the room.

You've been sent to ensnare him. It was nonsense, of course, but – could there be some grain of truth in it? Had Lionne, or even Louis, thought that Charles might take a fancy to me? It seemed incredible. And in any case, what would be the benefit? Even if I had been the sort of woman to encourage such behaviour, the idea that a king would change his policy just because of a woman was absurd. Even a king as absolute as Louis was surrounded by ministers, councils, petitioners. He barely listened to any of them; as for listening to his mistresses, from what I had heard it was more the other way round. And Charles II of England had his Parliament to contend with.

By the next morning I had convinced myself that Buckingham had simply been drunk and trying to trick me into his bed. I would wait for him to apologise, accept gracefully, and we would say no more about it.

But when I went to the window his yacht was already gone.

I spent the day in despair. I had failed already, and through no fault of my own. Of course, I could go back to Paris and explain what had happened, but the fact remained that there would be even less reason now for Louis to keep me at court. It would be quicker, and simpler, to get a fishing boat to take me straight to Brest.

At the thought of returning to my parents, my mission unful-filled, my spirits sank.

There was one other thing I could try. Taking a pen and paper, I composed a letter to Ralph Montagu, Charles II's envoy to the French court, and a frequent visitor to Madame's apartments at Versailles.

Five days later the innkeeper announced I had a visitor. I was flat-tered to find that it was Montagu himself.

'Mademoiselle,' he said, bowing low over my hand. 'I came as soon as I got your note.'

'I didn't know who else to write to—'

'You did the right thing,' he assured me. 'King Charles himself has been informed of your impending arrival, and eagerly awaits it. He intends to welcome you to Whitehall with all the respect due to a daughter of one of France's most ancient families.' There was a just a little inflection on the word 'respect', as if to say that he understood all too well what a man like Buckingham might have accused me of.

'I see,' I said, relieved. 'I must admit, I was rather anxious that the Duke of Buckingham had implied otherwise.'

'Please do not judge all my countrymen by his behaviour.' Montagu gestured at the harbour. 'Lord Arlington, one of Charles's principal ministers, is sending his boat for you. When you reach London, he invites you to stay with him at his home, where his wife will keep you company until accommodation can be found for you at court.'

'Then I am very grateful to Lord Arlington for the invitation.'

'Lord Arlington has asked me to make clear to you that he is pleased to have had this opportunity of being of assistance. He wishes only that you will mention it to your own king, should the opportunity arise.'

This was more like it. For the first time – again I will speak frankly – I felt the heady power that came from being associated with the greatest country on earth, a feeling that is now so customary with me I barely notice it, but which, if it is for some reason, such as a temporary failure of my diplomacy, withdrawn, I miss as much as I would miss my own arm.

'I would be pleased to. But I fear that corresponding with Versailles may be rather difficult in London.'

'Not at all. Arrangements have already been made. The confectioner will be able to pass messages for you.'

'May I ask how you know all this?' I said, surprised.

'Our countries are allies now. It is only proper that we should work together.' His smile did not slip, but his eyes grew more serious. 'Besides, there are some of us in England who have much in common with France.' He touched his chest, just below the breast bone, and I understood what he meant. It was where a crucifix might hang.

'Lord Arlington is one of us,' he said quietly. 'Although it would cost him his position if he were open about it. Buckingham, of course, is a Protestant. That, I am sure, is what really lies behind his change of heart. Someone has pointed out to him that bringing another Catholic into the king's –' he hesitated, just for moment – 'inner circle hardly helps their cause.'

Wheels within wheels. 'I am grateful to you for telling me so much about the political situation in England.' Clearly, I must be careful not to get pulled into their petty rivalries: there was only one king whose favour mattered to me, and he was ensconced in Versailles, not Whitehall.

There was an embarrassing moment just before we parted, when I was obliged to ask Montagu to settle my account at the tavern.

'His Most Christian Majesty has not given you any money with which to travel?' he asked, clearly surprised.

I shook my head. 'He must have assumed the Duke of Buckingham would cover my expenses.' And I had been too bashful to bring the subject up.

'I see.' For a moment he looked thoughtful, then the courtier's smile was back on his face. 'Well, I am happy to help. And I am sure that Charles will be able to arrange something with the French ambassador in London. Please, do not give the subject another moment's thought.'

A week after that I was in London. After all this waiting, suddenly there was no time. A new country, a new city, a new court – the roles of those around the king recognisably the same, only the titles and the people different, as if I were in a land reflected in a mirror.

My presentation to the king was as carefully managed as the entrance of any actor onto a stage. There was to be a ball at the Arlington's house, to which the king had been invited. Lord Arlington gave me over to the care of his wife Elizabeth, a friendly Dutchwoman, who had me fitted for corsets and dancing shoes.

'This is the first invitation the king has accepted since his sister's death,' Lady Arlington explained. 'Bennet – my husband – has told him of your arrival, and suggested that he might like to welcome you in person. But it is unlikely that he will want to dance, so we have arranged another partner for you. A good dancer, and as tall as you are, but of course you must not pay him too much attention. You will catch the king's eye—'

'How am I to do that, if I am dancing?'

'Bennet will point you out. There is no need for you to do anything at all. If the king decides to come over and engage you in conversation, Bennet will make a sign. But it will be best not to speak to His Majesty for too long. Say that you are still feeling tired from your journey.'

'I don't understand – what is the point of that?'

'If it looks too easy, he will certainly lose interest.'

'If what is too easy?' I said, suddenly on my guard.

Lady Arlington smiled. 'Your mission here is one that requires delicacy. If you seem too eager, I am afraid that the king will sense that he is being reminded to honour his obligations under the treaty – and believe me, he can be quite stubborn about such matters when he wants to be. It will be better if he thinks that it is him who is inviting you into his confidence, not the other way round.'

'What if he does not?'

'A charming girl like yourself? And with such a delicious French accent?' She shook her head. 'If anything can lift the king's spirits, it will surely be the sight of you.'

The night of the ball arrived. It was a glittering occasion, but – being well used to glittering occasions – I noticed how many of the fine paintings and French tapestries that proclaimed the Arlingtons' exquisite taste were brought in the day before, on loan from dealers and tradesmen.

For my part I rejected the dress Lady Arlington laid out for me in favour of one of those I had brought from France, a gown of grey velvet trimmed with black ermine and dotted discreetly with tiny pearls. The one she had provided was just a little too gaudy for my tastes.

The plan called for me to make an unobtrusive entrance, but as soon as I stepped into the room I saw heads turning in my direction. Why were they looking at me like that? I caught an admiring murmur: *Clever.* Did they mean me? It was a relief when the young man chosen to dance with me stepped forward and I was able to focus on the physical movement of the *galliard.*

You need not do anything at all, Lady Arlington had said. Well, if this was to be my only dance of the evening, I might as well enjoy it; although I was a little shocked to discover that the English danced country-style, each man paired to a woman, his arm slipped around her waist, with two bars of kissing on alternate cheeks worked into the measure. It was a far cry from the quiet formality of dances at Versailles.

Then I saw those around us faltering. My partner stepped back. 'Why—' I began, before I saw that his gaze was directed over my shoulder, and that he was bowing along with the rest of the court. I turned.

I had met Charles before, of course, at the celebrations of Dover, and his portrait had long hung in Madame's closet. The man who walked towards me now looked very different. Grief had etched deep lines into his face, so that his moustache was framed by an arch running from his nose to either side of his chin. His eyes, too, looked haunted, and his tall frame, dressed in deepest black, was gaunt.

Behind him Lord Arlington was bustling forward. 'Sir, may I—'

'I know that gown,' Charles said hoarsely. 'Oh God. I know that gown.'

I saw tears in his eyes, and realised to my horror that it was me who had caused them.

'She wore it at Dover. Not three months since, for my birthday. When I saw you dancing, I thought . . .' His voice trailed off.

Arlington too had stopped in mid sentence, unsure what to do. The musicians had come to the end of their piece, but no one was applauding. The silence lengthened.

'Sir,' I said desperately, 'I am Louise de Keroualle, your sister's lady-in-waiting. His Most Christian Majesty the King of France gave me this gown of hers before I left Versailles. It was thoughtless of me to wear it. Please accept my apologies.'

Charles only stared at me, his eyes blank.

'If your Majesty permits, I will go and change,' I added.

'Please do not,' he said. 'I remember you well now, mademoiselle. And it gives me great joy to see you here.' There was little joy in his expression. 'You must think me a poor fool, to greet you so ungallantly.'

Etiquette demanded that I respond to this pleasantry with a pleasantry of my own, some meaningless small talk that would cover my blunder and his display of emotion. But something made me say quietly, 'On the contrary, sir, I would not wish you so heartless. I loved your sister more than anyone in France, and not a day goes by when I do not weep for her myself.'

115

His eyes searched my face, and he said, so low that only I could hear, 'Then we will grieve together, some time more fitting, and share our memories of that wonderful woman.' Looking around, he said in a louder voice, 'Tonight I have business to attend to, but you must make merry, and tomorrow I shall hear of your adventures.'

He went to the door, nodding curtly at the musicians so that they started up again. Instantly, a knot of courtiers surged behind him, all eager to be at his heels. But I saw how he outpaced them, rolling his shoulders impatiently, as if he would physically shake himself free of the lot of them.

'So,' Lady Arlington said, coming to my side. To my surprise she did not seem as horrified as I was myself by my *faux pas*. 'I suppose you knew that dress was his sister's. You have your own strategy, it seems.'

'I knew, but did not think,' I said dully. How could I have been so stupid? I of all people, who prided myself on my quick-wittedness and sense of propriety. 'And there is certainly no strategy.'

But even as I spoke I recalled that it was Louis himself who had pressed those dresses of Madame's on me. Had he, or one of his advisors, hoped that this might happen? Was Lionne, or some other occult mind, even now plotting how events might unfold, manipulating me in ways I could not begin to understand, directing events from a suite of offices in the Louvre?

Across the room, a man was staring at me. He was very short, almost a hunchback, and he was leaning awkwardly on two sticks. I immediately saw why: his legs were twisted, one inwards and one outwards. Despite his short stature, the cripple's blond wig reached almost to his waist – an affectation, or possibly a sign of vanity, that together with his crooked figure made him look faintly ridiculous.

Seeing me watching, he bowed his head courteously. I inclined

116

my own head in return. 'Who is that?' I asked.

Lady Arlington looked over. 'Lord Shaftsbury, the Parliamentarian. I expect he came to get a look at you. Most people have.'

'He certainly did not come to dance.'

'You would have thought not,' Lady Arlington agreed. 'Although in some ways, despite those sticks, he is the nimblest of us all.'

Carlo

Infuse the rind of four or five lemons, peeled very thin, with the juice; add three half-pints of thick cow's milk, and three-quarters of a pound of sugar; simmer, sift through a napkin, and freeze, and you are done.

The Book of Ices

After the grandeur of Versailles, the sprawling warren that made up Charles II's palace of Whitehall came as a surprise. Some parts seemed almost derelict; others contained statues and sundials of quite remarkable workmanship, but placed without apparent thought or care. At one point we came across an ancient half-timbered cottage, seemingly embedded within the palace itself, as if in growing it had simply swallowed up the buildings around it.

'They keep saying they're going to pull the old place down,' Cassell said as he led me through the maze. 'Charles wants to build his own Versailles, out at Windsor, but Parliament takes the view it is granting him money for foreign policy, not foreign palaces. This way.'

The captain, clearly familiar with the route, opened a door, and we stepped into a cool, stone-flagged dairy. Four brown cows stared at us with mournful eyes. Under their bellies, maids pulled at their udders with a practised, fluent motion. The smell of warm milk and chewed cud filled the air. Cassell crossed the room without pausing and unlatched another door.

A narrow passage, then a gate. It led into a cloister that contained a small archery butts. A group of women were shooting at a straw target. 'The queen,' Cassell said under his breath, nodding at a slight figure. 'She practises every day, poor thing. It is all she has to occupy her.'

Yet another door. Now, without warning, we were in a grand salon, the walls covered with frescos. On an ornate chair sat a courtier, a woman straddling his lap facing him, her dress open to her waist. The woman gave us an incurious glance as we passed: the man did not look up. Cassell ignored them both.

At the next set of doors he halted. 'Money,' he said, snapping his fingers. I fumbled for the first of the three purses I had brought with me.

'Here, I'll hold this.' Cassell took the ice box from me.

'Don't open it,' I said anxiously.

'Don't worry, I know my orders. Do you have the purse?'

I found the tight leather ball that chinked of coins. 'Yes.'

'Give it to the servant.'

He knocked on the door. The footman who opened it pocketed the purse without a word.

We went up some stairs, emerging at the back of a balcony behind a group of people who seemed, from their dress, to be ordinary members of the public. They were gazing down at a vast banqueting hall, where a dozen or so courtiers were seated at a table that could have accommodated forty.

'The king,' Cassell said, nodding at the table. 'Are you ready?'

'I think so.'

'Give me the other purses, then.'

As I opened the wooden box, Cassell pressed the last two purses into the hand of another servant. Then he turned and gestured to me.

I eased the silver dish out of the box. Although the mound of ice had softened somewhat during the journey from Vauxhall, it was still intact, only a slight rounding showing that it was no longer as chilled as it once had been. The smell of lemons – clean and fresh – rose from the contents.

'Hurry,' Cassell said impatiently. 'Once he has finished eating he will not linger.'

'Does he always dine in public?' I asked as we clattered down another set of stairs.

'Only at midday. His evenings are his own. In here. And good luck.'

Cassell opened a final door and stood back to let me through. As I advanced towards the table I felt eyes on me – not just those of the dark, tall figure in the centre who was picking at a plate of fruit, but the servants who stood around him, the men-at-arms at the door, and the public upstairs in the viewing gallery.

Finally, I was close enough to bow. I did it in the Italian manner, one foot forward, the other knee bent, my left arm lifted in a flourish behind me.

'Your Majesty,' I said formally, 'I come from the court of His Most Christian Majesty King Louis the Fourteenth, by the grace of God King of France and of Navarre, and on his command offer you a most remarkable confection.' I proffered the dish and, finally, raised my head to meet his gaze.

From the descriptions given to me by Lionne and Arlington, I had been expecting some weak-chinned, weak-eyed fop. But the king's face was well-featured, his expression, despite the gauntness of his face, intelligent.

'Od's fish,' he said with a sigh. 'Well, I suppose it must be good, if Louis says it is. What d'you call it?'

I meant to say 'cream ice', but in my nervousness I got the English words mixed up. 'Ice cream, sir.'

'Very well.' He waved me forward.

I looked around for the servant who would taste the king's food. No one appeared, and for a moment I hesitated.

'Oh, the king does not fear assassination,' a voice drawled from the end of the table. A courtier dressed in the elaborate garb of a dandy was observing my confusion. 'If anyone were to poison him it would put his brother on the throne, and even in poxy England there is no one quite stupid enough to do that.'

The man was slurring his words, as if he had drunk too much, but there was a guffaw of laughter from some of those around him. I noticed, though, that the king did not join in. He indicated with a gesture that I should place the dish before him myself.

'You're French?' the king asked.

'By birth I am Italian, sir. But I have spent many years in France.'

'Then we have something in common. My sister . . .' He paused. Abruptly, the dark eyes were bleak. 'My dear late sister was at the court there too.'

'Indeed, sir. I met Madame on several occasions.'

'You knew Minette!'

'Only by sight. But I could see that she was a most virtuous and kind lady. The king himself was heartbroken by her death.'

'She died the most lamented woman in England or in France,' the drunk courtier said. 'Since when, dying has been quite the fashion.' This time nobody laughed, although the courtier appeared not to notice; or, if he noticed, not to care.

'I served an ice like this to her, amongst others,' I said, gesturing at the dish. I meant only to draw the king's attention back to the table, to prompt him to eat the ice before it melted, but I saw his gaze harden. Of course, Charles already knew the circumstances of his sister's death, and the rumours that had surrounded it. Was that part of the reason I had been sent here, I wondered? To show the king in person that it was not my ices that had killed her?

He picked up the spoon.

There was silence as he put the first spoonful in his mouth. I knew exactly what he was tasting: the pulp of Amalfi lemons, their sweetness intensified with a touch of ginger; a sprinkling of the lemon's rind, grated fine as powder; the whole left infused in rich cow's milk, twice-frozen and stirred; the resultant ice studded with tiny pieces of candied lemon peel.

I waited for a reaction – any reaction. He looked thoughtful, and it seemed to me that he frowned a little. But it was hard to be sure.

Then, after a single mouthful, he put the spoon down. 'You will have to forgive me, signor. I find have no appetite at present.'

Trying not to let my disappointment show, I bowed again. 'Of course. But perhaps I might bring you another, on a different occasion? I would be honoured to remain at court until Your Majesty is in better spirits.'

'Very well.' A shadow crossed his face. 'You'll want paying, I suppose?'

I shrugged politely.

'Well, I will attend to it,' he said wearily. 'Speak to Chiffinch. And in the meantime, perhaps . . . Yes: we have a lady-in-waiting here who is also recently come from France. Mademoiselle de Keroualle.'

'Oh, is that her name?' the drunk courtier drawled. 'I thought she was called Mademoiselle Do-Fuck-Me-Well.'

'I am acquainted with that lady,' I said, ignoring the drunk.

'You must send your ices to her, from me. Tell her it is to make her feel at home.'

'Tell her,' the drunk said loudly, 'that when she comes to court, she may have some royal cock.'

Something of my astonishment at the crassness of this remark must have shown in my face, because the king said mildly, 'You must not mind Lord Rochester. When he is sober he can be quite amusing, but when he is drunk he amuses only himself.'

It was a curious thing, but as he spoke these words I found some of the distaste I had felt at the drunkard's behaviour melting away. Where the Medicis had been austere, and Louis severe, Charles of England was charming – so charming he might almost not have been a king at all.

A lapdog had jumped onto the chair next to the king and was now stretching its neck surreptitiously towards the dish of ice cream. 'Sir . . .' I said, to warn him.

'What? Oh, Daisy, get down.' Charles gave the dog an ineffective push. 'Tell me, signor, what is your name?' he said, turning his attention back to me.

'Demirco, sir.'

'Do you know anything of ice houses, Demirco? How they are made and so on?'

'Of course.'

'I have built an ice house. Out there, in St James's Park. I shall place the ice within it at your disposal.'

'Thank you, sir.'

'Only my people can't get it to work, and the wretched stuff keeps melting.'

I bowed. 'I would be happy to see if there is anything I can do to improve matters.'

'Excellent.' Charles pushed back his chair. The audience was clearly at an end. I bowed again, my left arm raised behind me in the correct, formal manner.

Rochester sniggered. 'Lord, he looks as if he would produce a dove.'

'Speak to Chiffinch,' the king said to me, as a servant stepped forward and fastened a black cloak around the royal shoulders. 'Thank you, Signor Demirco, and welcome.'

'Signor Dildo,' Rochester said thickly. 'Welcome, Signor Dildo.'

Chiffinch turned out to be the servant on whom Cassell had pressed the final two purses. He was somewhat vague about how much I would be paid, or when. 'I will speak to the victualler. Or possibly to the pantry cook.'

'I am the king's confectioner. I answer to no pantry cook.'

He shrugged. 'Well, the king will attend to it.' I had the impression that, unless there were bribes in it, Chiffinch did not care very much either way.

Cassell, though, was pleased. 'It went as well as could be

expected, under the circumstances. You'd do well to sort out his ice house, though.'

'And I had better send his message to Louise.'

'What? Oh, of course. Mademoiselle Do-Fuck-Me-Well.' He was smiling. 'Rochester's an oaf, but he's a quick-witted one.'

'So the king said. I have not seen any evidence of it yet, myself,' I said sourly.

Cassell composed his features, but his mouth twitched. I guessed he was thinking of the fop's other quip. I sighed. There were many things about this country, I saw, that I was never going to warm to.

Louise

After the ball I am kept away from court. Nobody tells me anything. They seem to be waiting for something, some sign or command. Or perhaps they are simply wondering how best to respond to the king's reaction to seeing me in his sister's dress. I sense that there are conversations going on behind closed doors; subjects that are suddenly and smoothly changed when I enter a room. I spend miserable nights wondering if I am to be sent home after all.

After three days of this there is a loud knocking at the doors of the dining hall as the Arlingtons and I are having dinner. The doors are opened by two uniformed servants, who in turn stand to either side of a butler, who steps forward and announces, 'His Majesty has asked that Mademoiselle de Keroualle be sent this token of his esteem.'

'Ah,' Arlington says genially, swivelling in his chair. 'What did I tell you?' *Nothing at all*, I want to point out. Arlington waves the man forward.

The butler places on the table a small painted box about twelve inches square. On the side is a painted crest – something preposterous and without significance, the sort of thing that is concocted by those who do not actually understand the subtle codes of ancient families.

Even so, I think I recognise it from somewhere.

The butler opens it, and takes out a dish of fine glass. It contains a mound of what looks like snow, stained a deep port-purple.

Ice.

Lady Arlington looks puzzled. 'What is it?' she asks the butler.

'Madam, I believe it is a form of frozen dessert,' the butler says disdainfully.

It is clear from my hosts' expressions that even if I wanted to there would be no hope of keeping this gift to myself. By the time it has been divided there is just enough for two mouthfuls each.

Lord Arlington inspects his sceptically, before swallowing it down like a small boy taking medicine. Lady Arlington pokes at hers with the tip of a sharp, dainty tongue. I slide my own spoon into my mouth. Crystals of sweetened ice, already on the verge of melting, clash and crumble on my tongue as they dissolve.

The taste of damsons – subtle, ripe, the last fruits of the summer – fills my mouth, mingled with *crème fraîche*; followed, a moment later, by a welcome crunch of brown muscado sugar.

And I know, then, that Carlo Demirco has reached London.

I feel a sense of relief. Despite the fact that we did not part on the best of terms, it will be useful to have an ally at this court. I just hope that he is faring better at his task than I am at mine.

The next morning I wake early. Dawn has broken, and across the park that separates the Arlington's house from Whitehall there is a fine, translucent mist. Trees, their outlines hazy as if under layers of muslin, are turning golden yellow, the colour of pears. I open the window – there is a bite to the air, and a faint, earthy tang of woodsmoke.

Autumn is coming.

I will have to spend the winter in London, of course. Perhaps next winter too. I wonder if the winters here are as cold as those of Brest. Colder, probably.

Across the misty haze of St James's Park I see a tall figure, out walking. He must be cold – he is wearing only a short black jacket, unbuttoned, from which a white shirt billows at the waist and cuffs. Spaniels trail at his heels like a living, canine cloak as he covers the damp ground in long, easy strides.

The king.

He is quite alone. I watch him for a moment, then I realise he is headed directly towards the back of the Arlingtons' house. He is coming here, now.

126

Lady Arlington bursts in without knocking. 'The king is on his way.' She takes in the situation at a glance – me in my nightdress, staring out of the open window like a schoolgirl. 'There is no time to waste.' Behind her a maid runs in, brushes, water, and primping irons all spilling from her arms. 'Get ready as quickly as you can and join me in the breakfast room.'

'Of course.'

Lady Arlington nods, and I move to the centre of the room so that the maid can begin her work. The girl curtseys, and I raise my arms so that she can pull the nightdress over my head.

Lady Arlington does not move. For a moment she looks at me, her expression unreadable.

Then she gives another nod, as if I have passed muster. 'Five minutes, Susan,' she says to the maid. As she goes down the corridor I hear her giving more orders in a firm, unhurried voice.

'I would speak to Mademoiselle de Keroualle alone.'

Lady Arlington immediately gets up, curtseys, and leaves without a word. There is no protest of impropriety, of course. To suggest otherwise would be to impugn the motives of a king.

Only the servants, standing at either side of the breakfast side-board, do not move.

We are sitting on either side of the great table, empty now of its candelabra and its glasses. Charles gestures at my plate. 'Some coffee? Chocolate?'

'Thank you. I would prefer tea.'

'Of course. I understand everyone in Paris drinks tea now. Even Minette.' He grimaces. 'I mean – my late sister. I called her Minette. It was her childhood name.'

'I know. She let me read your letters. She used to look forward to those letters more than anything else in the world.'

He takes a deep breath. 'Tell me how she died.'

*

I tell him everything I know, and as I speak tears begin to stream down his cheeks. Soon he is openly sobbing, his hands brushing away the tears impatiently, dashing them from his face. I hesitate, wondering if I am distressing him too much, and he gestures wordlessly for me to continue.

I have never seen a man weep so openly in front of a woman. At one point he picks up a napkin and dries his face with it.

'And – tell me – was she murdered?' he says when I have finished. 'Did that brute, or one of his favourites, have her killed so that he could pursue his vices unimpeded?'

Now it is my turn to sound uncertain. There is only one answer I can give, but I am wondering how I can best convince him of it.

'In truth, he could pursue them unimpeded in any case. And although I am no admirer of her husband, I cannot see how it can have been murder.'

'But she was so well at Dover. I had never seen her so beautiful, or so well.'

I shake my head. 'She was in terrible pain. She was simply determined not to let you know of it.'

'How good we Stuarts are at dissembling,' he says, almost to himself. 'How little we show ourselves to those who love us most.'

'She loved you more than anyone alive.'

'And I her.' He is silent a moment, then pulls something from his shirt. 'I have brought her letters to me. Will you—' He cannot finish the sentence, but I understand what he wants.

'*En français?*'

'*Oui. S'il vous plaît.*'

I open the first letter and begin to read. '*Mon cher frère, votre Majesté . . .*'

Carlo

Find a room that is cool and clean, free from dirt and distractions of any kind.

The Book of Ices

Eventually Chiffinch found me a place in the palace kitchen. It was much as I imagined Hell might be: a vast, smoke-filled room where four great fires blazed day and night, and the stink of burning flesh hung in the air like a bitter fog. The cooks worked at long tables like seamstresses, banging with their cleavers at mounds of cow carcasses, or slicing morsels from animals so small they would have been discarded as inedible anywhere else. For the English, it quickly became apparent, were obsessed with meat, and thought it nothing strange to consume it almost daily. This beef or bear or boiled pork of theirs, however, was not actually 'cooked' in the sense that a Frenchman or an Italian would use that word; that is to say, made more palatable by the skills of an ingenious chef, with the clever addition of sauces, flavourings, herbs and so on, but was simply pushed onto a spit and roasted until it became tough and tasteless. Vegetables and herbs were apparently almost unknown, and although I was told the king himself sometimes ate raw fruit, in the French manner, this was considered a foreign affectation by his cooks, who would send along with the fruit bowl a board of 'proper' English puddings, such as taffety tart, stewed suet or plum duff. The courses were not even served separately: everything went out to the banqueting house in one chaotic rush of service, each cook carrying what she or he had made, soups and roasts and desserts all piled up in a heap for the king's guests to pick at. Chiffinch was quite surprised

129

when I told him that in France now the dishes were served one at a time, like the acts of a play.

But the real problem, as far as I was concerned, was that there was nowhere suitable to work. Even if I removed myself to the furthest possible corner of the kitchen, it was going to be impossible to make an ice that was not melted from the general heat almost as soon as it left the *sabotiere*. And, of course, there was the additional need to keep my process secret. By the end of the first day I had realised it would be better to take premises elsewhere.

I also considered whether to leave my lodgings at the Red Lion, where in general the food was almost as bad as that given to the king. However, there was one exception to this: each day they served a different kind of pie, and these simple dishes were, rather to my surprise, close to edible – that is to say, they usually contained a vegetable or two, and sometimes herbs such as lovage, marjoram or sage. On one occasion, in a pie of fish pieces simmered in milk, my homesick palate had even discerned a delicious whisper of tarragon. So I decided to stay, at least for the time being, and enquired from the landlord whether I might rent from him a cellar or cold store for my work. Now that he knew I had such powerful patrons, he hastened to oblige me, and immediately fetched the keys to the cellars.

In fact the cellars turned out to be damp, mouldy and windowless, while the kitchen was almost as hot as the one at Whitehall. Between the two, however, was a little store room or pantry, situated at a turn of the stair so that it was almost underground, and thus quite cool, but with a row of small high windows that admitted plenty of light. A stone ledge ran along one wall; a marble-topped table stood to the side, and at the rear was a windowless alcove where I could keep a stack of ice. I could discern no trace of damp, and the whole room was spotlessly clean.

'This was the dairy, when we made our own cheese,' the landlord, whose name was Titus Clarke, explained. 'Now it is where Hannah works.'

The room's present occupant was evidently a tidy worker: kitchen implements, rolling pins and so on, were neatly stowed along one wall, while bowls were stacked beneath the table. Trays of eggs were covered with a fly-cloth, and a sack of flour had been placed inside a raised drum for added protection from flooding or mice.

'It will do very well,' I said, gazing around. 'How much do you want for the lease?'

The landlord looked somewhat anxious. 'To share it? There is room for you both—'

I shook my head. 'I must have complete privacy.'

'Well, I am sure Hannah will understand,' he said nervously. 'After all, the king must have his ices. I will speak to her this afternoon.'

I had my chests taken downstairs, unpacked my things, and immediately began work on an ice of quinces. I had just reached the stage at which I was pouring crushed ice into the *sabotiere* when the curtain which served for a door was pulled back, and a woman of about thirty wearing an apron came in. By her side was the bootboy, Elias.

'What are you doing?' she demanded.

Hastily, I covered the mixture with a cloth. 'That is none of your concern.'

'Indeed it is,' she retorted, 'since Titus informs me that whatever it is, it means that I must leave my pantry.'

'I am His Majesty's confectioner,' I told her, somewhat surprised by her tone. 'The work I do here is confidential.'

'And the work *I* do here can be done nowhere else. Making pastry requires cold, as I'm sure you are aware, and the main kitchen is much too hot.'

Behind her, the landlord was edging into the room, clearly anxious to avoid a confrontation. 'Now, Hannah, the gentleman has leased the room from me, and there is an end to it.'

131

'Very well,' she said with a shrug. 'In that case, there is an end to my pies. Elias, fetch me a bag.' She began to take her rolling pins off their hooks. The landlord looked at me apologetically, as if to say that he regretted the interruption but everything was sorted now.

'Wait,' I said to the woman. 'You are the pie maker?'

'I was,' she agreed. 'Not any more, it seems.'

I now found myself in something of a quandary. For the fact of the matter, as I have said, was that the Lion's pies were one of the principal reasons why I wished to remain there, and the thought of being deprived of them was decidedly unwelcome.

'How long do you need the room for?' I asked.

'An hour or two each day, first thing.'

I made a decision. There was, surely, no danger in letting a servant use the room occasionally. 'Very well. You may continue to make your pies here.'

To my surprise, she did not thank me, but simply folded her arms across her chest, as if waiting for the catch.

'That is all,' I added.

'I won't pay you rent,' she said. 'Titus already takes more than enough profit on the pies.'

'Then you can repay me by doing some work, cleaning my pans and so on. And you,' I beckoned to the boy, 'how would you like to be my assistant? I will need someone to grate my blocks of ice every morning.'

His eyes grew round. 'Will I wear a fine coat like yours?'

I laughed. 'Indeed not, for you will not come to court. But I will pay you a penny every week.'

He nodded. 'All right.'

'Then that is settled. But you must both of you take a solemn oath that you will never reveal anything of what you see in here. The process is a secret one, and I intend that it shall remain so. Titus, would you fetch me a bible?'

Once again, I was surprised by their reactions to this simple request. For they neither of them moved, and in the woman's eyes there was – unless I was mistaken – a look of blazing defiance.

'For the oath,' I explained. 'You must swear on the bible that you will tell no one how I make my ices.'

The landlord was wringing his hands. 'If I might explain, sir, Hannah's position on the matter—'

'I am perfectly capable of explaining myself,' the woman interrupted. 'We do not take oaths.'

I looked at her, baffled. 'No oaths? Why not?'

'First, because we do not use God as a kind of superstitious talisman or bogeyman with which to frighten credulous people. And second, because an oath implies allegiance to an authority higher than our own conscience.'

'But if you do not swear, I cannot employ you,' I pointed out.

'Then you cannot employ me,' she said simply. 'I am sorry for it, but there you are. I will tell you now that I will not betray your confidence: but as for swearing, I will not.'

'I see.' I had never before been confronted by a situation such as this. Yet again it was borne in on me that France and Italy, for all that they were separated by the Alps, had far more in common than either had with this strange island just twenty miles off the coast of France.

She gestured at the walls. 'Well? Do you want me to remove my implements or not?'

'Leave them for the time being. I will have to think about this. In the meantime you can do some work for me, and we will see how you get on.'

'I am to be on trial?'

'Exactly.'

She shrugged. 'Very well.' She made it sound as if she was agreeing terms, rather than accepting a command from an employer. I wondered if all domestic servants in England were so lacking in deference. If so, it was a wonder anything got done.

*

133

The small amount of fresh ice I had brought with me from France was quickly exhausted. Even if the king had not suggested it, I would have needed to inspect his ice house.

St James's Park was a pleasant enough place, although of course nothing in comparison to Marly or Versailles. In the middle, aligned with the windows of the king's apartments, was a long, thin lake, only a little wider than a canal. Trees and copses dotted the parklands, in the natural style, and here and there a few deer grazed. But everywhere I noticed projects abandoned or half-built. A folly in the French style was still lacking a roof. A road, heading out to the west, started grandly between two stone gateposts but petered out after a hundred yards. And the wall encircling the park ran only halfway round, so that anyone who wanted to could enter without hindrance.

The ice house was at the northern side, near Piccadilly Hall, in a slight dip and under some trees – the worst possible location. However, the brick path that wound to the doorway was service-able enough, and the door was of a sensible size – low, small, and facing north. It was, however, ajar.

I had taken the precaution of bringing with me a bundle of tapers, to provide light, but I need not have bothered: a certain amount of daylight found its way under the roof, and there was already a lit taper set into one wall. Even so, I stepped ankle-deep straight into slushy, icy water. Drawing back my foot with a curse, I realised that I was not alone.

'We must have straw, John,' a voice was saying on the other side of the ice. 'Straw in bales, to pack around the edges. But straw will rot in this wet, so first the floor will have to be drained.'

'We drained it three weeks ago,' a rougher voice replied. 'And straw, surely, will make it even warmer.'

Footsteps were splashing through the water towards me. I still could not see anyone, because my view across the circular cham-ber was blocked by the stack of ice.

The first voice sighed. 'Straw has the property of keeping a warm place warm, certainly. But it will also keep a cold place cold.'

'So in effect, it becomes the warmth which is kept outside, not the cold inside?' a woman's voice asked.

'I had not thought of it that way, but yes – that is essentially correct, Elizabeth,' the first man replied.

Raising my voice, I said, 'Straw will not solve your problem here.'

'Who's there?' the rougher of the two male voices called. A lantern was raised, illuminating three faces. 'What are you doing here, sir? This is the king's property.'

'And I am here at his command.' I stepped forward. 'Carlo Demirco, at your service.'

'The confectioner?'

'The same.'

The group coming towards me consisted of three people, wrapped in thick coats against the cold. The man with the lantern was evidently the one called John: the other man, the one who had suggested straw, was being helped by a woman, who was supporting his arm at the elbow. In his other hand he held a stick, on which he leaned. It was this man who now eagerly addressed me.

'Tell us, Demirco. *Why* is straw not sufficient?'

'All the straw in the world will not make up for a poor design.'

'Mind your manners,' the rough man growled. 'It was the Honourable Robert Boyle here who instructed the architects, after the drawings brought back from Italy by Sir John Evelyn.'

I shrugged. 'The building is sound enough. It is the location that is flawed. And the central drain is either blocked or inadequate.'

'A central drain!' Boyle said. 'Of course! How do they drain such places in Italy, then?'

'In Florence they place a cartwheel over a central pipe so that it removes any meltwater. Ice keeps better if it is dry.'

'Is that so?' Boyle asked keenly. 'Now that I think of it, it may

135

be. Water is the natural element of ice, so it may facilitate the transition of the chilling corpuscles . . . We could determine it with a simple investigation. Come.'

He hurried outside, and crossed to a building immediately behind the ice house. We all followed, the woman because she was still supporting his arm, the rest of us – it seemed to me – simply because Boyle had a natural air of command.

'Be careful, uncle,' the woman said anxiously. 'You have already been in the cold for twenty minutes, and Dr Sydenham said—'

'If a man could get sick from cold,' Boyle said cheerfully, 'I should have been dead long ago. In here, Demirco.'

He opened a heavy door and we entered a room that was light and cold. It was, I realised, a workshop of some sort, the shelves lined with chemical apparatus: alembics, mortars, measures and so on. 'What is this place?' I asked, curious.

Boyle was by now weighing some small blocks of ice, and noting down the amounts in a pocketbook. 'My elaboratory. My second elaboratory, I should say. Here, with the king's permission, I carry out my investigations into cold.' He glanced at me. 'Perhaps you think it strange, sir, that a chemist chooses to work with ice rather than with a furnace.'

'Not at all,' I said. 'I have spent my life working with ice. And yet I believe I understand its properties only dimly.'

He nodded. 'Then let us take a small piece of ice, and place it in water, *so*, and then a similar piece, placed so it will drain. Which will melt faster?'

'It is a waste of time,' I said, shrugging. 'I already know the answer.'

'Perhaps, sir, but *I* do not, and until I have proved it to my own satisfaction I do not hold it to be true. *Nullius in verba*, yes?'

'It is the motto of their society,' the woman explained.

A dim memory from the schoolroom came into my head. '"There is no truth in words, and so I will not swear to the authority of any master." Horace, isn't it?'

'Very good,' Boyle said, nodding.

'But *I* think the results of this experiment may be the exact opposite of what Signor Demirco has described,' the woman said thoughtfully. 'Because ice in a drink makes the drink very cold, whereas ice in air does not cool down the room to the same extent.'

'Well, we shall see, we shall see,' Boyle said happily. 'But first . . .' He was hunting through a stack of papers. 'Here. Demirco, show us where we have gone wrong.'

He spread the architect's plans in front of me. With them were some sketches torn from a traveller's notebook.

'The drain goes here,' I said, pointing. 'But even if you make a drain, you will still have the problem of those trees. Better to have your ice house sunk into the earth, and in an open clearing.'

'Then we shall have to fell the trees, and bank the earth,' Boyle said. 'What do you say, John?'

The other man sighed. 'If it is necessary, we will do it. Although we have not yet started on the bridge for the king's new road to Chelsea, nor the birdcages on the walk.'

'Roads can wait. Ice melts,' Boyle said. 'Speaking of which . . .' He turned to the blocks of ice on the table.

'The one in water does appear to be shrinking faster,' his niece conceded.

Boyle consulted a pocket watch. 'I wish now I had thought to add a third bowl, with some salt. It would be interesting to compare the rate at which that speeds up the process.'

'You mean saltpetre,' I said, then bit my tongue. I should not have been discussing the secrets of my art with any Englishman, let alone one so clearly capable of understanding them.

But Boyle was shaking his head. 'Saltpetre? No, that is very old-fashioned. Saltpetre is of no more use than ordinary salt for this process.'

'Ordinary salt?' I repeated. 'But that cannot—' I stopped, confused.

137

Boyle shot me an amused look. 'I can assure you, sir: if you have been using saltpetre, you have been wasting a great deal of money. It is, as it were, the salt and not the petre that has been doing the job you require. The corpuscles within the salt are attracted to those within the ice, and thus release them from their solid state.'

'I thought not all the Fellows agreed with your corpuscular theory, uncle,' the woman murmured.

He frowned. 'They do not disagree. Some of the *virtuosi* require more proof. That is a different matter altogether.'

'"*Virtuosi?*"' I enquired.

'The invisible college,' Boyle said. 'The Gresham Gang.'

'He means The Royal Society of London for the Improving of Natural Knowledge,' Elizabeth explained. 'A group of natural philosophers, who investigate and debate such matters.'

Boyle nodded. 'Cold is one of our particular interests.'

'Though it is fair to say,' she added, 'that so many other natural phenomena also come under that heading, that cold is scarcely unique on that account. Or even particular.'

'I see,' I said. Then something occurred to me. 'Would your . . . philosophical investigations be able to tell you why certain liquids freeze thicker than others?'

'Go on,' said Boyle. 'I sense an interesting mystery.'

'It is simply . . .' I stopped, unsure how to put this. 'I wish to make an ice cream that is truly smooth. Not one that crunches between your teeth, with bits of frozen water in it. I managed it once, but I have been unable to discover since what it was that made it work.'

'An ice that contains no bits of ice?' Boyle said with a smile. 'Well, compared with designing the new cathedral, or understanding circulation, it is perhaps not so very pressing a matter. But if I know my colleagues, it is exactly the sort of problem that would capture their fancy. We could devise some experiments, set you on the right path, and then, if we were successful, publish our findings—'

'"Publish?"' I said quickly. 'What do you mean, "publish"?'

'My dear fellow, there is no point in acquiring knowledge unless it is made public. That is how our society operates: every experiment is faithfully minuted, debated, verified and subsequently published, for the benefit of all.'

'At which point,' Elizabeth added, 'the arguments usually start.'

'There are occasionally some small matters of precedence or originality to be determined,' Boyle conceded. 'The point is, we jostle for experimental prominence, not commercial advantage.'

'Perhaps it is not such a good idea after all,' I muttered.

'Commercial advantage being your *raison d'être*?' He shrugged. 'Very well, sir, that is a matter for you to decide. How fare our ice blocks, Elizabeth?'

'The one in water is almost melted, while the dry one has merely become cylindrical,' she reported.

'Excellent! What I would give for an accurate thermoscope, so that we could measure their relative temperatures.'

I watched as Boyle made some notations in his book, more stung by his previous comment than I cared to admit. 'It is not commercial advantage.'

'What is not?'

'Why I do this. It is not for money. Or not money alone.'

'I am pleased to hear it,' Boyle said mildly. 'But I would remind you of our motto. *Nullius in verba*. And whilst your words do you credit, it is not those but your actions from which I will draw my conclusions.'

'I cannot give away my secrets.'

'In that case, sir, you had better not consort too long with gentlemen like myself,' Boyle said. 'Secrets being, in our considered view, the sworn enemy of truth.' He turned back to his work bench, and I understood that, despite the man's courteous tone, I was being dismissed.

*

Back at the Lion I immediately called for salt. Elias brought a salt pot: someone in the kitchen had assumed I meant a little salt for seasoning.

'Bring me five pounds of salt, as quickly as you can,' I told him.

The child looked confused. 'We do not have so much.'

'Then send out for it. How much do you need? A shilling?' I tossed him a coin, and saw his eyes go very big. 'Go,' I said. 'And if there is a penny change, you shall have it, so long as you are back within the half-hour.'

By the time he returned I was ready to conduct my own experiment. I had been impressed by the logical manner of Boyle's test with the ice, putting the two cubes side by side so as to see which melted faster: I now proceeded to do the same, but with mixtures of ice and salts. In one *sabotiere* I had my usual mixture of ice and saltpetre – a crystal extracted from the urine of horses and humans; and, as the apothecary had noted, an essential and expensive ingredient of gunpowder; in another, I put a similar quantity of ice to which I added ordinary table salt.

Now I needed something to freeze. It hardly mattered what, so I went into the kitchen and helped myself to a jug of the ubiquitous custard which they made by the gallon every day, for their desserts.

I waited twenty minutes, then opened the lids.

Inside the first pot was a dense, smooth mass. I reached in and scooped out a shaving of frozen custard. I reached into the second and did the same.

I sat back on my heels, thinking.

Boyle was right: the saltpetre was not needed after all. Ahmad had taken it on blind faith, as he had taken so much else about this process. Now that I knew the truth, I would be able to freeze an ice mixture for next to nothing – for a few pennies.

Amazed, I permitted myself a brief oath in Italian.

'What is it?'

I turned. Hannah was standing behind me, wiping her hands

140

on a cloth. Without asking my leave, she picked up one of the bowls of ice cream and looked at it curiously. 'May I taste it?'

Quickly, I took the bowl away from her. 'It is not for vulgar palates.'

She shrugged. 'Well, I don't need to taste it, in any case. It wants more sugar.'

'I make these for courtiers. Not those who would pour sweetness into any dish if they could.'

'I only meant,' she said, moving away, 'that more sugar might set the custard better.'

'Sugar? Set the custard?'

'I see you are learning English by the method that hears it and then speaks it back again, signor.'

'What are you doing here, anyway?' I demanded. 'This pantry is supposed to be private when I am working.'

'I was looking for the custard I made earlier. But I see that it has been turned into ice cream.'

'You can have it back. Here, put it near a stove and it will be just as it was before.' I scraped the frozen mixture back into the jug. As I did so I tasted some, as was my habit.

It was good – surprisingly good: and despite the fact that I had not stirred it as it froze, creamy and soft. In fact, it was almost as soft as the one I had made in Versailles, the one that had got me banished.

Although it wanted a little sugar, to set it.

A knowing expression crossed Hannah's face. 'Well?'

I scowled. 'These are secret matters. Recipes that no one else has except me. I do not discuss them with anyone.'

Louise

'We must tempt him to pleasure,' Lady Arlington says. 'If we can drag him from despondency, the rest will surely follow.'

Her voice, with its sharp Dutch inflection, carries into the room where I am sitting. Her husband's voice does not penetrate so easily – a low rumble of which I can only catch a few words.

'But grief *is* a kind of pleasure,' Lady Arlington argues. 'At least, a form of self-indulgence. Charles is gorging himself on sorrow today: tomorrow it will be a different kind of excess. Both stem from the same immoderation of character that he has always shown.'

Another rumble.

'But we don't have to choose,' Lady Arlington says. 'For the time being at least, she can be both. As for the other thing – we can cross that particular bridge when we come to it.'

She comes to see me, all smiles. 'I have persuaded Bennet to let us go to court, to see a play. A private performance. The king is a great lover of theatre, usually, but since his sister's death he has been somewhat distracted. We are hoping that this entertainment may reawaken his interest.'

'That sounds wonderful,' I say dutifully. As their guest, I have little choice in the matter.

'And I will lend you a dress. Using his sister's seems to have piqued his interest, but it is something best not tried twice.' She goes to my closet, studying what I have brought with me. 'Dark clothes suit you, though. I will find you something grey.'

The play, frankly, turns out to be wearisome. There are only twenty or so of us watching, and most seem to find it hilarious,

142

although I find myself wondering if they are laughing because of the play's wit, or in the hope of making the king laugh too. It is something about a courtier who pretends to be a commoner in order to avoid marriage with a woman he affects to dislike but actually wishes to seduce. Rather than express merriment I do not feel, I adopt an expression of – I hope – polite but neutral curiosity.

The only other person not laughing is the king. While the others titter and guffaw, he is silent. After a while I glance at him, and find him looking at me. His stare is unnerving. I feel myself colour, and resolve to stare just as fixedly at the actors.

In the interval ices are served, but although Lady Arlington points them out to the king he waves the server away. He says to the person next to him, loud enough that I can hear, 'What do you think of the play, Lord Clifford?'

'Wonderfully amusing,' Lord Clifford assures him. 'The best he has done.'

'I find it contrived.'

'Indeed, sir. It is somewhat contrived.'

'And yet you think it hilarious.'

'Amusing, sir. I said amusing. It is amusingly contrived.'

'Both acts were overlong.'

'They were a little on the long side,' Lord Clifford agrees. 'But no less amusing for it.'

The king is looking at me now, not at his minister, and I wonder whether some of this baiting of the man might be for my benefit. 'It was tedious and superficial.'

'It repays careful attention, shall we say—'

'The jokes were coarse and the characters thin. What do you say, mademoiselle?' This last suddenly addressed to me.

'I could not follow all of it,' I say carefully. 'But in any case, I prefer tragedy. What Racine calls its majestic sadness. If I am to be moved, I would rather be moved to tears than to cynicism.'

His mouth twists into a wry smile. 'Then you have come to the

143

right place, mademoiselle. For in England tragedy is all we know.' He taps the chair where Lord Clifford is sitting. 'Come and sit by me. My French is still better than Lord Arlington's. I will translate the few jokes that are worthy of it.'

I sense the glances going back and forth across the room as I get up and move to the chair that Lord Clifford immediately and without protest vacates – the studied indifference on the faces of those who nevertheless miss nothing and who are instantly computing what this might mean.

As I sit down the king says under his breath, 'Your presence will make the thing bearable, at least.'

'Well,' Lord Arlington says that night at dinner, mightily pleased. 'It seems you are a success. The king asked after you three times this evening, after you had gone.' He tucks a napkin under his collar and picks up a fork. He is proud of his Continental manners, although in truth they would be considered effete in France. 'He wants to know when he can visit again. Of course, I told His Majesty that you are still tired from your journey.'

'You are very considerate,' I say politely. 'However, I am feeling perfectly rested now.'

'Even so. No point in rushing it.' He plunges his fork cheerfully into the plump leg of a chicken.

'But tell me, Lord Arlington,' I persist. 'If I am to be the queen's lady-in-waiting, should I not be presented to Her Highness?'

'The queen is rarely at court,' Lady Arlington says. 'Since her last miscarriage she has been in very ill health. She has been in bed most of this past month, and her doctors are close to despair.'

'I am sorry to hear it. I shall pray for her recovery.'

'Some in this country pray for exactly the reverse,' Arlington says mildly. He slips into French, presumably to prevent his servants from understanding what he is saying. I have already come to realise that this means a conversation about religion or politics, both of which are extraordinarily dangerous subjects here. 'Parliament would like nothing better than for the king to be free to marry a Protestant. Needless to say, that would be a disaster, not least for France. I wonder . . .' He glances at me thoughtfully.

'What is it, my dear?' his wife asks.

'Nothing,' he says in English. 'Just a passing thought.'

Carlo

There is no fruit so sweet it cannot be improved by being made into an ice. I have been fortunate to create *eaux glacées* from the rarest fruits, and can say that they freeze as well as, or even better than, the common fruits of the orchard.

The Book of Ices

I was summoned to a meeting with Lord Arlington – not at his house, where Louise was staying, but at the postal office I had visited before. Once again Cassell escorted me there.

'So,' Arlington began. 'The king declines your ices. It is not the best of starts.'

I shrugged. It was hardly my fault if the king would not eat.

'Perhaps he will feel differently if his sister is invoked.' That from Walsingham.

Arlington's eyes narrowed. 'Go on.'

'Just as we hoped, he seems to be quite taken with Mademoiselle Carwell. Perhaps—'

'De Keroualle,' I said automatically.

Walsingham paused. 'I'm sorry?'

'Her name is pronounced "De Keroualle". Not "Carwell".'

Walsingham nodded politely. 'He seems quite taken with the girl. Perhaps if she were to offer him an ice, and say it was his sister's favourite . . .'

'Good.' Arlington turned to me. 'What was it?'

'What was what?'

He frowned at my slowness. 'His sister's favourite ice.'

'Oh.' I shrugged again. 'She didn't have one. She drank chicory cordial, for her digestion.'

146

'Then make one up,' Arlington said. He made a dismissive gesture. 'Anything will do. After all, the ice is not important. It is merely a means to an end.'

'But let it be something special,' Walsingham suggested. 'He is less likely to refuse it if he knows it is a rarity.'

'One of those fancy fruits Louis of France so admires,' Arlington agreed.

I said hesitantly, 'That would be a pineapple.'

There was a brief silence.

'Pineapple!' Arlington said. 'You do realise what you are asking for?'

'I do. But if you want something truly tempting, something that the King of France himself would prize as remarkable, at this time of year it must be a pineapple.'

I knew, of course, that even in France a single pineapple cost almost as much as a new coach. Here in England, they would doubtless be even more expensive. But they were the epitome of aristocratic luxury. Louis's courtiers built heated pineries at their country estates where the fruit – which was imported from the colonies on the tree, roots and all – could be replanted under glass and ripened. Lesser people hired ripe pineapples by the day at enormous expense, just to adorn their tables and perfume their dining rooms, while only the very wealthy could afford to actually eat one.

'The Earl of Devon has a pinery at Powderham Castle, of which he is inordinately proud,' Walsingham said hesitantly. 'Last year, I believe, he boasted of producing four or five fruits.'

'Then he had better be inordinately proud to have his pineapples made into an ice and presented to the king,' Arlington said. 'I will speak to him.' He got to his feet. It was clear that the meeting was at an end.

I said, 'There is one other thing I am still confused about.'

'What is it?' Arlington asked.

'The girl – Mademoiselle de Keroualle. How do you know that she will play her part?'

'Oh, that.' Arlington gave me an amused look. 'We are not completely backward in such matters here, you know. It is already being taken care of. The information you gave us about her was most useful in that respect.'

I could not remember having given them any information about Louise that could possibly be of use, other than that she was not the kind of woman who would go along with their scheme. But they were already gathering their papers, and I had no opportunity to ask any more questions.

I went back to Vauxhall still thinking about Arlington's words. So Louise had, it seemed, agreed to go along with their plans. All those protestations of virtue, back in France, had been so much empty air, cast aside in her eagerness to bed a king.

It was as Olympe had said: all women are for sale. Which was not, in itself, a particularly startling discovery – indeed, it was almost self-evident. So why did I find myself almost *disappointed* in Louise de Keroualle? After all, it was to my advantage that she understood what was required of her. I could not return to France until our mission was achieved, and as things stood it was likely to be her, rather than myself, who was going to be the instrument of our success.

Louise

That night, as I lie in bed, Lady Arlington comes to see me. She is in her nightgown, as I am, her hair unpinned.

'Do you have everything you need?' she enquires with a smile, sitting down on the edge of the bed.

'Everything, thank you. You have been most hospitable.'

'And the bed is comfortable?'

'Wonderfully so.' I yawn. 'It makes me feel quite sleepy.'

'This was the bed in which I first lay with Bennet, after our wedding breakfast,' she says, placing a hand on the coverlet as if to indicate the very place. 'It is a happy day, when a girl becomes a woman.'

'When she is married, you mean.'

She does not answer me directly. Instead she reaches out and strokes my hair. 'You are a lovely little thing. But I suppose you know that already. And so charming! Who knows – perhaps you will attract the eye of a suitable husband, while you are here in England.'

My surprise must show in my face, because she smiles. 'You hadn't considered that possibility?'

'My parents might have something to say on the matter,' I say carefully.

'Of course. But much would depend on the position of your prospective husband, would it not? Alliances across countries are how these things are done, at a certain level. I myself was Elizabeth van Nassau-Beverweet before I was married to Lord Arlington.'

'I am not really thinking about anything like that,' I protest.

'But why ever not? Besides, if what I hear is correct, you do not have a great deal of choice in the matter.'

'What do you mean?'

'Just that you have already tried and failed to find a suitable husband in France,' she says simply. 'Nor, unless you succeed here in England, can you ever hope to return to Versailles. So what, or who, exactly, would you be saving yourself for?' She smiles ruefully, to show that she means no harm by it, and pats my leg through the bedclothes. 'Well, I will leave you.' She goes to the door, pausing only to blow out the candle on the bureau. 'Goodnight, Louise. Sweet dreams.'

For some time I lie in the darkness, thinking about what she has said. Clearly the Arlingtons have a plan in mind – some suitor or alliance whose cause they wish to further. But whose? And why are they being so elliptical about it? I have the uneasy feeling that I am being involved in some new, additional intrigue, the ramifications of which I cannot yet completely grasp, let alone control.

At breakfast they return to their theme. But they have clearly been talking overnight: their arguments are more polished now, their delivery less oblique.

'News from court,' Lord Arlington informs his wife, reading a note brought by the butler. 'I have here the latest report from the queen's physician. Unfortunately, it seems that our worst fears have been confirmed.'

'I must prepare our mourning clothes, and the black silks for the carriage. It seems certain that we will need them before the year is out.'

'Indeed. The poor woman.'

'Is there any more word,' Lady Arlington enquires, 'as to who the king is likely to marry, after she has passed on? God rest her soul.'

Arlington shrugs. 'There has been some discussion. Informally, of course. As you know, the king has the romantic notion that he would like to marry for love. But that is not a luxury kings are often given.'

'Indeed not. And Parliament will want him to marry a Protestant.'

'Ah!' Lord Arlington leans forward. 'But will it be Parliament's choice? It is Paris, not Parliament, which is in the ascendancy now. And Louis will want someone who cements the grand alliance.'

'A Catholic?'

He nods. 'Preferably, no doubt, a Catholic from France.'

Caught in the act of raising a piece of toast to my mouth, I do not at first realise the significance of all this. Then I understand. If I were not eating, I think my jaw would drop.

How stupid they must be thinking me, not to have realised before.

'So if Charles were already to favour such a person . . .' Lady Arlington is saying.

'Indeed,' her husband replies, nodding. 'Everyone would be delighted.'

He cannot resist giving me a brief, sidelong glance, to make sure that I have understood.

I walk in the garden, thinking hard.

So this is the Arlington's plan – to broker a marriage between myself and Charles II! At first glance it seems a breathtaking proposition. The wives of kings are princesses of the blood royal, not the daughters of impoverished old families. They bring with them vast dowries, strategic alliances, claims on distant thrones.

And yet, if Louis and Charles both wanted it, such a marriage might just be possible. So powerful is France in Europe now that a Frenchwoman of noble birth could be considered the equivalent of royalty from a lesser country. And from my own king's point of view, a Frenchwoman on the English throne would be a visible sign that the treaty is unbreakable. It would bind our countries together for a generation.

I consider what my parents would think, if I became England's queen. Of how Louis might reward them. My younger sisters would be amongst the most eligible girls at Versailles. There would be new lands for my father; money to rebuild our home at Brest . . . I would have achieved everything they sent me to Versailles for.

And my children – *our* children: the children that Charles and I would have together – would be of royal blood. They would have within them that portion of God's divinity which courses through all royal veins. I would be the mother of princes. As such, I would wield power – power even greater than Madame's. That great vision of hers – the vision of a Europe united under one faith – would be mine to achieve.

How could I possibly have known, when I contemplated being sent home from Paris as a failure, that this far greater opportunity would come my way instead?

Abruptly I shake my head, angry with myself. *Wait. Think clearly.* If that was really Louis's intention in sending me here, surely he or Lionne would have said so. They would not have left it to the charming but, I suspect, somewhat self-interested Lord Arlington to explain how things lie.

So. This is Arlington's scheme, not Louis's. But again, that does not necessarily mean Louis would not approve of it, should events fall out this way.

Should Charles wish it, in other words.

I consider, trying to see it clearly. Most obviously of all, there is the little matter that the present queen is not dead, and even to discuss the death of a queen, much less to wish for it, is treason. Of course, people do talk about such things – the succession in any country is a subject of grave importance – but to speak of it in the wrong way, or to the wrong person, is to risk disgrace.

And then, too, there is something almost too perfect about the timing of this, the way that it has been laid out so neatly before me, like a hand of cards with the king on top, almost begging to be picked up and played.

I think again of Buckingham's drunken words. *You've been sent to ensnare him*. Between that gross accusation and the Arlingtons' more welcome suggestions, where does the truth lie?

To be a queen. To be a queen. It is like a whisper going around and around in my head. Without meaning to, I find that I am carrying myself a little straighter than before, my bearing a little more regal, as I walk back towards the house.

Carlo

The difference between a simple *sorbetto* and an ice cream
is as great as the difference between chalk and cheese.

The Book of Ices

I had little to occupy me while I waited for my pineapple to arrive.
I sent chilled cordials and jellies to the court, and spent the rest of
my time in experiment.

In truth, I knew that I was as much a novice at this as I had
once been at making ices, and I sorely needed the guidance of
Boyle or some other natural philosopher. But Boyle had made it
clear that he would not help me unless I agreed to make my findings public, so for the time being I was on my own.

Determined to proceed using the same logical approach that a
chemist such as Boyle would employ, I began by returning to the
pear ice I had made in France and attempting to recreate it exactly
as I had done before. But it turned out not to be a straightforward
process. It seemed that the relationship between the various ingredients was almost impossibly complex – reducing the sugar made
the texture less icy, but also made it harder to freeze the mixture
at all: the *crème anglaise* sometimes froze smooth, but sometimes
cooked into lumps, like scrambled egg, while changing the proportions of pear and cream turned it from a smooth cream ice into
a sticky liquid mess.

During these experiments Hannah washed my dishes and Elias
grated my ice. Somewhat to my surprise, both were hard workers,
and I had no complaints about their diligence. I remembered the
words of the French intelligencer. *They believe in hard work, these
Protestants: religiously, one might almost say.* There had been no

154

repeat of the defiance over oaths, and so for my part I decided to say no more about it.

It was clear, though, that Hannah was not the kind of servant I had been used to in France.

'Why is a frozen cordial better than an unfrozen one?' Elias asked me one day.

'Because it cools the palate of those courtiers who are fortunate enough to eat it.'

'But why do they not simply take off their coats, and cool themselves that way?'

It was tempting to tell him to stop asking questions; but something about the boy reminded me of my own curiosity when I first started working for Ahmad. 'Because a cream ice is more delicious than taking off a coat,' I said patiently.

'Can I try some?'

'No.'

'Why not?'

'It is not a taste for children.'

'Then why do courtiers like it, if children do not?'

'Because courtiers are fools.' That was Hannah, interrupting unbidden. She saw my look. 'It is nothing but the truth,' she said unapologetically. 'And it is best he knows it now.'

I did not answer her directly, but spoke to the boy. 'Courtiers are used to magnificence. They can appreciate fine things, which they are entitled to in consequence of their nobility, and their service to the king.'

A tut from Hannah's direction indicated her disagreement. 'The court is the source of all our problems.'

'Without the court, there would be no government,' I pointed out.

'In this country we are fortunate enough to have a Parliament, which governed the country perfectly well when the king was living abroad.'

'When the last king was murdered *by the mob*,' I said pointedly, 'and his son forced *into exile*, this country, I am told, fell under the spell of a dictator.'

'Parliament isn't perfect,' she said. 'As for King Charles – there is no doubt that since his sister's death he has tried to throw off some of the rakes and leeches who surrounded him. But he is also weak, and when his grief has faded he will revert to his old ways again. That is to say,' she gave me a sideways glance. 'Catholic ways. He is easily led astray by pleasures and novelties of all kinds, especially if they have the stamp of fashionable approval from France.'

This, of course, was so exactly the assessment of those who had sent me that for a moment I did not know how to respond.

'He will not be led astray by my ices, at any rate,' I said at last. 'They are simply frozen waters and cordials. There is nothing about them that can change a person's character, let alone his religion.'

Louise

I am being dangled.

Every time Lady Arlington suggests a walk in the park, lo, there is the king, also out walking with his court. We pause, exchange pleasantries. *How are you settling in? Well, thank you, sir. I suppose you miss your friends? Sir, I am making so many new friends here I have not had time to think of it.*

We do not speak, in these public encounters, of his sister. But the grief – the pain with which he stumbles over these simple exchanges – is all too evident.

And then, just as he clears his throat to ask me something more, Lady Arlington bids him good day. The same when we are out riding, or playing *paille maille*.

Even on the river, where I am taken to learn to row, my splashing efforts attract a glance from an open window in the palace: there is the king with a pile of papers, a knot of advisors, state business, looking down. He waves to me, courteously; the royal wave, one open hand across the body, like a farmer scattering seed.

And yet, never having been dangled before, I find the sensation not entirely unpleasant. When I walk away from him I can feel his gaze on me, the way you can feel the sun's warmth on your skin even when your eyes are closed. Sometimes I even allow myself to glance back, to see if he is still watching me. *Am I being a coquette?* There is a part of me that is astonished at my own behaviour, another that finds the thought amusing.

And a part that thinks: *I must behave as a favoured confidante, but no more.* Buckingham's crass accusation has been useful: it serves as a warning. *They must have nothing to reproach me with.*

To be a queen. To be a queen.

*

Now the king is playing tennis. At one side of the building, a banked tier of benches allows his courtiers to watch.

He plays well, his tall frame moving surprisingly quickly as he leaps from one side of the court to the other. Even so, it seems to me that the younger man playing him could win if he wanted to. Every time he takes a point you can see him hesitate, wondering if he has gone too far.

The king knows it too. As soon as the man is beaten, he calls impatiently for another opponent.

'Do we play for love, or points, sir?' the next young man calls.

'Points,' Charles says shortly. 'Love has no place on the tennis court.'

'Only the Royal court?' the other player says dryly. There is a sprinkling of laughter, and a few eyes turn towards me. I pretend not to notice, but my heart beats a little faster.

This opponent is cleverer than the last: he builds up a commanding lead, and then gives the king the challenge of overcoming it. Beside me, Lady Arlington is murmuring into my ear.

'It's a good sign, he hasn't played like this for months. Doesn't he play well, such an athlete, a handsome man as well as a monarch. He swims too, and often walks all the way to Hampton Court. As well as his sport with the ladies.'

'"The ladies"?' I repeat, taken aback.

'Oh, the king is an accomplished lover,' she says with a mischievous smile. 'In addition to all his other talents.'

I blush. 'Lady Arlington . . .'

'I'm sorry. Am I being too frank? Perhaps I have been living too long in England. They are almost ridiculously relaxed about such things here. But then you are no child, are you? I am sure you know what's what, as they say.' She nudges me slyly. 'After all, from what I hear, Madame was no saint.'

I do not reply. It has not occurred to me before that innocence in such matters could be dismissed as a childish thing.

Besides, there is just enough truth in what she says to discomfit

158

me. For Madame, delicate and ill, her husband's attentions were, I knew, an increasingly unpleasant duty. But there was that one occasion when Monsieur was away, and I went into her closet for some pens. There was Madame, lying back on the divan, her frail legs wrapped around the king's hips as the monarch heaved himself into her, his long shirt unbuttoned, his own legs bare and hairy . . . I stepped back, appalled, and quickly shut the door. I could make no sense of it. Madame would not lie with Louis for advancement. Why, then? For love? I would not have said there was passion between the two of them so much as friendship; the deep understanding of those who had been born to similar positions.

I do not understand sexual relations, I think, and the realisation makes me cross. To be clever, and yet so ignorant – to be able to play instruments, and speak languages, and write diplomatic letters, and yet to comprehend so little of this, apparently the most fundamental of desires . . . it is like watching a game of tennis without understanding the rules.

Not that I fully understand the rules of tennis either, I think, forcing myself to concentrate on the game. The contest between king and courtier has become more intense now, like a duel or a rutting of stags. Charles sends a ball along the penthouse in such a way that it spins behind his opponent. The young man manages to get his racquet to it, but by now Charles is at the net. He smashes the ball straight up into the dedans, the window behind the server. I know enough to know that it is considered the most decisive way to win the point.

He acknowledges the applause of the spectators with a spin of his racquet. Then, still panting, he looks directly at where I am sitting.

'He plays for you,' Lady Arlington says under her breath, clapping furiously. 'Smile. Now you must play for him.'

As the players drink cold cordials, the court disperses. I recognise a figure in a French frock coat walking away, an ice box in his arms.

'Signor Demirco,' I call.

For a moment he hesitates – but then he hurries on, and I am obliged to break into a trot.

'Wait,' I call. 'Signor Demirco, wait!'

Finally he has no choice but to stop.

'Did you not hear me,' I begin, puzzled.

'I heard,' he says curtly.

'Then why do you glower like that?'

It seems to me that he almost says something, but thinks better of it. 'No reason,' he says at last. 'How do you fare? I have heard that your diplomacy here is meeting with great success.'

Is it my imagination, or is there a hint of a sneer on the word 'diplomacy'? A little put out, I say, 'And I hear that yours is not.'

He shrugs. 'It is thought that the king is more likely to accept my ices if it is you who proposes them.'

'And that is why you are so . . . surly? Your pride is hurt?'

'I am not surly, as you put it,' he says, still curt. 'Nor is it anything to do with my pride. On the contrary, your success will be my passage back to France. Speaking of which, how glad you must be now that you did not accept my proposal of marriage, back at Versailles.'

'I could not have accepted it, in any case,' I say carefully. 'Given the gulf between our births. But, since you have evidently been informed by our mutual friends of my possible good fortune in this regard, I will say that yes, it is a good thing. Although, signor . . . it might be better if that particular episode were to remain a secret between us. A proposal, even one that is refused, might be seen as tarnishing my good name, and my reputation is going to be more important than ever now.'

'Your reputation?' he mutters. 'Oh, please. Spare me. You mean that now you have bigger fish to fry.'

Angry now, I say, 'I am lifting the king's spirits – something that you, it seems, are unable to do with your ices.'

He bows. 'Indeed. You have my gratitude.' He walks away, his face like thunder.

160

I gaze after him, exasperated. The confectioner's feelings, it seems, are still somewhat bruised. Of course, I am sorry for it – although somewhat surprised – but it cannot be allowed to deflect me from my task.

That evening, Arlington and his wife have a conversation behind closed doors. Later, Lady Arlington comes to my room. She sends my maid away and combs out my hair herself, exclaiming over the thickness of the corkscrew ringlets that spring out from under her fingers, unruly as ever. I have never been able to tame them properly.

'I think we know someone who admires them, anyway,' she says teasingly, and I blush.

'Tell me,' she continues in the same calm voice. 'When are your monthly courses?'

A little embarrassed, I say, 'I have everything I need, thank you.'

'I don't mean *that*,' she says, unperturbed. 'I mean for the king. So that you go to him at the right time.' She smiles at me reassuringly in the glass. 'You do want him to fall in love with you, don't you?' Her hand on the comb never misses a beat, as regular as a groom brushing down a horse.

'I . . . don't know,' I say hesitantly.

'I think you do,' she murmurs. 'I think you must. The way he looks at you . . . He wants you as more than comfort in his grief. Much more. Lucky you!'

'No!' I say. 'I could not do that. Not ever.'

She holds my hair out to the sides in two bunches. 'Have you ever thought about wearing it like this?' she says, changing the subject as casually if we have been discussing nothing more important than a new *coiffure*.

Carlo

Alone among desserts, ices excite curiosity and wonder in
equal measure.

The Book of Ices

It might be thought as a result of my conversations with them
regarding oaths, courtiers and so on, that the servants at the Red
Lion were an unusually pious lot. But, in fact, I soon realised, the
place was little better than a brothel.

On the Continent, a man knows that he is visiting a house of ill
repute and, his business concluded, may close the door and forget
all about the dealings he has conducted there. In England the
demarcation between inn and stew, servant and trull, was rather
less defined – indeed, they have a word, *slut*, which describes
someone who occupies the lowest rank of domestic servant, but
which also indicates that she is likely to be available for whatever
else may be required of her. It soon became apparent that at the
Red Lion there were several sluts who supplemented their wages
in this way. These young women – Mary, Rose, and two or three
others – openly worked the main dining rooms of an evening,
going from patron to patron under the guise of bringing them ale,
engaging them in flirtatious conversation and so on, before slipping upstairs with them to one of the attic bedrooms.

I was, initially, somewhat annoyed when I discovered what sort
of place it was – not because I was bothered by the vice itself, but
because in France or Italy, to base your business in a brothel
would be grounds for an instant removal of the royal warrant. But
in England, clearly, things were not so straightforward. Indeed,
when I mentioned it to Robert Cassell, he seemed almost amused.

162

'Well, of course,' he said. 'What did you expect? It's a London tavern.'

'The authorities don't object?'

'In theory, yes – but in practice, they have more pressing matters to deal with.'

London's inns, he explained, had been hotbeds of dissent during the Commonwealth, often hosting informal parliaments of working men and women. Some had even had their own printing presses, and produced newspapers and revolutionary tracts which were eagerly devoured by the mob. After the purging that had necessarily taken place at the time of the Restoration, it had been decided that whoring was the lesser of the many evils that had to be dealt with.

'There isn't a tap-servant in London who can't be had for a silver sixpence,' he concluded.

'But I thought the people here were Puritans, before the Restoration?'

'Some were, but there were many sorts of dissenter, and they all had different views on what was or wasn't acceptable. Diggers, Quakers, Ranters, Levellers, the Family of Love, Muggletonians, Fifth Monarchists . . . They're all banished now, but for a while England had almost as many crazed sects as it had counties. Some of them, like the Ranters or the Family of Love, were virtually indistinguishable from libertines, except that in their case they dressed it up with a lot of nonsense about Christ Within and communality and brethrenhood. But whatever the sect, what they all had in common was a complete refusal to accept any authority but their own.'

I thought about Hannah's oddly defiant attitude to being thrown out of her pantry. In France or Italy a servant would have done as she was told without debate, but I could see how the people here, having tasted revolution, might find it a hard habit to break.

*

I had not actually considered, however, that Hannah herself might be among those servants who could, as Cassell put it, be had for a silver sixpence, and I was therefore surprised when I witnessed an altercation along those lines between her and one of her customers. The two of them were tucked away behind one of the stout beams of blackened oak that supported the ceiling in the front dining room, and speaking, despite their evident anger, in low tones; I probably would not have glanced at them at all had I not been waiting for her to bring me my food. Then I noticed two things. The first was that the man was better dressed than most of the Lion's other customers – almost as well dressed as I was myself. The second was that he had her in a tight grip by the arm.

'Don't go speaking to your betters in that way,' he was saying.

'I call no man my better, nor woman neither,' she retorted. 'And what exactly makes you better than me, in any case? Last night I was prepared to take your money; you were prepared to offer it. The difference is, I'll not make that mistake again.'

His reply was too low for me to catch most of it, but I could see that he was using the arm he had hold of to shake her roughly as he spoke, greatly jeopardising my pie, which almost slid from the plate she was holding onto the floor.

'. . . have you arrested, you ranter whore. Don't think I won't.'

To this she made no answer, but I could see she had gone white. He released her. 'We'll discuss this outside,' he said roughly, and turned away.

She came over to serve my food, but as she put it down on the table her hand shook, and the plate rattled, although her voice, when she asked me if I needed more beer, was hard and flat. I said that I did not, and she left me without another word. I saw her go to the door the man had left by, which led to the yard where the empty kegs were stored.

I shrugged and turned my attention to the pie. I had enquired what it was before ordering; the reply that it was 'cock-a-leekie' had left me none the wiser, but now, as I punctured the crust with my knife, it released a spurt of fragrant heat, revealing several soft, steaming pieces of potato, some pale garters of leek, slivers of chicken in a creamy broth, a good scattering of thyme, and even a few pieces of a dark currant-like fruit which I soon discovered were preserved plums.

However, there was something spoiling my enjoyment, and that was the knowledge that all the time I was inside eating a cock-a-leekie pie, the woman who had made it was outside, giving herself to a man she had clearly wished to refuse. She might be at fault, but I had not liked the look of the fellow, or the way he had shaken her arm, and I suspected that he was probably being no more gentle with her now.

Sighing, I put my plate to one side, got to my feet, and went to the yard door. Outside, it was dark, but I heard a noise from behind a pile of kegs to my right. I shouted 'Who's there?' A woman gasped, the sound instantly cut off, as if by a hand around the throat. I shouted, 'Bring the watch here, ho! Here's fornication in the streets!' – a phrase which surprised even me, until I remembered that these were the words shouted by the night beadles as they toured the streets in the small hours, looking for any mischief. I must have heard them a dozen times beneath my own window as I slumbered.

From behind the kegs there was the jingling of a sword belt, a muffled oath, and then the unmistakeable sound of a hefty slap. Hannah cried out; footsteps ran off, and I went behind the kegs to investigate.

She was sprawled on the ground where she had been hurled by his blow. From the way her skirts were rucked indecently around her waist, I had been too late to prevent the act which both parties had gone there to carry out; but perhaps, at least, I had prevented her from coming to further harm.

'Thank you,' she said flatly.

I noticed the absence of a 'sir'. But perhaps in the darkness she did not recognise me. Then she held out her hand. That too surprised me: on the Continent it would have been unthinkable for a servant to put out her hand to a gentleman. But she was clearly in need of it if she were to get to her feet, so I took hold of it and pulled her up.

'Thank you,' she said again when she was standing. She rubbed her cheek where the man had slapped it. I could see from the way she looked at me that she was wondering what I was now going to ask of her for helping her.

'You owe me no thanks,' I said. 'Nor anything else for that matter.' I turned to go.

'Signor Demirco,' she said.

I stopped.

'If you tell Titus Clarke what you have heard tonight, I will be dismissed.'

That was all. There was no question asked, no request made. She simply stated a fact, and left it for me to decide what to do.

It was on the tip of my tongue to say, 'You should have thought of that before.'

But I did not. I simply nodded, and went back inside. And when Titus brought me another pint of beer, I found that I had no inclination to tell him what had passed between Hannah and her beau. It was, I told myself, simply none of my business.

Louise

While the king swims, Lady Arlington walks me down the Stone Gallery, the longest and most ornate of the cloistered courtyards within Whitehall.

'Those are the king's apartments,' she says, pointing. 'The houses on the other side are for favourite courtiers. And here,' she pauses significantly, 'a new set of rooms is being prepared.'

She opens some wooden doors. Inside, four men in short wigs, court painters, are working on a fresco. On the opposite wall, a tapestry in the French style is being hung by men on ladders. Another workman, a cabinetmaker, is installing an inlaid bookcase of walnut and maple with the help of an apprentice. The smell of wood shavings and fresh paint hangs in the air. As we enter the men duck their heads respectfully, then go back to what they were doing.

'What a beautiful room,' I say truthfully, going to the window. The tall panes remind me of Versailles. Beyond is a pretty garden containing a large glass sundial, with the long glittering lake of St James's Park beyond.

'It's for you.'

I turn round, astounded. 'For me?'

'He is having it refurbished specially. And look.' She crosses to another door and opens it. It leads to a set of stairs. 'He can visit you directly from his own apartments.'

'Without anyone knowing, you mean?'

Lady Arlington nods. 'There may be times when he wishes to be discreet. To begin with, at least.'

I stare at her. 'But I would never permit him to visit me in that fashion unless he were my husband.'

'Don't be a fool, Louise,' she says softly. 'You must do what

167

is necessary, just as pretty girls have always done with kings. The only question is, what will *you* get out of it? Your Majesty.' She sweeps into a curtsey, and for a moment I think she is mocking me. Then, turning, I see that the king has come into the room.

'I was told you were here,' he says impatiently. 'Do the rooms meet with your approval? They will be finished by the weekend. Perhaps you will do me the honour of moving into them.'

'I cannot—' I begin, but Lady Arlington is quicker.

'That is very timely, sir. We are beginning some rebuilding works next week, so Louise would have had to leave us in any case.'

'Sir,' I say, 'I cannot possibly accept these quarters. They are far too good for a lady-in-waiting.'

'On the contrary. It is you who are far too good for them.' Charles is gazing at me with an intensity I find unnerving. 'Walk with me,' he says quietly, casting a glance at Lady Arlington. 'Let us talk a little.'

He leads me out into the Stone Gallery, and Lady Arlington walks fifteen paces behind us, pretending to be engrossed in the statues.

For a while, though, we do not talk much at all, the king only pointing out to me where various courtiers live. Then he produces a key and unlocks a small door.

'This is my privy garden,' he says, closing and locking the door behind him. Lady Arlington, I notice, is still on the other side of it. 'For my use alone.'

'It must be hard for Your Majesty to find solitude.'

'In truth, I never used to seek it. It is only since her death . . .' He glances at me. 'Tell me, Louise. You said she let you read our correspondence?'

'That is so.'

He says with a studied lack of interest, 'Then what do

you know about Dover? Besides that my sister was very ill, I mean?'

This is dangerous ground, but there is no point in denying it. 'I know about the treaty. Madame took me into her confidence from the outset.'

'I see.' He touches his moustache. 'Then presumably you are aware that it is a secret known only to a handful of other people. In this country there are six, besides myself. Seven, now you are here. Were it to become known more widely, it could affect the whole course of my reign.'

'I know. And I promise that I will never betray Madame's confidence.'

He nods. 'The fact that she trusted you is enough for me. But tell me . . .' He hesitates. 'Was it . . . honourable?'

'Sir?'

'Many of my subjects would say – if, heaven forbid, they knew about it – that when I signed that piece of paper, and took Louis's pension, I signed away my honour. I have been thinking about that a lot, these past months. I want to know what you think.'

He is asking what I think. I try to imagine Louis XIV having this conversation, and I cannot. It is extraordinary – to talk almost as equals like this.

I have to be careful.

'If a man had signed that document, then perhaps it could be considered dishonourable. But you are not a man. You are the king – you *are* England. You cannot be bound by the same considerations as ordinary men, just as you cannot be bound by the wishes of Parliament.'

'Yes.' He begins to pace, and I walk with him, trying to match his long stride. 'So I thought myself, at the time. But since her death . . . I see my people – they are weary of wars. Religious divisions too. Perhaps in my greed – my yearning to be an independent ruler – and my desire to please my sister, I have put my interests before theirs.'

169

'But Madame had no interest in this. She only wanted what was best for you.'

'True. But perhaps she was influenced by her own religious convictions. Not to mention her . . . admiration for Louis.' He glances at me, and I see that he knows, or at least suspects, about his sister and the king. 'She was like all of us Stuarts,' he says apologetically. 'Her appetite for life was large, and she sometimes allowed it to sway her judgement.' He falls silent for a moment. 'It is good to talk about this. Since her death, there has been no one I could discuss it with.'

I sense an opening. 'You can talk to me as often as you wish, sir. Indeed, I hope that you will.'

He gives me a rueful glance. 'I would not impose that burden on you.'

'It would be no burden. And it is only what they all expect.'

'Oh? Why is that?'

I hesitate, and find myself blushing a little. 'Some of your ministers think that I will catch your eye.'

'Ah,' he says softly. 'Of course.' He gives me a sideways look. 'I can see why they might think so. I confess that in the past I have often had a deplorable weakness for female beauty.'

My blush deepens. 'But I can help you without that. I can be your confidante, just as your sister was. I can get messages to Louis, I can make him aware of the pressures you are under. I have already seen how impossible it would be for you to announce your conversion now. I will report it to him.'

He raises his eyebrows. 'You would intercede with your own king on my behalf?'

'I would be a go-between, trusted by both. As your sister was.'

'Then let those be the terms of the Treaty of the Rose Garden,' he says laconically. 'But – just so I am quite clear – that is as far as it goes? To talk to me, and nothing more?'

I blush again.

'Forgive me,' he adds. 'More plain speaking. But I would

rather shock you now with my bluntness, than offend you with an unwelcome suggestion on some future occasion.'

'Then I will speak plainly too.' Plainly, I think, but carefully. 'I will never by my conduct bring disgrace to my family.'

He nods. Is he disappointed, or pleased? It is impossible to be sure. But it is important that he knows that I am not going to do what Lady Arlington is insinuating I should.

We have reached the sundial in the centre of the garden, an elaborate affair of glass orbs inlaid with stained glass. The base is carved with an inscription:

Each day all previous days forget:
Waste not these hours with regret.

'*Carpe diem,*' he says, seeing me read it. 'A good instruction for us both. You realise that if we are seen together, talking, people may draw their own conclusions? Your reputation, I am sure, would not invite such a response, but I am afraid that I have not always been so well behaved.'

'It will be better if they do,' I say frankly. 'It will worry them far less than the idea that we are discussing matters of policy.'

'A shrewd answer. And I see over your shoulder that Lady Arlington is spying on us from the windows of your apartment even now. She will be wondering what we are talking about.'

'Perhaps we had better make it look—' I stop.

'My thoughts exactly,' he agrees. He reaches for my hand, puts it to his lips, and kisses it at the wrist. Then, still holding my wrist, he pulls me easily into his arms. For a moment I find myself staring into his eyes. Is there a hint of amusement – of calculation, even – deep in their blackness?

'I meant what I said earlier,' he says softly. 'I will make no suggestions to you, I swear. But I do not deny that had you been a different sort of woman, I would have done so without hesitation.'

*

'Well?' Lady Arlington demands. 'What did he say?'

'He said . . .' I cannot tell her what he said. 'It was nothing. Flatteries and endearments and so on.'

Lady Arlington smiles. 'And I suppose you told him to keep his flatteries to himself?'

I do not reply.

'It's all right. I was watching from up here. I saw the way you were together. I knew you would be charmed by him. There's something about a crown that overcomes the most stubborn scruples, isn't there?'

Carlo

Take care that you serve your ices in small quantities, for
a surfeit of any pleasure soon wearies the palate.

The Book of Ices

'The game is on,' Lord Arlington said with some satisfaction. 'The
king is pleased.'

'The girl has done her duty?' Walsingham asked.

Arlington shook his head. 'Not yet. But she will: it is simply a
question of when.'

'Will she need further encouragement?' That was Cassell.

Arlington smiled. 'That is exactly the point – she knows she
must do it, but at the same time she is reluctant. It gives the king
the illusion that he must make the running, and it is precisely this
that stokes his interest. There's little sport in hunting a rabbit in
a barn: it's the running doe that makes for a satisfying chase.' He
glanced at me. 'Signor, your ices will soon be required. Make sure
that you are ready.'

'You have the pineapple?'

He nodded. 'It will be with you soon. Use it wisely. It cost me
a great deal of money.'

'I know my orders,' I said shortly. 'I will play my part.'

And then I will be gone, I thought; and good riddance to the
lot of you.

Louise

Two days later I move into my apartments. Sumptuous and vast, the rooms echo when I walk across the inlaid floors. But I am touched to find that Charles has tried to make me feel at home: the bookcase I saw the workmen fitting is filled with French books. And – a thoughtful touch – they are not just novels, but works of philosophy, drama, mathematics. A brand-new harpsichord stands to one side, the music case stocked with pieces by Blancrocher and Chambonnières. Next to it, the writing bureau already bears a neat stack of invitations.

As I look through them, the door to the apartment opens and two well-dressed young women come in. Seeing me, they curtsey.

'Hello.' I gesture at the empty rooms. 'If you have come to visit me, I'm afraid you are a little premature. I have only just arrived myself.'

The older of the two girls, a brunette, looks puzzled. 'We have not come to visit. We are your ladies-in-waiting.' She indicates her companion. 'This is the Honourable Lucy Williamson, and I am Lady Anne Berowne.'

'Ladies-in-waiting!' I catch myself. 'Forgive me, you are very welcome. It is just that I was not expecting to have anyone wait on me. Rather the other way round, in fact. Please, take a seat.' They are both very pretty: presumably that is all part of the Arlingtons' design. The king will be even more likely to visit me if I am surrounded by attractive faces.

After an hour conversation is becoming stilted, not least because we are all now ravenously hungry.

'Tell me,' I ask Lucy, who is pale and fair, 'what does one do to get some food in this place?'

She looks even more confused than Lady Anne did earlier. 'Is your chef not bringing lunch?'

'My chef!'

'Everyone at court has their own chef.'

'Well, I have not appointed one as yet. Nor am I entirely sure how I would set about doing such a thing.'

'Perhaps you would ask your steward to appoint one for you?' Lady Anne suggests helpfully.

'Perhaps, but I have not yet got a steward either. Or a butler, or a footman, or a dresser, or maids.' And neither do I have the money to pay for them if I did.

'Oh,' says Lucy, whom I am quickly realising is the less clever of the two. 'Does that mean we are not going to get any lunch?'

I sigh. 'Perhaps the French ambassador will lend us some staff. I will write to him.' I stop. 'I suppose I am going to need a servant, to take my note?'

The girls nod.

'Lunch in France is often skipped by the ladies of the court,' I say decisively. And perhaps by supper, I think, I will have worked out what to do.

But it is long before supper when a servant in royal livery enters and whispers something to Lady Anne. She spins round to face me. 'The queen is coming.'

'Now? Here?'

She nods, her eyes large.

'*Mon Dieu*,' I say faintly. 'What about Lady Arlington?'

'On her way also.'

'That is something, I suppose. What will the queen expect?'

Lady Anne shrugs helplessly. 'She likes cards. And she will expect to be fed.'

'Fed what?'

'Supper,' she says vaguely. Clearly Lady Anne's upbringing has not included much household management.

'For how many?'

'She'll bring her ladies-in-waiting. Perhaps a dozen all told. And if she is visiting, others may too.'

I think for a moment. 'Send a message to Signor Demirco, the confectioner. Ask him to send ices for twenty. Tell him there is no time to lose.'

Carlo

In a hurry, a simple ice may be fashioned from eggnog, or
custard, or fruit, or any mixture of the three.

The Book of Ices

'Twenty! I cannot make twenty ices by dinner time.'

The man who had brought the message shrugged. 'That is the
request.'

I sighed. 'Very well. Say that I will see what I can do. And have
a carriage here at six.'

It is not possible to make cream ices in a hurry, but a good quantity of *granite* may be prepared in a few minutes, if you have a syrup
to pour on them. Cordials, too, can be boiled up in no time, if you
have a supply of ice with which to cool them down. And even
creams can be approximated, if you have preserved fruits with
which to flavour your milk as you churn it. In Paris I could have
responded to Louise's request with a snap of my fingers, and my
apprentices would have rushed to get everything ready in time.

But here in London, I had no apprentices. And no one I could
trust not to steal my secrets.

'Why are you shouting?' Elias enquired.

'I am uttering profanities in Italian,' I told him. 'But now I am
going to utter instructions in English. Put on that glove, and grate
as much ice as you can.'

'*Si, signor*,' he said happily.

'Not like that, or we will be here all night,' I said, showing him.
'And I must get some syrups on to boil. Who is there who can go
to the market for me?'

'Mary is free,' he said, pulling on the grating glove.

'Then send Mary for oranges. And more sugar.'

'What is going on?'

It was Hannah, having heard the commotion.

'The queen is coming to supper with Madam Carwell,' Elias told her.

'You cannot possibly make enough orange syrup in time,' Hannah said, taking in the situation. 'Send Mary out for oranges by all means, but you must squeeze the juice fresh and serve it with some sprigs of mint and a little cardamom.'

I had not, at that time, heard the English expression beginning 'Too many cooks', but I was quickly becoming familiar with the sentiment. 'There is no time to debate this. I need to serve ices to Her Majesty—'

'I have made a posset,' she interrupted. 'You can have it.'

That brought me up short. 'How much?'

'A gallon. Enough for twenty, if you freeze it.'

'Making ices is not quite as simple as that.'

She sighed. 'I do not mean to suggest that it is. But I think, all the same, that the posset will freeze adequately, just as the custard did. Think of it as a kind of cook's short cut.'

By now Mary, Rose and the landlord, Titus, had all joined us. I had to make a quick decision. 'Very well,' I said. 'I will freeze the posset. But get some oranges as well. We will squeeze them for juice. And lemons too – we will make a syrup.'

'Do not pay more than sixpence for the oranges,' Hannah added to Mary. 'Go to Robin Marchmont, and tell him I sent you. Rose, tell Peter to get the stove hot. And I will fetch the posset.'

Posset, I should explain, is a concoction the English are especially fond of, a kind of eggnog made with wine and spices. It was often served in the taverns, both as a warming drink and as a kind of dessert. This one was flavoured not just with lemon juice, sweet wine and nutmeg but also another taste I could not at first identify.

'What is that?' I asked. 'Some kind of herb?'

Hannah nodded. 'Sweet cicely. Just a pinch.'

I put down the spoon. 'Well, it will have to do. Elias, how does the ice?'

'I have nearly done the whole block,' he reported, his cheeks pink from the effort of grating.

'We will need at least twice that.' I picked up the paddle, and hesitated. Now I had to pack the *sabotiere* with ice and salt so that I could freeze the posset. At this stage I would usually have asked everyone present to leave, but today I could not afford to have them stop what they were doing.

Making the best I could of the situation, I took the various ingredients off to a corner. To confuse an eavesdropper even further, I spoke some Latin over the pail as I stirred it.

'*Dominus virtutum nobiscum,*' I added, recalling some words from a Catholic psalm.

And so we proceeded for the next two hours, making the orange cordial and thickening a lemon syrup for the *granite* while I periodically turned back to the *sabotiere* to work the ice mix as it froze. Hannah suggested that we send out for some jellies as well, so Rose was despatched to purchase quiddanies from Mrs Lamb around the corner, and by the time the carriage arrived we had almost pulled together a respectable collation. I was not in such a rush, however, that I neglected to taste the frozen posset: to my surprise, it was possessed of a smooth, rich texture that I had only achieved twice before, once on the day of Madame's funeral, and once when I froze Hannah's custard.

Louise

'They're here,' Anne says, looking down from her position at the window. I go to her side.

The procession coming towards us down the Stone Gallery makes a strange sight. The queen is unmistakeable – a tiny woman, she is nevertheless dressed in a fine Spanish gown, her bearing upright as only a princess's could be. Her ladies-in-waiting, though, are another matter. They wear strange, tall hats like nuns, and their skirts are sewn with hooped farthingales that make them sway from side to side as they walk.

'Lord help us,' Lady Arlington says behind me. 'She's brought the whole Portuguese fleet. I can't wait to see the looks on their swarthy faces when they realise they've been usurped.'

I can believe the queen is dying. She looks even more frail than Madame did in the months before her collapse, the streaks of grey in her hair suggesting that she has been suffering like this for years.

Lady Arlington's curtsey is so perfunctory she might simply be ducking something thrown at her head.

'Your Highness, may I present Louise de Keroualle. I believe at one point she was going to be a lady of your bedchamber,' she drawls, with just a little emphasis on 'your'. 'Although the king has now been pleased to find another place for her at court.'

If the queen notices the insinuation, she does not show it. 'The king is most considerate,' she says to me. 'I remember how kind he was when I first came to this country. If there is anything I want, I only have to ask him.' She may sound weak, but the meaning is clear. *Do not attempt to humiliate me, or I will have you removed.*

There is an awkward silence. Fortunately, the ices arrive. 'This is the latest fashion in France, Your Highness,' I say as Lucy arranges them on a side table. 'It means one does not have to interrupt one's card playing. One simply eats the ices at the table, and carries on refreshed.'

She beams. 'That sounds very pleasant.'

The game itself presents a different problem. I know how to play her favourite game, basset – it is also popular in France – but I have no money with which to gamble.

'I'll lend you some,' Lady Arlington says under her breath. 'After all, you should soon have more than enough.' In a louder voice she says, 'Shall I shuffle, Your Highness? The queens are all together.'

There is little skill in basset; it is simply a game of nerve and luck. A winning card pays out whatever has been staked on it. But if, instead of taking the winnings, you leave your card on the table and it wins again, your winnings are seven times the stake; the time after that, fifteen, then thirty. It is possible to win a fortune, but the odds against doing so become increasingly slim. Within a quarter of an hour I have lost fifty guineas, most of it to Lady Arlington.

'I'll lend you some more,' she says immediately.

'No, thank you – I will sit out for a while, and watch.'

I see how Lady Arlington, having relinquished the bank, becomes flushed with excitement when she makes *le quinze*, the fifteen-fold payout, only to lose it all on the next turn of the card. That tells me something about her, I think: not only a gambler, but a reckless one.

'You do not play?' a voice murmurs behind me.

I turn. The king has entered, unnoticed and without ceremony. The others start to get to their feet, but he cuts short the formalities with a wave of his hand. 'Please, do not let me interrupt your game. I shall sit over here, and speak to Mademoiselle de Keroualle.'

The queen darts her husband an anxious look before returning obediently to her cards.

181

'Tell me, why do you sit this out?' he asks quietly. 'I can't flatter myself that it was on the off-chance I might come by.'

'I do not care greatly for games of risk.'

He raises his eyebrows. 'The plans my sister hatched were bold enough.'

'I meant, risk for its own sake. In diplomacy, surely, one tries to make the gamble as small as possible. In basset it becomes the whole point of the game.'

He nods. 'I myself prefer *poque*. It requires a certain talent for bluffing.'

'In France *poque* is known as the cheating game,' I say, a little mischievously.

'I flatter myself I have a certain talent in that direction also,' he says, the ghost of a smile appearing deep in his eyes.

'Sir, you keep Miss de Keroualle from the table,' Lady Arlington calls. 'And she needs to play, if she is to recoup her losses.'

He looks at me interrogatively. 'I think she means to get me away from you,' I explain under my breath. 'She has some idea that the more you are held back, the more eagerly you will pursue my friendship.'

'Then you had better go to her,' he murmurs. 'But while they are playing basset, we shall be playing *poque*.'

As I go to the table he follows. 'How much does she owe, Lady Arlington?'

'Fifty guineas, sir.'

'There is a hundred.' Charles tosses a pouch onto the baize. 'And if she accrues any other debts, I hope I am good for them.'

Lady Arlington's eyes almost reach the top of her head.

'Madam, I bid you good night,' Charles says, bowing to the queen. 'And you, Lady Arlington. Mademoiselle.' He bows to me last of all, as protocol demands, but it is on me that his eyes remain, a glance of complicity travelling between the two of us.

Carlo

To make a pineapple sherbet: add two cups of sugar to two cups of buttermilk, or more if your pineapple be sharp. Stir in a spoon of fresh minced mint, and the juice of a lime, and stir it as you freeze. The principle is no different from any other fruit.

The Book of Ices

The next day, when I went to Whitehall to collect the empty goblets, I found Louise in her apartments. She seemed somehow adrift in the great space, lost, like someone wearing a ballgown several sizes too large.

I had no wish to speak to her, but I bowed anyway.

'Don't be like that,' she said sharply.

'Like what?'

'Carlo . . .'

I waited.

'I was truly grateful for your help last night,' she said. 'Were it not for your ices, it would have been a difficult situation. A more difficult situation, I should say.'

'You and the queen? I can see how that might have been a little awkward.'

She shrugged. 'That is the point of manners, isn't it? To make awkward situations bearable. Besides, I suspect she has had to suffer worse, in this terrible country.' She was silent a moment. 'I mean it, signor. We find ourselves reluctant partners in this task, but I am grateful that Louis has sent someone who I know I can rely on.'

'I will do my duty. No more, and no less. And then we will return to France, and there will be an end to our association.'

She seemed surprised. '*You* will return to France, you mean.'

'You might stay here?'

She gave me a sharp glance then, as if wondering why I asked. 'Possibly. We shall have to see.'

'Your enthusiasm for your task is even greater than I imagined, then,' I said dryly.

'I have an opportunity. I would be a fool not to take it.'

'Indeed.' I bowed again. 'Reluctant partners, then.'

As I closed the door of her apartment behind me, I saw a note fluttering on the wood. Someone had pinned it there with a fruit knife. Two lines of verse.

> *Within this place a bed's appointed*
> *For a French bitch and God's anointed.*

I went back and handed it to her. 'You have been sent a *billet-doux.*'

She read it, her face ashen. 'Barbarians. How could they?'

'It is probably a man called Rochester. The king indulges such behaviour, I believe.'

'They hate us. That is to say, they hate me. And they will only hate me more when—' She shook her head. 'It does not matter. It means nothing. If I could handle the French court, I can surely handle this.'

'And this,' I said, pointing at the note, 'is exactly the sort of merriment that we are here to encourage, isn't it? We will know we have been successful when Lord Rochester is as celebrated in England as Moliere or Racine are in France.'

Finally, my pineapple had arrived, and for a time I was able to put Louise de Keroualle from my mind.

For all that I had spoken casually of pineapples to Lord Arlington, I had never before been able to use one for an ice. Even at the court of Louis XIV, they were too precious for that.

So I was both curious, and a little excited, to get my hands on one now.

The pineapple came in its own coach-and-four, direct from Lord Devon's pinery. The chest was carried into the Red Lion by two of his footmen, with a third standing guard with a pistol in case of robbers. A curious crowd, meanwhile, gathered in the coaching yard to watch its progress from coach to kitchen.

'I had better place someone to keep watch,' Titus said nervously. 'I would not like to be responsible if it were stolen.'

In my pantry, I had already had Hannah scrub the stone ledge that ran the length of one wall in readiness. The chest was set down and the locks undone. A few people had managed to follow the chest's progress indoors, and now craned forward eagerly to see the contents.

Inside, on a red satin cushion, lay a strange fruit: half coronet, half hedgehog. The skin was scaly and patterned, like the shell of a tortoise, while from the crown sprang an extravagant headdress of prickly plumage. The aroma – which had something of the perfumed fragrance of strawberries, and something of the sharp freshness of limes – escaped from the chest where it had been trapped and filled the air around me. As one, the onlookers made an ahh-ing sound.

'And now you must all leave,' I said firmly. 'I have work to do.'

When there was no one left in the pantry but Hannah, Elias and myself, I reached into the chest and pulled out the pineapple, using the tips of my fingers to avoid being pricked by the curved, talon-like spikes that protruded from each scale. Placing it on the ledge, I picked up a cleaver. With a certain trepidation – this must be how a surgeon feels, I thought, in the moment before he slices open a patient – I lopped off the top, revealing the pale, sweet-smelling inside. Carefully, I placed the crown to one side. Then I sliced the pineapple in two lengthways, before taking a smaller filleting knife and carefully cutting away both the scaly

185

skin and the hard, husk-like inner core. I did this last part over a bowl: even so, drops of priceless pineapple juice ran down my fingers.

'That fruit,' Hannah observed suddenly, 'would cost more than I will earn in my lifetime.'

'What of it?'

'Nothing could be worth so much.'

I shrugged. 'It is worth what men are prepared to pay.'

'But it is not even particularly pleasant.'

'How do you know?' I said sharply, wondering for a moment if she had taken some to taste when I was not looking.

'From the smell. It is almost as sour as a lemon. Can't you feel it?'

It was true – my own nostrils were pricking from the fruit's sharpness too. Experimentally, I lifted my hand and licked my finger where the pineapple juices dripped along it. It was very sharp indeed: bitter, almost. It would need a great deal of sugar to make it palatable.

'I cannot help thinking,' she went on, 'that these pineapples are like gold, or precious stones – their value comes principally from the fact that they are rare.'

'It is rather more than that.' I hesitated. 'The pineapple is known to be an aphrodisiac – to stoke the passions of love.'

To my surprise, she hooted with laughter.

'What is so funny?'

'Only that it is strange how it is never common-or-garden herbs or fruits that are said to do that. If a simple blackberry or an English apple had the misfortune to look so strange, and to be so elusive, then perhaps those too would cost men fortunes, and be considered a source of potency.'

'No one would be so foolish as to pay a fortune for a blackberry,' I said. The pineapple now lay in eight pieces in my bowl, together with its juice. I separated it into two, and handed one lot to her. 'Cut it as fine as you can.'

186

She nodded, and we began to slice and reslice the pineapple into cubes barely larger than crumbs of bread. I will say this for her: she kept a sharp knife, and she could use it quickly.

'People – that is to say, *men* – prize what they cannot have.' She gave me a sideways glance. 'For you, I suppose, that is all to the good.'

'What do you mean?'

'Only that your ices are expensive for exactly the same reason.'

'My ices are sought after because of their excellence,' I said. 'Enough of this chatter, woman. We need to slice and sift the fruit very fine.'

'I can talk and chop at the same time.'

I sighed. 'Perhaps, but I cannot. This fruit is, as you have rightly pointed out, more precious than gold, and I would like to give its preparation the attention it deserves.'

When the sifting was done, and I had a mound of fine-textured pulp and juice, I considered what to do next.

I had been planning to make a simple *sorbetto*, but the fruit's sharpness persuaded me that I would do better to aim for a richer dish. So I sent Hannah to get some buttermilk, the creamy, thick liquid left over from churning butter. Meanwhile, I readied my other ingredients: crushed mint leaves and a little lime juice, to act as a flavour base for a sherbet.

When Hannah returned, I mixed together equal amounts of buttermilk and sugar, and added that to my pineapple and the other ingredients. Then I poured my mixture into the *sabotiere* – Hannah by this time having been ordered out of the pantry – and stirred it every half an hour, initially with a whisk, and later, as it became heavier and more snow-like, with a fork to break up the crystals.

So simple, and so quick. I tasted it – just a morsel: there were barely three cupfuls in total. It had a sweet, delicate flavour, like pale sunshine, the sourness balanced now by the sugar and the richness of the buttermilk. It was very fine – but as to whether it was any better or worse than a blackberry or an apple, I really could not have said.

Louise

Every day now he comes to visit me. If there is anyone else present – the ambassador, Lord Arlington, one of the many French exiles who seem to assume that my apartments are their *salon* – he abruptly bids them good day.

And then . . .

All we do is talk. Talk, and tears.

That is to say, he talks about his sister. But we also speak of the Great Affair, this plan for a united Europe, a kind of second Holy Roman Empire, stretching from Ireland to Russia. One continent, united under one faith. A place without wars, almost without borders.

And little by little we switch to talking about Louis. How he has stamped his authority on what was, once, the most divided and squabbling kingdom in Europe. How he has slowly reclaimed those portions of his lands owned by foreign powers. How, even now, his borders are being pushed outwards – to the Netherlands, to Alsace, to the Pyrenees.

It is clear that Charles is fascinated by his French cousin – fascinated and a little envious.

L'état, c'est moi.

I tell him about the glories of French art, the musicians and philosophers and poets who add such lustre to the court of Versailles.

'I have my poets too,' he says, a little defensively. 'I have my painters and my wits.'

'Of course,' I say soothingly.

'Well? Has he made love to you yet?' Lady Arlington says with a smile.

189

'Elizabeth! What a question to ask.'

'I'll take that to mean yes, shall I?'

I don't reply.

'You French, with your shrugs!' she exclaims. And then, more quietly, 'Well done!'

Why do I not tell her the truth? After all, she has never laughed at my scruples, even if she has made it clear that she thinks them irrelevant. But I sense that on this point she may yet become insistent.

As may he.

For it is becoming all too clear that his interest, whatever he says, is not only because of Minette. Grief has given way to something more. When he looks at me now it is not always with the chaste eyes of a brother.

And yet he keeps his word. He does not make any suggestions that would embarrass me. It is all in the space between the words: the glances, the unspoken intensity of his eyes, the sudden smiles, the silences.

Is this what I want? What force am I unleashing? Is this a monster I can ride, or one that will destroy me?

'Sir, I have an ice for you.'

I hand him the goblet. Tiny, exquisite, it has been made especially for this moment: an eggcup-sized pineapple of gold and painted glass, latticed like a pineapple's eyes, its brim adorned with golden leaves.

'Is this . . .?'

I nod. 'Pineapple, yes. It was your sister's favourite.'

He takes the tiny glass, dips in the even tinier spoon, like something you would use to serve salt. Touches it to his lips.

And, a moment later, nods approvingly. 'Remarkable,' he breathes.

The next spoonful he holds out to me. I reach up to take it from his hand, but he does not let go, and I find my fingers closing around his.

His eyes on mine, dark and unreadable.

He guides our hands towards my mouth. I suck icy crystals from the spoon. The taste is sweet, lemony, elusive.

'Wonderful,' I agree.

He reaches into the tiny glass for another spoonful. This time I guide our hands towards his mouth. Obediently he opens, closes.

We alternate – one for him, and one for me, our hands working together. When it is all gone he says quietly, 'I never saw the point, until now.'

He is looking at my mouth. I feel my throat go dry – I want to swallow, to draw a breath. I see his lips part, and then his head inclines a little to one side, and moves imperceptibly closer.

'What were we talking of?' I say quickly, getting to my feet. 'I was going to find you that book of verse, wasn't I?'

Above reproach.

One afternoon, he asks me to sit beside him at court, in the presence chamber. I am uneasy – it seems too public, too exposed, but this is the whole point of me being here, to coax him back into public life, so I can hardly refuse. And so I sit at his side, being shown off like a queen, while ministers and petitioners come and make requests. Those who are diseased with dropsy or ague even ask if he will touch them, to heal their sickness. As God's representative on earth, he has some of God's powers. He accepts these people with patient courtesy, but over their heads he catches my eye and wrinkles his nose.

One of the petitioners offers him a bribe – not a present, such as a snuff box or a jewelled brooch, but actual money. There is a murmur of disgust from the courtiers around us.

Charles makes a joke of it. 'Give it to someone else,' he says. 'Give it to . . .' He looks around. 'Louise. She is always losing at basset.'

The petitioner follows his gaze, and brings me the purse.

'I cannot accept this,' I say firmly.

'Please, madam?' the man says faintly, aware that he has made a terrible error.

'I would rather cut my own throat than besmirch my own honour,' I tell him.

'Bravo,' Lord Arlington murmurs. 'Well spoken, Louise.' He prompts a small patter of applause.

At the side of the court I notice a woman watching me. Small, redheaded, quite pretty, but dressed in a most extraordinary get-up – her gown so gaudy it might be a doll's. Indeed, she is so tiny that for a moment I think she is a child, come to court to look at the grown-ups. She watches me fixedly, almost as if she is studying me. Oddly, she pulls a face, then turns her head on one side and squints. She looks from me to Charles and back again, puzzled, as if she is trying to work out what is going on. Then I see her lips move, as if she is whispering something to herself.

I mean to ask Charles about her later, but it completely slips my mind.

Carlo

The English hedgerows provide much that is good for ices.

The Book of Ices

The king was eating ices at last. But only with Louise. Each day I sent a different one to her rooms. Damson, rosehip, pear, blackberry, and the large, sweet hazelnuts called Kentish cobs. Nuts posed their own challenges, of course – they must be chopped fine, then roasted: I longed to match their crunchiness with the creaminess I had created in my pear ice cream, but although I had tried many times to replicate that smooth texture, it still remained something that seemed to only come about by chance. At one time I thought it must be something to do with eggs, since both the *crème anglaise,* the posset and Hannah's custard had contained egg whites or yolks, but when I tried adding beaten egg to my syrup I simply made a fruit-filled omelette.

There was enough work now that I could employ Elias every day. Although he was young, he was no younger than I had been when I started working for Ahmad, and from the point of view of secrecy, the younger the better, since he was unlikely to understand enough to explain the process to anyone else. In fact he proved an eager pupil, happily grating ice for hours on end, and although he was liable to ask questions I was careful not to tell him too much.

I was less pleased, however, when I entered the pantry and caught him in the very act of dipping his fingers into the last remaining bowl of pineapple sorbet.

'What is this?' I cried, appalled.

He jumped back, his face scarlet.

'I told you never to taste the ices,' I reminded him furiously.

He hung his head. 'I am sorry, master. I was only curious.'

'You have stuck your dirty fingers in a dish intended for the king,' I said. 'That is very possibly treason. What is more, you have disobeyed your master, which most certainly is. Now you shall be beaten – and be grateful that it is only by me, and not the watch.'

I picked up a wooden spoon and began to beat him. He cried out: I raised the spoon to strike again, and suddenly found it gripped by someone behind me. I turned. Hannah was standing there, giving me a furious stare.

'What are you doing?' I said, trying to pull the spoon from her grasp. But her grip was surprisingly firm, and I could not.

'I should ask you that,' she said calmly.

'Isn't it obvious? I am beating him for a thief.'

'Whatever he has done, you strike too hard.'

'I am his master, and I will strike as hard as I like,' I retorted.

'And I am his mother, and will not let you.'

'His mother!' I was so surprised that I relaxed my hold on the spoon; she, meanwhile, had not relaxed hers, and it slipped from my grasp. No one had ever mentioned to me that Hannah was Elias's mother.

'Yes.' She tossed the spoon to one side. 'Why do you look surprised?'

'But then – where is his father?'

She hesitated. 'Elias has no father.'

'None you can name, you mean,' I muttered.

'That is exactly what I mean,' she replied defiantly. 'None I can name. And what of it?'

I ran a hand over my brow. 'What of it? Madam, I have the royal warrant. And yet now I find I am employing a whore's bastard as my assistant. In France or Italy that would be enough to have me banished from court.'

For a moment her eyes flashed angrily. 'Then the courts of France or Italy must be very different to our own,' she said. She turned to Elias. 'Is it true? Did you steal?'

'Yes,' he said in a small voice. 'I tasted the ice. The pineapple one.'

She sighed. 'I am disappointed in you. First, for taking what was not yours, and second, for believing all this nonsense about ices and pineapples in the first place. I have not brought you up to be so foolish.'

'I am sorry,' Elias said, his lip trembling.

'Your punishment will be to work for a whole week without any pay. But if he beats you again, tell me, and you will work for him no longer.'

I was so astonished at this unheard-of interference in the relationship between master and assistant that I barely knew how to respond; by the time I had collected my wits, she had gone.

'I am sorry, master,' Elias said hesitantly. My anger had abated by now: indeed, something about his hangdog expression was almost amusing.

'And have you learnt your lesson?' I said, with as much sternness as I could muster.

'I have.'

'Will you eat the king's ices again?'

He shook his head.

'And what did you think of it, now that you have tasted it?' I said, curious. I was expecting him to screw up his face and say that it was not very pleasant after all: but to my surprise his eyes lit up.

'Oh! It was wonderful!' he exclaimed.

I raised my eyebrows. 'Well, don't get too used to it. It may be a long time before I let you taste another.'

'Why so glum?' Cassell demanded. The soldier came round every week or so, to pass on letters or pump me for information about the court. But today he had found me in an ill humour.

195

'I have always suffered from melancholy,' I tell him. 'Particularly at this time of year.'

'You Italians are notoriously moody. You should try some horse riding, or fencing.' He brightened. 'I know! I'll take you to the theatre. Come, I insist.' And so I found myself taking a boat with him to Charing Cross, and then walking up Drury Lane to the King's Theatre.

This was the grander of the two theatre companies in London, he explained as we queued for our seats, the other being the Duke's, under the patronage of the king's brother, the Duke of York. It was my first visit to either establishment. To my surprise, men and women were sitting together in the stalls quite openly, while down in the pit some of the women wore masks. This, Cassell told me, was a sign that they were there for sport, and would acquiesce in being groped. Meanwhile, urchin girls ran up and down the aisles with baskets of china oranges; the smell of these as they were peeled, together with the wax candles that illuminated the stage, fortunately mitigating the stench caused by so many common people being crammed together in one place.

Before the play began, two trumpeters announced the king, and the people rose with a kind of cursory respect as the royal party took their seats in a box to one side of the stage – once again I was struck by the lack of formality with which this was done, compared with France or Italy. Louise was by the king's side, wearing a fashionable – that is to say large – French hat: there was an audible muttering amongst the audience at the sight of her.

The main female role that day was taken by an actress listed on the handbills as Mrs Eleanor Gwynne, although as far as I could tell from what Cassell said she was not actually married, and the audience – who clearly adored her, even going so far as to call out to her during the performance – called her 'Nellie' or 'Miss Nell'. The bill was a double one. First came a serious play about the martyrdom of Saint Katharine; I thought it rather good, although the audience were restless, hurling orange peel at some of the less

196

impressive actors, though never at Nellie. They only really applauded when, after the action was over and Nell lay dead upon the stage, with the pall-bearer approaching to carry her away, she suddenly leapt to her feet and stopped him.

> *'Hold! Are you mad? You damned confounded dog!*
> *I am to rise and speak the epilogue.'*

At once the theatre erupted with cheers and laughter, only silenced when Nellie herself held up her hand. There followed a speech full of lewd innuendo, until eventually she advanced to the side of the stage and addressed the king himself.

> *'But farewell, sir, make haste to me:*
> *I'm sure ere long to have your company.*
> *As for my epitaph, when I am gone*
> *I'll trust no poet, but will write my own:*
> *"Here Nelly lies, who though she lived a slattern,*
> *Yet died a princess, acting in Saint Cattern."'*

Then she started to dance, lifting her skirts and spinning around so that they rose even higher, an exhibition that the audience encouraged with whistles and applause. She was a pretty enough little thing, with shapely legs and a face that seemed full of jest and exuberance; but I could not myself see the appeal.

The second play was called *The Conquest of Granada*. This time Mrs Gwynne made her entrance in an outlandish get up, with a hat the size of a coach wheel, a vast black wig down to her shoulders, and oversized boots on her feet. The audience roared with laughter.

'Why is that funny?' I asked Cassell. He was laughing too, but he only shook his head.

Still wearing the enormous hat, the actress slouched over to where a male actor with a paste crown on his head was going through a jewel box. Then she started to speak. Her voice had changed since the last play – she was speaking in a kind of broken, drawling English. But there was something familiar about it, all the same.

I suddenly realised what I was witnessing. That huge hat was a send-up of French fashion, and the accent was meant to be Louise's – indeed, it *was* Louise: with a precision that was uncanny, the actress had somehow transformed herself into the Frenchwoman. At one point she crossed the stage, her tiny frame somehow taking on Louise's lissom, long-legged stride; a faint touch of something determined in Louise's posture now comically exaggerated into a parody of a bossy, pouting, hip-swaying coquette.

'Me no bad lady!' Mrs Gwynne lisped, pushing the actor away. 'If me tort I was so weckid a lady, I would cut my own trote!'

'Madam Cartwheel! Can't you see that I love you?' the man implored, going down on one knee and winking at the audience, who were by now in stitches. Even the orange sellers were doubled up with laughter, their wares spilling unnoticed from their baskets to the floor.

'Oh, Your Majestay, I cannot lurve you. For I am a gweat lady of Fwance.'

The man offered her some jewellery from his chest.

'Well . . . per'aps I can lurve you just a *leetle*,' she said, squirreling jewels into her bosom. The audience went wild.

I looked up at the king. He was shaking with laughter. Beside him in the Royal Box Louise's own face was expressionless.

'I have had enough of this,' I said curtly to Cassell.

He was holding his ribs as if in pain. 'No – wait,' he gasped. 'They will get on with the play soon.'

'I have seen enough fooling for one day.' Angrily, I pushed my way outside, shoving my way past the helpless Englishmen and women, Cassell following me reluctantly.

'You wanted me to see that,' I said when at last we were standing in Drury Lane.

He nodded, unapologetic.

'Why?'

'Come, let us find a tavern.' He began striding down towards the Strand, and I fell in beside him.

'It is one thing to seduce the king,' he said calmly. 'It will be quite another to hold him. As you saw just now, there is no shortage of women eager to share in the spoils.'

'Nell Gwynne?'

'Amongst others. The Duchess of Cleveland earned her titles in his bed, and may yet add a few more to her collection. The actress Moll Davies has a fine house in Pall Mall. Peggy Clift has a pension of eight hundred a year. And those are just the ones he's already had. There are a score of young women at court even now, all eager to fill Madam Carwell's boots.' He turned towards a tavern overlooking the river. 'It will take more than mere acquiescence: she'll need all her filthy French tricks if she's to—'

He never finished the sentence. I swung around with my fist, driving it into his face. I felt my knuckles meet his teeth, and then I was on the ground, Cassell's knife at my throat, the blade as steady as the eyes that were now boring into mine.

'Careful, signor,' he whispered. 'I have become fond of you, but I will not take an insult like that from any man.'

'And neither will I,' I said, staring him out.

After a moment the knife was withdrawn. 'Christ's wounds,' he said incredulously. 'You're sweet on her yourself.'

I got to my feet. 'Don't be ridiculous. I merely resent the suggestion that I am in some way her pimp. If you wish to speak to her of what she must or must not do, do it yourself.'

He began to brush the dirt off my back, as calm now as if our quarrel had never happened. 'Indeed,' he said. 'If I inadvertently gave you any offence, signor, please accept my apologies.' His tone was courteous; but I saw that his eyes were thoughtful, even so.

Louise

I am almost breathless with the directness of it. I am used to malicious *bon mots*, cutting remarks, the smiling but barbed asides of Versailles, but the sheer shameless barbarity of Nell Gwynne's attack is something else altogether. It is all I can do not to cry out as I watch.

And then they all applaud her. Laughter I can forgive – anyone can laugh, and then regret it – but to applaud!

I pointedly keep my hands folded in my lap. Charles notices, and leans across. 'They can seem a rough lot here at first,' he says apologetically. 'It is only their way of welcoming you.'

'But why does she hate me so much?'

He gazes down at the stage, where Eleanor Gwynne is even now performing another dance, the audience's applause beating out the rhythm. 'She doesn't hate you. It's just Nelly's way of having fun. Please don't mind it, Louise. Nell does love her fun.'

Carlo

For a grand occasion, nothing beats an ice.

The Book of Ices

'It is an attack on all of us,' Arlington said. 'Nell is Buckingham's creature. He has not forgotten how he was made a fool of over the treaty. He has been waiting his chance.'

'It is particularly an attack on France,' Colbert said. The little French ambassador had joined our meeting on this occasion. 'We cannot afford to ignore it.'

'We should do nothing.' That was Walsingham. 'Nell's satire may have made the king laugh, but its only effect is to have driven him further into Madam Carwell's arms. He has not visited Nell since his sister's death. Nor any of his other habitués, come to that. The Duchess of Cleveland has been reduced to satisfying her carnal appetites with a tightrope dancer.'

No one asked how he knew. Walsingham's information was always assumed to be impeccable.

'*You* can ignore it,' Colbert conceded. 'But *I* cannot. The reputation of France is at stake.'

'What will you do?' Arlington said ironically. 'Strike back with a play about the Siege of Orléans?'

'A ball,' the ambassador said firmly. 'I will give a ball. After all, it is only fitting that we celebrate His Majesty's return to good health. And it will be an opportunity to show your countrymen how these things are done. No effort will be spared, none.' He looked directly at me. 'We will have ices, signor. Ices, for eight hundred guests. We must remind everyone where the king's pleasures come from.'

It was not a request.

But in truth, even if the ambassador had given me a choice, I would have leapt at the opportunity his ball presented. I was going mad here in England, cooped up in this little court, this little country, making ices for such a small circle.

It was not only the ambassador who wanted to show them how these things were done in Versailles.

Gradually, the plans fell into place. We would take over St James's Park, and fashion it into a replica of the pleasure gardens at Versailles. There would be a great palace of canvas and papier mâché, erected for one night only, just as they were for Louis XIV's *divertissements*. An orchestra of French musicians, brought in for the occasion. The noble guests themselves would all be masked, as if for a carnival.

Even the ices would be especially remarkable. Colbert would be serving the *pétillant blanc* wine of Champagne which was such a symbol of Anglo-French co-operation: the wine French, the extra-strong bottles which made it possible invented by a member of the same Royal Society to which the Honourable Robert Boyle belonged.

And I – I would serve champagne sorbets.

The inclusion of alcohol, I knew well, made ices harder to prepare. Wine was particularly tricky; sparkling wine even more so. But I was becoming confident enough in my own abilities that I wanted to try.

That was not to be the only ice on the menu, of course. After much thought, I settled on a pomegranate sorbet with a champagne sauce; an apple and chrysanthemum jelly, and a fennel-milk *granite*. The ambassador's kitchens were to provide the main course, a collation of French meats, but the desserts would be mine: a selection of sherbets, along with – at last! – the first public appearance of my pear-and-*crème-anglaise* cream ice, that noble alliance, served in a double coronet of brandy snap to represent the happy union of kings.

Louise

The French ambassador wants to know if the king will attend his ball.

'I have no idea,' I say. 'He is still in mourning for his sister.'

'Of course,' the ambassador murmurs. 'How regrettable that lady's death was – and yet I find I cannot regret it, because it brought you here. How fortuitous for France that the king has found solace in the companionship of one of our countrywomen.'

All his speech is like this – airy and overblown and assumptive. He makes some insinuation, and waits for me to contradict it; if I do not, he thinks that I have confirmed what he has in mind, when the truth is that it is simply none of his business.

'I have ordered ices,' he says after a moment. 'Ices, in the hope that the king honours us with his company.'

'Indeed,' I say. 'Let us hope that he does.'

Sure enough, two days before the ball three packages arrive, brought by liveried footmen. With them is a note.

Enough mourning – CR

Carolus Rex. Charles the king. A royal command.

Inside the first package I find a mask sewn with tiny red diamonds. The next contains a costume – a highwayman's breeches, a short jacket like a conquistador's, a three-cornered hat, all glittering with silver thread and made of shimmering silks. In the final package there are boots, a belt, a silver pistol.

I tie my unruly hair back into a man's ponytail and paint my lips the same deep red as the mask.

Carlo

For a champagne sorbet: mix four cups of champagne, one cup of water and one cup of sugar in a pan, and boil with the zest of a lemon until all the sugar is dissolved. Cool, and add the lemon's juice. While it freezes, fluff the sorbet with a fork.

Chrysanthemum and apple jelly: simmer five or six green apples and a dozen chrysanthemum flowers in a pan, then sieve. Once it has cooled, add a cup of sugar syrup and a small amount of gum. Pour into goblets and chill, but do not freeze.

The Book of Ices

Still mindful of the need for secrecy, I employed only the staff of the Red Lion as my assistants. There was much to be done, and I threw myself into it, happy for once to think of something other than politics. For two weeks we laboured, storing the completed sorbets on ice to keep them fresh.

I left my arrival at the ball itself as late as I dared – I knew that by the end of the evening the heat would be immense, and I wanted my ices to stay cool for as long as possible. So I was not surprised to find the crowds three deep around the park. What did surprise me, though, was the discovery that, far from being there to enjoy the spectacle, they were hostile.

'Why do they shout like that?' I asked.

Hannah, riding at the back of the cart with the ice chests, said quietly, 'They think France means to lure us into fighting the Dutch, and then, when we are weakened, turn on us herself.'

'No war – no pope' was the crowd's chant, as well as 'Send them home' and 'Catholics out'. As we tried to get into the park the cart itself was jostled, and it was all I could do to keep the ice chests safe. 'Can the soldiers not keep order?' I cried in exasperation.

A man thrust a pamphlet up at me. 'See the pictures, read the rhymes! The scandalous seductions of Madam Carwell, with etchings. See what old Rowley's getting now—' I pushed him away with my foot, and he went down into the muck.

Inside the tent, by contrast, all was decorum and elegance. Bewigged footmen stood at every turn, ready to serve my champagne sorbets from silver platters; there was French music and French conversation and the slow, stately dances of Versailles. I saw how the light from the four vast candelabra glittered on the cut-glass goblets, making the sorbets within flash like diamonds. Even the champagne bottles were being cooled in urns made from sparkling blocks of ice.

I was busy – the first guests were already starting to arrive as I went round dispensing ice chests, one to each pair of footmen. 'Keep the ices as fresh as you can,' I instructed. 'When your platter is empty, refill it from the chest, but keep the lid closed, or you will soon have only cold soup.' They looked at me, uncomprehending: they had never heard of ices before, and more than once I had to patiently explain why the drinks they were serving were meant to be this cold, and that it was not a good idea to warm them up. The orchestra tuned, and then struck up: the trumpeters announced the first arrivals; the ambassador himself took a tray of ices and positioned himself by the entrance, to greet people and press on each one this novelty of France.

Still I did not stop – I was hurrying around, trying to get the footmen to understand that once a sorbet was melted it was ruined. Some were running out of sorbets faster than others, and the ice chests needed to be redistributed to make sure that all had enough—

And then I saw her. I saw her, and the world stood still.

Louise

The other women have come as shepherdesses, nymphs, figures from Roman and French mythology. Even the dances are French – menuets and glides and pasacalles. Everyone of any consequence in London is here, and every French noble and courtier in England. An attack on France is an attack on all of them, and now everyone waits to see if the king will show his support for France by attending the French ambassador's reception.

If he does not, it will be a sign that the alliance is broken, for certain.

And then – at last! – a tall, masked figure appears at the top of the stairs, accompanied by a small group of favoured courtiers. The noise of the throng checks, like a beast looking around, then surges, louder than before.

The king. The king is here.

And . . .

He is dressed, no longer in black for his dead sister, but in the three-cornered plumed hat, silver-threaded coat and rolled-top boots of a French musketeer.

The king inclines to France.

As he comes towards me, the people bow in a great undulating ripple, any pretence that he is incognito in his mask instantly abandoned – the force of his passage spreading obeisance through the crowd like a scythe passing through corn.

They bow to his back, and he ignores them, pressing forward.

He stops before me.

Instead of curtseying, I lift my pistol, aiming at his chest. At his heart. There is a collective gasp before the room goes quiet.

'A forfeit, if you please,' I say calmly.

The masked face looks down at me. 'There are three things I

could give you, pretty highwayman. Can you guess what they are?'

His courtiers laugh, their minds running to the bedroom. I shake my head.

'I can give you a dance, I can give you a kiss, or I can give you my heart. Which is it to be?'

I put up the gun. 'A dance, then.'

'Very well.' And he escorts me onto the floor, the musicians immediately resetting the measure so that the whole company is forced to begin again.

As we reach the end of the dance he places his hands against my own, palm to palm, interlacing our fingers. His eyes, dark behind the mask, bore into me.

Then he opens his arms a little, our fingers still entwined, so that I am pulled towards him. Once again I sense the room around us go still.

Is this part of our game? Or something more?

The gentlest of kisses, on the very corner of my mouth. The smell of his cologne, musky and French. Bristles from his moustache. And then his lips press harder, enveloping mine.

I stiffen involuntarily, and he steps back.

A buzz of conversation from those around us.

He puts his lips to my ear. 'For a kiss such as that, I would fight a thousand wars.'

Carlo

To make a pomegranate sorbet: squeeze enough pomegranates to give two cups of juice. Add half a cup of sugar to make it sweet, then stir all together and freeze. To serve, pour champagne over the sorbet, garnishing with pomegranate seeds and pieces of candied orange.

The Book of Ices

The highwayman's costume suited her, emphasising the narrowness of her waist, her slight hips, the length of her back, her elegant neck. But it was the way she stood that marked her apart from the English ladies around her. From her posture alone you would have known her a well-bred daughter of France.

The king danced with her. I could not tear my eyes away. Neither could anyone else: but for me it was different.

From the way the others looked at her, she could have been a chicken and they a pack of hounds, ready to tear her apart. It was her against them all, and yet she never wavered.

I looked at her, and I knew that I loved her.

How could I ever have denied it? It had been so ever since I met her under the medlar trees in Versailles.

Perhaps we will meet again.

If we both keep looking for places to be alone, signor, you may be sure of it . . .

The dance ended. Time resumed its inexorable march. But still I watched her, as the king let her go. She walked back to the side of the room. She had no one to go to, no one to be with.

I have heard love compared with a fire. But that is all wrong. If

208

you touch a flame you draw back. The pain is quick and sudden, and then it is gone.

Love is like ice. It creeps up on you, entering your body by stealth, crumbling your defences, finding the innermost recesses of your flesh. It is not like heat or pain or burning so much as an inner numbness, as if your heart itself were hardening, turning you to stone. Love grips you, squeezing you with a force that can crack rocks or split the hulls of boats. Love can lift paving slabs, crumble marble, wither foliage from trees.

I loved her, and I would never have her.

Then something made me turn my gaze, and I saw a tall, dark figure watching her too, over the heads of his courtiers. They were laughing and joking, but he was paying them no attention. He was staring at Louise, as motionless as a statue. As motionless as I was myself.

The king.

I saw that he loved her, just as I did.

Carlo and King Charles. Two peas in a pod. Reflections in a mirror. Rivals, and yet not rivals.

For he was a king, and I was not. He could have her, and I could not. The ice would eventually leave his heart, and would always be left in mine.

Louise

The masks fool no one. Yet I do not recognise the woman in a chequered vizard who stands beside me later at the supper board.

'So you are my replacement,' she says.

'I'm sorry?' I turn to look at her. Tall, well-figured, older than me. But there is something about the way she carries herself – confident, strong, commanding – that puts me on my guard.

'Oh, don't worry,' she says. 'I've had a good run. Besides, as you've doubtless discovered by now, some of his . . . *peccadilloes* can be rather wearying.'

'Who are you?'

'Don't you know?' She sounds amused. 'Well, I suppose there *are* plenty of us to choose from. But I'm the only one so far who's gained a title from it. Mind you, I had to let him watch me with three of his guardsmen before he made me a duchess.'

My shock must be evident, despite my mask. 'Oh, has he not sprung that one on you quite yet?' she murmurs. 'Give it time, my dear, give it time. But don't be fooled by his perfect manners. For all his charm, he is a libertine just like the rest of them.'

A footman steps forward with a platter laden with langoustines. Spearing one on a knife, he thrusts it into my face. I look round. The other woman has vanished. 'Where is the closet?' I ask the footman. 'Quickly – I think I am going to be sick.'

PART THREE

'The affection of the King of England for Mlle. de
Keroualle increases every day, and the little attack of
nausea which she had yesterday makes me hopeful that
her good fortune will continue, at least all the remainder of my embassy . . .'

Colbert de Croissy, French ambassador to England, to
Louvois, French Minister for War

'The king was surprised at what you wrote me concerning Mlle. de Keroualle, whose conduct while she
was here, and since she has been in England, did not
inspire much expectation that she would succeed in
achieving such good fortune so quickly. His Majesty is
anxious to be informed of the connection which you
believe exists between the king and her . . .'

Louvois to Colbert

Louise

'His Most Christian Majesty wants to know *what*?'

'If there is any, ah, happy news. Whether the King of England is to be blessed, perhaps, with a child.'

'You will have to ask the queen that yourself. I have heard nothing about it, nor am I likely to.'

'As it happens, mademoiselle, I did not mean the queen.'

'Who, then? What are you talking about, Your Excellency?'

The ambassador has the good grace to look embarrassed. 'I had formed the opinion that your excellent relations with the king, perhaps, might be . . .?'

I stare at him. 'Entirely proper. And will remain so.'

'I see.' The ambassador seems to have gone a little pale. 'So there is nothing that I should be reporting to Versailles? The king himself has asked for a . . . clarification.'

'You may tell his Most Christian Majesty that I am entirely aware of the fact that France's honour depends on the honour of every one of her citizens. And that I will never, ever, do anything to bring the reputation of our country into disrepute.'

'Yes. Yes, of course.'

'I am Louise Renee de Penacöet, Dame de Keroualle, the eldest daughter of the oldest family in Brittany. Not some common flower girl.'

He bows icily. 'We are indeed fortunate to have amongst us one of such distinguished lineage. And such irreproachable manners, of course.'

*

213

Bennet, Lord Arlington, to Ralph Montagu, English envoy:

Colbert is a fool: he has promised the King of France that the game is almost over, and now has the unfortunate task of telling him that it has barely begun. However, Louvois appears to have sources of his own, and knows far more of what is really going on in Whitehall than his ambassador – certainly he knows what the girl in question has done or not done, and to judge from the letters we have had sight of, he was able to tell Colbert in no uncertain terms to get his facts right next time before sending gossip through the diplomatic post. But all this has had the consequence that the ambassador is now embarrassed, and wishes for us to speed matters along. Naturally, I have made it clear to him that he can rely on us to help, but that it is also time for his master to play his part. This makes him even more anxious, for of course he may not tell his king what to do, but he would not be an ambassador if he were incapable of finding some way of framing my suggestion so that it appears to be Louis's own idea . . .

Colbert to His Most Christian Majesty, Louis XIV:

Sir: It is certain that the king of England shows a warm affection for Mlle. de Keroualle, and perhaps you may have heard from other sources what a richly furnished set of lodgings has been given her at Whitehall. His Majesty repairs to her apartment at nine o'clock every morning, and never stays there less than an hour, and sometimes two. He returns after dinner, shares at her card table in all her stakes, and never allows her to want for anything. All the ministers court eagerly the friendship of this lady, and milord Arlington said to me very recently that he was very pleased to see that the king was becoming attached to her;

and that, although His Majesty was not the man to communicate affairs of state to ladies, nevertheless, as it was in their power to render ill services to those whom they disliked, it was much better for the king's good servants that His Majesty should have an inclination for this lady, who is not of a mischievous disposition, and is a gentlewoman, rather than for actresses and suchlike unworthy creatures, of whom no man of quality could take the measure; and that it was necessary to counsel this young lady to cultivate the king, so that he might find with her nothing but pleasure, peace and quiet. He added that, if Lady Arlington took his advice, she would urge this young lady to yield unreservedly to the king's wishes, and tell her that there was no alternative for her but a convent in France, and that I ought to be the first to impress this upon her. I told him jocularly that I was not so wanting in gratitude to the king, or so foolish, as to tell her to prefer religion to his good graces; that I was also persuaded that she was not waiting for my advice, but that I would, none the less, give it her, to show how much both he and I appreciated her influence, and to inform her of the obligation which she was under to milord . . .

Carlo

The serving of an ice is the highlight of any gathering.

The Book of Ices

The ball was a success. Such a success: King Charles was once again the merry monarch, the prince of pleasure. Every night there were parties, masques, high-stakes card games, escapades and frivolity and wit. And it was France who had effected this. Once again, France was the epitome of all that was fashionable. French plays were shown at the Royal theatres; French dishes were served at every high-born table; French ices – which is to say, *my* ices – graced every dinner dance and ball. The nobility began feverishly building pineries, potagers and ice houses on their estates, and the great houses of England had their *façades* remodelled in the style of French *chateaux*. Ceilings were painted as at Versailles, and every woman of quality clamoured for a *salle des miroirs* in which to sip her porcelain cups of *thé*.

Only the common people were sullen and uneasy, wondering where it would end. Every last mechanic or servant could tell you what was happening in Europe: they clubbed together to buy the penny newspapers that were sold in taverns and coffee houses, and then sat together to discuss the news, grim-faced. Louis wanted war, that much was clear. But would it be Spain or the Netherlands he swallowed up first? And if victory was inevitable, was it better to be his ally or his enemy? He had made alliances before, and then turned on his allies when it suited him.

Parliament ratified the Treaty of Paris, but the Treaty of Dover remained a secret known only to a handful.

Busy now, I bought a sedan chair to hurry me through the

216

crowds. I saw Hannah's disapproving glances, and thought it was only at the extravagance. But then I saw her berate one of the bullies I had hired to carry it as a useless lump who was always in her way, and asked her what the problem was.

'The problem is treating Englishmen as slaves and beasts of burden,' she told me furiously. 'Chairs like that weren't seen in England before the king came back.'

'Then it's progress, surely?'

'It's men setting themselves up as better than other men.'

'If my fortunes have risen,' I pointed out, 'Then yours have risen with them. Elias's too.' It was true: I was paying her an extra shilling a week, and Elias now had a smart uniform with which to accompany me to court.

She only muttered darkly, and turned back to whatever she was doing.

As for Louise, her star had risen even more than mine. Where the king was, she was, helping him to take his ease at the soirées and the parties, her clear French laugh cutting through the buzz of gossip and the musicians' drums, her smile drawing every eye.

You would have thought, to look at her, that she was triumphant; that having coaxed the king from his mourning, she had done enough. But it was not so, and they only pressed her more than ever.

Louise

I have a letter. A letter from Louis XIV himself.

I read it sitting at my harpsichord, the ambassador standing at my side. A pained smile plays across his lips, as if he is a music master and I am a particularly recalcitrant pupil.

'Do you know what it says?' I ask when I have reached the end. I put it on the music stand, so that he will not see how my hand shakes the page.

'I do not presume to guess the thoughts of my king.' I note the way he does not actually answer my question. 'Perhaps he has some paternal advice for you . . .?'

'"The King of France commends you to please the King of England." Now what do you suppose he means by that?'

Colbert does not reply.

'Although naturally, as a loyal subject, he would be delighted to welcome me back to France whenever I wish to return. And, as a token of the esteem in which Madame held me, he has spoken to the Abbess of the Convent at Marseille, who has graciously offered me a place as a novitiate; if, that is, I decide that I would really rather turn my back on diplomacy and pursue a life of virtue and reflection instead. Well, he has not actually spoken to her, the order in question being a silent one, but they have corresponded. Apparently the nuns there are doing admirable work among the lepers. That is why they can be sure of a vacancy, the sisters being rewarded for their virtue by being reunited with God rather more rapidly than most.'

'His Majesty is generous with his counsel, as always,' he murmurs.

'Oh, yes – and there are some lands at Brest, formerly belonging to my family, which have reverted to him. He is wondering how to dispose of them. So. What would you have me do, Your Excellency?'

Colbert's smile is inscrutable. 'Mademoiselle?'

'His Majesty ends by suggesting that I seek your advice – yours and the Arlingtons'. Well, I know what theirs will be. Lady Arlington thinks I should yield unreservedly to the king. Those were her very words to me this morning. "Yield unreservedly". What do you say to that?'

He looks pained. 'They have a way of speaking here which is sometimes abhorrently frank. Coarse, even.'

'And yet there is this to be said for it: it is also commendably clear. It is only now, for example, that I realise the full extent of my own king's designs.' I speak calmly, but it is all I can do not to let my anger show.

He contrives to look both ignorant and enquiring, all with a lift of his eyebrow.

'Oh, I think we both know what I mean,' I say. 'Or would you have me be even coarser than Lady Arlington?'

'Ah. Yes, I see. Well, you must do what you think best.'

'So I must.' I fold the letter and hand it back to him. 'It is clear to me that His Most Christian Majesty has not been made aware that there is another possibility.'

'Which is?'

'I am referring to Lord Arlington's suggestion that I become England's queen, when Catherine of Braganza passes away.'

The ambassador goes pale. His eyes dart to the door, as if to check that no one is listening. '*Lord Arlington* has proposed this?'

'Yes. Were you not aware of this plan? The thinking is simple. A Frenchwoman – a Catholic – on the throne of England would mean—'

'Do not speak of such a thing!' he hisses. 'Do not even think it!'

'I had assumed you knew—'

'There is no plan!' he squeaks. 'Nor do I believe that Lord Arlington, of all people, would ever have suggested there was.'

'He said—' I stop. What has Arlington actually said? I think back. With a sinking feeling I realise that, in fact, he has said nothing. It has all been implied, inferred. Pictures painted in the air. 'He said that the queen's health is very grave.'

Colbert nods. 'That much is certain. Naturally, France hopes that Her Highness will make a full recovery.'

'And he said it might be Louis, rather than the English Parliament, who decides on her successor.'

The ambassador looks at me as if I am babbling nonsense. '*If* there were a successor, and *if* His Most Christian Majesty were to be consulted, naturally he would give his cousin the benefit of his advice. But any queen suggested would be of royal blood.'

'I am a de Keroualle, and thus descended indirectly from the ancient kings of Brittany on my mother's side—'

'You are a lady-in-waiting! And an impoverished one, at that.'

'My breeding—'

'Breeding! What is all this about breeding? Breeding is for spaniels and parakeets, not queens and princesses of the blood.' He passes a hand over his face. 'Queens have *dowries*. Catherine of Braganza brought the English king Tangier and Bombay. Without her, he would have had nothing. He could not have been a king.'

I stare at him, stunned into silence. All this time, while I have been tempting Charles, they were tempting me; luring me on with the illusion of a future they had no intention of seeing happen. 'But if Charles *were* to marry me—'

'Of course King Charles will not marry you. He cannot. Parliament would not allow it. His advisors would not allow it. His Most Christian Majesty would not allow it.'

I am almost crying now: I can feel the tears pricking at my eyes. 'If he wants to marry for love—'

'Marriage is not what kings do when they love,' he says quietly.

So we are back to that. 'Then what would you have me do?' I ask numbly.

He bows. 'It is as we said. You are fortunate enough to be the subject of a king's regard, and thus in a position to do France a great service. But if you feel that this . . . honour is not one with which you are comfortable, then you have an alternative. He nods at the letter. 'The nunnery. So now you are doubly fortunate. Few women in your position are given the luxury of a choice.'

Carlo

An ice that is too sweet, or too rich, will never freeze.

The Book of Ices

'Not deceived,' she said. 'Misled. Oh, they have been so clever. Clever, clever, *clever*.'

'But . . .' I stared at the letter, my head reeling. 'I don't understand. Does this mean that you have not become the king's mistress after all?'

'Of course not,' she said sharply. 'Did you really think I would dishonour my family's good name so easily?'

'I was not sure what to think.' But my spirits soared at her words. 'So you were tricked? You never agreed to anything?'

She nodded, shamefaced. 'They knew how to play me so that I would go along with their plans.'

'That was me. I'm so sorry, Louise: I told them you were virtuous, that your parents had sent you to Versailles to make a good marriage. That must have been when they decided marriage would be their bait—'

'It was hardly your fault. After all, five minutes' conversation with me would have revealed exactly the same thing. And I would not have been the first girl so dazzled by the prospect of a crown that I forgot the inconvenient necessity of needing a wedding in order to get it.' She sighed. 'They almost succeeded, too. Had Charles been just a little more determined, or I a little less . . .'

'But now it is not only Charles's determination you must contend with.'

'Yes. That is what appals me most – the fact that Louis is part of all this. Since I arrived at Versailles he has been like a father to me.

222

'And fathers do not sell their daughters to the highest bidder?' I said dryly. 'Besides, no one knows better than Louis that a king can sometimes prevail where others cannot.'

'True. But you must not feel bad, Carlo. It is me who should be apologising to you. When I told you in France that you were too low-born to marry me – now the boot is on the other foot, I realise how insulting that was. I behaved abominably.'

'It hardly matters now.' I held up the letter. 'Not compared with this. What are you going to do? Will it be the king's bed, or a nunnery?'

'Neither.'

'Neither!'

She lifted her chin. 'I am still Louise Renee de Penacöet, Dame de Keroualle, the eldest daughter of the oldest family of Brittany. I am no man's concubine, king or otherwise. And certainly not because some jumped-up errand-boy of an ambassador tells me I should be.'

'Then you must stand aside, surely?'

'There may be another way.' She began to pace up and down the inlaid floor. 'I think Louis does not really care whether I am King Charles's mistress or not – that is simply a means to an end. And the end is influence – that is to say, holding Charles to the terms of the treaty.'

'War against the Dutch.'

'Exactly. If I can achieve that without giving myself to the king, even Louis will have to admit that being his mistress isn't necessary.'

'But how will you do that?'

'I have Charles's ear. And I have his confidence. He has talked to me already of the treaty, and his doubts about it. It seems to me that I can put the case for war just as easily without . . . without all this nonsense about yielding and mistresses.' She looked at me. 'Will you help?'

'I am not sure how I can.'

'I'm not sure either, at the moment. But I do know that it will be the two of us against all of them. And that I cannot do it alone.'

'Then I will do whatever I can.'

Of course I would: I would do anything, rather than see her in the king's bed. But in my heart I was uneasy.

For who knew better than me that men want most the one thing they are told they cannot have?

Louise

I inform the ambassador of my decision. He looks pained, but does not actually order me onto the next boat back to France. For the moment, at least, it seems I am their best hope.

'And how do you mean to achieve this?' he wants to know. 'Through reason and learned debate?'

'Partly. And partly by invoking his late sister's wishes.'

'It is not merely a matter of persuading King Charles of the need for war. He will have to defy his own Parliament. That will involve considerable risk to his own position.'

'Parliaments can be dissolved.'

'*Mon Dieu* – have a care,' he says faintly. 'That was how his father lost his head.'

'Bribed, then. From what I have seen of England so far, they all have their price.'

'All this bribery, just to spare your honour, mademoiselle?' he says laconically.

'All this bribery to achieve our objective. After all, I do not think my honour alone would have persuaded Parliament of the need for war, do you?'

When he has gone I go to the window, calming myself.

This is something new: to meet with an ambassador, and bend his will to mine. And, what is more, to reframe a suggestion – almost a command – from my own king. I have not defied Louis, exactly – that would be a most foolhardy thing to do – but I am making it clear that I, a mere woman, am going to go about this in my own way.

At best, I will be allowed to try. If I fail, the consequences might be even more unwelcome than being shut up in a convent.

Something else I consider: Madame would not have spoken to an ambassador like this. Madame's way was always to trust people, to believe in their goodness, fixing them with the radiance of her gaze until the person she was speaking to became caught up by the force of her conviction.

But that, I am starting to realise, is not my way.

I go back to the harpsichord. The seat doubles as a chest, for storing sheet music. I lift up the cushioned lid and feel at the bottom of the pile, then draw something out.

Aretino's Postures: being a true Account of the lewd Methods and divers Positions employed by a so-called Lady, lately come from France.

Pornography, slipped under my door. They have not even attempted to make it look like me, but that is the suggestion.

Why, I wonder, flicking through the pages, is there so much fuss about which way one lies to be coupled? What can it possibly matter if one is on the right or the left, or standing up, or sitting? And what could convince any woman that squatting over a man as if over a pot is a decorous way to behave? I shudder. As for the later pictures, the ones with more than one woman, or more than one man . . .

Yet, somehow, I have not been able to throw it in the fire. There is something about the etchings, for all their crudeness, a kind of vulgar relish, that both repels and fascinates.

And there is instruction here, of a kind.

I hear Lady Arlington's voice in my head. *The king is an accomplished lover.* Perhaps coupling is quite like tennis after all; a game which must be learned like any other, initially baffling, but simple enough when you master the rules.

And I have never yet come across a game I cannot win at.

I think: do I really want to marry – to become some nobleman's brood mare, obliged to do *this* for him whenever he wants – when I could be the confidante of a king instead?

And at the thought of how the stakes in this game are rising –

how the abyss on each side is deepening – I am surprised, and not a little curious, to find that what I feel is not so much fear, or disgust, but excitement: the thrill of someone who walks onto a tennis court, and feels a racquet in her hand.

Louise

Charles listens to me play, lolling in a chair beside me, his long legs almost touching mine. In his lap a spaniel scratches lethargically with its hind leg at one tangled ear.

'Have you given any thought to the Dutch?' I ask, as if it is no more important a subject than any other we discuss.

He glances at me. 'Why? Does your king become impatient?'

I play another phrase. '*My* king? I have two kings now.' I smile at him. 'But if you mean Louis, I believe he is always mindful of the need for haste.'

Charles grunts. 'I have heard that he is sometimes over hasty.'

'As a statesman?'

'In all respects.' He leans forward. 'I prefer to take my time.'

'As a statesman?'

'In all respects.'

In response, I drop the speed of my playing, comically, from *andante* to *adagio*.

'I have been in wars, you know,' he says. 'They are rarely as glorious as people think. As a young man – a boy – I fought Cromwell, my army against his, pikes against swords, Englishman against Englishman . . . It left me with a lifelong aversion to the shedding of human blood.' He smiles ruefully. 'Don't tell my ministers. But I have always preferred negotiation to conquest.'

There is an edge to his last comment: we are not simply talking now about wars.

'I like to watch you play,' he says idly. 'Did you know that you lift your chin at the start of every measure?'

'Louis believes that delay will only make the war more arduous. To strike quickly and decisively will save more lives than it costs.'

'I am familiar with the argument,' he agrees. 'But it does not explain why we must strike in the first place.'

'To have peace in Europe—'

'We must first have war? But there will not be peace in Europe if there is civil war here in England.'

I smile, and play a little more. We both know that it is not for me to comment on the policy of France.

'Will you dine alone with me this evening, mademoiselle?' he says abruptly.

I keep my eyes fixed on my music. 'Your Majesty knows I cannot.'

'Why not?'

'People will talk.'

He makes an impatient gesture. 'Let them.'

'I thought Your Majesty had just suggested that he is not, by nature, one to rush things?' I suggest, with what I hope is an attractive mischievousness.

'And yet you would have me jumped into this war.' Suddenly, he is petulant. 'You must not be hurried, it seems, but I must. You must keep your honour, but I must discard mine.'

I play without speaking for a minute. These flashes of irritation come on him sometimes. They usually pass just as quickly.

Not this time.

'God's nails, woman, how is this fair?' he thunders. Across the room, Anne and Lucy look up from their sewing, startled. The spaniel, given no warning, scrambles hastily to the floor as Charles gets to his feet. 'You would have me fight the Dutch, but with you . . . with you . . .'

I keep playing, anxious not to make this more of a scene than it already is.

'With you I must play the lapdog,' he says, aiming a kick at the dog. 'I will dine elsewhere. As for your war – tell Louis I will attend to it.'

*

But he does not attend to it.

'He is a man used to wielding power,' Lady Arlington says. 'His desire for you is such that you have the power now, not him. No man likes to be in that position.'

'What must I do?'

'Yield, of course. Nothing restores a man's temper better than undressing a new mistress.'

But I will not yield. Neither will the king.

'You have lost him,' Lady Arlington says. 'I hear that he has been seen going into Nell Gwynne's house in Pall Mall. You might as well go back to France.'

I must be careful how I handle this. I see it in their faces – Arlington, the ambassador: they all think that to make him declare war, there will have to be a trade.

My body, for an army. It is a deal which almost everyone involved would consider a bargain.

Carlo

An ice, properly stored, will keep for a month without
spoiling.

The Book of Ices

The effort it was costing her, I was all too aware of. At the balls
and ballets and suppers she smiled and joked and you would not
have thought anything wrong – not unless you saw her, after the
carriages had all departed, and the laughter left her eyes as
abruptly as a candle being snuffed.

'What must I do to regain his favour?' she asked me wearily one
evening, when I was clearing the ice goblets away from her apartments.

'Nothing at all.'

'You think it impossible?'

'On the contrary – I simply meant that to do nothing is the
best course. I think Charles is divided within himself. There is a
part of him that would like to stop wanting you. But there is
another part that knows he cannot. So he is angry, not with you
for being virtuous, but with himself, for caring so much.' I
avoided her eye as I spoke. 'Sooner or later that battle will be over,
and then he will know what he feels.'

Her voice when she spoke was quiet. 'And what is that, Carlo?
What will he feel? Will the king love me, or hate me?'

I shook my head. 'He will not hate you.'

'I wish to God it could be neither,' she muttered. 'Oh, for a
world without all this love.'

Louise

It is almost two weeks before he comes back to my rooms.

'Your Majesty,' I say, curtseying.

'Oh, there you are,' he says – as if I have been away; as if it is me, not him, who has been avoiding this moment. He holds out his fist. 'Here. I have something for you.'

'I do not need gifts, sir.'

'Not "sir". "Charles". Unless we are in company, which I am glad to say we are not.'

'Charles.' The word slips from my mouth a little awkwardly, a 'sh' where there should be 'ch'.

He smiles. 'My sister could never pronounce it either.'

I try again. 'I do not need gifts . . . Charles.'

'Better. But it is even prettier when you misspeak.' He lifts his hand. 'Now then.'

He leaves his fist closed, so that I must turn it over and open his fingers for him, unpeeling them one by one from his gift. A pocket watch, the smallest I have ever seen, an oyster of polished gold.

'Open it.'

I open the lid that covers the face. It is like no pocket watch I have ever seen. There are three hands, one of which is racing round the dial.

'It tells the seconds,' he says proudly. 'A coil inside the mechanism that is wound tighter than any pendulum. And look at the reverse.'

I turn it over. An inscription, *Waste not these hours with regret.* A date.

It is the day I came to England.

'My calendar started then,' he says simply.

*

232

He wants to show me his apartments. We pass the royal bed-chamber, where he never sleeps, and go through a door almost hidden behind a curtain. Inside there is a working room, no bigger than Madame's, filled with clocks. The noise they make is like rain, a deafening downpour of time; seconds and minutes tumbling around our shoulders.

He brings out his favourites – the watch that tells the phases of the moon, the carriage clock that contains a carousel of tiny silver horses chasing a fox. They were made by one of his *virtuosi*, his gang of philosophers and men of learning. He has many gangs, I am coming to realise. He likes to slip between them, changing roles as he does so: here the rake, here the philosopher, here the statesman, but always eager for entertainment, for dialogue, for enthusiasm. Almost like a boy.

Certainly it is hard to believe that, of his brother James and he, Charles is the older. Or that he is more than twice as old as me. But a king is young at forty-two, a woman old at twenty.

He is called away on business, but bids me wait. As the hour comes, a dozen chimes ring out, the moment jumping from time-piece to timepiece.

Curious, a little bored, I inspect my surroundings. There is a door that leads to a padded privy stool. Another room contains his chemicals and machines. And then there is a light, square room in a tower, lined with wooden panels that reach from floor to ceiling.

One of the panels is ajar. I look more closely: it is hinged, like a cupboard.

I swing it back. Hung on the inside, so that he may choose whether or not it is displayed, is a painting. A woman, completely naked, reclines on a bed of cushions and velvets. Her pale skin seems to glow like moonlight against the dark, rich cloth. Around her are stage props, some painted theatre scenery. Red hair, a mischievous smile.

The actress.

Does he have all his women painted like this, I wonder? I swing open another panel. Another naked body, the face haughty. I recognise the woman who spoke to me at the French ambassador's ball. And another – a woman with her gown rolled down beneath her breasts, smiling saucily. I turn back another, then another . . . the panels sway and crash gently against each other, like the pages of some giant wooden book.

I hear voices from the other room. Quickly I swing them back again, one by one, ending with Miss Nelly. Hidden again behind the wainscot, the brown respectable wood, for the king's pleasure alone.

Louise

He dances with me, and I feel the urgency of his desire. He kisses me during the dance, along with the rest, and his lips linger a little longer than they should.

When he has to release my hand so that I can turn to another partner, I sense his reluctance, my fingers slipping through his, until, with a sigh, he turns away.

And yet he keeps his pledge. Never does he try to make me feel I have no choice.

That, did he but know it, is being done by others. Colbert reminds me almost daily that I overstretch the patience of not one but two kings. Lady Arlington tells me that I must act before Charles's eye alights on someone else. Lord Rochester looks at me with cynical drunken eyes and declares that I am playing a shrewd game.

'I did not know that French bitches made such clever hunting dogs,' he says.

And Charles treats me with such courtesy that it is only when I am with him I do not feel besieged.

But this unrest over his son has given him something new to worry about. Just as it has given me, perhaps, a new way into his favour.

It is Lord Monmouth – his eldest son, illegitimate of course: the product of a union with a woman called Lucy Walters during the first years of his exile. Now the boy is twenty years old, and a hothead.

In Parliament recently, there was a debate on raising money – there are always debates on raising money, to clear the king's debts. Someone had proposed that taxes could be levied on the theatres. A member of the court party pointed out that the theatres gave much pleasure to His Majesty, and should thus be exempt. To which a member of the parliamentary faction, one John Coventry, wondered aloud whether it was the theatres which gave His Majesty much pleasure, or those who acted in them – a clear reference to the king's fondness for actresses.

The silence which followed this observation persuaded him that it was time to sit down, but the damage was done: by nightfall his sally was being reported in every tavern and coffee house in London.

It was also being talked about at Whitehall, where one of those outraged by John Coventry's impertinence was Jemmy Monmouth. Declaring his father insulted, he gathered together three of his cronies, intercepted Coventry on his way home, and slit his nose open with a sword.

In response, Parliament passed an act making it a criminal offence for any person to lay hands on, or assault, a member of that body. They could not charge Monmouth, of course, as the attack had taken place before the law was made; but they were saying that in future, they would have the right to.

This, in turn, caused further outrage – the notion that laws made in Parliament could be applied to those of royal blood. Instead of keeping a low profile, Lord Monmouth and his friends decided to make a public display of their defiance. After an evening's drinking, they went out looking for amusement, which they found in the form of a ten-year-old girl and her grandfather. The girl was pretty, and they decided to have their way with her. The grandfather protested, and they kicked him to the ground. A night beadle appeared. He too protested; both at the girl's youth, the taking of her by force, and the treatment being meted out to the grandfather. So they kicked the beadle to death.

Those who had defended Monmouth before now found themselves in a difficult position. For if he was entitled to slice open a man's nose without being subject to the law, surely things were no different now that he had committed the attempted rape of a child, and murdered an elderly public servant?

The king's ministers are divided. Those who say Monmouth must be punished fear the people will riot if he is allowed to go free. Those who say that Parliament must not be appeased say that riots can always be put down with bullets.

Charles is reluctant to use the army. No one knows better than him that riots have a way of turning into revolutions.

'It is one thing to keep my crown upon my head,' he says. 'Quite another to keep that head upon my shoulders.'

I begin to see an opportunity here.

The issue is a subtle one. Monmouth, for all that he believes himself attached to his father's faction, is the natural ally of the Parliamentarians. As a Protestant, and the king's acknowledged son, he could be the mob's choice for king if Charles were to convert to Catholicism.

So, the less popular Jemmy Monmouth is, the better for the interests of France.

And – more importantly – if I can demonstrate my own influence over Charles in a small matter such as this, I may have gained a measure of freedom.

Finally, Charles talks himself to a standstill. Between those of his advisors who say that Monmouth must be dealt with, and those who say that Parliament must be stood up to, he is caught in a dither of indecision.

Walking with him in his privy garden, I say mildly, 'It seems to me that your dilemma is that you cannot decide whether to pardon Jemmy, or punish him.'

'Yes,' he says with a sigh. 'That is it exactly.'

'Then why not do both?' I suggest. 'Pardon him first, so that he is not imprisoned by the courts, but then punish him in some other way, so that everyone can see you will not tolerate such behaviour.'

He considers this thoughtfully. 'But how would I punish him?'

'He could be banished. After all, he is scarcely an adornment to your court. And it would have the effect of making it clear to the people that the king is a higher authority than the law.' I hesitate. 'In fact, you would come out of this with your own position strengthened.'

'Louise, that is excellent advice,' he exclaims. 'Now, why couldn't my ministers have thought of that?'

I shrug. 'Sometimes it is easier to give advice when one is neutral. Tell me, is it true that de Grammont has invented an amusing new dance?'

The next day my rooms are full. Ministers I have barely met arrive to pay court to me. Lord Arlington shows me off, fussing around and calling for more chairs. The young rakes come to flirt with my ladies-in-waiting; the older ones to size me up.

I serve them ices in tiny glass goblets. I discuss theatre with Mr Dryden and theology with the Bishop of Chester.

This, I think, is what influence tastes like.

Soon it will be time to talk to Charles again of war. But not directly this time. I have learned my lesson. I need to be more subtle, my approach circuitous.

Carlo

Wardens, like quinces, must be softened before using, and are best sweetened with cooking or the addition of other fruit.

The Book of Ices

The king had asked to see me. We walked in St James's Park, spaniels darting under our feet. His Majesty was in a mood for idling today – *sauntering*, I had heard the courtiers call it, the long royal legs effortlessly covering the ground, but to nowhere in particular.

I had taken him a new ice I had been working on, a cream worked with white currants and the hard winter pears the English call 'wardens'.

'This is excellently made,' he commented as we walked.

'Thank you, sir.'

He pointed with the spoon at the far side of the park. 'My ice house is being rebuilt according to your instructions. I have told them to prioritise the work.'

I nodded. 'It must be finished before the frosts come, or this year's harvest will be ruined as well.'

He smiled at my choice of words. 'You are not familiar with our English winters, I think.'

'No, sir.'

'Ice is one of the few crops in which we rarely suffer a famine.' He handed me the empty goblet. 'My ministers are all building ice houses now, did you know that? Arlington at Newmarket, Clifford at Chudleigh. You and I have started a fashion, signor, and now they all want to outdo me.'

'Or perhaps, sir, they simply want to outdo each other, in being as much like you as possible.'

'Yes,' he said thoughtfully. 'Yes, that is exactly it. You put it well.'

I shrugged. 'It is the way of courtiers everywhere.'

He turned down a gravel walk. 'Next year will be a special anniversary for me. It will be ten years since my coronation – my second coronation, that is, the restoration of my throne. I intend it to be a celebration: a summer of pageantry and feasting. Starting with a great feast – a *divertissement*, I believe Louis would call it. For the Order of the Garter. Over a thousand guests.'

'A thousand!'

The king nodded. 'Every noble-born man and woman in my kingdom. I am going to have Windsor Castle rebuilt especially. There will be a new Great Hall, as big as anything at Versailles, where the feast will be held. And it will all be modern – that is to say, French. No griffons or songbirds or dried-out *rosbif* for us, signor. I will have ice – great beds of the stuff. Chilling my crayfish, my strawberries and asparagus; ice tubs cooling my champagne . . . Perhaps even some of those clockwork ice fountains I have been hearing about.'

'I could not—' I began, then stopped. One did not say no, directly, to a king. 'It would take a great deal of ice, sir – more than has ever been used in this country before.'

'And, signor, I want you to create a dish for the occasion,' he continued as if I had not spoken. 'Something even more splendid than the ices you created for the Sun King.'

'Would this be in honour of a particular guest, sir?'

'Indeed it would.' He paused, but I already knew what he was going to say. 'It is for Mademoiselle de Keroualle. I want you to make something for her.'

'And this will be served to everyone?'

The king shook his head. 'To the royal table alone. It will be like sturgeon, or porpoise, or swan – a dish reserved for me, and those whom I favour. For her and me, and no one else.'

I saw, then, what he was about. For every banquet, whether it is stated or not, has a theme. Every meal expresses its host's vision of himself and his place in the world. From the head of the household carving his family's Sunday fowl, to a silent circle of puritans blessing their daily bread, every meal, humble or ornate, speaks a language of ceremony to those who can decode it.

What better way for Charles to express his allegiance to the fashions, the policies and the pleasures of France, than through an extravagant display of the finest, most fashionable French foodstuff of all?

And what better way to symbolise his own status than by serving as the meal's centrepiece a dish his own guests were forbidden to eat?

He was not simply displaying his Continental tastes. He was making a political statement. By dedicating the dish to Louise, he was saying that he did not care what anyone else thought about him openly favouring France. Just as Louis XIV was the undisputed, autocratic ruler of France, so Charles's dish of ice cream would say that this was the course he intended to take in England – as its absolute, arbitrary monarch.

It was everything Parliament had made him renounce, when they restored him to his throne. And it would be my job to provide it.

I bowed again. 'I will endeavour to create something worthy of the occasion, sir.'

'I am sure you will, signor,' he said, with that charming smile. 'I want this feast to show the world what we are capable of, you and I. I know you will not let me down.'

'It's a good thing,' Lord Arlington said immediately. 'He can't afford it.'

'He will have to rein in his plans?'

Arlington shook his head. 'He considers economies beneath him. No – if he commits himself to rebuilding Windsor and holding a feast for a thousand guests, he'll have no choice but to go to war. Without Louis's pension, he'll be bankrupt within six months. Do as he bids you, Demirco. And make sure no expense is spared.'

The water in London was notoriously foul, and the Thames black with ordure. Well before the rivers were frozen, I started scouting for a source of good fresh ice.

Beyond Hampton Court I found it. A series of lakes fed by their own spring. Flat ground, easily reached by cart, and already in the king's ownership. I explained to the bemused steward what I would need.

'You want to cut the ice? And store it?'

'Exactly. It will require labourers – a large quantity of them. And special tools that will have to be made up by a blacksmith. I will draw you some sketches.'

I ordered the construction of a barn, in which to store the ice as it came off the lake, and he point-blank refused me.

'There's no money for building. The king hasn't paid his own household for three months.'

'He will pay for this,' I said confidently. 'It is necessary, if he wants his ice.'

I told Elias we would be spending the winter out at Hampton, and his face fell.

'What is it, boy?'

He said hesitantly, 'It is just that we will miss Christmas.'

'Elias!' his mother said, overhearing. 'Christmas! What is this I hear?'

He hung his head in shame. 'Some of the other children are saying that it will be a holiday.'

Without asking my permission, she whisked him off into a corner. I thought she must be scolding him over his lack of enthusiasm for his work, until I realised that her objection was a different one. She was trying to speak quietly, but anger made her voice carry.

'. . . bad enough that you work for a papist. But I will not have you celebrating papist festivals as well. Now be off with you, and let us have no more talk of Christmas.'

I waited until the boy had gone, and Hannah was angrily clashing pans together, before I spoke. To tell the truth, I was amused: it had not occurred to me that, while I was worried about the propriety of employing a whore's bastard, the whore in question was worried about the propriety of him working for me.

'You don't celebrate Christmas, I take it?' I said neutrally.

'We do not.'

'May I ask the reason?'

'Under the Protector, it was seen that there was no need for it.'

'Whereas the Protector's own birthday, no doubt, was a public holiday?'

She glared at me. 'Show me where in the Gospels it says that December the twenty-fifth is Christ's birthday, and we will celebrate it. Until then the Sabbath is enough Lord's Day for us.'

'Indeed,' I said. 'It seems to be more than enough. Since I've been here, I've not seen any of this inn's servants go to church, even on a Sabbath.'

Her voice when she replied was flat. 'We go when we have to. That is how it is in England now. You must go to church when and where you are told to, or you will be listed as a dissenter.'

'Then it seems to me that you need more festivals, not fewer.'

'Why?' she said angrily. 'So that we can be preached at by men in holy dresses who claim that they alone know the word of Christ? Who mumble prayers as if they were spells, and talk about the Holy Ghost as if God were some kind of invisible sorcerer?'

'And it also seems to me,' I said mildly, 'that while your bishops would no doubt call me a deluded papist, they would not be much happier with you.'

'Bishops!' she said in disgust.

'You cannot have a church without them.'

For a moment she seemed to be struggling to keep silent. Then she said, 'But we did. For a while at least, we did.'

'What – no Christmas, and no bishops either?'

'We were building God's kingdom,' she said with a kind of strange, defiant pride. 'A holy experiment. That was what we were told. And we could see the truth of it – could *feel* it, when the Spirit moved in our own breasts. A kingdom without kings. A church without churches. A country where there were no bonds: not of property, nor privilege, nor birth. A place where no man was born with stirrups on his back, for other men to ride him. Where every man could choose his way of worship; yea, and every woman too, and the only laws to which we paid allegiance were written in our hearts.' She spoke all this in a kind of sing-song, as if it were a litany she had spoken many times before, and knew she should not be speaking now. She looked at me levelly. 'And I still believe that one day it will happen here again, whether I live to see it or not. King Charles will leave us, and in his place King Jesus will sit on the throne. We will kneel to no man, and we will all be free.'

'Enough of this,' I said, suddenly fearful. 'This is treason as well as heresy, woman. Guard your tongue, and let us hear no more.'

Louise

One morning Charles brings me a gift. Another gift, I should say, for there have been several in recent weeks. But none like this.

A necklace. Rubies. Darker than currants, darker than blood. He fastens it around my neck himself, then turns me to a mirror.

I see him stroke the side of my neck with the back of his finger, so softly I can barely feel it, tracing a line from my ear down to where the necklace sits against my throat.

'It wants earrings, in the French style,' he says abruptly. 'I'm a fool not to have thought of it. I'll get you some.'

'Your Majesty has been generous enough already. Really, there is no need for jewels.'

'You are a great lady of France,' he says ironically. 'How else should I woo you, if not with jewels?'

'*Is* Your Majesty wooing me?'

A silence. In the mirror, his eyes meet mine. 'I suppose I am.'

'Then I cannot accept this, because I cannot keep my side of the bargain.' I reach up to take the necklace off, but the clasp is stiff. 'Would you help me, please?'

He reaches up as if to help, then puts one hand on my hands to keep them there. With his other he reaches around, placing it on my stomach.

And I feel – I feel . . .

I cannot write it down. What are the words for this, this blossoming of warmth and trepidation? I am aware of a sensation – a kind of silkiness – something unknown, unanticipated. Unguents dissolving inside me, as a candle softens underneath the flame.

His lips brush my neck – tentatively, as if he knows he should not, but cannot help himself.

My chin lifts. I feel my back arch, involuntarily.

He increases the pressure of his hand, pulling me against him, and I realise that he is aroused. Startled, I draw in my breath.

'Keep the necklace,' he says, releasing me. 'There is no bargain to keep or break. It is a gift without conditions.'

Once he says: 'Tell me this.'

'What, Charles?'

'If it were not for your virtue – if the world were a different place, and you and I were free to do as we pleased – would I be the sort of man . . .'

This is unlike him, this hesitancy. I think: a woman was cruel to him once, and for all his charm he has never got over it.

'Charles, you are a handsome man, and a kind one too. Any woman would be lucky to have you as a husband. But I cannot answer your question. My virtue is as much a part of me as my hands or my head. How can I imagine what I would be if I did not have it?'

Brusquely, he says, 'Then keep your virtue. I love you too much to wish you any different.'

He turns away. But even I, with my court manners, cannot altogether contain my surprise at his first use of that word.

Carlo

Gather ice in winter, that you may have the pleasure of ices in the heat of summer.

The Book of Ices

'A harvest', I had called the gathering of ice in conversation with the king; and that is exactly what it was. Seeing the first frosts in St James's Park was like spying the first small sprouting of a long-awaited crop. Each day the shoots grew a little sturdier, a little stronger, nourished by the dark and the increasing cold. Men hurried through the streets now wrapped up in furs. Dray horses stamped their hooves where they waited to unload, and blew trumpets of warm breath as they laboured over the uneven roads.

Then the snow came. If the frosts were the shoots, this was the blossom. Great, fat petals of snow, drifting over the city, turning roofs white; settling a little longer, a little deeper, every time it fell.

The ice did not harden yet, though. The ice was winter's fruit, ripening slowly. First a tiny brûlée of clear toffee on the surface of a puddle. Then a disc of glass. And finally a thick, white plate of porcelain, crazed with cracks where children had tried to stamp it through and found they could not.

'Ice,' I told Elias, 'even ice that seems frozen, needs time. It sets slowly, over the course of a week or so. And the harder the ice, the more slowly it will melt. We want iron, not porcelain.'

'We wait?'

'We wait,' I confirmed.

After a week, the ice rang hard and true as iron. It was time to move out to Hampton. Where, of course, all was chaos. The steward had neglected our arrangement; the labourers were idle; the

247

barn I had ordered was being used by cattle. Only the ice was perfect, thick enough to ride a horse across, as hard and unyielding as the frozen ground itself.

I invoked the king's name, and swore volubly in Italian. Little by little, my harvest was gathered in.

One morning I awoke to find that the air itself had turned white. A freezing sea mist had come in from the east, bringing with it a cold so bitter that holly leaves could be snapped in two like biscuits, and every twig and branch was furry with ice.

I remembered Louise talking about Brest, and wondered what she was doing now. I tried to put her from my mind. But sometimes, through the frozen mists, I thought I glimpsed a figure in a threadbare gown, dancing in the snow.

Louise

Now the canals and lakes in St James's Park are frozen. Charles and his brother James teach me to slide on the ice – 'skating' they call it, a Dutch word. They learned how to do it during their years in the Low Countries. James is the better of the two, something Charles is irked by, since in all other sports he far excels his younger brother.

Sometimes James skates beside me, holding me up: one hand pressed against my side to steady me, the other reached around me so that I do not fall, speeding me along in a great sweeping arc, the two of us propelled only by the swishing of his long legs, while I concentrate on keeping my own legs braced and steady so that I do not fall.

'Od's fish, he looks as if he's about to tumble you into his arms,' Charles grumbles.

He's jealous. And not entirely without cause: James holds me a little harder than he needs to, his hands a little higher or a little further around than is strictly necessary.

He is a strange man. Physically, he looks like Charles – that is to say, handsome: yet somehow what in Charles has turned to charm, in James has become dourness. Questions of faith and policy trouble him. On his face there is a perpetual expression of anxiety or regret. Yet it is said that he is cleverer than his brother, and does much of the painstaking work of government when Charles loses patience with it.

His taste in mistresses is a Whitehall joke: it is said that as a kind of penance he makes sure they are always uglier than his wife.

Yet he is also Admiral of the Fleet. As such, no one is more important in advising Charles whether or not to go to war. It is also said that he secretly inclines to the True Faith. If so, he will not have the same concerns about making war on a Protestant nation that some of the king's ministers do. This war might even be seen as a test. Does he save his soul, or help his brother stay on the throne? It is a difficult dilemma for a man of devotion.

And who better to talk to him about such matters than a Catholic lady of great virtue, lately come from France?

We spend long afternoons reading *Lettres Provinciales*, and discussing Pascal on the soul.

Charles is not amused. 'Why do you spend so much time reading with my brother?'

'Your Majesty is most welcome to join us.'

'I can't think of anything more tedious than discussing religion with James. Even if there's precious little else to occupy any of us at the moment. If the ground doesn't unfreeze soon, the racing will be over this year before it's even started.'

'Take care you do not stretch this out too long,' Lady Arlington warns. 'The king is irritable when the weather is like this. It would be perfect time to spend in bed, in fact. A warm fire and a fur coverlet, and his apartments would be the cosiest place in the kingdom.'

My tactic now when she talks like this is to look vague. 'My own fire is perfectly warm, thank you. The sea coal here in London is very good, don't you find?'

That winter, one of his Parliament men circulates a poem that begins:

> *Had we but world enough and time,*
> *This coyness, lady, were no crime . . .*

Charles sends it to me with a note: *This man is one of my enemies, and a scurrilous pamphleteer, but somehow he expresses my own thoughts more eloquently than I can myself.*

*

In the evenings, entertainment. The great fad this winter is for masquerades. In the Banqueting House, in the mansions of Pall Mall, we dance and gossip in disguise. I have a dozen different masks, fashioned from lace, from feathers, from silver leaf and worked leather.

And one that I am still wearing when the other masks come off.

So many layers of dressing up. I have seen the king without his mask, but not without his wig. Does he take it off, I wonder, when he takes a woman to bed? I have a sudden image of him in his nightshirt, the luxuriant hair pulled away from his head, a soldier's crop beneath. Dark stubble. It should be comical, ridiculous, the monarch stripped of his dignity – but instead I feel a kind of tenderness at the thought.

At the dances the king and his brother are easily picked out, both by the fineness of their clothes and their great height. But sometimes it can be hard to tell them apart. Only the king's posture – that athleticism in the dance – distinguishes them.

And this: James flirts, a little awkwardly. He tries to talk with me, to catch my interest in some current event or gossip.

Charles only stares at me from behind the vizard, his dark, glittering eyes more eloquent than words.

Carlo

Cinnamon, galangal, sassafras and cloves are all good spices for ices. Nutmeg ice cream, indeed, can hold its own with the very grandest of gelati, and makes an excellent ice in winter. Serve it with some warm apple pie and a glass of mulled ale.

The Book of Ices

England was glutted with snow now, groaning with it, surfeited. My workmen grew desperate, forcing carts laden with ice through the endless deep drifts. The horses' hooves had to be wrapped in scraps of fur; even so, picking their way through the cold and wet, some got the rot and had to be turned loose to fend for themselves as best they could. Sometimes we were trapped for days by howling blizzards that scoured the skin from our faces and pushed pellets of snow inside every crevice of our clothes. At other times the sky was blue and brilliant and calm above a world turned white, the still air sparkling like the dust from a marble-cutter's drill; pillars of snow heaped on every cottage and frozen cart like the freshly baked crusts of pies.

I was in my element.

It was not only ice to fill the king's ice house I required. That might have provided enough for his own household, but the court, and his feast, had greater needs. That meant finding and filling caves where the air would stay cold all year, granaries of ice from which I would refill the larder in St James's.

Caves are rarely near good roads, and even good roads were impassable now. The horses' withers were soon striped indelibly with the marks of our whips.

It was mid-January by the time Elias and I returned to London, at the head of a caravan of carts. Although it was not long after noon, darkness was falling – there were few good hours of daylight in those midwinter days. We passed through Ludgate, and saw the great river below us. For a moment I thought they must have lit the famous beacons that warned London of invasion. Then I realised that – a thing of wonder – the bonfires were on the river itself, actually on top of the ice, a line of flames that stretched away towards the west as far as the eye could see.

It was like the gathering of a circus, or the encampment of an army. There were castles made of canvas; fire eaters and dancing bears; jugglers and fools; fire balloons, and the glittering sparks of coloured gunpowders illuminating the faces of the crowds. Pennants fluttered in the breeze, and the sound of music drifted towards us.

'It's the wherrymen's doing,' Elias said, from his perch by the carter. 'When they can no longer work their boats, they declare the frost fair open. No one has jurisdiction between the riverbanks but them.'

The road we were on led down to the river. Soon I could smell roasting chestnuts and the warm, spicy odour of mulled beer.

'Want to stop?' the carter said, licking his lips.

'No,' I said shortly. 'We must get our ice to its destination.'

When we finally reached the Lion, exhausted after a night spent unloading the ice carts, I found the place deserted except for a solitary tap-man. Titus Clarke had opened a fuddling tent at the frost fair, he explained, and Hannah was selling her pies.

Curious, I accompanied Elias down to the river, where a coach and six was taking passengers from one bank to the other. The driver assured me that it was perfectly safe, but I had too much respect for ice to toy with its dangers, and stayed on foot. At the Red Lion's tent Elias was reunited with his mother: she hugged him and told him that he must have grown at least a foot. He looked a little uncomfortable at this display of affection. Not all his growing-up had been done on the outside, I thought, amused.

To me her smile of welcome was warm. 'Thank you for looking after him,' she said. I nodded, and left them to catch up.

Each tent bore the sign of an inn, and, by agreement, sold only one style of drink. The Three Bells was an arak tent; the Coach and Horses dispensed wormwood, while the Red Lion was serving mum.

'Why is it called that?' I asked Titus Clarke.

'Because mum is what you become if you drink enough of it,' he said cheerfully as he handed me a foaming tankard. 'Has the power to take away speech, mum does, as many a man has found out to his cost before now.'

I tried some: it was a frothy mulled ale spiced with sassafras and cloves, pleasant, if a little too aromatic, in a way that reminded me of a linctus for the cough. All around me Englishmen and women were taking great drafts of the stuff. I drank mine a little more moderately – in Italy we are not inclined to drunkenness, as the English are. Rather to my surprise, it felt good to be back in London: I had not realised, out in the countryside, how much I missed its rough, perpetual energy. I strolled on. There was some bull-baiting going on, and a cockfight or two, which diverted me for a while. People were eating apple pies and sweetmeats, and the warm smells of nutmeg and cinnamon filled the air.

Then I heard a shout: *The king*. I looked up. A procession of a dozen coaches was driving down the ice from the direction of Whitehall. As I watched, they pulled up and the court disembarked from them, men and women spilling onto the ice. Many were wearing skates beneath their fine clothes, and as they set off, as graceful as dancers, the crowd gave them a cheer. I saw Louise among them, skating backwards in a circle, her dress of golden silk billowing. Then the king stretched out his hand to her, and the two of them went speeding down towards the Great Bridge together, outstripping all the rest, their legs moving in perfect unison, her long black hair streaming behind her; as if they were two gorgeous birds, flying away downriver.

I turned back to the fair, which suddenly seemed a little darker, a little colder, without them there.

The next thing I can remember I was waking up, painfully, in my room at the Lion. Someone had undressed me: whoever it was had folded my clothes neatly beside the bed, and even put my boots outside for cleaning. I swung upright, alarmed, then wished that I had not: my head ached unbearably, like a rock that had been split open by a mason's hammer. It seemed that I had succumbed to the vice of the English after all, and drunk too much.

Groaning, I made my way down to the dining rooms. I could tell the kitchens were open – the smell of baking pies was wafting out from the back – but there was no one about, and I was in no condition to shout. Eventually my breakfast was brought to me by Rose, the lowest of the sluts.

It took me a little while to realise that she had sat down at a nearby table and was now watching me eat.

'How're you feeling?' she enquired, with what was clearly intended as a sympathetic smile.

I frowned. 'My head is a little thick.'

'Not surprised, if that was the first time you'd tried mum.'

So she had seen me the night before. 'I take it I became speechless? Stupefied with drink?'

She threw her head back and laughed. 'You? Speechless? No. You it took the other way. Speechifying like a priest, you was.'

Needless to say, I had no recollection of this. 'What was I . . . speechifying about?'

'You really don't remember?'

'If I did,' I pointed out, 'I would have no need to ask.'

She nodded. 'Fair enough. Let's just say most of it went over my head. Mary's too. Especially the bits in Italian. Pretty, they

255

were, and very persuasive, but not in any way that was what you might call intelligible.'

I wondered at that 'persuasive'. But at least, it seemed, I had not blabbed any of my secrets. It was another reason to vow never to touch mum again, had the condition of my head not already resolved me to just such a course.

Whatever had happened that night, it had another unforeseen consequence. Far from being horrified by my lack of self-control, the regulars at the Lion seemed to take it as evidence that I was now, as they put it, 'one of them'.

'We thought you were stuck up to start with,' the other slut, Mary, confided to me. 'But you're all right really, aren't you?'

I was rather in two minds about this. On the one hand, I was tempted to point out that, as the confectioner to His Majesty, I was hardly one of them; on the other, I was glad these people no longer considered me an outsider, and so I judged that the best thing to do would be to accept their friendship in the spirit in which it was offered.

Mary and Rose, in particular, loved to gossip about the court, and now that I had – somehow – signalled to them that I was more approachable than I had hitherto given them reason to believe, they often came to bother me as I worked.

'What about Lady Castlemaine? Is she as beautiful as they say?'

'I have not had the pleasure of seeing that lady yet.'

'What about the king? What's he like?'

'His Majesty is very gracious. And tall. That is his most distinguishing characteristic: his height.'

'Is it true that Lady Arlington has a hundred gowns?'

'I have not counted them myself. But at Versailles, a hundred gowns would not be considered so very many, by a true lady of fashion.'

In particular, they were fascinated beyond all imagining by Nell Gwynne – 'Our Nell,' as they called her. I might look askance when I heard the name, and venture the opinion that the actress was a coarse and unappetising creature, but for them that was simply part of her fascination. The fact that Nell had started out as a common whore – 'a coal-yard cullymonger' Mary called her – graduating to the stage, fame, and thence to the royal bed, seemed to them a kind of fairy tale, all the more so for the way that in its sordid beginnings it reminded them of their own lives.

'I was an orange girl like her, only at the Duke's, not the King's. Eleven, I was, when a gentleman decided he wanted to unpeel more than he'd paid for,' Mary said. I quickly changed the subject, although the discomfort was all on my side, not hers.

They had heard of Louise de Keroualle, but their impression of her was formed by a different prejudice: that as a Frenchwoman, she had been sent to the English court for the sole purpose of bewitching their king. All my protestations that this was not in fact the case were met with polite but stubborn disbelief. One of the girls even had a book purporting to be Louise's biography, and, not being able to read, asked me if I would describe its contents to her. It was, of course, more filth, and after taking one look I declined in no uncertain terms.

There was more gossip and chatter to which I paid little heed; but to my surprise, when Robert Cassell dropped by on his regular visits, it was this tavern gossip, and not my progress with making a smoother ice cream, in which he seemed most interested.

'Anything else?' he said, leaning across the table and fixing me with his bright military gaze. 'What about talk of other nations, for example?'

'Well, they are quite convinced that the Dutch started the Great Fire.'

'Are they indeed?' he said, with a slight smile.

'I told them that it is far more likely that God is punishing their country for its regicide.'

257

'Hmm,' he said. 'I think, for the time being, you should perhaps keep that point of view to yourself. Opinions are going to get rather heated on subjects such as that one in the coming months. In fact, it would be better for many reasons if you were to say that you have heard several eminent people at court also say that the Dutch were behind the burning.'

One person who took little part in the gossiping was Hannah. Yet, perhaps surprisingly, I found myself disputing with her almost as much as with the other two. For if Rose and Mary were too credulous, Hannah was too dismissive.

'Hann,' they would call to her as she passed through the front rooms, 'Come and listen, do. Signor Carlo is telling us about the time he served goblets of snow mixed with a rosewater conserve to the Countess of Sedburgh at a ball.'

'The Countess of Sedburgh is not an acquaintance of mine,' Hannah said without stopping. 'So I am not very interested in what she has to eat.'

'But she is beautiful—' Rose called after her; but it was too late; Hannah was already out of earshot. It seemed to me that she was shorter with all of us since the night of the frost fair; then again, winter was the busiest time of year for her pies, so she might simply have been pressed for time.

Then there was the occasion when I was repeating some remarks the king had made concerning the forthcoming feast for the Garter Knights at Windsor, and my own central role in those festivities.

'So he has money enough to spend on palaces and banquets, but none for wells or hospitals,' Hannah said, overhearing me. 'And every single penny of it paid for from our taxes.'

'What the king spends his exchequer on is a matter for His Majesty and his advisors,' I observed mildly. 'How can we, with our limited information, presume to question the decisions of great men?'

She did stop then – stopped dead, in fact: a rare enough occurrence for me to mark it. 'And what, pray, makes one person great, and another not?' she demanded.

'His birth, his manners and his blood,' I said immediately. 'You may not always like those whom God has set above you, but you surely cannot doubt that He has the means to do so. Just as the king is entitled to some of the respect that is due to God, whose representative he is, so his courtiers are entitled to some of the respect that is due to the angels.'

Perhaps I did not express myself very clearly, because Hannah simply threw her head back and laughed sarcastically.

'And I suppose you include yourself in that?' she said when she had stopped laughing. 'Because if you're an angel, then I'm a Frenchman's arse.'

I stared at her, baffled as to where this new animosity had come from. I was certain she could not be referring to my own humble birth: that was a shameful secret I never alluded to. Unless I had somehow betrayed my lowly origins when drunk? I watched her, trying to gain some clue from her expression. But she had already turned her back on me and moved away.

Carlo

To make a sorbet of medlars: simmer two pounds of
medlar pulp with one cup of sugar and the juice of a
lemon, working it smooth with a spoon or stick. It will be
improved by adding a glass or two of cordial made from
the blackthorn or sloe berries that grow wild in northern
climes.

The Book of Ices

Of all the orchard trees, the medlar must be the strangest. On the
tree, the fruits are hard and bitter. But if they are left over winter,
frosts break down the hard flesh. Only when the skin turns brown
is the pulp soft enough to eat, with something of the smoky,
musty richness of hung game, or cheese that has been aged in
damp cellars. In England they call this process *bletting*, a word
that suggests both ripening and rotting.

I had first spoken to Louise in a copse of medlar trees.

I made an ice of medlars, and sweetened it with a fragrant,
slightly medicinal liqueur made from blackthorn berries. I set it in
a bed of fresh snow from the countryside, and took it to her.

In her apartments, all was activity. A wall had come down, knocking the rooms into those next door. Workmen were repainting
walls with frescoes and *trompe l'oeil* columns. Another painter was
making her portrait. And a whole cluster of ladies-in-waiting
watched and gossiped from the other side of the room.

'I have brought you an ice,' I said with a bow.

'Signor Demirco.' To the painter she said, 'I will be with you
presently.' He looked furious, but put down his brush with a nod.

260

'Come.' She drew me towards a private alcove.

'What is going on?' I asked as I handed her the ice.

'This? Oh, he is having my apartments refurbished. Apparently I must have a bedroom as big as a ballroom, for my morning *ruelle*, when he visits me with his friends. And a ballroom for when he wants to dance.' *He*, I noticed. No longer *the king* or even *Charles*.

Her gown was sown with hundreds of pearls. She was dressed up for the portrait painter, of course, but she had changed, too. No longer a girl, a child, but a lady – a great lady of France, polished and poised.

Or were these differences not in her, but in the way I saw her, because of the props she was surrounded with – the gown, the silks, the ladies-in-waiting, the painter of portraits, the sumptuous apartments themselves?

'Have you had a good winter?' she asked. 'You got your ice?'

I nodded. 'Enough to keep all of Europe in ice creams. And you? How are your relations with His Majesty?'

'Oh, Carlo,' she said heavily.

'What's wrong?'

'The king is in love with me.'

'So? He was in love with you before I went away.'

'But now he seems almost – *crazed*. As if he is in pain. I have mishandled him. Now we are both trapped. He can't marry me; he can't bear to let me go: none of us can go home until we have this war. What am I to do?'

'What brought this on?'

'His brother's wife, Anne Hyde, passed away.'

'I heard.' It was said that on her deathbed she refused her priest, saying that she would rather die unshriven in the True Faith than blessed in a false one. The people I spoke to in the countryside were more certain than ever that the Stuarts were secret Catholics.

'The question is, who will James marry next? Someone young, he says, beautiful, and of course, a Catholic.'

261

Suddenly I realised. 'You?'

She nodded. 'He spoke to Charles of it, anyway. There was such a row . . . Charles thought I had encouraged him. I hadn't, of course. I was simply trying to get his support for war.'

'So what happened?'

'I told both of them that I couldn't possibly accept.'

I knew what this must mean to her: to turn down an offer of marriage from the heir to the English throne.

'I had no choice,' she added. 'Colbert and Arlington made that perfectly clear. It is Charles's mistress or nothing.'

'And the war?'

She shrugged. 'I fear it is further away than ever now. I have managed to influence him in some small things, certainly. But not that.'

She looked so despondent, sitting there, that I made a sudden decision.

'Run away with me,' I said. 'Now. Today. We'll take a ship to Spain, or Sicily. Marry me or not, it is up to you. But we could be in Dover by dawn. Madrid within a week. My ice creams are the best in Europe: the Spanish are great lovers of ice, we will not starve . . .'

She shook her head.

'You must not,' she said quietly. 'Carlo, you must not do this. The king loves me.'

'And you him?'

She shook her head again, and I knew that she was not answering me, but only warning me that I should never ask her that again.

I went back to the Red Lion. I admit it: I stopped at another tavern on the way, the nearest one, and sank three tankards of mum.

Then I strode into the Lion looking for a woman.

It could have been any one of them. It happened to be Hannah who I met on the stairs.

262

'Come,' I said abruptly. 'I have need of your services.'

'Making custard for your ices?'

'I meant your other services. The services you give to certain men. How much do you charge?'

She looked at me levelly for a moment. Doubtless she was wondering how high a price she could name. 'A shilling,' she said at last.

'Good. Let us go to my room.'

She followed me upstairs without a word. I pointed to the bed, and told her where to arrange herself. And then—

O, I am ashamed to write this. But I have sworn to set it down without embellishment or evasion.

I had her on the bed, like a beast of the farmyard, without even taking off my boots.

She made no sound while I did it, and for that I was grateful. I could not have borne it if she had squeaked and groaned and flattered in a feeble simulacrum of pleasure. There was no pleasure in that coupling. None for her, and none for me. All I felt was a little of agony of desire purging from my loins, like the letting of a vein, which only left the ache in my heart all the clearer.

Afterwards I lay on the bed, staring at the ceiling.

'Why do you weep?' she said. They were the first words she had spoken since we had begun. Carefully, as if I were a fire she might be burned by, she put a hand to my face.

'I do not weep,' I said, turning my head away. She did not say more, but only got to her feet.

'There is money by the window, in my purse,' I said. I heard her go to it, the chink of coins, and then I was alone.

Louise

There is no let-up. On the contrary, they snap at my heels from every side. Arlington, Louis, Louvois ... Even my ladies-in-waiting have been bribed to whisper in my ear as they brush my hair or hang by the windows of my apartments, hoping for a glimpse of him. *How handsome he is, how lucky you are, I remember my first time, it is a pleasure to lie with one like him ...*

Colbert attends me every afternoon. Today, though, he has something delicate to tell me. He waits until we are alone.

'His Majesty did me the honour of attending a small supper at my residence yesterday,' he murmurs.

'I trust the evening was an enjoyable one?'

'Indeed.' Colbert seems unsure how to continue. 'King Charles became increasingly relaxed.'

'Relaxed?'

'That is to say, he unburdened himself.'

'He talked about me?'

'Not directly. That is to say, there was a young servant girl who served us at dinner. From Gascony. Perhaps you have seen her? A pretty little thing.'

I assure him that I have not given any especial notice to the ambassador's serving girls.

'His Majesty certainly noticed her. Indeed, he felt so ... comfortable in my company, that towards the end of the evening he asked if this girl could join us.'

I raise my eyebrows.

'His Majesty did me the honour of showing me that he trusted me *to the utmost.*'

'I see.'

'What followed . . . There was a most unfettered debauch,' he says faintly. *Une débauche très libre.*

Indeed I do see, a little. The words of his masked ex-mistress echo in my ear. *A libertine, like the rest.*

'I eagerly look forward to the day when His Majesty's ardour might be tempered by your influence. I feel sure that you will be a force for morality in all this darkness.' He continues hesitantly, 'The thing is, we seem to have reached something of an impasse.'

'Oh? In what way?'

'His Majesty appears to have realised that you are not the only one with bargaining counters at your disposal.'

'He wishes to *bargain?*'

'In a manner of speaking. That is, before he left my residence, he made his position clear.'

'Yes? What does he intend to offer me, that he believes is more valuable to me than my honour?'

Colbert looks positively uncomfortable now. 'It is not to you he makes the offer, mademoiselle. It is to our king – to His Most Christian Majesty. Charles has asked me to make it absolutely clear to Versailles that, while there is no mistress, there is no alliance. And vice versa. He is making a quite straightforward proposal. When you are amenable to his entreaties, then he will listen on the subject of the Dutch war. But until then, nothing.'

Carlo

To a pint of blackcurrants, add four sprigs of mint, chopped, a cup of sugar, and the white of two eggs. This ice, a little sour, is in my opinion even better than the fruit from which it is made.

The Book of Ices

She would not do it.

She would not be blackmailed into his bed, she said, any more than she would be bribed into it.

Arlington said, 'It is entirely her own fault. She has enflamed him beyond what any man could bear.'

'A woman has a right not to be coerced.'

'Why?' Arlington demanded. 'If a girl cannot choose her own husband, why should she have the right to choose whom she is bedded to?'

I was given a letter to take to her.

'Her last chance,' Colbert told me. 'Even now it may be too late.'

I looked at the linen envelope in which the letter was wrapped. The seal bore the insignia of a sun, surrounded by molten rays – the personal arms of the Sun King himself, Louis XIV.

She read it ashen-faced.

'What does it say?'

Silently she handed it to me. After the usual courtesies, the matter was short and to the point. Louis's anger was evident even in the few lines that were written there.

We now consider that there is no more you can do. It is time for you to return to France. You leave next week, from Dover.

'They will send someone else in my place,' she said heavily. 'Someone more amenable. And me to a nunnery, or worse.'

'At least you will be free of all this.'

She shook her head. 'I have failed. My promise to Madame – the Great Affair – all of it. I have failed. I will never be free of that.'

She looked so despondent, sitting there, that I longed to take her in my arms. But I did not.

'It's over.' She looked around – at her sumptuous apartment, at the king's gifts: the clocks, the books, the paintings and tapestries and furnishings and the gorgeous marquetry. 'Over before it has really even begun.'

And I heard myself saying the words I thought I would never say.

'Perhaps you should yield to the king.'

'Your virtue does not consist of your virginity,' I said gently. 'No woman's does. It lies in your character, your disposition, who you are and what you believe. But this is the choice you have to make: which is more important to you, your maidenhead or your promise to Madame?'

'You don't understand. My family – we earned our titles on the battlefield, serving kings. Honour is what makes us different from other men. However poor we are, we have that.'

'You can be a king's mistress, and still have honour.'

'I will have surrendered—'

'No!' I said. 'You will have *won*. Don't you see? Once you are his mistress you will have power – such power! – not just over Charles, but over Louis too. Once you are Charles's mistress, Louis will never again be able to order you back to France. You will be able to do what you set out to do. And what you have lost – what you have discarded – does it really matter, compared with that?'

Her shoulders lifted as she took a breath, and in that moment

267

I saw that she would do it. And I saw, too, that I was the only person who could have spoken to her like this; because no one else knew her, or loved her, well enough to consider her own happiness in all these intrigues.

She was a woman to whom love was of secondary importance. I did not love her any less because of it, but it helped, a little, to know that it was not out of desire for him she would do this, but for an aim – a patriotic endeavour – to which she had committed herself long ago.

We talked for a long time – arguing it back and forth, weighing up the pros and cons. It was, we both knew, an irrevocable step.

'If I do it,' she said, 'you should know that I will do it to the utmost. I will not be his mistress in some hole-in-the-corner, furtive manner. It must be acknowledged, open, in the French way, so that all are aware of my position. I will make him depend on me for every judgement and decision he must make. I will be nothing less than a queen, even if I do not have that title.'

'I know it.'

For a long moment neither of us spoke. Then she said in a different voice, 'How would I make them aware that I have changed my mind?' and I knew the decision was taken.

'Speak to Arlington,' I said. 'Let him be the go-between. He will be only too eager to take the credit for this.'

At the Red Lion I found Hannah making pies.

'When you are done,' I said hoarsely.

She took in my meaning with a glance at my face. 'I have to get these in the oven.' She indicated the trays of pies.

'Well, do not spoil them on my account. I will be upstairs.'

When she came to my room she was still wearing her apron.

Always it was the same: her on her knees across the bed; my hips working; my groan of release. Not a word from her. The chink of coins – I checked: she never took too little, or too much.

The only difference this time was a faint smell of pies, and a little puff of flour in her hair, like a streak of grey, where she had patted it absent-mindedly as she cooked.

I found myself staring down at it as we rutted. I was thinking of a couple long-married, a couple who did this act out of companionship, or love, instead of pain. Presumably there must be some such in the world.

Louise

I invite Lady Arlington to cards. It is easy to beat her now – she always plays the same hand in the same way. But, for the same reason, just as easy to let her win.

The usual questions about the king. Does he still come to me every morning? What about at night?

'Of course, I only permit him to visit me during the day,' I say. 'Unless we were married, anything else would be improper.'

She snorts derisively. 'But you cannot be married. Not while the queen still lives.'

I say idly, as I put down a card, 'You know, I sometimes think it is a pity a king cannot have two queens. That would solve so many problems, wouldn't it?'

I place the queen of diamonds and the queen of hearts together, one on either side of the king, as if my comment might have been no more than a remark about cards.

Out of the corner of my eye, I see her eyes widen as she takes the bait.

It is barely a day before her husband comes to see me. 'I have had an idea,' he tells me genially. 'A suggestion, rather.'

'I am sure you have many ideas, milord Arlington. All of them excellent.'

'I do indeed,' he agrees. 'Many ideas. But, ah, only one wife.'

'One is the usual complement, is it not?'

'For ordinary men, it is.'

'Oh, come, Lord Arlington. You are no ordinary man.'

He accepts this with an inclination of the head. 'But not a king. No,' he continues, almost to himself, 'if I were like His Majesty – an absolute ruler, head of the Church, and God's anointed representative on earth – I could certainly have a second, official . . . *consort*, if I chose.' He regards me, pleased with himself.

'Really? How interesting.' After a moment I add, almost as an afterthought, 'I am surprised the priests would sanction it – I know how difficult they can be about these things. But naturally I trust to your expertise in such matters.'

'Priests!' he says, his eyes widening. Clearly, he had not bargained on my requiring priests.

'A ceremony of that nature would require a priest, would it not?' I say vaguely. 'For it to be official, and recognised in the eyes of God? Of course, I am not *au fait* with all the customs of your English church.'

A slight pause, and then he sees the opening I am creating for him. It is obvious when you think about it: they already have a made-up religion, with made-up ceremonies, their psalter and liturgy and rituals in a constant state of flux. What difference will one more make?

'As it happens, I am not aware of the precise ceremony for such an . . . unusual occasion,' he says slowly.

'But then, you are not a bishop.'

'No.' Another pause. 'It is an interesting theological question. I will put it to a bishop of my acquaintance. Do you know, I would not be surprised to find that such a ceremony exists after all.'

'Nor would I,' I say. 'Not surprised in the least.'

And so, by hints and innuendoes, a deal is brokered.

Not a marriage, but a *union*. Not a queen, but a *consort*. There will be a wedding, after a fashion. Vows will be made, prayers said, a blessing given. There will be madrigals, a specially composed epithalamium in our honour, a masque. And then we will be put to bed, and the stocking thrown, just like any other bride and groom.

271

And Louis will have his war.

As for the venue, Arlington suggests his country palace, Euston Hall, near Newmarket. There is a chapel – of ambiguous style, neither plain Protestant nor extravagant Catholic – within the house. Of course I know why he is suggesting it: he wants this done out of London. That way, if it ever becomes known, he can dismiss it all as a frolic, a rustic masquerade held to entertain his guests. But equally, he wants it done under his auspices. He intends to get rich on the back of this. The chancellorship, at least, the gift of a grateful king.

A bishop is produced who swears that this is all quite proper. That is to say, no more improper than the alternative. That is to say, if something improper is to take place, it is better done in God's plain sight than not. That way the king is almost asking His forgiveness and understanding. Which forgiveness is, in one sense, a kind of blessing in this world of sin.

I believe the bishop wants to be an archbishop, and soon. His arguments are nonsense – a child could blow them down. But nobody chooses to disagree. Especially not Charles. He does not care what rules are bent so long as he gets what he wants.

The ambassador, Colbert, is even more impatient than the king. 'We need war now. Why this delay?'

'There are thirty-two warships being hammered together at Chatham docks as we speak. The delay is for your benefit, not mine.'

'But why cannot the yielding happen first, and the ships follow after?'

I turn my mild gaze on him. 'You may know a lot about diplomacy, Your Excellency, but you do not seem to know very much about men and women. Who do you think those ships are being built so urgently for – Louis, or Louise?'

He sees the sense in this, and bows.

'Let us hope, then,' he says quietly, 'that King Charles never sees fit to regret the high price he has paid for your companionship. Madame.'

I note that 'Madame'. And for that slight, Your Excellency, I think, and the small frisson of distaste with which you condescend to look at me, I will make sure that once I am his mistress, you are recalled to France.

Carlo

However sharp your rhubarb, the juice of a lemon will strengthen its flavour.

The Book of Ices

In the very midst of winter, the English grow a strange crop: half vegetable, half fruit. It looks a little like celery, but the stalks are bright pink, a curiosity made all the stranger by the fact that they have to force it, as they say, growing it in upturned buckets and dark sheds. It seems to thrive in the dark and cold: indeed, it is necessary, if the rhubarb is to develop the sharp, almost strawberry-like flavour that they prize.

I made her an ice of winter's fruit, the first forced rhubarb of the year, its bitter shoots a reminder of all the harvests yet to come.

Once the decision was taken, she did not waste time regretting it. It was too late to change her mind, and besides, any sign of indecision would only have weakened her position.

Only once did I see her worry about how it might be seen.

'Can you make sure this reaches Brittany?'

I looked at the envelope she had given me. It was addressed to the Compte and Comptesse de Keroualle at Brest.

'You know it will be read anyway? If not by the English spies, then by the French?'

'I know it. I have tried to be circumspect. No doubt they will hear the story from others soon enough, but I wanted them to know that, despite everything, I am still their daughter.'

Other than that, she was all business. Until one day she said, 'Carlo?'

I waited.

'How does a lady who . . .' She hesitated. 'How does a lady who is in love behave?'

Her voice was as practical as ever. But her pale skin had a little more colour in it than was usual.

'To the man she is in love with, you mean?'

She nodded.

'In his bed?'

She nodded again.

'Do your novels and books of letters not tell you?'

'Oh – those.' She made a dismissive gesture. 'Apparently I must sigh and swoon. Or I must protest shrilly every minute he is not with me. Or act the jealous shrew. None of which, I suspect, would endear me to Charles.'

'Nor would they seem much like Louise de Keroualle,' I agreed. 'But do I take it from your question you are worried that, because you do not love him, he will know it?'

'He has so much more experience than I.'

'Well, I am not the best person to ask, since I am not sure that I have ever been loved by a woman in the way you describe. Nor should you be too quick to disparage your own innocence, since for many men that is itself a kind of aphrodisiac. But I can tell you what little I do know.'

'Then please do so.' She was quite pink now.

I thought back. Olympe had not loved me, but she had had an ease with herself, a confidence, that had made lying with her a kind of feast. She had made me feel like a person of the world, a sophisticate, for whom sex was just another of the sensual pleasures a cultivated person should enjoy.

With Emilia there had been no coupling, yet when I recalled the eager delight of her kisses, the excitement we had both felt, the joy of discovering that the loved one felt the same way about you as you did about her, there had been something even sweeter than Olympe's perfumed skin.

I thought how it might have been with Louise, if fate and fortune had been different.

I said, 'You must make him feel that you are both new continents, waiting to be explored. That every time he touches you, it is like some new discovery – that like Hooke's microscope, or Newton's telescopes, some new wonder is being revealed which was previously hidden. You must be eager, but your eagerness must seem to astonish even you. Your kisses must be as exciting to him as the first pineapple his gardeners ever grew, and when he kisses you, you must think of the most surprising, most delightful, the most extraordinary thing you ever saw or did.'

'Then I will think of the first time I tasted ice cream.'

'But do not gulp, or shriek, or clasp your throat and say it has gone numb, as people who try my ices often do.'

She smiled.

But I could not.

'Like this?' she said softly, kissing me.

She kissed me.

She kissed me.

'No, not like that,' I said hoarsely, when at last we pulled apart. 'That was too gentle, and too sad. If you kiss him like that he will think you pity him.'

Back at the Lion I said to Hannah, 'Upstairs.'

Silently she followed me to my room.

A wordless coupling, as of animals.

Except that this time I could not finish. A great weariness came over me. I stopped, fell limply to the bed, and lay still.

I said to the ceiling, 'You can go.'

Perhaps she was worried that I would not pay her for this failure, or that I was becoming bored with her and there would soon be no more. Whatever the reason, I heard her say softly, 'I will bring you a cordial.'

It was on my tongue to retort that I was a maker of cordials myself, and hardly had need of more.

But I did not.

Later I heard the door open as she returned. 'Here.' She handed me a tankard. The smell was of fragrant herbs – something grassy, like the taste of spring wheat when you pull a fat white stalk from its sheath of leaves, and crush its milky richness between your teeth.

Something bitter, too, in the aftertaste.

'Valerian,' she said, guessing my thoughts. 'Willowbark, and klamath weed, and extract of nettles.'

'Physick?'

'Of a kind.'

I grunted. 'I am not usually so unmanned.'

'It is not for—' She stopped. 'Drink it anyway.'

I swallowed it down. 'Thank you,' I said grudgingly, handing the tankard back.

As I lay down I heard her go to my purse, the chink of coins. Then, surprisingly, I fell into a deep, dreamless sleep.

Later, when I woke, all was silent. I went downstairs. Hannah was not there. I was glad of that.

On the counter in the pantry, something caught my eye. A book.

I picked it up. *The Compleat Herbal*, by Nicholas Culpeper. I glanced at the shelf where she kept her books of recipes. There was a gap where it came from, between *Excellent Receipts in Cookery* and *The Housemaid's Companion*.

I picked it up and flicked through the pages. It seemed to be about astrology as much as herbs. *You know Mars is hot and dry, and you know as well that winter is cold and moist; then you may know as well the reason why nettle-tops, eaten in the spring, consumeth the phlegmatic superfluities in the body of man, that the coldness and moistness of winter hath left behind . . .'*

I flicked through until I found a reference to klamath weed. Oddly, Culpeper did not seem to prescribe it for impotence, but for heart sickness.

Carlo

Even plain white rice makes a surprisingly delicate ice cream.

The Book of Ices

'Is there anything you need?' Louise asked me.

'In what way?'

'I am making a list. After all, I can ask for anything I like now. I am going to bring over a whole retinue of painters and musicians . . . Even a philosophy tutor. If there is anything you want, you may as well throw it in as well.'

'There is one thing, as it happens.'

'Yes?'

'There is a man here in England who knows about ice. Boyle, his name is. A chemist. A member of the Royal Society.'

'And?'

'I think he can help me make an ice cream for the king's feast. An ice that is truly worthy of its recipient.'

She gave me a strange look. 'And that is really all you want? You were instrumental in this, you know – you could ask for anything. Any favour or gift. Even,' she hesitated, 'even your passage back to France.'

I had not thought of it like that. But of course I could not leave her now.

'Boyle's help is all I want,' I said. 'At least, that is the only thing it is within King Charles's power to give.'

'I was wrong, wasn't I?' she said quietly. 'When I said that you were just a libertine, and a maker of tidbits . . . I had not realised at the time that a man can be so serious about the pleasures he creates. I will make sure you get your chemist.'

She was as good as her word. What inducements were necessary I do not know, but a few days later I received a message from Boyle inviting me to his laboratory, where, he promised, I would make the acquaintance of two other men of experiment – Christopher Wren and Robert Hooke – who had agreed to help us in our task, all under conditions of the strictest confidence.

Of that day, and the experiments we undertook, I will write little. This is not because I could not understand the methods of the *virtuosi*; on the contrary, they were admirably clear, and differed from common sense only in their great diligence and thoroughness. Nor was there any rank or distinction between us as we worked. Boyle, I knew, was the son of the Earl of Cork; Hooke, it turned out, had been a penniless orphan; Kit Wren was the son of a mercer. Yet although they deferred to Boyle in philosophical matters, I believe that was only because of his superior knowledge; when it came to mathematics, it was to Wren they turned, while for anything practical or experimental, Hooke was the undisputed master.

We made over a score of different ices; varying the cream, little by little, and then the sugar, and then the temperature, and finally the eggs. As we worked I told them what I knew, but could not necessarily explain, such as the way that a pan of milk, left to steep overnight, makes a thicker ice than does milk that is fresh. From these scraps of information they *hypothesised*, as Boyle liked to call it: each hypothesis was then handed over to Hooke for him to devise an experiment which would prove or disprove its truth. And—

There was no great moment of illumination, such as schoolboys are taught of. Archimedes may have once leapt naked from his bath, Isaac Newton (who was not of the company on that occasion, although the others spoke admiringly of his work with telescopes) may have seen a falling apple – although Hooke claimed that this was a fable created by Newton to disguise the fact that it was he, Hooke, who actually discovered the forces governing the rotation of the earth: the Fellows of the Royal Society were nothing if not disputatious about such matters – but in my case it was simply a time of quiet but remarkable discovery, as one who sails to a new land does not suddenly arrive at his destination, but must first glimpse it on the horizon, and then wait patiently for the various features of the country to make themselves more visible, and only after many hours seek a suitable spot for landing. It was a voyage, indeed, that took more than one day to complete. Even with the *virtuosi*'s remarkable powers of concentration, experimenting in the cold of the ice laboratory became too much for them after a few hours. After that they insisted it was time to repair to a coffee house, and took me to Garraway's, where they cross-questioned a sea captain about the best method of propagating cabbage trees; then to Will's, where there was a fierce debate about whether the Dutch would open the dykes if the French invaded; and then to Scott's, where they joined a competition to create a new mill wheel for London Bridge. And everywhere we went – not only the coffee shops, but the streets and places between them – people came up to my companions to ask them about the progress of this or that building project, or to enquire after an experiment, or to press an observation on them. I began to see why they generally preferred coffee to wine or ale, for they habitually moved and spoke and thought, these *virtuosi*, with a lively but good-humoured impatience which coffee seemed only to exacerbate, quite unlike the stupefaction that I had experienced with mum.

By the end of three days, we had made such progress that it was with some surprise that I looked back and saw just how far we had come. It was apparent that eggs were, in one sense, the answer, for we could now consistently produce an ice cream made with eggs – or hen's testes, as Wren insisted on calling them – that was so smooth and rich, it seemed to contain not a single crystal of ice. But my friends were not content with this as a solution: they wanted to know *why* eggs produced this effect, and whether it could be replicated with other ingredients. First we tried substituting the eggs of geese and gulls (the former were very good, the latter less so), then we separated the eggs into whites and yolks to see which part of the egg was responsible; then we gradually reduced the eggs altogether, and started working once more with cream.

It was the avowed intention of Wren, as a geometrist, to come up with a mathematical formula to express the solution. 'For only by mathematics,' he said, 'can recipes be recovered from the chaos and superstition of cooks. When I go to Garraway's, I insist that my coffee be made with sixty-eight beans; when I eat a beef steak, I demand that it has been on the grill for exactly four minutes. Your ice cream, signor, may be more complex in its constituents, but it is surely no more impervious to the laws of the physical world than motion or light.' It was because of this gentleman that I subsequently got into the habit or recording exactly what quantities and methods I had used to make my ices, thus enabling me to replicate each one without relying on my recollections.

Hooke, conversely, was more interested in devising a practical machine to make the process more efficient. Having watched me prepare the first batch, he announced that we would be here all winter if we were to proceed in this manner. Taking my paddle from me, he drilled half-a-dozen large holes in it, ignoring my protests that the implement in question had been specially made for me in Paris. 'Now try,' he said, indicating the *sabotiere*. I did so, and immediately found – of course! – that the mixture passed through the holes as it thickened, thus speeding the movement of the paddle, and working the ice cream more effectively.

Nor did he stop there. While Boyle, Wren and I performed the next batch of experiments, Hooke repaired to his workshop 'to run something up', as he put it. What he returned with was a lid for the *sabotiere* through which was inserted a simple crank. Turning the handle of the crank caused the paddle to sweep around the inside, making the labour easier.

'It will not be of much use to you,' he pointed out, 'since you make your ices in tiny quantities. But for us, having to make so many for these experiments, it will make the work quicker.'

When it became clear that he meant me to have the apparatus as a gift, I asked how I could ever repay him.

He shrugged. 'If anyone asks, say that Mr Hooke invented it. That is all that I, or anyone, could ask.'

What, then, was the result of all our deliberations? It turned out to be no secret formula, no magic ingredient or incantation, but simple exactitude and balance. We found that ice cream is like a triangle with three equal sides: the sides being the fruit, the sugar mixture or custard, and the stirring. When all three were in perfect proportion, you made an ice cream that was as smooth and creamy as freshly churned butter.

I recalled the words Hannah had spoken, about more sugar setting the custard. As it turned out, she had been right, although it must have been a lucky guess, since she could not have understood the process as I now did.

'We are done,' Boyle said at last, setting down his spoon. 'Gentlemen, to Garraway's. I have heard there is interesting news of a peace treaty in the Rhine.'

We went to Garraway's, where we were joined by a man who had invented a more efficient cider press, and another who drew pictures of the disturbances of the heavens. The talk then turned to alchemy, and whether there was a fundamental difference between it and the New Method. Hooke and Boyle differed on this point, Boyle, that fine and gentle man, being of the opinion that God had made nature deliberately mysterious, while Hooke – who despite his personal generosity to me, I could not help disliking, for he was a difficult and prickly individual – took the view that the universe was no more than a mechanism, a kind of giant watch whose cogs and purposes we were only now beginning to discover. But what intrigued me was that they engaged in the most furious debate, neither giving ground, for over half an hour; although each thumped the table, neither thumped each other, and five minutes after they had finally agreed that neither could prove their hypotheses, they were back to examining a strange dead beetle that someone had brought in from Epsom, once more the best of friends.

We made space for the serving girl to set down another round of drinks. Most of us were drinking coffee, but Boyle and I were having chocolate, for our health.

'Now there would be a fine fashionable flavour for your ices, Demirco,' Kit Wren said, turning to me. 'A plate of ice cream that tasted of coffee.'

'Indeed, it would be very easy to prepare,' I replied. 'The beans being excellent at infusion in water, they would surely do so just as easily in milk.'

'I should prefer mine to be chocolate,' Boyle said. 'Coffee disagrees with me even more readily than Hooke does.' He smiled at Hooke to show there had been no offence intended. I mention this exchange both to show how readily these gentlemen shared their ideas, and where the origins of two of my most curious recipes came from. The public, I am aware, think that those particular confections prove I am a little mad, and there was much joking and adverse comment when they became known; all I can say is that those who sneer at their strangeness have not tried them, and that as well as being fashionable they are remarkably good.

Soon it was time for them to repair to a meeting of their Society, and to my great pleasure they invited me to accompany them as their guest. I have to say that I could not understand much of what was discussed that night. There was a debate about whether an opaceous or foggy air was heavier than a clear one; Hooke passed around some beautiful drawings of snowflakes, which he had caught on the felt of his new hat and observed with his microscope; there was a letter read by Henshaw on the unravelling of a dormouse's testicle, and a lengthy discussion about why a door that does not stick in summer sometimes sticks in winter. Wren described a way to make a smoking chimney sweet, and they debated a paper on motion. Finally, they performed an experiment, devised by Hooke, to blow air into the lungs of a fish; to my surprise, the king himself was present for this part of the evening.

'Signor Demirco,' he said, catching sight of me. 'I was not aware that you were a philosopher.'

'Sir, some of the Fellows of your Society have been helping me to create a better ice cream.'

He raised his eyebrows. 'This is the dish for my feast, I take it? The one that is to be dedicated to Mademoiselle de Keroualle?'

I hesitated – and then nodded. 'Indeed, this will be a fitting dish to dedicate to that lady. For it is a dish, not just of one flavour, but which is capable of being many flavours, depending on what you choose to put in it. One day it might be strawberries, another peaches, and another nuts or posset or tea. Only the texture is always the same: cold and hard in the bowl, it melts on your tongue like the softest of creams—'

'An ice that is cold in the bowl, but yields in the mouth?' he said with a smile. 'Indeed, signor, it sounds very appropriate. I shall look forward to trying it.'

Later, as we left, I expressed surprise to Boyle at seeing the king in that company.

'Oh, he attends quite regularly,' Boyle assured me. He was accompanied now by his niece; she had come to meet him, she said, as on Society evenings he was liable to forget that he was infirm, and spend all night in philosophical debate unless she was there to fetch him home. 'Every day, no matter what affairs of state he has to deal with, His Majesty performs at least one experiment. He is an able chemist, as it happens.'

The freeness of the discourse emboldened me to say something further, that had been on my mind recently.

'I was told,' I said, 'before I came to this country, that Charles was a weak-willed and effeminate ruler. I have seen myself how he surrounds himself with drunken oafs and self-interested ministers. And yet he seems to me to be a charming, and indeed a clever, man.'

'Rochester has the liberty to be offensive, and Harvey has the liberty to dissect the human brain,' Boyle said. 'Perhaps they are much the same thing, at heart.' He looked thoughtful. 'I met Galileo once. I was a young man, studying my way around the universities of Europe, and he was under house arrest in Florence. I went to see him, but by then he had lost his mind, thanks in no small part to the way he had been treated by the authorities. England has many faults, but that, at least, could not happen here. I don't think it can be a coincidence that we now have among us scholars such as Halley, Harvey and their ilk.'

'Not to mention Boyle,' his niece murmured.

He made an impatient gesture. 'I might have done some useful work, were it not for my infirmity.'

'You are too modest, uncle. Your vacuum pump—'

'A start, nothing more.'

We had reached his carriage now, and the footman came round to help him up. 'Thank you, Edwards,' he said, settling himself with a sigh. 'I was not always so frail,' he added to me. 'An apoplectic seizure. What they like to call a stroke of God's hand. Although I had always imagined that His caress might be rather more gentle than this was. Would you like those pamphlets?'

It took me a moment to recall what pamphlets he was talking about: earlier he had offered me a copy of his own publications concerning cold. 'Indeed.'

'Good – I will send them. And when you have read them, perhaps we could resume our conversations.'

'I should like that very much,' I said. 'There are many things I would like to understand better about what I do. It may take someone like yourself, I think – a natural philosopher – to unpick them.'

He nodded. 'In my present condition, it is just the sort of investigation I should undertake. We will leave the secrets of the cosmos to others for a few months, perhaps, and eat ice creams. What do you say, Elizabeth?'

Elizabeth was placing a blanket over his legs. 'I do not think it sounds so very trifling, to be sloshing about in ice-cold water.'

She stepped back, and I noticed that she smiled in a familiar way at the footman, Edwards. To my surprise, he smiled back, equally familiar. It was clear to me that there was some kind of romantic intimacy between them, something that on another occasion would have shocked me. But I had heard, and seen, so many strange things that night that I simply found myself thinking, 'Why not?'

After Boyle had driven off I walked back towards the river, deep in thought – not least about what he had said. For it was certainly true that there was something the people in this country all had in common, from the Honourable Robert Boyle right down to Hannah Crowe. It was not pride exactly, although it was something they were proud of; it was not stubbornness, although they were certainly capable of being stubborn about it if they chose. Rather, it was a fierce regard for getting to the truth of a matter; a love of disputation, and a refusal to accept another person's point of view without first robustly testing it against your own, just as a coin might be bitten, bent, and finally flung to the ground to test its mettle, before being accepted with a grudging 'Very well.' For such a quarrelsome and libertarian people, perhaps government by debate was not such a bad idea after all.

I had noticed, when I began to read books and newspapers in English, that whenever they wrote the word denoting the person giving his opinion – 'I' – they habitually used a capital letter, as if to stress its importance. This, of course, was not something that a Frenchman or an Italian would ever do with *je* or *me*. At first this had struck me as just another example, almost an amusing one, of the presumption of the common people here, who each considered their own opinion as good as anyone else's.

There was a fashion amongst them, I had been told, for writing diaries: not necessarily for publication, but simply to give their fleeting thoughts a lasting form. That, too, had struck me as comical. But perhaps I had been too quick to draw these conclusions. Perhaps an ordinary person's opinion really could be of as much interest as the judgements of great men: perhaps, indeed, the only difference between great men and others was that great men took the trouble to form those opinions in the first place . . . I realised that my head was buzzing, but whether it was from the effects of so much coffee, or so many new ideas, I could not have said.

Carlo

White strawberry ice cream: the delicate flavour of these
fruits needs no adornment, save perhaps for a dusting of
white pepper.

The Book of Ices

Charles's great banquet, the beginning of his summer of festivities, was to be held on the feast day of St George, England's patron saint. The irony of this, of course, was not lost on those who knew who the king's patron really was, or which country was actually paying for his celebrations.

Almost a month before the feast, I moved out to Windsor to supervise the arrangements. The new Great Hall was still being worked on by the builders, while carpenters were making the last of the tables at which the king's guests would be seated. The yeomen of the pantry were also at work, unwrapping thousands of pieces of tableware that had not been used since the coronation. The candelabra alone would take a team of eight two weeks to clean.

There were no ice houses, but I requisitioned a cellar, and had ice brought directly from the caves where I had stored it. First I began the work of carving the ice sculptures, and set workmen to preparing the great beds of crushed ice on which the cold food would be served.

But as to exactly what ice cream I would serve to the king's table, I still had not decided.

In the weeks since the *virtuosi* and I had perfected the technique of making a perfectly smooth ice, I had experimented with every flavour under the sun. As soon as a new fruit or vegetable

289

became available in the markets, I froze it. Asparagus, Jerusalem artichokes, celeriac, even cabbages . . . Radishes turned out to be surprisingly good, and over-wintered spinach; sorrel had its merits, too. I went down to the docks and bought strange fruits off the boats that returned from the Colonies. I made ice creams of peppers, of melons, of mangos, and fruits so ugly they did not even have a name.

They were none of them right. Not for a dish made in her honour.

I toured the orangeries and pineries of the great nobles' estates, a letter of *carte blanche* from the king in my pocket. More than one pineapple was pulled from its tree, sliced open, sniffed at, and discarded.

Elias said, 'There is a man at Sonning who has grown some white strawberries, they say. They are as big as gulls' eggs, and perfectly sweet.'

'I hardly think that is likely.'

'He is a sailor. He brought the plants back from America.'

I did not believe it, but I rode out to Sonning anyway to see for myself. And found that Elias was right: there was an old sailor, his boots covered in mud, who grew strawberry plants in a raised bed warmed by vents from a fire. As he fondled the berries in his calloused hands he muttered to each plant, stroking it and apologising for the loss of its children. He was quite mad, but his strawberries were remarkable. The fruits were completely without colour: I thought at first they must be unripe, but then he gave me one to try, and I realised it was not just sweet but completely different from the normal kind of berry – as white as cream, heavily fragrant, and with none of the tart sharpness that most strawberries have. Each one nestled under a leaf that was covered in fine prickles, like a gooseberry or a nettle: they stung a little when you handled them.

I recalled that there was an old custom that any white beast or albino belonged to the king. The white hart or stag was the ancient symbol of kings; swans were reserved for the royal table, while a coach pulled by white horses was a sign that the occupant was connected to the royal family.

Louise, too: that white, white skin, reserved for the king alone.

I took all the strawberries the man had, and divided them in two. One half I would serve plain; the other I would make into ice cream, with a little white pepper, for the king's pleasure alone.

The day of the feast arrived – or rather, the first day, as the celebrations were to last the better part of a week. Flags fluttered from every point and turret of the castle; fanfares were blown, and everywhere you looked soldiers paraded in ceremonial display. There were exhibitions of horsemanship to entertain the guests, and a mechanical statue that sang. It was not Versailles – the castle was too much of a castle to be completely elegant, and the atmosphere was altogether more like a rural fair than the formal, choreographed ceremonies of France – but there was no mistaking the majesty of the occasion. The frescos on the ceiling of the Great Hall might not be dry, but it was vast, and it was painted, and as the thousand noble guests walked through the carved doors you could see them looking up and wondering at it.

And then Louise made her entrance.

The gown she wore that day was remarkable. It fitted her like a glove, and indeed her waist was so slender that a pair of gloved hands could almost have encircled it. The cloth was sown with a delicate pattern of diamond shapes; the skirt and bodice were separate, in the new French style; the skirt itself had a split at the side, so that as she walked one slender leg could be glimpsed amongst the folds of drapery, which was swept up to one side and pinned with a brooch. Only her hair – that unruly thicket of dark curls – was not French in the least: it was not pinned up under a hat, but simply parted in the middle. It was as if she were saying: *From now on I will be the arbiter here. I will copy what I want, and you will copy me.*

The king bowed and led her to his table, which was separate from the others on a little raised dais. The queen was nowhere to be seen.

Shortly before I was due to serve the ice cream, one of the stewards came over. 'This is to go into the ice,' he said. 'At the king's command.' He opened a small velvet pouch, and shook something out of it into my palm.

It was written on the menu that stood by each guest: *For the king's pleasure alone: one plate of white strawberries and one plate of ice cream.*

But it is not written how it happened: the blast of trumpets, the shout of the heralds, a sudden hush: all eyes on me as I walked, at the head of a solemn procession of servants, towards the figures at the topmost table.

My eyes made contact with hers, I believe, as I bowed low over the damask. But with that lazy eye, it was hard to be sure.

I stepped back. The king reached into the platter of crushed ice on which the bowl of strawberries rested and pulled out the end of a fine chain. He pulled again, and this time it swung free; laden, pendulous, heavy with flashing nuggets of what looked like ice: ice that suddenly caught flame in the glow of the candles.

A necklace of white diamonds, the stones as big as strawberries, dripping in his fingers as he lifted it from its icy womb.

Only now did I notice that her neck had been left bare in preparation for this moment. As he fastened it there, whispering something only she could hear, I could imagine the goose-skin on her shoulders and collarbone from the jewels' cold; the soft, almost velvet texture her skin would have beneath his hands.

She looked at him, adoring yet bashful, and then she turned to smile at the whole room: an innocent delighted, the happiest girl in the world. Instinctively, they applauded her, many of them rising to their feet as they did so; and if there were a few, like Rochester and Buckingham, whose claps were just a little slower, a little more cynical, it was swallowed up in the general buzz of approval.

For the king's pleasure alone.

And even I – courtier, confectioner, accomplice to my own heartbreak – even I put my hands together, and called a cheer I did not feel.

PART FOUR

'It was universally reported that the fair lady was bedded one of these nights, and the stocking flung after the manner of a married bride; I acknowledge that she was for the most part in her undress all day, and that there was fondness and toying with that young wanton; nay, it was said that I was at the former ceremony; but it is utterly false.'

Diary of Sir John Evelyn, September, 1671

Louise

It is done. I lie in the royal bed, wet with the king's seed. Anointed by the Lord's anointed. My thighs bloody, streaked. My maidenhead mingled with the fluxions of his desire.

The blood of Louise, spilled so that Louis might have Dutch blood spilled in the Netherlands.

In a daze, in a bed, words spilling around my head. I am a burning fortress, a ransacked village, scorched earth.

'Please, do not cry, my love,' he croons. 'My love, my dearest love.'

Please Louise.

I am done, dishonoured, fallen. I am Eve, Magdalene, the Whore of Babylon, the wanton *Lady lately come from France* the pamphleteers have always said I was. My precious honour plundered, stained along with the bedsheets. I am, quite literally, shattered.

But mostly what I think is—

Really?

All that fuss, for this? Are you sure?

Oh, of course it hurt. I was expecting it to hurt. But the first time it was over so fast that I scarcely had time to tell myself that it was not as bad as I had been expecting.

But perhaps that is the nature of his famous skill as a lover? Is it like being a surgeon – if you can saw an arm off in under a minute, patients will beat a path to your door?

I lie here, unable to move, all my limbs sawn off, scattered around the room where he has thrown them. Charles the surgeon, wiping the sweat from his forehead with the back of his hand.

Yes, he does take his wig off. Underneath, his stubble is turning grey. No, he does not kick out the lapdogs. Thank God the three he has brought to Newmarket were too small to jump up into the bed. All night I heard them snuffling beyond the curtains.

Charles the surgeon was a lot slower with the second operation than the first. Perhaps he tires. His fingers on me, cold with seed, working between my legs. Why is he doing that, inside? Does it somehow prepare the way?

Sawing, sawing, sawing away.

I think of Aretino, all those pictures I studied so carefully in preparation for this night, trying to understand what would happen. I even made notes. But there is no chance whatsoever of me doing anything of that nature now. Nor, thankfully, does he seem to expect it. It is all I can do to lie here without sounding winded, much less squat or kneel or any of those other contortions.

'My love, my love,' he says, flopping into me again. And again. Squashing me. I think with sudden envy of the mechanism of a clock, cool and mechanical and clean.

With a groan he anoints me a second time. A sudden shuddering in his legs. The first time I thought it was some kind of fit, that I had killed the king. This time it is less alarming. But hardly less unpleasant.

Seven hundred years of loyal service to France. For this.

His thumb touches my cheek, stroking me.

'They are tears of joy,' I whisper.

Satisfied, he sags over me, a dead weight. I feel his heart thudding against my breasts. Every bit of him is as hard and unyielding and solid as a statue. Except for the wet softness now where we are joined. Where the statue melts inside me.

The third time, dawn is breaking. I wake with him kneeling over me, his yard looming into my line of sight, thick and terrifying. The hair on his broad shoulders and belly is as dark as an ape's.

I turn my head to the side and he plants a kiss on my cheek, slowly and deliberately, as he enters me.

298

Like a flag. I am his territory now. Conquered.

This time the sawing is slow and sonorous.

Afterwards he says, 'How was it?'

He might be asking my opinion of a play.

I consider. 'Not quite what I expected.'

'Oh? In what way?'

'It was more like horse riding or tennis than poetry or music.'

A frown crosses his face, and I remember where I am. Who I am with. Why. 'That is to say, it was wonderful. I was the happiest girl in the world; now I am the happiest woman.'

Mollified, he pulls back the bed curtain on his side. Instantly there are two valets there, one holding water, the other a cloth.

The one holding the bowl, the younger, stares straight ahead. Then, as if he cannot help it, his eyes flick down to where I lie, my breasts damp with the king's sweat. Yesterday, I might have had him whipped for his temerity. Today, I am a fallen woman. Let him look.

Charles gets to his feet. I watch as the royal cock is sponged, the royal undergarments held out for him to step into. By now there is a quite a crowd around him, spraying and snipping and primping until, at last, it is no longer the man who stands there but the monarch, tugging at the lace cuffs of his frock coat.

Finally, the wig.

He takes a step forward, towards the door, which opens as if by magic.

Music. Applause.

On my side of the bed, the curtain is also pulled back. Two maids stand there, eyes downcast, waiting to do the same for me. I hear a buzz of conversation from the other room. A shout: 'To Newmarket, Your Majesty? Or have you had enough riding for one day?' The laughter erupts, male and hearty. It spurts into the room, thick and wet. There is a chant, singing, a dozen gruff voices roaring the refrain.

'With a heigh-de-de-ho, old Rowley!'

I swing my own legs to the floor, stiff and a little sore. Lady Arlington is standing there, waiting.

'There is work to be done,' she says simply.

I am to stay in my *déshabillé* all morning, as a sign that I am wedded. My hair is brushed out, but not too much. A portrait has been commissioned of the two of us, a gift from the ambassador – or rather two portraits: the proprieties must be observed. I will reach out with my right hand, Charles with his left, across the divide: we are not quite handclasped, but when the paintings are hung together, the symbolism will be clear. The painter will have little luck making the king sit today, though. An hour at the most, and then he will be off to the races.

Lord Arlington appears at my side. 'All well?' he says quietly.

'All well.'

'Ask him this morning. Before he does any other business.'

'As you wish.'

I walk up to Charles. He turns to face me with a smile, the courtiers beside him melting into the background.

'Lord Arlington wishes me to ask a favour.'

He raises his eyebrows.

'The timing is also at his request.'

Charles nods, noting that I have understood – as Arlington has not – that this lack of subtlety is ill suited to the mood of the occasion.

'He wishes to be Lord Chancellor.'

Charles looks genuinely shocked at the size of Arlington's demand. Then he says thoughtfully, 'You pass on the request, Louise, without petitioning me to grant it.'

I shrug.

'Arlington is a fool,' he says quietly. 'He should have had you ask me yesterday. Yesterday I would have given you anything you wanted.'

'I know,' I say. 'That is why I did not ask you yesterday.'

Charles's chuckle makes some of the courtiers look up. 'You would not have me appoint a fool to the highest office in the land?'

'I would not.'

'He is my oldest friend.'

'And he has built your kingdom's newest palace on the strength of it,' I say, glancing pointedly at our surroundings.

'If not him, then, who?'

'For chancellor? Shaftesbury.'

'Shaftesbury!'

'If a Parliamentarian finds that even he cannot balance the books, Parliament will have no choice but to vote more funds. And it will be hard for Shaftesbury to oppose the war if you have put him in charge of it.' Also, his appointment will annoy Lord Arlington more than anyone else I can think of.

He nods. 'And I suppose you were thinking about this even while we were in bed?'

'Of course not,' I lie. 'I was far too busy thinking about you, my dearest love.'

'Well, I will attend to it. Now?'

I smile across the room, to where the Arlingtons are pretending to talk to each other. 'Oh, I think we can keep Lord Arlington in suspense a little longer, don't you? Today I want to go the races and meet this stallion I have heard so much about. After all, I have already become well acquainted with his namesake.'

Carlo

Raspberry ice cream: make a quart of custard; when cold,
pour it on a quart of ripe red raspberries, mash them in it,
pass through a sieve, simmer and freeze. But do not over-
sweeten them: the taste of raspberries is all the better for
being a little sharp.

The Book of Ices

She held out until September – a full year after she first arrived in
England. I have heard it said that she always meant to be seduced;
that her scruples were just play-acting, her coyness a stratagem.
That does not account, surely, for the fact that it took the most
determined men in Europe twelve months to get her into his bed.

I hardened my heart, and tried not to think what the two of
them did there.

The political consequences, however, were immediate. A pretext was found for war: the little royal yacht passed by the Dutch
fleet and was not saluted with all with the solemnities due to a
great warship. The Dutch apologised for their oversight, but the
English announced hostilities nevertheless. The government
called a halt to its debt repayments so that money could be
diverted to the war. And Charles personally drafted a bill he called
the Declaration of Indulgence. All men and women were from
now on to be free in their hearts. Free to worship as they pleased,
free to think as they pleased, free to say what they pleased.

You would have thought he had announced that henceforth all
English babies would be put to the sword and all English virgins
raped. The country erupted. The apprentices rioted, and burnt
down the brothels. The prostitutes marched, and burnt down the

302

shops. Shopkeepers boarded up their shops; bakers could not sell their bread; priests denounced their own king's libertinism from their pulpits. It was said that the army was on the verge of rising; though for who, or what, was never very clear.

'But this, surely, is exactly what you wanted,' I said to Hannah in exasperation. 'You are always talking about the rights of Englishmen. Now Charles has turned them into law.'

'Don't you see – that is the whole problem. We have those rights because we are born with them. It is not in Charles's power to indulge them or take them away.' She sighed. 'Besides, everyone knows this Declaration is suspect not because of what it says, but what it does not say.'

'Meaning?'

'It's Catholics, not dissenters, whom the king actually means these freedoms to benefit. Then, when England is Catholic again, the Inquisition will return and torture the dissenters.'

I began to see people in the streets wearing green ribbons on their lapels. It was a sign, Cassell explained, that they were for Shaftesbury and the Parliamentarians.

'They're little better than Whigs, some of them,' he said with a sniff.

'Whigs?'

'Gypsies. Tinkers.' But he looked worried. 'The situation is more serious than I have known it since the Restoration,' he admitted. 'With most of the army away to France, there is little to prevent an uprising at home. If that happens, Parliament will almost certainly side with the insurrection.'

'What is the answer?'

'I suspect the king will have to withdraw the Declaration. The question is, what else will Parliament demand? Once they have the upper hand, why should they stop at repealing just one unpopular law?' He gave me a sideways look. 'You must take precautions for your own safety, signor. I suspect that any Catholic could easily fall victim to the mob just now.'

Indeed, I had already done so. The roads around Whitehall were often blocked by disaffected crowds; hardly a day went by when I did not hear a stone hitting the woodwork of my carriage, and on more than one occasion I had to turn back altogether. I hired two burly servants to ride on the outside, but they were more for show than for safety. I knew that in a real confrontation they would be unlikely to save my life at the expense of their own.

You would have thought, therefore, that the atmosphere at court would be tense. But in fact the reverse was true. It was as if the Declaration had ushered in a new mood of pleasure and ease. Now that he finally had Louise, Charles was carefree; and just as she had succumbed to him, so the court now succumbed to her. Every lady of quality wore their hair *au naturel*, parted in the middle; every dress was remade so that it was slit open at the side. More Frenchmen appeared in London. Le Nôtre came over from Versailles to remodel St James's Park, and shuddered at the Dutch-style canal. A tailor called Sourceau arrived to dress the king, Monsieur de Pontac had charge of his wines, while Louise's dresses were made by a milliner called Desborde. I even heard some of the younger ladies-in-waiting speaking with an affected drawl, as if – like Louise – English was not their native tongue. She was not liked by them; indeed, I believe that she was hated and resented in equal measure, but she had the king's favour, and that was all that mattered.

And I was there. I moved amongst them, dispensing my cordials and my *granite*, almost as if I were back at Versailles. I was there at the balls, at the card parties, at the collations and the private performances and the masquerades. I was there – God help me – when the king and his new mistress cavorted: I was even there in her apartments when they lay together.

For the king was a physical man: exertion made him hot, and when he was hot he liked to call for refreshment. Every day I made the lovers cool cordials of elderberry, lavender, borage or gillyflower. I made them sweet infusions of mint-and-ginger, poured over crushed handfuls of ice. I made them ice creams of lemon and apricot, of quince and apple, of blackberry and vanilla and fig. I made them goblets of lemonade freshly squeezed, sweetened with dandelion honey and chilled with pressed snow. I carried my ices on silver platters into her bedchamber, with its carved French bed; behind the drawn curtains, into the bed itself, onto those tumbled sheets. I smelt him on her; I smelt her on him; I served them both, with an inscrutable smile, and she thanked me with a smile that was just as oblique.

Only once in those first weeks did I manage to talk to her alone. He had been called away – he refused, mostly, to listen to his ministers' pleas for his attention to state matters, but if they were persistent enough he would go with ill humour to hurry through a pile of papers or join a council session, although he rarely stayed to the end. On this occasion he left her bed just as I arrived, snatching up a glass of iced peach juice from my tray and calling to her over his shoulder, 'I'll be back – stay there,' barely bothering to button his clothes for his ministers.

For a moment we neither of us spoke.

'So,' I said at last. 'Is it what you expected?'

'This?' She shrugged. 'This would have been my duty in any case, whether I did it as a wife or a mistress. At least I do it now with someone for whom *I* am not just a duty. It makes it easier to pretend.'

'Pretend? So that is all you do?'

I should not have asked – it was like touching a wound: you cannot help it, although you know no good can come of it.

'Sometimes it is,' she said softly, 'and sometimes it isn't.'

'But do you love him now?'

'I do not think of it as love, or pleasure,' she said. 'I only know that now I am in a position to achieve what I came here to do. Is that love? Is that pleasure? Whatever it is, I am grateful to him for that.'

*

305

My own position at court, of course, had once again risen along with hers. There was nothing more French than ice; and nothing was therefore now more fashionable. Since Newmarket, my services had become as indispensable to a grand gathering as the presence of Louise de Keroualle herself.

And yet there was one dish I never provided. Cordials, *granite*, sorbets and even milk ices I would serve; but unless the king was present, there would be no ice cream. Ice cream, as created by myself and the *virtuosi*, was the royal dish; unless the king himself offered it to a guest, no one else could eat it.

There were many who tried. I lost count of the number of times I was asked to prepare some 'as a curiosity'; my response was always to frown and say, 'I am afraid that will not be possible.' Some, of course, could not be shamed in this way. Lord Rochester strode into the Red Lion one morning and threw a purse onto the counter of the pantry where I was working.

'I want to try the raspberry ice cream the king enjoyed last night.'

'I am afraid that will not be possible.'

'He said it was the finest thing he had ever tasted.'

'Indeed.'

He gestured impatiently at the purse. 'There are twenty *pistoles* in there. Take as many as you wish.'

I picked up the purse and handed it back to him. 'I have already done so.'

He stared at me. His eyes, I might add, were like the eyes of a lizard, utterly bereft of humanity, and even at that hour he stank of wine. 'Do you defy me, Signor Dildo?' he whispered.

I stared back, quite calm. 'I think perhaps that you defy the king.'

After a moment he nodded. 'You think that because your French friend has the king's ear, people like you are protected from people like me. And in a way, that is true. But remember this: she has the king's ear because she has the king's cock. When the cock tires, the other organ may too. And what will become of poor Signor Dildo then?'

Others were more circumspect. I saw Chiffinch, the steward, lift a bowl in order to pass it to the king: there were some elaborate flourishes, the getting of napkins and so on, and by the time it was presented, moments later, the bowl contained significantly less ice cream than it had done before, although Chiffinch's face was as inscrutable as ever.

The infamous Barbara Villiers, Duchess of Cleveland, Charles's former mistress, ordered me to her house – or rather, her palace, for Charles had given her Nonsuch, one of the finest of the royal residences, as a pay-off for her services. Ostensibly our meeting was to discuss the cordials I could provide for a ball; it soon became clear that she actually wanted ice cream, and that in return she intended to provide me with the same favours the king had once enjoyed. When I made it plain that I was not to be so easily bought, she flew into a rage – I have never seen such fury; she was like a woman possessed, hurling any object that came to hand at me, her beautiful face contorted with anger.

It was this – the fact that only Charles and Louise ate my ice creams – that gave me an idea I should probably not have entertained.

I was working in my pantry during the late part of the afternoon, when no one else was about. I glanced into Hannah's alcove next door, and observed that it was deserted.

I hesitated, then slipped inside and went to the shelf where she kept her books. I ran my fingers along the spines. *The Cook's Guide: Or, Rare Receipts for Cookery . . . Physick, Beautifying and Cookery . . . Excellent & Approved Receipts . . .*

The Compleat Herbal, by Nicholas Culpeper.

I drew it out, and began to turn the pages.

'What are you doing?'

It was Hannah, entering the room behind me.

'I mean no harm,' I assured her. 'I am simply looking for some information.'

'Then you had better tell me what you need. I know that book from cover to cover, and it is not one that should be left out.'

'The physick I need is not for me. It is for . . .' I hesitated. 'For one of my noble patrons. He wishes to avoid the passions of love.'

'To *avoid* them?'

I nodded. 'Most definitely. He is a busy man, with many important calls upon his time. He wishes not to be troubled by thoughts of a libertine nature.'

'Well, that is certainly unusual,' she said. 'Since most people ask if there is a herb which can do exactly the reverse. But yes, as it happens there are several infusions which have the effect you require.'

'That my patron requires,' I corrected.

She made an impatient gesture, as to say it was all the same to her. 'I take it we are talking about the desire, rather than the performance?'

'Both, if possible.'

'Well, let me see,' she said, taking the book from me and rifling through the pages. 'Yes . . . Chamomile is good for this, and, and elderflower when the moon is full. But the most effective treatment would be feap-berries.'

'"Feap-berries?"'

She nodded and read aloud, '*Sometimes called gooseberries, these berries subdue the passions, particularly the passions of Venus whose dominion they are under. An infusion of the leaves will further cool the blood, and calm all forms of choler and immoderation.*'

'Do you have some?'

'I can get you some preserved, in jars. But if you are going to use them for ice cream, you had better let me show you how to make a gooseberry fool. It is all too easy to try to mask the berries' sharpness with too much sugar, and if you do that the ice cream will never freeze.'

Again I wondered at the knowledge she seemed to have of such matters, and caution made me hesitate. With the merest hint of impatience she said, 'Do you really still think I am going to steal your secrets? In any case, showing you how to make a gooseberry fool is surely the other way around.'

After a moment I nodded. 'Thank you.'

And so she showed me the method of making this simple English dish: boiling the fruits in water, along with a couple of elderflower heads; then crushing, sieving and sweetening, and finally mixing the puree with custard and a little grated nutmeg. It was so easy, and so perfect for ice cream, that I marvelled my fellow confectioners in Europe had not yet discovered it.

As if guessing my thoughts she said, 'Perhaps one day anyone will be able to freeze a mixture such as this.'

'And destroy my livelihood, you mean?'

'Are cooks paid for their secrets, or their skill? There is no secret to making pies, and yet mine are more sought after than any others in Vauxhall.' It was said matter-of-factly; without false pride, but not meekly either.

I grunted. 'Perhaps that is why there is no pie maker with the royal warrant.'

She shrugged. 'Perhaps. Anyway, I will leave you. It is time I was about my other work. And I hope,' she hesitated, 'I hope that your friend finds some relief from his longings. If the gooseberries do not work, will you let me know? There are various other remedies he could try.'

I made my gooseberry ice creams, and sent them to the king. When I asked Louise a week later if his ardour was any lessened, she looked at me in a strange way and asked why I wanted to know. I tried to imply that I was simply concerned as to whether her obligations were still as onerous as before.

'Well, he is a little slower than he was,' she said. 'It is better,

309

actually. Sometimes now he is actually concerned for my pleasure.'

That was an outcome I had not anticipated, and after that I sent no more gooseberries to the king.

Louise

He needs to be handled, and this I am learning to do. Business bores him – the process of government, the careful alignment of interests, building consensus. He is a man for bold strokes, sudden decisions. In that respect, we complement each other.

Problems he loathes. The finding of answers he leaves to others – that is, to me. *Louise, why couldn't anyone else have thought of that?* To which the honest answer, if I were foolish enough to give it, would be: *Because you did not give them a chance.*

And then, if the problem was a large one, there will be some gift: a necklace, say, or a piece of silver. I have employed a steward, Hawton, to sell them off discreetly.

My own expenses are enormous. For the king, I have realised, does not want me only as a mistress. Nor am I quite a queen. Rather, I am to be a kind of princess, as Minette was – spendthrift, cultured, delightful, my rooms always full of art and amusement and good French food. He positively encourages me to order Gobelins tapestries, glass goblets, Parisian silks, perfumes from Grasse and wines from Champagne.

My apartments are the court he always dreamed of. When he is with me he is the king he always wanted to be – that is to say, not Charles of England, but Louis of France, all-powerful in his kingdom. He is no longer king by condition and the consent of Parliament: he is Carolus Rex, absolute and arbitrary, England's emperor.

This is the final masquerade: to be able to pretend that things are not as they are. It explains, I think, his love of the theatre: he is a kind of actor himself, and as his fellow players our task is simply to keep the play in progress. The king does not want his illusions disturbed by unseemly reality.

*

And yet he is kind when I am discomfited by others. At a ball I find myself standing near to two women about my own age. One of them is Lady Sedburgh; another, Caroline de Vere. They are clever, at ease with court ways but not in thrall to them, speak four languages, play music, dance and write. In short, they are just the sort of women with whom I might have hoped to be friends.

As I take a step towards them they turn away, pretending to be deep in conversation. I check, and make it look as if I am simply strolling past.

And think: once I would have done the same as them.

Charles asks me why I am distracted. Foolishly, I tell him: immediately he has the two of them summoned to his presence.

'I have decided that you are to join Madam Carwell's train,' he tells them peremptorily. 'From now on you will be among her ladies-in-waiting.'

I see the disdain on their faces and think: *This is not the way.* I smile approvingly, but my heart is sinking.

'Do you have any objections?' he thunders.

Meekly, they shake their heads.

'Those I lie with are fit company for the greatest ladies in the land,' he says crossly. 'You may go.'

As a result, of course, I am hated even more. It does not help that Arlington is openly calling me an ungrateful bitch. Ungrateful! Lady Arlington walks around court in a diamond necklace reportedly worth six thousand pounds. When I admire it she says simply, 'Oh, it was a present from your king, for getting you into Charles's bed.'

I smile back just as sweetly and say, 'Then I must give you a present too, Elizabeth, for I cannot imagine being any happier than this.' I will not give her anything, of course. A diamond necklace is more than enough recompense for being a bawd.

And then, in short order, everything changes again.

Carlo

Burnt ice cream: melt your sugar in a pan over the fire until it scorches: meanwhile, prepare a mix of six eggs, one gill of syrup and one pint of cream: stir all together, pass through a sieve, and freeze.

The Book of Ices

'Pregnant? Are you sure?'

She nodded miserably. 'I have been sick twice today already.'

'Will this alter things?'

'For me? I don't know. The ambassador certainly thinks it is good news.'

'But you're not so certain?'

She shrugged. 'Charles has had bastards before: there seem to be dozens of his children running around the place. I suspect it may mean that my position will be established, and therefore make it more difficult to change.'

I saw what she meant. 'You still hope he might make you his queen.'

'If Catherine dies, yes. Why not? It is my only way out of this now – the only way my position can become an honourable one. But somehow I think even the English might have a problem with a fat, pregnant Frenchwoman waddling up the aisle to claim their king.'

'What does Charles say about the baby?'

'Oh, he's delighted. More, I think, because it proves his continued potency than because he really wants another child.' She hesitated. 'There's something else. As I soon as I told him, his interest in me lessened.'

313

'You think he has somehow been put off?'

She shook her head. 'He still visits me – but to sit with me, or walk, or listen to conversation. You would not think anything different from his manner – he is still as attentive as ever – but when we lie together, it is only the once now that he covers me.' I noted the matter-of-fact way she spoke: there were no blushes these days; her copulations were matters of politics and strategy, to be analysed in the same way as any other court matter. 'It is almost as if, having got me with child, he feels he has done his duty, just like any husband getting an heir on his wife.'

'Perhaps that is the case. And it is only normal for a man's desire to wane after the honeymoon.' Perhaps, I thought, Culpeper's gooseberries had had some effect too, after all. 'After all, he will need to forego you completely once your belly is bigger. After a period of enforced abstinence, he will return to you with even more vigour.'

'If abstinence is truly what he is experiencing,' she said dryly.

'You think he has other women?'

'I am sure he does,' she said quietly. 'And I can hardly mind, if it reduces his demands on me. But this is different. It is not merely Will Chiffinch showing some servant girl up the backstairs. He dines away from me.'

'With the queen?'

She shook her head. 'When he goes to her he does it publicly, so that it can be noted. I fear that Arlington has found someone with whom he intends to supplant me.'

Cassell was even more direct. 'The king tires of her,' he said bluntly. 'I would not be surprised if he sends her back to France, to have her bastard there.'

'So who does he favour instead?'

'The word is that he has gone back to the actress.'

'The actress! Why her?'

314

'He always goes back to her in the end. She amuses him. His Majesty is not made for constancy.'

'Then he may yet come back to Louise.'

'It is possible, I suppose. Do not let them squabble over him, though. The king likes nothing better than ease, and we have had squabbling women before.'

'Louise will not stoop to fighting. Least of all with a play-actress.'

'Oh, she will certainly have to fight,' Cassell said. 'I just meant that she must do it quietly. The actress has seen off rivals before, and your Madam Carwell would do well not to underestimate her.'

Louise

In St James's Park I walk up to a knot of courtiers, thinking the king is amongst them, but instead I find the actress marching up and down with her nose in the air, talking gobbledegook in a French accent and calling herself 'Madam Squintabella'. Some of them manage to stop laughing when I approach, but the actress turns to me without breaking a stride.

'Oui? Bonjoo?' she enquires. More laughter. I notice that she is holding her head off to one side, one eye half-closed, as if squinting through a telescope. Mocking my lazy eye.

'I was looking for the king,' I say calmly. 'But I see he is not here. I will seek him elsewhere.'

'Oh, His Majesty is quite well,' she says, reverting to her normal voice. 'In fact, I never knew him on better form than he was with me last night.'

'Thank you,' I say icily. As I leave the group I hear them applauding her performance. 'Merci, merci,' she thanks them, curtseying prettily. 'But Madam Squintabella prefer jewels to applause.'

It seems astonishing that she is allowed at court, given how coarse she is. But he has installed her in a house at the back of St James's, with a gate connecting her garden to the park.

I remember those ladies-in-waiting. Was Charles's rebuke to them also a coded warning to me? *Those I lie with are fit company for the highest in the land.* Must I expect not only to have to share his favour, but to have the fact of it thrown in my face?

There is only one course of action open to me: ignore her, and hope that this will pass when my pregnancy is over.

It is another of the ways in which I must behave like a queen, it seems.

Meanwhile there is Jemmy Monmouth, the king's first bastard, to deal with – back from his all-too-brief exile, and eager to make trouble.

He comes to the king while I am with him, and abruptly asks if they might speak alone.

'Jemmy,' Charles protests, 'I have no secrets from Louise.'

'Nevertheless, I will leave you,' I say graciously. And, to rub it in a little, added, 'Perhaps, though, I will see you again in a little while, Charles?'

'A very little while, I hope.'

Monmouth's furious gaze follows me out of the room.

Of course, Charles tells me afterwards what he wanted. Now that the army is fighting, Monmouth wants to be given command of it.

'I tried to dissuade him,' Charles says. 'But like all young men, he wishes to prove himself in the dangers of battle.'

More likely, I think, he wishes to prove that he is worthy of the Crown. Aloud I say, 'I suppose from his point of view it is only fair. After all, your brother has command of the navy. Why should your son not have the army?'

Charles's face darkens. 'It is very different. My brother is the legitimate son of a king, and my heir.'

'You think it might give the wrong impression if Jemmy were to command the army?' I say thoughtfully. 'Yes, that had not occurred to me.'

'It had not occurred to me either, until you and I began to talk it through. I am clear now – he should not go.'

This is good – but it could be better. 'Perhaps there is a middle way,' I suggest. 'Let him go to Holland and fight, but only in an honorary capacity. Then he can prove his courage, without you suggesting that he is anything more than one of your loyal subjects. It

317

would be a kindness, I think, to let him redeem himself for those terrible things he did last year.'

'You are very good to him, Louise.'

'If I am good to him, it is only because I know how much he matters to you,' I say with a smile.

The dangers of battle. I like the sound of that: a most satisfactory place for the king's eldest bastard to be.

Buckingham, too, is angling for the position.

'I am inclined to give it to him,' Charles muses. 'Even though it will put Jemmy's nose out of joint.'

I have not forgotten Buckingham's insult to me in Dieppe. *You've been sent to ensnare him.* As it happens, he was right, but the man's casual assumption that he could tumble me into his own bed still rankles.

'Buckingham? Is he reliable?'

'George is reckless, certainly, and somewhat vainglorious, but these are qualities which are useful in a soldier. No, I think he should have it.'

He speaks as if the decision is already taken. I think quickly.

'He's a Protestant, isn't he?'

'Yes.' Charles shrugs. 'As am I myself.'

'For the time being,' I point out. 'But a Protestant leading the army against the Dutch . . . will Louis think it a sign that you intend to delay your own conversion?'

'That is not my intention.' Charles looks uneasy. He is always vague on the subject of exactly when he will convert. He has already written to Louis suggesting that he wishes first to discuss certain matters that may arise from it with the Pope: sadly, the Pope is too ill to travel just now.

'If Buckingham leaves England, half the ladies in the court will have their hearts broken,' I add teasingly. 'Not least poor Lady Shrewsbury.' This lady's infatuation for him is legendary, despite – or possibly because of – the fact that he killed her husband in a duel.

318

Charles looks relieved. 'Very well. I will tell him that the ladies of England cannot spare him.'

Buckingham is furious, and goes so far as to accuse the king in my hearing of being swayed by me: the king, equally angry, tells him that the decision was his alone.

This is how it works, I am discovering: you do not tell a man what to think, you simply tell him what he himself is thinking. Nine times out of ten, he realises that he agrees.

So if I can deal with Monmouth, and Buckingham and Arlington, why not Nell Gwynne? She claims never to have read a book, much less a play – she learns her lines by having them read aloud to her; her voice is shrill and common, although when she chooses to mimic one of the grand ladies of court she is uncannily accurate. When I hear her speaking in the voice of Elizabeth Arlington – 'No, Bennet, we absolutely must build another house by Christmas, or we shall have to stay in the same palace two months running!' – there is something about the mannerisms, the timing, that is both Elizabeth and yet, somehow, funnier than Elizabeth. I suppose her imitation of me must be equally accurate: I cannot see it myself.

But if she can speak like a lady when she chooses, why on earth does she not choose to all the time?

I have not cried for many months. Not for her, or for myself. But now, with the baby coming, I cry.

My honour is an invisible thing, and besides, it is sometimes possible to forget that I am dishonoured. But a baby – a child – is something tangible. Will he be known forever as a mistress's bastard? Or will he be the son of England's queen?

The ambassador calls on me, and in my confusion I allow myself to cry over him. The prissy fool immediately takes it upon himself to issue a rebuke.

'It is not seemly,' Colbert opines, 'to speculate on the health of

Her Highness. Particularly as there is good news in that respect. It seems that her physician might have been too hasty. Dr Frazer now considers that it is not consumption she suffers from after all, but rather an over-susceptibility to pleasure.'

I cannot believe what I am hearing. 'An over-susceptibility?'

He nods. 'As you will be aware, the king is blessed with the means to give ladies exceptional satisfaction. It seems that the queen suffered such paroxysms of happiness when the king was with her that she bled. Now that she is relieved of the necessity of lying with him, her health is much improved.'

'But you said—'

'Medicine is not an exact science. Happily, in this instance.'

'Then she is not going to die,' I say numbly. 'The queen is not going to die.'

'We are all going to die,' he says piously. 'But the queen can, by all accounts, look forward to many years of better health.'

'You lied to me. You and Arlington. You told me she would die.'

He frowns. 'I think I said at the time that it was irrelevant, since you are hardly the cloth from which queens are cut. My point is that it does not behove you to speculate any further—'

'Behove? Behove?' My tears have given way to rage. 'You have done little else but speculate about such matters for years. Don't you dare tell me what does or does not behove. My family were courtiers when yours were tilling the fields like beasts.' A little unfair, perhaps, but I simply want to wound.

'I will leave you,' he says with a stiff bow. 'I can see you are upset, and it is well known that ladies in your condition need to remain calm, for the good of the child. His Most Christian Majesty, incidentally, authorises me to pass on his personal congratulations at your great good fortune.'

Colbert. I am more determined than ever to have him recalled, but not yet: one enemy at a time.

*

I try a different approach: making friends with her. The king is away, inspecting the fleet at Portsmouth, so the court is quiet. Walking in the park amongst the other ladies, I see Nell is wearing a new dress.

I say pleasantly, 'Why, that dress is very fine, Miss Gwynne.'

It isn't true, of course: she has no taste or restraint; she can't see an expensive ribbon or a piece of silver thread but jackdaw-like, she must have yards of it.

She smiles back. 'Fine enough to be a lady's, you mean?'

'I was wondering who your dressmaker is. You must give me her name.'

'Why? You already look perfectly fine enough to be a whore.' Even for the English court, this is strong talk; there are some indrawn breaths, but those around us are transfixed. Nell looks around. 'If she is a lady of such quality, why does she demean her-self to be a jade?' she demands insouciantly. 'She ought to die for shame. As for me, it is my profession; I do not pretend to be any-thing better. And yet the king loves me as well as he does her.'

I feel a little faint, but I manage to say, 'And such nice shoes. Your English shoemakers are the best in Europe, I think.'

I have this small victory: that whatever she says, whatever I now am, she cannot provoke me to a fight, like common fishwives. That is what my honour, my breeding, consists of these days. While I still have my manners, I am not what she is.

Carlo

To season custard with vanilla, take your vanilla pod and
scrape out the seeds, and add them to the custard.

The Book of Ices

The pride of England sailed with its fleet, under the Duke of
York's command, an armada of sixty ships and twenty thousand
men. The plan was for them to join up with the French fleet at
Solebay in Suffolk, and together blockade the Dutch ports.

Yet the Dutch, although their navy was far smaller, went on the
offensive. While the allied armada was still at anchor, the Dutch
appeared on the horizon with the wind behind them. The allies
immediately broke in two, the French ships turning tail and sail-
ing south. The English, meanwhile, had no choice but to stay and
fight. Over a thousand cannon pulverised each other for the best
part of a day before the Dutch withdrew.

It was put about that the absence of the French from the battle
was a simple mistake, due to poor signalling, but most
Englishmen preferred a different explanation: France had wanted
the English to take the brunt. It was as they had always feared.
England was being lured into this war with the deliberate intention of leaving the country weakened, to pave the way for a
Catholic invasion.

Press gangs now roamed the streets, taking any able-bodied
youths they came across for the navy. Taxes had been raised, and
order was only kept through a sharp increase in public floggings
and hangings.

I made an ice cream of spring asparagus, packed into an aspara-
gus-shaped mould, and contrived it so that one end of each spear

322

was white, the other green, just like the real thing. Charles, who loved anything that was not what it seemed, pronounced it the finest ice I had yet served. He liked to press some on his guests, to see their astonishment.

Louise, pregnant, summoned me for a different purpose. 'Can you make me something? I have a hankering for sweet gherkins and a rich ice cream.'

I sighed. 'It is well known that women in pregnancy eat curious foods. I will see what I can do.'

I made her an ice of fresh, creamy custard seasoned with vanilla seeds; the vanilla would at least counterbalance the sharpness of the gherkins. But she was still not happy.

'You are making me fat,' she grumbled, even as she ate it. 'Fat and deformed.'

'It's the baby that does that. You'll lose the fat soon enough after it comes.'

'No man in London will look at me, much less the king. I am like a pregnant sow. He has started calling me "Fubs".'

'Fubs?'

'Or "Fubsy". It means chubby-cheeked, apparently.'

'Then it sounds as if pregnancy has not diminished his fondness for you.'

'He pinches my cheeks, exclaims over my belly, and then saunters off to spend the night with his actress. Fondness is no good to me. Fondness will not compensate for the perfidy of the French fleet. I don't need fondness. I need *desire*. I need *infatuation*.'

'On the contrary. Any man can be infatuated; to be fond as well suggests that his feelings will last. Be patient. When the baby is born he will come back to your bed soon enough.'

On another occasion she said, 'I have been too naive. If I am to keep him in future, I must learn some tricks.'

'Tricks?' I said, although I knew exactly what she meant.

323

'Before, I trusted to my innocence, just as you suggested. But now I can no longer be innocent, I will have to be cunning.'

'And how do you intend to learn these tricks?'

'You must teach me, of course.' She saw my look. 'Not like *that*. You must explain it: where I am to go, how I lie, what I must say. I know the basics now: it will be easier for me to grasp what you are talking about.'

I could refuse her nothing. And so we clambered onto her bed, the door shut and bolted against the spies amongst her ladies, and she puffed and waddled her way through the various postures of love under my instruction. We were both fully clothed: she was heavy and pregnant; perhaps not surprisingly, there was not a scintilla of amorousness in either the occasion or her manner, until at last I could not help but add, 'Of course, with him you will be loving, as well.'

'Loving?'

'You know – eager. Smiling. Murmuring endearments.'

'That too?' She seemed perplexed. 'It is not enough that I do all this? I have to seem as if it delights me?'

'Of course. Your eagerness is the greatest compliment you can pay him.' I took a gherkin from the plate. 'Imagine that this is the king.' I dipped it into the dish of ice cream. 'Imagine that he is covered in the flavour you most desire – that you are craving him more than anything you have craved in your pregnancy.' I handed it to her. 'Now try.'

She tried: her tongue came out, and licked around the gherkin's head, she glanced at me, to see if she was doing it right, and for a moment the green eyes were filled with such unmistakeable lust that I could not breathe.

Then, her mouth still full of ice cream, she started to laugh. She put the back of her hand to her mouth as she swallowed. When she could speak she said, 'So that, I take it, from your face, is an appropriate look of overwhelming desire?'

'Yes,' I said hoarsely. 'What were you thinking?'

'I was thinking of the ice cream, and that it would soon be all gone. And then I felt a bit serious, and I rolled it around my mouth, and it *was* all gone.'

'Do that,' I said with a sigh. 'Do it just like that, and he will think that you adore him.'

Back at the Lion, I ordered Hannah to my room.

'I suppose you know some tricks?' I said curtly.

'Tricks?'

'Embellishments. Extras. Like they do in France.'

'I know how to make a fricassée, if that is what you are asking.'

'You know very well it is not.'

'Yes, I do know. But I wanted to see if you would smile,' she said mysteriously.

I grunted. 'I will pay you extra.'

'That is very generous, but I am afraid I cannot help you. If you want French tricks you will have to find a Frenchwoman.' She hesitated. 'But perhaps you already have.'

I glanced at her. 'What do you mean?'

'Only that whatever it is you do at court does not seem to make you very happy.'

'That is none of your business.'

'Of course,' she said, her expression unreadable. 'It will just be the usual, then, I take it?'

'Yes. The usual.'

The usual, conducted in the usual silence. The usual chink of coins. The usual tears on my cheeks, before the brief oblivion of sleep.

When I woke I discovered to my surprise that it was past three o'clock. I went to the window, and for a long time I sat there, on the window seat, looking down at the people going about their business in the street.

Then I saw Hannah, coming out of the inn yard. I would probably not have noticed her – she was wearing a dark cloak with a hood that was pulled up over her hair – but as she turned to look up and down the street I happened to glimpse her face quite clearly in profile.

In her hand, clasped tight, was a purse.

Something, I do not know what, exactly, made me curious about where she was going. Putting on a coat, I hurried downstairs. I had seen the direction she had taken, and it was no great difficulty to catch up until I was walking about ten paces behind her.

I noticed how many people greeted her as she passed, not effusively but with a nod or a small gesture of recognition. And then there were some, both men and women, who stopped, and shook her hand.

I remembered Cassell's words. *They refuse to bow to any man, since they say all are created equal.*

Hannah was evidently in a hurry, however, and did not pause long to exchange pleasantries. After about five minutes she turned into an alley which was lined with tiny shops selling books and maps. At the far end, she slipped into one of the smallest. It seemed that whatever she was doing in there was the purpose of her journey, as she did not come out for several minutes. I waited until she had turned the corner, then went into the shop myself.

It was even smaller than it appeared from the outside. Books covered almost every surface. But on the counter, unrolled as if it had recently been placed there, was a map. I bent down to examine it. At the top was an inscription.

A New and Accurate Map of the World. Drawn according to the truest descriptions, latest discoveries and best observations that have yet been made by Englishmen or strangers.

'It is the one they are all after,' the shopkeeper said, seeing me looking. 'Based on John Speed's own projections. Look, it even shows the island.'

'The island?'

'Of California.' He pointed. 'And here – if Sir William Penn has his way, all this will be New Wales.'

I looked at the map, searching for some clue as to why Hannah should have been interested in it.

'Have you a passage booked?' the bookseller enquired. 'Well, when you are ready to book one, come to me. We do easy terms. A deposit, and then a small payment every month. The boat belongs to my brother-in-law: it is the finest in Bristol—'

I suddenly realised what this must be about. 'The woman who was here just now. Was she buying a ticket?'

He shook his head. 'She bought hers a year ago. She should have sailed last May, but she fell behind. Now she only has another six to make, and she'll—' He stopped, suddenly aware that my interest might not be just that of a casual customer. 'Was there anything in particular you were interested in?' he said, rolling up the map with that chilly politeness the English do so well.

So Hannah was emigrating to America. I should not have been surprised: it was where all the malcontents and miscreants ended up. And if she was paying for it by whoring, well, that too, was hardly any of my business.

All the same, I felt uneasy. Now that I knew why she needed the money, I felt somewhat ashamed of what she had needed to do to get it. And – rather to my own surprise – I found I was a little envious of her too: not of what she had done, but that she had been able to do it: that she had been able to see a choice and take it, instead of being always at the beck and call of ministers and kings.

Louise

It seems all London is talking about my rivalry with Nell. And not just London: the ambassador lets slip that Paris, too, watches agog.

Men can duel with swords, or tennis racquets, or compete for honours on the battlefield. But I must battle Nell Gwynne with nothing more than smiles and words.

Words, unfortunately, are her forte. Even in my native tongue I do not have her wit. The latest story to do the rounds is that she found out her house on Pall Mall, given to her by Charles, was only leasehold – and the lease no more than twenty years. The implication is obvious: while the king shares her bed she will be kept in state, but when the affair is ended, she goes back to the gutter. For some reason the people of London have adopted this cause as their own, and the Matter of Nell's Freehold is being reported in all the newspapers and scandal-sheets.

Nell, it is said, informed the king that she gave herself to him freehold, not leasehold, and she expects the same courtesy in return. Charles was apparently so amused by this that he gave way. To celebrate, she is having a *salle des miroirs* built – in her bedroom, along with a carved silver bed, engraved with busts of the king and her, and their initials entwined! Surely Charles, whose own taste is impeccable, must shrink from such gaudy show?

I tell him that I am going to have my apartments rebuilt so that they more closely resemble Minette's rooms at Versailles. Of course he agrees. More tapestries, more carpets, more silverware, but all of the highest quality – that is to say, French. When he finally has to choose, it must be clear what he is choosing between: brashness and breeding, coarseness and refinement.

Apparently Nell found her footman fighting in the street: when she asked him why he was brawling, he said he was fighting a man who had called her a whore.

'Then you must find another reason,' she said. 'For I am.'

How does one combat someone who is not ashamed of what she is?

If she has a weakness, it is that she does not see the difference between us. To her, whore and mistress are the same thing; orange girl and lady-in-waiting only different in degree.

For all her shamelessness, she has pretensions to a title, and that, surely, will be her undoing. If Charles makes her a duchess, every noble family in England will believe themselves demeaned.

My strategy, then, is to remind Charles of my birth. An opportunity comes up when a distant relative of mine, the Chevalier de Rohan, dies. Admittedly, he has been executed by Louis for plotting with the Dutch, but he can be mourned all the same, and he is descended from the old kings of Brittany, which means he is a distant relative of Charles's as well.

Charles sees me in black, and asks me in front of the court what is wrong.

'I am mourning our cousin, the Prince of Rohan,' I explain.

I intend to wear black for a week, no more – the length of time appropriate for so distant a connection. But when I go to court the next day, Nell is in black as well. As the king talks to some of his advisors, the sound of muted sobbing comes from her direction. Eventually he calls out, 'Why, Nell, how now! Has your mother died?'

'No,' she says. 'It is not her.'

'Who, then?'

'The Cham of Tartary,' she weeps. 'He's dead. Dear Lord, he is dead.'

'But what relation is this Cham of Tartary to you?' he says, mystified.

'Exactly the same,' she snivels, 'as the Chevalier de Rohan is to Louise; that is to say, none at all.'

There is a moment's silence, and then a guffaw of laughter rolls around the court. Like a dog escaped from the kitchens with a string of sausages in its mouth, it scampers from corner to corner, from group to group, and although I chase it furiously with my eyes I cannot pin it down.

'Well then,' the king says, wiping his eyes, 'Perhaps, Nell, you and Louise had better divide the world between you, for between Tartary and Rohan there will be an awful lot of strangers to be mourned.'

'We have already done so,' she replies matter-of-factly. 'The only thing not settled is which of us shall have England.'

They are laughing openly now. I am ashamed: I had not realised my approach was so obvious. But what she does not understand is that every time she makes one of these outrageous displays, she plays to my strengths. They may laugh with her, but they see even more clearly that she is not one of them: sooner or later they must close ranks on her, and I shall be triumphant.

Carlo

Parmesan ice cream: take six eggs, half a pint of syrup and a pint of cream. Put into a stewpan and boil until it thickens, then rasp three ounces of Parmesan cheese, mix and sieve, and freeze it. This is a rich and nourishing ice cream, well suited to nursing mothers.

The Book of Ices

Louise did not retire for her lying-in until the last possible moment. She could not afford to: they sniggered enough to her face, but behind her back they laughed even more.

'Oh tell me, where is Carwell?' Rochester enquired of me one day in the king's hearing. 'Has she not whelped yet?' For that, at least, he was banished for a few days, it being one thing to denigrate the king's mistress, quite another to include the king's unborn child in the joke.

Meanwhile, just as Cassell had predicted, Parliament was tightening its grip. The Declaration of Indulgence was withdrawn and replaced with the Test Act, a law by which anyone holding public office had to swear a Protestant oath. Lord Clifford, the Treasurer, was one of those forced from public life: he committed suicide at his country home. Lord Arlington, whom Louise knew to be a Catholic, took the oath without demur. The Duke of York hesitated, then stepped down from the post of Admiral of the Navy, effectively confirming to the country that the king's own brother was indeed a convert.

Once again I had reason to be thankful that no one but I had the secrets of ice cream: it meant there was no Englishman who could replace me, and I went on serving the king and his favourites just as I had done before.

331

And yet, if Parliament had thought to restrict the influence of Louise, it was mistaken. Her baby was born in July: by Christmas she was once again resurgent, and in a way that Nell could not hope to emulate.

Louise

My child is born. Charles. Even in his naming, politics takes precedence, and the world must know who his father is.

Childbirth, of course, is agony. And yet it is nothing to the pain of giving the baby up to a wet nurse to suckle as her own. My own breasts, engorged, leak milk into my fine French gowns. But this would be my duty were I a wife, too: to report back at court as if nothing has happened, as if bearing sons were such an easy thing I can take it in my stride.

Charles likes children. That is a surprise, since he is himself so easily distracted, so indulged. But he likes to sit and hold the baby, teasing his puckering lips with a finger. Only for a short while, mind. When the baby cries, he is handed back to the wet nurse.

'What a lusty cry,' he says mildly. 'You had better take him away.' He does not relish anyone who makes demands, let alone so noisily.

'Tell me,' he asks. 'What religion will he be raised in?'

I have already thought about this, of course. For me to be England's queen, my children would have to be Protestants. But if I choose that path, I will be saying that I do not believe Charles will ever honour his own promise to convert.

'He will be raised in the True Faith,' I say. 'Perhaps one day you and our son will be able to worship together.'

'Perhaps,' he says non-committally.

I write to my parents with the news, inviting them to come and meet their grandson. With quiet pride I describe the favours that the king bestows on me, the size of my apartments, the jewels he has given me. I make it clear that they would not be inconveniencing me in the least.

333

By then, I hope to have seen off Madam Gwynne. That is something I would rather my parents didn't see: their daughter being called a whore by an English play-actress.

Politically, the intrigues just now revolve around who the king's brother will marry. The English have given up hope of him accepting a Protestant bride. Louis XIV still favours the fecund but ugly Duchess de Guise, but James himself, the king tells me, is holding out for a beautiful virgin.

'Does he have one in mind?' I ask.

Charles throws up his hands. 'That is the whole trouble. He says it is beneath his dignity to choose his own wife – but then he rejects every one who is chosen for him. So far he has turned down the Archduchess of Innsbruck on account of her figure, the Princess of Württemberg on account of her mother, Princess Maire of Alsace on account of her red hair, and two German princesses on account of their being German. My ministers are at their wits' end. I have told him it is a nonsense to marry for beauty. One gets so accustomed to a face that in a week it neither pleases nor displeases in any case.' He hesitates. 'Not yours, of course.'

I smile to show that I know he meant no insult. 'I have a very beautiful young cousin.'

The king raises his eyebrows. 'Of good family?'

'Francoise Marie is the daughter of the Duchess d'Elboeuf, and a princess of the house of Lorraine.'

'Of course,' he murmurs. 'I sometimes forget that you are related to all the best families in France.'

Is he teasing me? 'I have her portrait in my apartments. Perhaps if your brother could be persuaded to come and see his new nephew, it might happen to catch his eye . . .?'

Charles laughs and pats my knee. 'Oh, how I have missed you, dearest Fubs. We are so very alike.'

'Of course,' I say. 'It is our breeding.'

*

James visits, and professes himself intrigued by the portrait of Francoise Marie. Within hours, a furious Colbert has stormed into my apartments.

'His Most Christian Majesty has expressly ordered me to work for the betrothal of de Guise,' he almost shrieks.

'I am sure he has,' I say calmly. 'But James is both a lecher, and newly religious; as a result he wants to marry a girl the same age as his own daughters. Only a fool would think that he is going to marry an ugly widow.'

'Are you calling Louis XIV a fool?' Colbert splutters.

'Of course not. I was referring to those who have advised him. Who, when the de Guise plan fails to happen, he will almost certainly blame.'

I can see Colbert considering this. If he can use me to switch Louis's aim to a more achievable target, he can take the credit if it works, and blame me if it does not.

'Let Louis find another Catholic girl,' I say. 'But let her be young, attractive and unmarried. Then you and I will work together to secure the marriage.'

'There is another candidate, as it happens,' he says hesitantly.

'Who?'

'Princess Mary of Modena. Thirteen years old, and going to be a great beauty, they say. But she has expressed a desire to enter a convent rather than marry someone so much older than herself.'

'A pious young beauty?' I say. 'She sounds perfect. Have someone send over her portrait at once.'

Within a month it is all arranged. They will marry next year, as soon as she turns fourteen. In return, James has agreed to have two wedding ceremonies – a private, Catholic one, and a public one according to the Anglican rites.

'How do you do it?' Charles wants to know. 'For me he is as stubborn as a mule. But you, it seems, can get him to do anything.'

'Perhaps he is jealous of you.'

'Jealous?' Charles seems surprised.

'He is still a little in love with me, you know.' I shrug modestly. 'I don't know why.'

'Yes, of course.' Charles stares at me, and I can tell that he is seeing me through his brother's eyes: desirable, marriageable, but above all unattainable. 'Will you dine with me this evening, madam?' he says abruptly.

I smile. 'I would be pleased to, Charles.'

That night he takes me as if I were a virgin again, and he an eager young blood.

Afterwards he says, 'My God, but you were keen.'

I kiss his chest. 'You're so delicious. I can't keep my mouth off you.'

He lies back, content. I carry on kissing him: the hard chest, the ribs that stand under the skin like the hull of a ship. Whether it is the baby, or relief at being back in his favour, or something else, I don't know, but I feel a kind of tenderness for him, a yearning, that I have never felt before. I twist myself over him, kissing his nipples, exclaiming at the taste of him, the feel, the strength of the hands that lace themselves around my head.

And so everything is in alignment again. I am in Charles's bed and Louis's favour. Colbert has been made to look ineffectual, and my apartments are once again the real parliament of England.

Charles wants to give me a necklace. There is one that Nell has been angling for, my spies tell me – literally: she has been teaching the king to fish in the hope of snagging it. The necklace costs over eight thousand pounds. How sweet it would be to snatch it from her grasp!

But I am playing a longer game than that.

I say, 'My love?'

'Hmm?'

We are lying in bed after a bout of lovemaking.

'I don't want expensive presents.'

'Really?' He seems surprised.

'To be loved by you is all the recompense I need. But if you really wish to show me favour . . .'

'Yes?' he says, and I can tell he is steeling himself for some outrageous demand: a pension, perhaps, or a gambling debt that must be settled.

'As you know, I come from an old and noble family.'

'Indeed.'

'My maternal grandfather was a marquis. The de Keroualles have been Seigneurs of Brest for over seven hundred years. Yet I don't think some of your court are really aware of my background. They see only that I am your mistress, and because I don't have an English title, they think I am hardly better than a common orange girl.'

He nods thoughtfully. 'You want an English title?'

'If that would please you.'

He considers. It is, on the face of it, a cheap gift, but he knows as well as I do that titles usually come with pensions or other revenues.

'I could be minded to give you something of that nature,' he says slowly.

'Thank you.' I kiss his cheek, the rough end-of-day stubble. 'Of course, you will have to make me an English citizen as well. Otherwise I could not be a duchess. Or whatever it is you decide to make me. Really, it is completely up to you.'

I think I am beginning to understand the mistress's role a little better now. It is not merely to listen, but to reflect; not merely to be available, but to act as a proxy for all the other, unavailable women – the women he would have too, if he had opportunity and time. To be the woman whom every man desires but only one can have.

I understand, now, why Nell Gwynne has her bed set up in a Hall of Mirrors.

I was wrong when I told Carlo that I did not know any bedroom tricks. The subtlest tricks are not played with the body; nor can they be drawn in a book of postures.

Louise

He wants to have me painted. 'Now that your figure has returned,' he says casually. 'And before you are pregnant again.'

'My figure hasn't returned. I am like an elephant.'

'My dearest Fubs,' he murmurs. 'I like you like that.'

From the reference to my figure I understand that it is not my face alone that he wants painted. 'You wish me unclothed?'

'Why not?' He looks at me sideways. 'I was thinking of Sir Peter Lely. A most discreet gentleman, and an excellent painter. Besides, hardly anyone will see it.'

For the king's pleasure alone. But the king's pleasure, I am coming to realise, lies partly in what is his alone, and partly in imagining how others will see it. 'In France it is considered very lewd indeed to be painted without clothes.'

'I know what an extraordinary favour you would be granting me. I would endeavour to find some extraordinary way to make it up to you.'

A title? 'Imagine the shame if my family heard of it.'

My protests are exciting him. He has something new to chase, a new maidenhead to take.

'For actresses or orange girls,' I add, 'it is nothing, of course. But would a king ask a queen to do such a thing? I think not.'

'Unless he loved her very much,' he murmurs.

We both know how this dance will end. I cannot afford to resist him for too long. Not while he has Nell Gwynne.

In the end we compromise on a silk chemise, unbuttoned. It covers nothing, but it means that I am not, strictly speaking, naked. I recline on a divan, spread open to Lely's gaze as he pecks and dabs and flourishes at a canvas I cannot see.

If I drop my eyes, even for a moment, he murmurs, 'Look at me.' My gaze, you see, must meet that of the men who view the painting. How strange to think that when I look at Peter, at his dark impersonal frown of concentration, I am looking directly into the eyes of every man who will stare at me. There could be dozens, hundreds who will stand before that painting, some even after I am dead.

And every single one will look at me and think how shameless I am, that I do this for the king's private gratification.

Not realising that it is them, not me, who do that.

Charles comes to chat. He was worried that I might be bored, he says. He strolls across to look at the painting. Peter stands aside, as patient as the king is impatient. Occasionally he involves his patron in some detail of design or technique. *Here. This is called impasto. Do you prefer the green, here, or this aquamarine?*

There is something about all this that excites Charles: the two men, fully clothed, glancing at my naked body, discussing me. Almost as if I were a bone that Charles might drop from his mouth, for another dog to sniff at.

I remember Colbert's words. *A most unfettered debauch.*

Lely suggests some fruit, on the left, to balance the composition. 'Not oranges,' I say firmly.

He raises his eyebrows, a little.

'Oranges make me think of orange girls.'

He smiles at that. It was him, of course, who painted Nell.

'I know,' Charles says. 'Ice cream! There should be ices in the picture.'

'They would melt before Peter had painted them,' I say.

'They could be replenished,' the artist says. He taps the canvas, thoughtfully, with the blunt end of the brush, to show the king where they might go. 'Just here, at the side, they could be replenished without disturbing the *mise en scène*. It would be interesting, actually. People would wonder how it had been done. A moment captured. The illusion of instantaneity, in the midst of frozen time.' It is the longest speech that I have heard him make in five days of painting.

Another woman, I reflect dryly, might be a little offended that he is so much more excited by the technical challenge of painting an ice cream than by her naked figure.

'Indeed,' Charles breathes. 'A platter of ices. Will you paint them just as they are thawing?'

'Just as they start to, sir. The ice softening. Like a fruit ripening in the bowl, caught at the very moment before it rots. Anticipating the inevitable corruption of the flesh.' He glances at me, and I realise that it is not only the technical challenge that interests him. There is symbolism here too, of a kind.

And so they send for ices. *Hurry. Tell him it is for the king. At Lely's studio.* Carlo enters with the ice chest. I cannot move, cannot warn him. I am fixed and immobile on my divan, like Daphne rooted to the spot as she turns into a bush.

'Ah, Demirco. Put them over there.'

He has stopped dead, staring.

'Come on, man. Anyone would think you'd never seen a naked woman before.'

He recovers himself quickly. 'Never one as beautiful as this, sir.'

'Yes.' Charles strokes his moustache, pleased. 'She is quite lovely, isn't she?'

He glances at Peter, then at me. Peter has stopped, his brush raised from the canvas, startled. They both stare.

A blush – deep and crimson, like the turning of a vine leaf in autumn – has travelled up my pale skin, all the way from my exposed legs to the tips of my ears.

Nell, at court. 'Oh, Madam Carwell. I hear you were recently painted in nothing but a silk chemise.'

'Indeed, Nell. Sir Peter's portrait is very fine.'

'Perhaps we will hang next to each other in the king's gallery

341

room. So that his gentlemen friends may compare us, side by side. As a whore, of course, I should consider that a great honour, to be compared with a grand lady such as yourself.'

I do not reply.

'Tell me, have you seen Charles the Third this morning?' she enquires.

I sense some kind of trap here, but even so I blunder into it. 'Why do you call him Charles the Third? He is Charles the Second.'

She ticks them off her fingers. 'My first Charles was Charles Hart, my second was Charles Sackville, so Charles Stuart is my Charles the third. You have only had two Charlies then, I take it?'

There is nothing to be done when she is like this but to remain calm. It is like having a child who refuses to be sent to bed, whose only way of talking with the grown-ups is to shock. I say gently, 'Before I met the king, Nell, I had not had any other men.'

'Oh well,' she says with a shake of her head. 'There's still time. He never minds, you know. Barbara Villiers took four at one sitting, and the king only said that what was sauce for the gander was sauce for the goose.'

A simple, obvious insult, like so many that she makes. But it sets me thinking.

The crown jewels are on display in the Tower of London, where any man can view them for a penny. They were almost stolen a few years ago, but Charles will not lock them away, out of sight. Why not?

An actress. A woman who plays many parts. A king who is forced to do the same.

A whore. A woman who has had many lovers, and few of them for love. A king who chooses to do the same.

Playing me off against Nell Gwynne – could it be, in some way, deliberate? Is it all part of the same trait?

There is in Charles, I am coming to realise, a deep, deep cynicism – almost a darkness. To his natural scepticism has been added the effects of his experiences in exile: wandering from court to court, welcomed in case he might prove useful, tolerated only until shifting political considerations made his hosts wary of letting him

Nell and I have this in common, I realise with a start, both with each other and with Charles himself: we have known what it is to be penniless, powerless, and cold.

Is that why he keeps men like Lord Rochester around him – does he find in their bitter, mocking sarcasm an echo of what lies within his own mind?

And when he says that he and I are alike – is this what he means? Will he only truly be happy when I have given him the satisfaction of proving him right?

Does he need me to show him that I can stoop as low as he?

Carlo

Barberries and bergamots are amongst the fruits which
make better ices than eating.

The Book of Ices

Louis XIV led the advance on the Dutch personally, riding almost
unopposed at the head of a great Franco–English army up
through the Spanish Netherlands. But the Hollanders, realising
they could not beat him in open warfare, opened the dykes and
flooded a vast area of the country he had hoped to conquer.
Frustrated, the Sun King was forced to play a waiting game.

Armies are expensive things, and armies that are not marching – that are not plundering and pillaging as they go – are more
expensive still. For Louis, of course, it was nothing to snap his fingers and demand another tax. For his ally Charles, with his
Parliament to consider, it was a different matter.

The Great Stop of the Exchequer, when his government had
grandly announced that it would be paying neither interest nor
capital on its debts for a period of a year, now looked like a terrible miscalculation. For what banker would lend more to a king
who did not keep up his payments? What debt was safe, if a king
could subsequently alter its terms as it pleased him?

His only income now was his pension from Louis, and what he
could raise from Parliament. Parliament made it clear that it would
vote no more without results. The king was on the verge of bank-
ruptcy.

That was the month he gave Louise a sedan chair upholstered
in silver silk, and two negro footmen to carry it; a necklace worth
three thousand pounds, a rope of pearls worth twice that, and

rebuilt her apartments to include a hall of mirrors. That was the month he gave Nell a carriage with six white horses, to show that she was the lover of royalty, and a silver table to match her silver plates. That was the month he ordered the building of a new state apartment at Windsor, and flooded St James's Park for a mock battle on the water.

It was a summer of ice creams – of course it was. The king was much taken with his new glasshouses; his gardeners had succeeded in growing a fine crop of pineapples, apricots and musk melons, and he gave orders that I was to have whatever I desired. I made an ice cream that looked exactly like a pineapple, sweetened with a little sugar and grape must. I surrounded it with real pineapples and sliced it open with a flourish in front of the king himself, declaring that he would find it the sweetest, ripest fruit in his kingdom. This event occasioned more amazement at court, I believe, than the capitulation of Utrecht.

I found myself running out of ideas. Once I had served the king and his guests every fruit that England grew, every cordial of Europe, every seed water of the world, what then?

Sometimes I found myself wishing I was like Hannah, who served no more than five or six pies in any one month, depending on what had taken her fancy at the market.

'What is this?' I called to her across the inn's dining room one day, as I lifted a steaming crust on something rich and deep-red and unfamiliar.

'Umble pie.'

'I am still none the wiser.'

'Venison offal. A deer's heart, tongue, brains, and stomach, with onion gravy and thyme. All the parts that wealthy people don't want to eat.'

Yet even wealthy people, I noticed, now sent their servants to the Red Lion to buy a few pies for their supper. Hannah's renown was spreading.

'And tomorrow?'

'Cock-a-leekie. On Thursday, ale-and-kidney. And on Friday, cheese-and-onion. Why?'

I grunted. 'I need some new flavours for the king.'

'Send him a pie,' she said facetiously.

I could not, of course, but the next time I was in the pantry I pulled out her cookbooks and thumbed through them, looking for ideas.

'What are you doing?' Hannah asked, coming in.

'I mean to make some herb sorbets. This sounds interesting, for example. Culpeper speaks of the culinary uses of nettles—'

'You should be more careful. I have told you that book should not be left out,' she said quietly.

I looked at her, perplexed. 'I thought you meant, to keep the pages clean.'

She shook her head. 'Culpeper's books have been banned by the Stationer's Office. If they find them, they burn the book and arrest the owner. And that's if you're lucky. Sometimes they burn both. Herbals make good witches' pyres, they say.'

'But why?'

She took the book from me and slid it back into the shelf. 'Culpeper was a Fifth-monarchy-man – that is to say, one of those who believed that the time of kings was coming to an end, and the time of freeborn men beginning. That was partly why he published his knowledge, and in plain English – so that ordinary people could have the information that physicians and apothecaries were trying to keep to themselves, with their Latin and their guilds. Much good it did him. Or those who followed him.'

I remembered those herbs in her pies – sage, sorrel, a delicious whisper of tarragon, onion gravy and thyme . . . 'You were one of them? A herbalist?'

She nodded. 'Among other things.'

'Then will you help me devise some ices?'

She shrugged. 'I suppose so. Why not?'

346

'Good. I will pay you something extra—'

'I do not want paying,' she said quietly. 'Culpeper gave his own knowledge away for nothing, in the hope that people would make use of it. It is not for me to make a profit from it.'

And so began another stage of my culinary education. For while we began by making simple herb sorbets – nettle, sage, fig leaf, pelargonium and lemon balm – it soon became apparent that herbs were even better in combination, either with each other or with other tastes, and that by employing them in this way an almost infinite variety of flavours could be created.

This, truly, was no longer engineering. This was cookery, pure and simple. For certain flavours married, and others did not, and it required both imagination and skill to envisage what such a marriage might be like – whether it would be a fruitful union or a barren one. Who would have thought, for example, that pippin and rose petal ice cream would be so good, the deep, sweet richness of the apples and the voluptuous scent of the flowers making the ice cream almost ridiculously sensual and heady in the mouth? Who would have thought that celery – the mildest and most watery of vegetables – would, when its seeds were toasted and combined with hibiscus flowers, have the clean, piercing, dry flavour it did? Who would have paired blackcurrant and mint, or oranges and basil, or made a cordial of maidenhair fern and black pepper?

Fig and bay leaves, peach and hyssop, clotted cream and lavender, apricot and cardamom – these were among the ice creams we made that day. They were majestic, fascinating, even remarkable – yet the ingredients were as simple as an English summer's garden.

I could not ask Hannah not to taste them, of course; I needed her expertise and her palate. And when she in turn wanted to get the opinion of a third person, someone who did not know what to expect, she quite naturally turned to Elias and gave him a spoonful, and he told us what he thought.

347

'It's wonderful!' he cried of an ice cream straight out of Culpeper, made with cucumbers and celery.

'It is, isn't it!' his mother replied. And the two of them danced a little jig around the pantry.

'I thought you would be against such things,' I said, surprised.

'Why? We are not opposed to pleasure, only to privilege.'

'Yet these are for the king alone,' I reminded her. 'The king and a few of his favourites.'

'Yes,' she said, a little deflated. 'Of course.'

'Perhaps if you met him you would not be so against him. He is a charming man.'

'Perhaps,' she said flatly, and danced no more.

Later that month, as the king ate an ice cream of barberries and lemon balm, he said to me thoughtfully, 'You are a man who knows about ice, Demirco.'

'Indeed, sir.'

'Louis's plan is to wait for winter. After all, if we can ride coaches across the Thames, why should he not drive his cannon across the frozen polders?'

I hesitated, and he said, 'You think it will not work?'

'The issue is how much salt there is,' I explained. 'Just as the Thames does not freeze below The Great Bridge, so allowing in seawater would immediately cause the polders to unfreeze again. It all depends how determined the Dutch are to resist the invasion.'

'William of Orange has stated that every Dutchman will drown before they see their country Catholic.'

'Then I certainly would not trust to ice alone to win this war.'

A few weeks later Arlington and Buckingham were sent to Holland to try to conclude a separate peace. The French, furious, accused the English of betrayal. In the event, no peace was forthcoming, and we were back at war, with the added complication that now Charles's own allies did not trust him either.

'Do you think we will ever get back to France?' I asked Louise one day, when I took her an ice of jonquilles and lemons.

'I don't know,' she said wearily. 'In any case, it is different for me now. Who would marry me and take on a royal bastard as well? It is one thing to turn a blind eye to a scandalous past, quite another to have that past growing up in your household.'

I said, 'Perhaps you will marry someone of lowly birth, who will love you and love your son as well. Perhaps you will be happy together without titles, or wealth.'

She looked at me and smiled. 'Do you know of such a man?'

'I have heard rumours that some such do exist.'

She said gently, 'You are too loyal, Carlo. I have done nothing to be worthy of this adoration.'

'On the contrary. I don't adore you in the least. I find you maddeningly practical; hard-headed, haughty, proud—'

'Thank you. I was not actually inviting a catalogue of my failings.'

I shrugged. 'Better to admire someone whose failings you are aware of, than a stranger.'

'And the king?'

'What about him?'

'The fact that that I am his mistress. Does that not change how you feel?'

'Why should it?' I busied myself with some glasses. 'I know you do not do it for love.'

She was silent a moment. 'I used to think love was only a fancy. But now I realise that it is a force almost as strong as an army.'

'Charles loves you.'

She shook her head. 'He likes me, and he desires me, and he likes to see me happy. He loves me in the same way he loves Windsor, or tennis – I am necessary to his well being, and his sense of being a king. And I am useful, too, in that I give him good advice. He loves Nell Gwynne far more than me.'

'Nell!'

'Certainly. At any rate, she is the one woman he can never give up, even though he knows that Louis or any other king would be appalled at the notion of keeping a common whore as a mistress. So yes, I think he does love her.'

'While she, presumably, is only after his money.'

'Oh no – that is to misunderstand her. She may be an actress and a whore, but she genuinely delights in their connection.'

'And you,' I said, 'who are neither actress nor whore . . .'

'Must play a part, and lie with a man I do not love. Yes, that irony had occurred to me as well.'

'Can you beat her?'

'Perhaps. But there is so much else to do. We must find a way to make him keep fighting this war. Parliament must be prevented from forcing him to sue for peace. James must be married before he changes his mind. More money. More battles.'

I went back to the Red Lion that day feeling a little melancholy. Hannah was in the pantry, making pastry for her pies.

'What are you looking at?' she asked.

'Nothing.'

She measured out a jar of flour, broke two eggs into it, and began to mix it all together. After a while she turned to face me. 'I really cannot work with you staring at me like that.'

'I was not staring,' I explained. 'Or at least, not at you. You happened to be standing in the general direction of my gaze, that is all.'

She sighed, and turned back to her pastry.

'But since you ask,' I added, 'we could go to my rooms, later.'

Her voice when she answered was flat. 'You have been at court today, I take it?'

'Yes.'

'With Madam Carwell?'

'What does that have to do with it?'

'Only that I have noticed it is after you have been with her that you are most likely to invite me to your rooms.'

I shrugged, but since she was not looking at me she could not see it. 'I invite you to my rooms because the arrangement suits both of us. You can come or not, as you choose. It is up to you.'

It seemed to me that she was struggling to decide whether to say something. 'Tell me,' she said. 'When you first came here, how did you know what I was? That I would go with you for money?'

'An acquaintance told me what English inn servants were like. And then I found you with that man. He knew what you were.'

'Yes,' she said. 'He called me a ranter whore. But that was a figure of speech. He was referring to the fact that I was a dissenter.'

'He threatened you with arrest.'

'He was a spy. He was trying to coerce me into spying on you.'

'On me!' I said, bemused.

'I was meant to find out how you made your ice creams. But I had already given you my word that I wouldn't tell anyone, so I didn't.'

'But . . .' I said, perplexed. 'When I told you to come to my room, that first time, you came. You took my money.'

'Yes.'

'So Cassell was right. You *are* what he said you are.'

She addressed the pastry. 'Perhaps. But I have decided that in future, signor, I would be obliged if you would ask Mary or Rose instead.'

'Why?'

She did not answer me for a long time, only working her fingers into the mound of dough. Eventually she said, 'It would not be fair on Elias, if he were to discover what we do.'

'Oh. I see.'

'He admires you. He might . . . misunderstand our association. He might read into it more than there actually is.'

'Well, in that case I will make sure that I do not ask you again.'

351

'Thank you.'

'I will ask Mary. Or Rose, as the case may be.'

'Exactly.' She took her rolling pin and banged her mound of pastry, so hard that a cloud of flour jumped into the air.

Louise

It is an open secret that Parliament will insist on peace as soon as it assembles. Every night Charles sits in meetings, debating with his ministers what to do. His objective is to buy time: a policy which his brother, in a rare flash of wit, has described as being indistinguishable from wasting it.

The only solution is for Parliament to be prorogued – that is to say, suspended by the king's authority. But to defy in this way the very Parliament to which he owes his restoration might trigger armed rebellion. His ministers – with one eye on their own popularity with the mob – urge caution.

They do not know him as I do. Reckless gestures appeal to him. He prefers the bold course, the high-stakes gamble. And his loathing of Parliament runs very deep. Publicly, he has to appear grateful that they restored him to his throne. Privately, he does not forget that the throne was only vacant in the first place because they murdered his father.

I think there is a way. But first I must match him boldness for boldness.

I throw a party, a supper in my apartments for the king and forty of his closest friends. I even invite some of the wits, those frivolous libertines whose influence over the king is stronger than he likes to admit.

A feast of French food, French wines, French ices, French thoughts expressed in the French tongue. Only the wine flows in a way that is not quite French, and the talk quickly reverts to English and descends – as it always does in this country – from the flirtatious to the bawdy. Soon the courtiers and court ladies stumble off into dark corners for assignations, unbuttonings. Debauchery becomes the order of the night.

But not, of course, for Charles or me. He casts glances into the shadows, and I sense that on another occasion he might have liked to have joined them, but he cannot be seen to leave my side for such a purpose at my own party.

By dawn, exhausted or ashamed, they have all crept away: all except for my own ladies-in-waiting, the Honourable Lucy Williamson and Lady Anne Berowne. The king yawns, and says he must go as well. That is when I suggest a last round of Questions and Commands. But no one has any money.

When the king asks what the stakes will be, I say, 'Our clothes.' The girls look uncertain, but do not dare protest.

Each time one of us loses, we take something off. Lucy is the first to be naked. In her nervousness she clutches at herself, giggling, trying to cover herself with her hands. The effect – is it intentional? – is to draw attention to her state of undress even more.

Anne is not far behind. I am the last to be unclothed. Charles, of course, has had a run of luck. Indeed, as the banker, he has won most of Lucy's clothes, and is now wearing her petticoat over his shirt.

'Come.' Pushing back my chair, I take each girl by one hand and get to my feet. They do not demur as I lead them around the table to stand in front of him.

'Well?' I say lightly. 'Which one deserves the apple?'

Of course he knows the story, and the reason I allude to it. The Judgement of Paris. A contest of beauty that led to a war.

'Such a judgement should not be lightly made,' he says with a hungry smile, getting to his feet.

I wait, as if we are a living statue, for him to examine us. Which he does, slowly, a connoisseur's gaze travelling slowly over bare skin. He walks around us: fingers brush my back, the curves of my waist, my hip. I feel his breath on the nape of my neck. His hand cups my buttock, compares it with the other—

One thick finger touches me *there*. Next to me, Anne gasps, and I know he has done the same to her.

He slides his hand up to my breast, resting his thumb on the side of it briefly, before withdrawing it with a sigh.

He turns to Lucy, who is still giggling with nerves. On my other side, Anne stares at him with an intensity that makes me want to smile. Doubtless she is hoping that this display of her charms may lead to something more.

'Your question, Lucy,' he murmurs.

She does not know what to ask. 'Do you like what you see?' she says at last.

'Of course.'

'Do you,' she blushes. 'Do you desire me?'

'Of course,' he says again.

'Then I command you to drink a toast to my beauty,' she says with a little coquettish toss of her head.

'With the greatest pleasure,' he agrees, reaching for a glass. 'Madam, you have ravished me. I hope one day to return the compliment.' He drinks the toast, bows, then turns to Anne. 'And you, Lady Anne? What is your question?'

She too hesitates – but in her case, I sense, it is because she is wondering how best to turn this to her advantage.

'Who do you desire most: Lucy or me?' A clever question, I think: she knows that if she had included my name, he would have felt obliged to choose it.

'That is hardly a question which a gallant man should answer,' he demurs.

'It is Questions and Commands,' she reminds him. 'You must.'

He nods. 'Very well: I desire you both, but Lucy less than you.' Through our clasped hands I feel, rather than hear, Lucy's gasp of protest. 'What is your second question?'

'How many lovers have you taken this year?'

He smiles. 'That I truly cannot answer, for I never keep count.'

'Then my command is that one day you take another,' she says,

355

her meaning unmistakeable despite my presence.

He nods, and drinks the toast before turning to me. 'And you, Louise, what do you want to ask?'

'Who is the happiest monarch in the world?'

He looks surprised at this, but says, 'Louis, of course.'

'Why is he happy?'

Still he doesn't see where this is going. 'Because he is the undisputed power in his kingdom.'

'Then here is my command,' I say. 'Send Parliament home.'

He blinks, though whether it is at my effrontery or the subject, I cannot tell. I smile, and start to turn: with their hands in mine, the other two must turn with me, wheeling about my axis, until we have performed a complete about-turn.

'I command you to do only what yourself would like to do,' I say when we are facing each other again.

'Because you alone are the anointed king of England,' I add, on the second revolution.

'And only in a game such as this one,' I say, facing him for a third time, 'should anyone in this country be permitted to tell you what to do.'

I can feel Lucy trembling beside me. Debauchery she was prepared for: politics terrify her.

'Od's nails,' he breathes. 'I'll do it.' He takes a step towards me. I am still holding the hands of my naked ladies-in-waiting. He looks at them hopelessly. 'Louise . . .'

I give the smallest of shrugs. I see his nostrils flare, as if he would inhale the aroma of our skin. He puts his hands on my waist.

'Ladies, you may go,' I say, letting go of their hands. 'I bid you goodnight.'

Parliament assembles later that day, and he immediately sends them away, back to their constituencies. Prorogued until further notice. The country holds its breath – but there is no armed rebellion. The gamble has paid off.

The French fight on. The frosts come, but the Dutch break down the sea-dykes and melt the frozen polders. Those that do not melt, Louis advances across, inching forward with his cannon and his cavalry across the creaking ice. Out of nowhere, Dutch regiments appear and sweep through their ranks – they have taken the sailors from their frost-locked warships, armed them with muskets and put them on skates. Then the Dutch blow holes in the ice, sinking the cannon under the French gunners' feet. The French retreat – retreat! The French army has not retreated like this in living memory.

The Sun has been first halted, then made to go backwards. The Dutch are cheered on the streets of London, by those who are meant to be their enemies.

Meanwhile James's child bride has arrived, brought upriver by boat so that she will not hear herself being booed. It is – somewhat unfortunately – Gunpowder Night, the night when all England burns papists in effigy to celebrate the failure of a plot.

This year as well as Guido Fawkes they burn the Pope, the French king, and, for good measure, me. The stomachs of the effigies are filled with gunpowder and live cats, which squeal hideously as they feel the flames. One is burned directly opposite my windows, in the royal park. Arlington warns me with a smile that I should not go out of the palace without an armed guard.

'I rarely go out of the palace,' I inform him. 'Everything I need comes to me.'

'You are very fortunate, madam.' There are daggers in his eyes now when he looks at me. He still believes that I cheated him of the chancellorship.

The princess steps off the boat, takes three paces towards me, and sinks into a graceful curtsey. 'Your Highness.'

At once there is a ripple of laughter. The poor girl looks confused. Quickly I curtsey in return. 'I am not the queen, Your Highness. She is not at court today. But on her behalf, I am pleased to welcome you. Come, let me present you to some of your new relatives.'

Charles, stepping off the boat behind her, sees that I have taken steps to avert an incident. He nods gratefully. James does not even notice. It is said that he has been so overcome with piety that he has not yet spoken to the bride alone. Yet tonight he will deflower her. No wonder the poor girl looks terrified; no wonder she mistook me for the queen. Under cover of showing her around the court I squeeze her arm reassuringly.

All the same, I cannot help reflecting that no one ever mistakes Nell Gwynne for royalty.

When, a month later, Princess Mary is finally presented to the queen, Catherine snubs her. It seems a harsh thing to do to a child.

This court is a savage place, far more brutal than Versailles. I wonder how easily I will adjust, when I go back. If I go back. It is increasingly hard to see what will become of me if I do not succeed in England.

These gloomy thoughts are strangely timed, for I have not just succeeded here – I am triumphant. Finally, Charles has made me a duchess.

I am to be Baroness of Petersfield, Countess of Farnham, and Duchess of Pendennis. Then a few days later, he adds Duchess of Portsmouth as well.

'A naval town,' Nell Gwynne says loudly in my presence. 'Full of whores. And very close to France. How fitting.' But nobody laughs. It is clear that she is beside herself with envy. For his part, Louis responds with an equal honour: the ducal fief of Aubigny. The message is clear: I am the honoured protégée of the French king, just as I am the honoured favourite of the English one.

And yet, and yet . . . If it were possible for such a gift to have a disadvantage, it is that Charles could not have chosen a worse time to bestow it. The war is no less expensive for being stalled. The French are loathed beyond measure. It is almost as if Charles wished to draw attention to my presence at court.

Has someone advised him of this course? And if so, who? Do they hope that the people will attach their blame on me, rather than him?

In theory, the lesser ladies of the court should curtsey to me now. Many do not, or try to get away with something so perfunctory as to resemble a shrug. Let them turn their noses up. My family were nobility when England was nothing more than an outpost of barbarian Celts.

I write to my parents and tell them of the titles. They have not yet replied to my previous letter, the one informing them of the arrival of their grandson. Perhaps it would have been better to have waited, and softened the blow with this. No matter: soon I may be able to do something for them, some grand gesture that makes it plain how much our family's fortunes have altered.

One night a figure in a dark coat slips into my apartment. A secretary of some kind. Polite, self-effacing, inscrutable. I recognise him vaguely: a Parliament man, one of Arlington's party.

'I thought you should see this,' he says, handing me a letter.

It is a dispatch, or a copy of one, from Colbert de Croissy to Versailles. It takes the form of a diatribe against a certain woman.

I confess I find her on all occasions so ill-disposed for the service of our king, and showing such ill-humour against France (whether because she feels herself despised there, or whether from an effect of caprice), that I really consider she deserves no favour of Your Majesty. But, as the King of England shows her much love, and so visibly likes to please her, Your Majesty can judge whether it is best not to treat her according to her merits . . .

'Why are you showing me this?' I ask. 'You are Arlington's man.'

'I was,' he says. 'I am looking for a new patron, now.'

I raise my eyebrows. 'Me?'

'I need someone who is minded to dispense wealth, not merely to accumulate it. And Lord Arlington is not going to rise any further.'

'This is not worth a great deal, though,' I say, tapping the letter. 'An ill-considered rant, perhaps, but of no political account.'

'No,' he agrees. 'But read the final section.'

I turn over and read on. It takes a moment for it to sink in.

One risks offending Arlington by drawing close to his rival Buckingham; but for what? It must not be imagined that with two-hundred thousand crowns we can bring so large a body as Parliament to follow a course which reason alone should dictate . . .

'Buckingham has approached a middleman at the French court, and offers to sell his party's votes to Louis,' he explains. 'His intention was that Colbert not be informed, but as you can see he has been, and he is not happy.'

'What does Louis say?'

'Nothing, as yet. But he has sent a man called Ruvigny, an ex-soldier, to London as his negotiator.'

I think hard. If this scheme goes ahead, Buckingham will replace Arlington in influence. But equally, Buckingham will have betrayed Parliament by selling his party's votes. It might be possible, later, to destroy him by revealing it.

As if reading my thoughts, the polite young man says, 'Arlington will be replaced by Buckingham. Colbert will be replaced by Ruvigny. France will make terms with the Dutch. Once there is peace, perhaps the French will no longer be as hated in England as they are now. As for Buckingham, who knows what may happen to him?'

I fold the letter. 'What do you suggest I do, to bring about this happy series of events?'

'Make it clear to Louis that you do not support Colbert. Without him, Arlington will sink.'

'And Buckingham will rise.'

'Buckingham will rise,' he agrees. 'For now.'

English politics is a constant merry-go-round of betrayal and counter-betrayal, of bribery and intrigue and ambition. Nothing is fixed; everything is possible; every outcome can be manipulated. Possibilities dance in front of men like will-o'-the-wisps. But this young man seems to have a gift for seeing clearly through these chimeras of chance and favour. 'What is your name?'

'Thomas Osborne, Your Grace. At your service.' He bows.

'Thank you, Thomas. I will write to his Most Christian Majesty immediately. And I will tell Charles what Buckingham is plotting. He will, I think, be very interested to learn of it.'

Carlo

Ices, like revenge, are best served cold: but like revenge, too much cold will blunt the taste.

The Book of Ices

It seemed that nothing could stop her conquest of that court. By the end of the year, Arlington had been removed from office. In January it was Buckingham's turn to be impeached, tried by the very same Parliament which he had helped to make so powerful, and whose votes he had tried to sell to France. At the last minute he tried to curry favour with his accusers, declaring that the fault was not his but the king and his brother's. 'I can hunt the French hare with a pack of dogs, but not with a brace of lobsters,' he told them: a foolish remark, for it lost him the support of the only two people who now stood between him and the Tower. In desperation he then announced that he had seen the error of his ways. He banished his mistress Lady Shrewsbury to a convent, reconciled himself with his wife, donned a hair shirt, and adopted the dress and habits of a Puritan. It saved his life but not his pride, and from then on he was a man without influence.

Charles stood by, and did nothing to help him.

Nell Gwynne got one of her cronies, old Tom Killigrew, to dash into the king's presence in full riding gear, complete with a cape and a horsewhip. When the king asked him where he was going in such a hurry, the man cried, 'To hell, to fetch Master Cromwell back to govern us, for he could do no worse than this.' Charles looked on stony faced: for once his good humour abandoned him, and he said curtly, 'Politics does not suit you, Nell, any more than it suits your friend George Buckingham. You would do well to leave these matters to those who understand them.'

It was only Louise who could advise him now, along with Osborne and the new ambassador, Ruvigny. On her he lavished gifts – not simply jewellery, but fiefs, pensions, revenues and lands. She was the acknowledged mistress of his palace, his unofficial first minister, and the unacknowledged queen: the woman through whom all requests must pass, whose opinions became state policy; who made decisions for a king who would rather make none.

Carlo

For a celebration: bombes, flags, fancies, layer-cakes, and
other extravagant ices.

The Book of Ices

'I intend to hold a ball,' she told me, one day in early April.
'Something special. Something they will still be talking about long
after Nell Gwynne has been forgotten.'

'What do you have in mind?'

'A festival of ice,' she said promptly. 'A frost fair . . . but in
summer. Perhaps at the beginning of June, to celebrate the king's
birthday. Is it possible?'

I considered. 'It may be. If we take all the ice I collected for the
year, and use it in one go.'

'Can you make the Thames freeze over?'

I smiled. 'That would be beyond even my resources. But we
could lay ice blocks side by side on the grass, and seal them
together with water to make a kind of skating pond.'

'What about a building? A palace of ice?'

'I don't see why not. Buontalenti once made an ice grotto for
the Medici in the midst of summer. He had the sculptors carve
beasts out of ice, and trees for them to crouch amongst—'

'Yes! Let us have beasts, and trees as well,' she interrupted.
'And an ice garden, along the banks of the river. Arlington denied
me a coronation: this ball must equal that.'

'Perhaps a triumphal arch of ice, then, for you and the king to
pass beneath.'

I was half joking, but she nodded. 'And tables of ice to eat
at . . .'

364

'Frozen fountains . . .'

'And fires amongst the ice, and lanterns. As for the food, let it be a feast of ice creams, for those the king and I have honoured with an invitation.'

'It will cost a fortune,' I warned.

'He likes to spend money,' she said simply. 'It makes him feel like a king.'

I should have thought it extravagant, ridiculous even, to use up a year's supply of ice on a single night's pleasure. And yet there was a part of me that was thrilled. It was intended as her triumph; but it would be mine as well. After this the name Demirco would be as famous throughout Europe, surely, as that of Buontalenti or Varenne.

A spectacle of this nature required an army, and in the king's name I was able to command one. It was exactly the kind of fantastical, ephemeral illusion that appealed to him. Midwinter in the midst of summer, breathtaking cost, a gift from his favourite mistress, an event that would be talked about across Europe – it had all the right ingredients. I was ordered to spare nothing, no detail or expense. If I ran short of ice, I was to requisition it from those nobles who had already built ice houses, or have it shipped in from France. If I needed anything else, any special talent or expertise, I was to come straight to him.

I think he always remembered the day of his Restoration: riding into London at the head of twenty-thousand soldiers; the people weeping with joy, the streets strewn with flowers, the church bells ringing and the fountains running with wine.

In dark, cold cellars men started to cast the trees, beasts, fountains and other decorations I ordered. Dryden and Marvell were put to writing the masques. Kit Wren put aside the plans for St Paul's in order to sketch out a great pavilion of ice, a cathedral of pleasure whose carved, glittering facade would excel any wonder the country had ever seen. Hooke and Boyle, those ingenious men, devised a system of pipes carrying chilled seawater, to be laid underneath to keep it from melting. And Charles himself chose the location – Barn Elms, three miles out of London, where a bend in the river would give the impression of a frozen flood plain.

It was impossible to keep an idea like this secret: indeed, Louise did not want it to be – this party was, as she had said, a kind of coronation, and she believed the hatred the public had for her could eventually be turned to support. 'It will be a circus,' she said, 'and the mob loves a circus.' She ordered the week declared a holiday, and the maypoles decked out. Louis XIV himself sent a glass coach, so that Charles and she might arrive in suitable style.

'And make us something special,' she said to me. 'One particular ice cream, in honour of His Majesty, just as you once made one for me.'

When I look back, that spring was one of the happiest times I had in England. I was with Louise almost daily, planning the details of her ball. I was engaged in a great undertaking, which I knew would make my name. I had mastered the art of making ice creams to such an extent that I probably had no equal in the world. There was even the possibility that, if a lasting peace between France and the Dutch could be negotiated, one day she and I might be free to return to France.

Nor did it disturb my good humour to learn that Rochester had been banished from court.

'He wrote a satire that went too far, even for the king,' Louise said.

'What was the subject?'

'That the king is impotent.'

'I can see why the king would not want a slander like that to go unpunished.'

'On the contrary.' Looking around to make sure that we were not overheard, she said quietly, 'Rochester has made similar jokes

366

before, and not been banished. The difference is that now it is true.'

'The king cannot perform?'

'Only rarely.'

'That must make things easier for you, surely?'

'Not exactly.' She made a face. 'He does not want to admit it, so he tries . . . And the more he tries, the harder it is. Or not, as the case may be.'

'But is this just with you?'

'Apparently not. Wait here, I'll fetch the poem. A copy was pushed under my door, as usual.' She went to her music stool and found it.

It was the usual filth, but there was one section in particular that made me draw in my breath.

> *This you'd believe, had I but time to tell ye,*
> *The pains it costs to poor laborious Nelly,*
> *While she employs hands, fingers, mouth, and thighs,*
> *Ere she can raise the member she enjoys.*

'Even Rochester knew he had gone too far this time – he did not mean the king to see it: he handed it to him by mistake, along with another poem. But of course, now that he has been banished people are saying it must be true.'

'Will it affect your position?'

'I don't see why. He relies on me too much to dispense with me now.'

'I am sure Arlington once said the same,' I warned. 'Or Clifford, or Clarendon, or Buckingham, or any of the other ministers he has dispensed with over the years.'

'Don't worry, I know what I'm doing.'

She was right – to an extent: she had her hands firmly on all the levers of power now; but that did not stop her enemies from trying one last attempt to dethrone her. Even as we planned the occasion that would celebrate her ascendancy, those she had thrown down were plotting. They knew they could not beat her by themselves; they needed a champion, and they found it in the lovely shape of Olympe de Soisson's sister, Hortense Mancini, Duchess of Mazarin.

'The Duchess Mazarin is one of those Roman beauties in whom there is no doll-prettiness, and in whom unaided nature triumphs over all the arts of the coquette. Painters cannot say what are the colour of her eyes: they are neither blue, nor grey, nor yet black, nor brown, nor hazel. Nor are they languishing or passionate, as if either demanding to be loved or expressing love. They simply look as if she has ever basked in love's sunshine. Her complexion is softly toned, and yet warm and fresh. It is so harmonious that, though dark, she seems of beautiful fairness. Her jet-black hair rises in strong waves above her forehead, as if proud to clothe and adorn her splendid head. She never uses scents.'

César de Saint-Réal, *Memoires de la Duchesse Mazarin*

Louise

It is Nell who first alerts me, appearing at court one day dressed all in black. Expecting a repeat of the Cham of Tartary hilarity, at first I take no notice.

'Why are you in mourning, Nell?' someone says at last, feeding her the line.

'Not for any person,' she says in that peculiar nasal accent of hers. 'I am in mourning for Madam Carwell's ambitions, which are dead and buried now the Duchess of Mazarin is here.'

My ears do prick up at that – not at the nonsense, but at the title. Mazarin . . . I have heard it somewhere before, some sliver of gossip from my days in France.

And then it comes to me. Something Madame once said, discussing her brother.

He fell in love with an Italian beauty called Hortense Mancini, but those were the days of his exile, and her uncle the cardinal thought him too poor a prospect. So now he is married to Catherine of Braganza, and Hortense is scandalising all Europe as the Duchess Mazarin . . .

A love he could not attain. An old flame. *That's clever*, I think. I wonder which of my enemies has brought her to England. I am willing to bet all my not-inconsiderable pensions it has not happened by chance.

Of course I am right. A few discreet enquiries by my people, and it soon becomes apparent what is really going on.

Mazarin has left her husband and squandered all her money. She has been living off various wealthy lovers – of both sexes, they say – in different parts of Europe ever since; now, having been told by Montagu that there may be a vacancy in England for the position of king's mistress, she has been shipped over here at his expense. She has a great hatred of France: she feels Louis should have forced her husband to return her dowry.

All this I learn before I meet her. I am prepared for someone cunning – knowing that she is the sister of Olympe de Soissons, I suppose I am expecting some plump, pretty, malicious little thing.

Lord, how mistaken can one be?

I see her first walking across St James's Park at dawn, with Annie Fitzroy, the fifteen-year-old Countess of Sussex, trotting by her side. She wears a man's clothes, half undone: two swords are tucked casually under her arm, and in her other hand she carries leather fencing masks. As she comes closer I see her properly and almost stop dead.

She is beautiful. Utterly, utterly beautiful.

There is an unadorned clarity to her face, an intelligence, that makes me immediately want to like her. She is tall, slender, as long-legged as a man, but in her stride there is a rolling gracefulness, a suppleness, that is entirely feminine.

Seeing me stop she stops too, waiting to be introduced. I feel a pounding in my ears. 'Hello, Annie,' I say to the girl beside her.

'Hello,' she replies. There is a brief pause. 'May I present the Duchess Mazarin,' she adds, a little sulky at having to share this woman whom she clearly idolises.

Hortense and I exchange amused curtsies, in the French manner. 'I see you have been fencing,' I say to break the ice, but all I want to do is to feast my eyes on her, on the unadorned freshness of her face.

Her eyes light up, and suddenly she is even more beautiful. 'Do you fence?'

'Alas, no—'

'We have been fighting for my honour,' Lady Anne interjects.

'Goodness. That sounds dangerous.'

'I am teaching her to defend herself,' Hortense says with a smile. 'You never know when it will come in useful.'

The girl takes one of the swords and makes some passes in the air. Instantly Hortense drops into the *en garde* position, graceful as a cat, and parries Anne's amateurish lunges with three casual flicks of her blade.

'I myself have never learned to fence,' I say weakly.

'I will teach you too, if you like,' Hortense says eagerly, without taking her eyes off Annie's sword. 'Then we can fight a duel. That would be fun, wouldn't it?'

Perhaps she is trying to disarm me, but I have no sense of ill will from her: I am simply an obstacle that stands in her way. Perhaps not even that. She must be used to the fact that every man she meets falls in love with her. Women, too. Other women – wives, mistresses, lovers – are not really rivals. She has the luxury of not needing to try, of not having to fight for what she wants.

Of course Charles will succumb. Of course he will tell himself that he must have this extraordinary woman, just as he once told himself he must have me. The cure for his impotence is courtship: in the battle to possess her, he will rediscover his lost vigour.

All I can do is be patient, and hope that afterwards he will return to my bed, rather than be impotent in hers.

I have my strategy. A waiting game. It is the correct approach, I am sure of it. And yet, these mornings, as I pull myself from my bed and sit before my mirror to begin the necessary work on my face, I feel a great weariness, as if I have barely slept at all. As if the effort of putting on my gorgeous gowns, my jewels, my ropes of pearls and my sapphire brooches, is almost more than I can bear.

But still I do it. I would not be beaten by the common, loathsome Nell Gwynne, and I will not be beaten by the well-bred, lovely Hortense Mancini.

And so I paint on my face, primp my hair, line my eyes. For what? The king rarely comes to me these days. When the court moves, as usual, to Newmarket for the spring races, his steward does not even allocate me lodgings. When I ask Charles, with a smile, whether he has forgotten me, he says, genuinely surprised, 'I thought you would rather stay in London, dearest Fubs, and run the country for me while I am gone.'

I have become a sort of second wife, as forgotten as the queen. I stay in London and run the country. Word comes back that at Newmarket, Hortense Mancini is up early every morning, riding the fastest, most dangerous horses over the gallops.

No one seems certain whether she and the king are lovers yet. Anne Sussex has the use of an apartment above the king's, where Hortense visits her; it is said the king visits too, but as for what goes on there, no one knows. The ambassador believes that the duchess is having an affair with Lady Anne, and the king holds back for that reason alone. Others think it is all a game, to inflame him.

I carry on planning my ball. Perhaps by then she will have gone.

Another poem, pushed under my door.

> *Methinks I see you, newly risen*
> *From your embroidered bed and pissing;*
> *With studied mien and much grimace*
> *Present yourself before your glass*
> *To vanish and smooth o'er those graces*
> *You rubbed off in your night embraces.*

Rochester, of course; back at court, loathsome as ever. It is said that while he was banished he wrote a play called *Sodom* that surpasses in vileness anything that even the Romans wrote. There are scenes involving six men and six women, dildoes, buggery, and the rest. A private performance was staged for Charles and a select group of his wits. A gift to titillate the waning virility of a king.

*

'The fact is,' the ambassador says, 'we are entering a delicate phase.'

I drag my attention back to him. Courtin, his name is. Small, dapper, discreet. Ruvigny, it seems, asked to be withdrawn. 'A damn filthy traffic,' was how he summed it up, this court of England.

The sight of the French handing out bribes, they say, disgusted him even more than the sight of the English accepting them.

'Why is it delicate?'

'His Most Christian Majesty is inclined to sue for peace. As a temporary measure, you understand. A tactical withdrawal. His negotiators are assembling at Nimeguen even as we speak.'

'What has that to do with Hortense Mancini?'

'His Majesty's greatest bargaining tool is still the alliance with England. If it were known abroad that Charles had cast you out, and taken an enemy of France into his bed instead . . .'

'He will not cast me out,' I say. 'My position is more secure than ever. Soon all Europe will be talking of my ball. My ice palace. My birthday party for the king.'

He smiles, thin-lipped. We both know that it is now much more than a birthday party.

Carlo

Of all extravagant ices, the *gelato luminoso,* an ice surrounding a fountain of fireworks, is one of the most spectacular.

The Book of Ices

I had seen her weary before, but in all her time in England I had never before seen her downcast. There was a kind of sadness about her now, a calm resignation – not because she was beaten; far from it; but perhaps because she had realised that this would be her lot: a lifetime of fighting off prettier, or younger, or more exotic rivals.

'It is certain now,' she said to me one day in early May. 'Mazarin and he are lovers. Lady Anne has been sent off to the country, but Charles spends almost as much time in her apartments as he did before.'

'Here, I have made you a cordial,' I said, handing it to her. 'It is what the apothecaries call sambooch – distilled elderberries. It is said to be reviving.'

'Thank you.' She drank a little, but I could tell she had barely tasted it.

'Do you think he will come back to you?'

She shrugged. 'I have come to suspect that I am only a kind of symbol to him now. He does not actually want me; he simply wants everyone to think that he does. I am the French mistress, as necessary to him as a French tailor or a French chef, no more.'

'Then he is a fool,' I said.

'Oh, he will not be faithful to Mazarin either. He is no more capable of standing by a woman than he is of standing by a treaty.'

'Then he is a double fool.'

'I should not mind, really, should I? I have influence now without the need to lie in his bed for it. There was a time when that was all I wanted. Besides, it means,' she hesitated. 'It means that I am free in other ways, too.'

'What do you mean?'

She did not answer me directly, but went to the window, looking down at the park. 'Do you remember what I said, that time at Versailles when I told you I couldn't marry you, and you asked why we couldn't love each other even so?'

'Of course. You said that you were not like my friend Olympe.'

'Yes.' She spoke calmly enough, but her remarks were still addressed to the window. 'I was so proud in those days . . . But I am like Olympe, now, aren't I? I am exactly like her. A cast-off lover of the king.'

I stared at her. 'Are you saying—'

'Now that I have no honour to protect, and no one to be faithful to, I can take a lover for myself. If I want to.'

'And do you want to?' I said quietly.

She had coloured a little. 'I thought I might as well see what all the fuss is about.'

'Do you have anyone in particular in mind?'

'I thought I might place an advertisement in the *London Register*. 'Whore of Babylon – most hated woman in the country – seeks lover. Must be able to make ice creams.'

'There is only one person in this country who can do that.'

'Then I will have to hope that it is him who responds to my advertisement.'

I said nothing, my heart suddenly too full.

'If you still want me, that is,' she added. 'Everybody else seems to have decided that I am not worth the bother. I will quite understand if you have too.'

'Oh, Louise,' I said. 'Louise . . .' And then I had stepped towards her, and pulled her into my arms. 'Are you sure?'

She was nodding and gasping and laughing all at once, but she had not forgotten the need for caution. 'Wait,' she protested. 'Not here, someone will see us. But yes, I'm sure. I have never been surer of anything. We will have to be discreet—'

'Of course. I would not risk your reputation.'

'I have no reputation, you ninny. I would simply like to avoid being gossiped about yet again.'

'When shall I come to you?'

'Tonight. No one will be watching then.'

'I'll come,' I promised. 'But – why now? What changed your mind?'

She shrugged, and would not say, but I pressed her, and eventually she told me.

'My parents are in England.'

'Your parents! Where?'

'They are staying with Sir Richard Browne, in Hampshire. An old friend of my father's. They fought together against the Spanish.'

'When do they come to court?'

'They don't.'

'Why not?' I said, puzzled.

'They don't answer my letters. But I have been told that they intend never to speak to me again.'

'What! How dare they—'

'No, it is all right. I understand: they think I have disgraced them. They have a rather old-fashioned view of what is honourable, you see. And they will never see that it was partly their own fault. They thought that dukes and lords should be queuing up to marry me because I bore their name. They couldn't understand that without money, their precious name was worth nothing.' She was crying: it made me realise that I had not seen her cry for many months. 'Well, I am free of them now,' she said angrily. 'I did my duty, and look where it got me. From now on I shall look out for myself.'

Carlo

Strawberries and white pepper ice cream; blackberry and
cream sorbet; chocolate and vanilla custard . . . No matter
how many new combinations we invent, the greatest ices
remain the simplest.

The Book of Ices

I walked through the darkened corridors of the palace, an ice
chest in my arms. If anyone asked, I was taking an ice to the king's
cast-off mistress, to console her. Anyone who bothered to check
would have found in the chest an ice cream of red strawberries
and white pepper, nestling in a garland of strawberry leaves.

Nobody stopped me. Nobody asked. The king was elsewhere.
Those left behind were of no account.

Her apartments, usually so crowded with courtiers and ministers, were empty. 'I've sent them away,' she said, seeing me glance
into the shadows. 'We won't be disturbed.'

She was wearing her hair loose, twisted in a kind of rope over
one shoulder of her *déshabillé*. Her feet were bare, and she had
removed the king's jewels. But it was not that which was so different about her. She seemed somehow younger, as if some of the
weariness had lifted from her shoulders along with the weight of
the king's rubies.

'You're happy,' I said, wondering. 'I don't think I've ever seen
you happy before.'

She stepped towards me. Without her court shoes, she was
shorter than usual. I put my hands on her shoulders—

'Wait,' she said softly, kissing me and stepping back. 'I want
tonight to last for ever.'

'We've waited long enough.' And I picked her up and carried her bodily into the bedchamber.

Her white, white skin: the colour of candlewax, of white strawberries, of ice cream.

I spooned a shaving of strawberry ice onto her belly, and carried it to her lips with my mouth. We passed the sweetness back and forth between us, until it had melted away to nothing on our tongues.

She melted more slowly. The ice cream was soon all gone, but I kept licking it from her belly anyway. From her belly, and the soft downy dish at the top of each thigh, and her mouth, cold and creamy with kisses and ice.

I had waited all these years. I could wait a few minutes longer.

Until eventually, with a sigh, she pulled my head to hers, and kissed me with a sudden desperate passion, and I knew that she was ready to feel pleasure.

This was a new Louise. Her eagerness that night – her *greed* – almost took me by surprise. It was as if she had been starved of sensations for so long that now she must feast on them without restraint.

And yet. And yet.

I did not tell her this, but as we lay together I sensed the presence of a third person in the room – or perhaps it is truer to say, I sensed his absence. When she turned her head, like so, it was because he kissed her just *there*, on the cheek: when she looked at me with those sleepy, smiling eyes, it was because he liked her to look at him that way. When she gasped, it was a gasp that he had heard a thousand times.

And when the paroxysm gripped her, all her muscles clenching as she strained for the moment of release, whispering imprecations in French too fast for me to catch, it was almost as if she had left us both, pleasure bearing her away to a place where neither could follow.

It is well known, of course, that in the midst of love's ecstasy one may experience a moment of unexpected sadness. I felt it that night. I had achieved my heart's desire, and I was not disappointed – far from it – but there was something missing, something I could not put my finger on, or name.

Carlo

White peaches, perfectly ripe, redolent of the final days of summer. Chocolate, thick and smooth and rich with cream. Truly, there is no more heavenly combination of ices in the world.

The Book of Ices

I threw myself into the preparations for the ice ball. Nothing was left to chance. I made a miniature of the skating pond, to make sure it worked, and a scale model of the ice palace, in which a paper Louise and a paper Charles sat on tiny thrones to welcome a line of paper guests. As for the ice creams, I experimented with some extraordinary flavours. I made an ice cream that was smoked, gently, by lighting a small pile of tobacco leaves under a perforated *frigidarium*: as the leaves smouldered, the fragrant smoke seeped through the mixture, scenting it. I made an ice that was encased in a warm pie of meringue, and another that contained at its core a hot, spurting ball of caramel sauce. I even made an ice cream from apples that were just starting to rot: the taste was utterly decadent, rich with the juices of mortality, yet sweet as brandy wine.

But for the king, I created an ice that was both simple and extraordinary. Indeed, the idea was Wren's, that day in Garraway's when he had idly suggested that I turn the newly fashionable drink of chocolate into an ice. When I combined eggs, syrup and cream with cocoa powder and a dozen chocolate tablets, I made an ice cream so voluptuous, so thick and so smooth that nothing else could possibly be my centrepiece.

I remembered the board of pear sorbets I had made for Louis

XIV. How primitive those seemed now! But there was virtue, as Louis had said, in simplicity. I made a board of chocolate ices – first a plain chocolate ice cream; then one of chocolate scented with rosemary; another that combined chocolate with mint, then chocolate and orange, chocolate and raspberry, chocolate and cherries, and finally a dark, pungent ice based on the *sanguinaccio* of Florence, chocolate with blood and pine nuts.

Every few days, I went to see Louise, to show her what I had done. And under the guise of secrecy – 'This part is to be a surprise: you must leave us now' – the ladies-in-waiting and the ministers of state and the painters and the hangers-on were shooed out of her apartments, and we eagerly took my ices to her bed.

I made an ice cream of white peaches and musk – her taste – and scented it with a drop or two of the rosewater perfume she wore.

When I looked at my model palace, there was something missing. I made a snowman, and placed him on a plinth in the foyer of the ice palace, just behind the king and his mistress. As the revellers entered the pavilion, tiny crystals of frozen scented snow would float and glitter about their heads, while the snowman smiled his inscrutable smile, and welcomed them to the dance.

Hannah came to see me.

'I am giving notice,' she said without preamble. 'My ship leaves from Bristol in three weeks.'

I looked at her, surprised. 'But what about the ice ball?'

'I will miss it. And I am sorry about that, for it sounds as if it will be a memorable occasion. But if we do not take this boat we will lose our passage to America.'

I noted the plural. 'Elias is going too?'

'Yes. He will be quite sad to leave. He has enjoyed his time working for you.'

'But this is most inconvenient,' I said angrily. 'We are busier now than we have ever been. The king himself is relying on us—'

'I am sorry for it,' she said patiently. 'But we have been planning this for years. You never asked how long we would be working for you, or I would have told you sooner.'

I heard myself say, 'Then if you must go, leave the boy behind.'

'Leave Elias! How could I possibly do that?'

'I was younger than him when I left my parents. They let me go because . . .' I paused. 'Because they knew that I would have a better future. That I would become a man of the court. As Elias will. I will teach him my secrets, Hannah, just as I was taught them by my own master. He will be a wealthy man. A favourite of kings and emperors. After this ball, our fame will spread even further, I am sure of it. I will take him to Paris, to Naples, to Spain—'

'But that is not the future I choose for him,' she said.

'Why not? What more could you wish for?'

'What more could I wish for?' she repeated, a sad smile touching her eyes. 'A kingdom without kings. A church without churches. A country where there are no bonds; not of property, nor privilege, nor birth. A place where no man is born with stirrups on his back, for other men to ride him. Where every man can choose his way of worship; yea, and every woman too, and the only laws to which we pay allegiance are written in our hearts.'

I sighed. 'Your new country will be like a pack of animals, then. Without laws or leaders, you will simply fight each other.'

'If we need leaders, we will choose them. If we need laws, we will make them ourselves.' She hesitated. 'Perhaps you should come too.'

'Come to America!'

'Why not? There is ice a-plenty in winter, and they say the summers are hot. Perfect conditions for an ice-seller, it seems to me.' She shrugged. 'Ice creams and pies. They go together, almost, don't they? Perhaps we could set up in business together, you and I.'

I stared at her. 'My ice creams are bought by kings and cardinals. Neither of which, as I understand it, America is yet supplied with.'

'Of course,' she said quietly. 'Forgive me. It was a stupid suggestion.'

Going round the pantry, she packed her things in silence for a while. Then, as she went to the door, she said, 'This is my last chance to say this, so I will say it. What you have now, with Louise de Keroualle – that is enslavement, not love.'

I said stiffly, 'That is none of your business.'

'But it is,' she said, a little sadly. 'Oh, it is.'

'Why?'

But she did not answer me directly. She said, 'It seems to me there are two kinds of love – the love that happens to us, and the love that we invite. The love that happens to us uninvited is a physical thing, as a sickness is, and like a sickness it makes us weak. It is a love that must hurt us, because it based on the need to possess someone, rather than on affection or respect. But the love that we invite – that two people choose to have together – that grows, daily, from small beginnings. It is like a fire that can be kept just hot enough to cook on, and to warm the house, but is not allowed to rage until it has burnt down the whole city, as the great fire of London did. But you cannot do it alone. It takes two.'

I said angrily, 'What is this mad talk of fires and cooking? Go to America, woman, with your bastard. Go and be damned. You will end up a whore there, just as you have been a whore here in England.'

She said slowly, 'You asked me once why I came to your room, that first time. I did not tell you the real reason. I did it because I liked you. And I thought that I could lift your melancholy. But I came to realise that no woman could do that.'

'One can,' I said shortly. 'Indeed, she has.'

'Then it is not love which makes you sad, for you are no less melancholy than you were before,' she said quietly. 'It must be your secrets. Until you choose to give those up, I do not think you will ever be free.'

She stood looking at me, and then without another word she turned away.

The next day she left for Bristol, without saying goodbye.

Louise

The king, back from Newmarket, calls on me solicitously. But only in the afternoons. At night, he is elsewhere.

One afternoon we attend a concert by some visiting musicians. They invite the king to choose a song.

'Ask Fubs,' he says. 'She knows these French ballads better than me.'

'Sing the one that begins, "Let me die of grief, but not of jealousy,"' I say. He smiles wryly, acknowledging the joke.

Later, the musicians strum their guitars. 'Are we to dance?' he asks.

'I could not dance to this tune, sir,' I answer. 'It is too rough and wild for dancing.'

He turns to those behind us. 'Is there anyone who will dance?'

'I will,' calls a voice, and Hortense Mancini steps forward, into the space between the musicians and our chairs. Without a trace of self-consciousness she adopts a position: one leg cocked, her arms above her head.

I am reminded of the way she crouched *en garde*: supple, poised, waiting.

Then the music starts – fast and giddy. She spins and stamps and snaps her fingers – there is a part of me that wants to say, *Oh look, Charles, she dances like a Neapolitan gypsy*; but the words stick in my throat. The dance is nakedly sensual, pagan. But she does not dance for him alone: it is me, too, at whom she directs her flashing gaze, her glittering eyes. I can hardly breathe. I glance sideways at the king. He is staring at her, fixated.

When she has finished, bowing insouciantly to the applauding court, it is us, not her, who are short of breath.

Carlo

Chocolate ice cream: this is not an easy ice to make, but it repays the effort. Mix together half a cup of chocolate powder and half a cup of sugar. Add enough cold milk to make a paste, then two cups of hot milk. Simmer very gently, stirring all the while, for eight minutes. Then remove from the heat and stir in six one-ounce tablets of chocolate, chopped very fine. In a separate bowl, beat together six egg yolks and half a cup of sugar and beat until pale. Pour in the chocolate mixture, beating vigorously. Heat, but do not boil; add half a cup of sugar syrup; cool in a cold-water bath, and finally beat in two cups of heavy cream before you freeze.

The Book of Ices

The king had asked for an ice, his first in many months. I made an ice of chocolate and raisins, and took it to his apartments.

'He is in his laboratory,' the footman told me. 'You are to go straight in.'

I found the laboratory full of a stinking smoke, and the king coughing. 'Ah, signor,' he said cheerfully. 'Never mix sulphur and magnesia.'

'Indeed, sir.'

There was a large glass prism beside the window. It had been arranged in such a way that it caught the sunlight, scattering it into a rainbow of colours. I could not help wondering how it was done, for the glass itself appeared to be completely plain, with nothing inside it.

Seeing me looking, the king nodded. 'You can pick it up.'

I picked it up and peered inside the prism, but the colours instantly vanished. It was only when it was placed in the sun again that the rainbow reappeared.

'One of my *virtuosi* fashioned it,' he said. 'It shows what light is made of.'

'Light, surely, comes from God?'

'So we were taught. But this man has dared to look inside God's light, and now finds that like any other substance it has its composition and its quantities. And so another of our childish illusions is pricked by the cold scepticism of science.' He was silent a moment. 'How fares the Duchess of Portsmouth's ball? She has everything she needs?'

'Yes, thank you, sir.'

'I am very fond of the duchess, signor.'

'Of course,' I said, not entirely certain how else I should respond.

'That is to say, I would not want her to be without anything that she requires for her entertainment.' He turned back to his bench. 'Or, indeed, her comfort.'

I nodded, unable to speak, for I saw now what this conversation was really about.

'I have been unable to attend Her Grace recently as much as I would have wished. The pressure of business. . .'

He looked at the chocolate ice cream where it sat on the table. One of his lapdogs clambered onto the stool, put his head on one side, and eased his tongue into the bowl. A few licks later, and the ice cream was gone.

'I am not, by nature, a jealous man,' he said softly. 'Take care that you are not either, signor, and we shall do very well.' He touched the glass prism, spinning it so that the rainbow whirled around the room. 'Sometimes it does not do to enquire too closely into the nature of things. Sometimes there can be altogether too much light.'

*

I walked through the streets of London, thinking. I walked for several hours, until it was dark.

Then I turned back towards Whitehall.

I went to Louise's apartments. But although it was by now very late, my way was blocked by two unfamiliar footmen.

'You can't go in,' one of them said.

'Tell her it is—'

'No one enters. Including us.'

I stepped back. 'I am her confectioner.' I realised how feeble it sounded. But just then the door opened and the French ambassador came out. He cast me a shifty look before scuttling off.

I waited. A few minutes later Thomas Osborne came out – or Lord Danby, as we were to call him since he had become Lord Treasurer. He, too, glanced at me quickly and then turned away.

Assuming that whatever the meeting was, it was over, I once again stepped towards the door – only to find my way still barred.

'His Majesty does not wish to be disturbed.'

'His Majesty!' I stared at the door, trying to imagine what was happening behind it. 'I will wait until he comes out.'

The footman shrugged, as if to say it was all the same to them.

I went to a nearby window seat and waited. Dawn was breaking when at last the door opened and a familiar figure stepped out.

I did not move, but the light from the window must have caught my face, because he came to stand at the window. Down below us, in St James's Park, a small group of deer moved silently through the early morning mist.

'Another fine day, signor,' he said, looking out. Then he was gone, the long stride echoing down the corridor, the footmen marching at his heels.

Her apartments were grown so large that just to reach her bed-chamber took an age. Every surface was covered with paintings and tapestries: every corner contained some ornate French cabinet or priceless vase. Candles burned low in great glass chandeliers above my head, chandeliers shivered and chimed softly as I passed below them.

She too was standing by a window, wrapped only in a long woollen chemise, her hair tumbled over one shoulder, looking down at the mist where it wreathed on the surface of the lake.

As I entered she turned. She did not seem particularly surprised that I was there.

'I came to warn you,' I said. 'To tell you that the king knows about us. It seems I was too late.'

She nodded.

'What's going on?' I asked.

'Last night, in these rooms, he signed a new treaty with France.'

'A secret one, I take it?'

'Yes. It replaces the Treaty of Dover. In return for a new pension from Louis, Charles will prorogue Parliament and commit England to another war with the Dutch.'

'Another! The blood is hardly dry from the last one.'

'He gets four million gold crowns. Enough to pay for all the mistresses he could ever want. Enough to rebuild Windsor Castle. Enough to live like a king.'

'*Like* a king?'

She shrugged. 'From now on, France will make all decisions affecting England's foreign policy. What Charles does at home, of course, is of no concern.'

'And his conversion? The conversion of his country? All Madame's hopes for his soul?'

'Madame was not pragmatic in these matters. In my treaty, Charles simply promises never to set aside the queen. His heir will thus be his brother James, who is already a Catholic. England will become Catholic after Charles is dead.'

'But your own hopes of becoming queen—'

'Were impractical as well,' she interrupted. 'I should have

accepted that sooner. I have my work cut out just being what I am.'

'And what is that?' I demanded – pointlessly, for the tumbled bedsheets already told me.

'He has returned to me,' she said simply. 'I am the king's mistress again.'

'And – that's it?' I said desperately. 'He walks in and claims you, and I am just put aside?'

She gave me a look then of sudden pity – not pity that I felt this way, but pity that I had not understood.

And with a sudden realisation, I did understand.

'It's no coincidence, is it?' I said slowly.

She did not reply.

'The king had grown bored with you. You needed to find some way of rekindling his interest. Some *game*.' Another thought struck me. 'Are there spy holes?' I eyed the painted panelling above the bed, the mirrors artfully placed in the corners of the room. 'Did you tell him when to come and watch? When I would be here? Where to stand, to reinvigorate Old Rowley's withered yard?'

'I did not tell him,' she said wearily. 'You are wrong about that, at least.'

'But you allowed others to.'

'I can't help it if the palace is full of spies. Carlo, you should be pleased at this outcome. Far from being jealous, the king has made it clear that you have his blessing. Not all men would be so understanding. It is a sign of how important I am to him now.'

'You will be the most loathed woman in the kingdom, if there is another war.'

'I am not here to be popular. Besides, my children are to be given titles. Little Charles will be raised as a Protestant. He is to become Baron Settrington, Earl of March and Duke of Richmond.' She rolled the English titles off her tongue, savouring each word. 'Ample recompense for a little jeering, don't you think?'

'Tell me one thing,' I said. 'When we lay together – in that bed . . .' I could hardly bear to look at it now. 'Was any of that real, or was it all simply to excite the king?'

'Oh, that was real. You must believe that. It was a greater pleasure than any I have ever felt.'

'And?' I demanded. 'Surely that means something to you?'

She shrugged.

'Pleasure is pleasure,' she said simply. 'It means nothing. It changes nothing. Enjoyable, yes, but compared with the important things – planning, and achievement, and making all Europe march to one drum – compared with shaping the world, it is nothing.'

'Then you don't love me.'

'Not as you love me, no. And you know something? I am glad of it. How I would hate to have my judgement clouded by a passion such as that. It is like tennis – when you play for love, you play for nothing. And so love comes to mean nothing, in the end.'

She put one hand on my shoulder.

'This will all be all right. You'll see, Carlo. Come to bed. We should celebrate this.'

I left her then.

I turned and walked out of her apartments, the outer rooms already filling with petitioners eager to get the best position at her *ruelle*. I walked out of that decrepit, sprawling palace, past rakes still drunk from the night before and grand ladies hurrying home in their ballgowns. I passed courtesans tiptoeing from ministers' apartments, and yawning footmen removing the burnt-out stubs from silver candlesticks. As that great hive of cynicism and debauchery came to life for another day, I left it without a backward glance.

I walked through St James's Park. One of the deer lifted his head to watch me: a single stag, his head crowned with antlers, guarding his does.

The kitchens at the Red Lion were quiet, now that Hannah had gone. There was no smell of baking pies wafting through the dining room, no aroma of fresh herbs steeping on the stove.

She had left the alcove where she worked very tidy. Her perishables had been given away to neighbours or friends, the saucepans and tools sold in the market for ready cash.

On the table was a book. I picked it up, wondering why she had left this particular volume behind.

Culpeper. *The Compleat Herbal.* I opened the cover. On the flyleaf she had written,

Signor,
   This book is freely available where I am going. So you had better have this one, and I will buy another. But please keep it safe, and do not let them burn it.
   Your friend, Hannah Crowe

I turned the pages.

Musk melons . . . Cucumbers . . . Burdock . . .

Nettles are so well known that they need no description; they may be found, by feeling, in the darkest night.

Chamomile . . . Penny-mint . . . Cress . . .

Did a book of herbs really deserve to be burned?

Was Charles right, when he talked to me about the prism? Is it really knowledge that is dangerous, or secrecy?

I took my cart and drove down to Barn Elms. Builders wearing gloves against the cold were hard at work, hoisting into place the great blocks of carved and moulded ice that would make up the facade of the pavilion. Next to it, the skating pond was already complete, covered with straw to keep it fresh.

I walked round, inspecting their handiwork. Even now, the sun's rays were making the surface of the blocks damp. When it was finished the ice palace would last a few days, a fortnight at the most.

It would be a triumph – of course it would: everything she did was a triumph. People would talk about this extravagance for years. As for the tastes of my ice creams, what would be said about them? Nothing – for how could anyone talk about something so few had experienced and none could imagine?

They would disappear, like snowflakes in summer. Like Michelangelo's snowman, washed away by the rain.

Two apprentices were playing amongst a pile of discarded chippings. As they hurled fistfuls of ice at each other the chips scattered and caught the sun above their heads, a flashing, glittering rainbow of colours. The children shrieked and whooped, before the foreman stopped them with a growl.

I loaded up my cart with ice and tools. To the east lay the road back to London – the new King's Road, still unfinished, but sure to be a recipient of some of those French *livres* soon. To the west lay the great road that led to the far coast of England: the ports of Plymouth, Bristol and Torquay.

I went west, towards the setting sun.

Carlo

Few pleasures, indeed, can be made so cheaply as an ice.

The Book of Ices

Beyond Slough I came across a small country horse-fair. It was nothing special, but it was all the more special for that: children on ponies were showing off their prowess over tiny jumps; there were jugglers and lace-sellers, a competition for the biggest marrow, and another for the cow with the fastest milk. At the market stalls they were selling gooseberries, blackcurrants, apricots and nuts.

I made a blackcurrant ice cream, and served it with the sweet, rich cream from the milk.

At Maidenhead I made an ice of lemon-cream and penny-mint, and sold it on market day for a ha'penny a glass.

At Newbury I bought gooseberries, and made an ice-cream fool.

At Hungerford I almost caused a riot with an ice cream of Barcelona nuts. I had prepared two gallons, but such was the demand that many had to share. I saw country lasses and country boys licking spoons together, and by the time I left that place there was dancing around the maypoles.

At Castle Combe I spent the evenings writing down my recipes, and how to make ice colder with salt.

At Marlborough Fair I gave a demonstration – they thought it was a trick, and kept asking each other how I was fooling them. I had to give away the ice cream for nothing before they would believe me.

At Bath I parked my cart outside the Assembly Rooms. I made

an ice of nectarines, and another of pistachios, and watched the fashionable lords and ladies skip like country folk for joy.

By the time I reached Bristol I had used up all my ice, except for a final pint or so. I put it in my rooms, and as I wrote my book of ices I watched it turn to water – clear and cool and pure.

I drank it with a few drops of lemon-pulp, and a sprig of sweet cicely.

Bristol is a big town – the biggest in England, after London. It is said good ice can be got here, for use by the gentry. But I have had enough of making ices for now.

I have found a Mr Gregory, a bookseller, who has agreed to print the book. He seems a little surprised that I do not want money. But I have my tools, and my skill: it is enough for me.

I wonder if I will find Hannah in America. It seems unlikely – even according to the unfinished map I have purchased, it is clearly a vast country. But somehow it does not seem impossible. Somehow nothing seems impossible, in a country so new and fresh it has not even been properly mapped yet.

A place where no man is born with stirrups on his back, for other men to ride him.

A new and accurate map of the world.

Even if I do not find her, I will find love. Of that I am sure. I will be moved by the spirit of God's grace within me, just as she described.

And as I sit here scribbling in this inn, waiting for my boat which is still two weeks away, I take a draught of water and I feel, somewhere deep inside me, a sliver of something hard and cold, something that has been there for as long as I can remember, finally start to melt.

Louise

Of course you hate me. Why would you not?

It is certain that I am now the most hated woman in England. Now that English boys have once again been dying with Dutch musket balls in their chests, and drowning with Dutch cannon ringing in their ears. Now that Hortense Mancini, tiring both of Charles's attentions and his vacillations, has skipped off to Europe with the Prince of Monaco, taking all the king's presents with her.

It is rumoured that Thomas Osborne, Lord Danby, shares my affections with the king these days. It is not true – he has a shrewish wife, and it seemed politic to charm the man – but many believe it, including the king.

Danby and I have something much more interesting in common. We divide between us the sale of the minor offices of state. No one cares greatly whether this squire or that one gets appointed Sheriff of Hampshire or Keeper of the Royal Ducks, so we decide according to the emoluments we are offered. Who can object? Every Member of Parliament is taking bribes. If any of them cause trouble, I simply ask the French Embassy to provide me with the receipts.

And yet the irony is that all this corruption has turned out to be a waste of France's gold. The wars against Holland which almost bankrupted her have not been won – and such territories as France has managed to acquire belonged to Spain, not the Dutch. It is the English who have somehow ended up with the greatest prize: New Amsterdam, now to be renamed New York.

It is the Dutch war, too, which has alerted the English to the extraordinary abilities of Charles's nephew, William of Orange. If he can defend Holland against the French, people think, could he do the same for England? And so Danby has arranged a secret marriage between William and Anne, the Duke of York's oldest daughter, a betrothal which I have long known all about, but which – for reasons of my own – I did not bring to the attention of my masters in France.

Hedging my bets, you see.

But even that alliance has not brought peace. Buckingham and Arlington may be finished, but Lord Shaftesbury is still machinating in their place. His Whigs are stirring up fantastical plots: I have lost track of the chapbooks, ballads, satires, and pamphlets that have been pushed under my door, the pornographic engravings that purport to show the Whore of Brittany being pleasured by her regiment of papist lovers.

Nell Gwynne likes to tell the story of how she was attacked by a mob while out driving in her carriage. Realising from their shouts that they had mistaken her coach for mine, she leaned out of the window and shouted, 'No, good people – I am the Protestant whore!' Whereupon they gave her three cheers, and an escort home.

If it had been me, as she smugly observes, there might have been one less Catholic in England by nightfall.

But if you hate me, ask yourself this: what else should I have done?

I could have married gentry, and produced a string of heirs. I could have entered a convent, and become – I suppose – a Mother Superior. I could have been the companion to some great lady, helping her with her sewing and her household accounts.

I could have married an ice-cream maker whom I did not love, and lived a comfortable bourgeois life in the shadow of a court, surrounded by our children.

As it is, there are queens who do not wield the influence I do, and ministers who do not have my reach. Whatever happens in this strange, barbarous little country – whatever shifting allegiances may crack and splinter beneath my feet – I will keep moving forward, and I will thrive.

Read on for an historical note from the author and reading group questions for *The Empress of Ice Cream*.

For background, reading notes, a message board and information on Anthony Capella's other books, please go to www.anthonycapella.com

Historical Note

It is a heresy according to a true lover's creed ever to forgive an infidelity. But where mere nature is the motive, it is possible for a man to think righter than the common opinion, and to argue that a rival taketh away nothing but the heart, and leaveth all the rest.

George Savile, Marquess of Halifax, on Charles II

At the time of Charles II's death in 1685 Louise de Keroualle was thirty-four. She returned to France a wealthy woman, retiring to her ducal fief of Aubigny and living there quietly until her death at the age of eighty-five. Voltaire met her when she was seventy and described her 'with a face still noble and pleasing, that the years had never withered.' She never married, devoting herself instead to good works and high-stakes gambling in equal measure.

'Pretty, witty Nell,' as Pepys called her, died in 1687, at the age of thirty-seven. By the time of her death she had amassed considerable debts.

Charles's throne was inherited by his brother James, but the English Parliament rebelled, arguing that he had abdicated by virtue of his choice of religion. The army refused to give him their support and he had no choice but to flee the country. Parliament then invited the Protestant William of Orange to be their ruler. It was the first time in Europe that an elected body had effectively appointed their own king, an almost-bloodless coup that became known as The Glorious Revolution. One of the first acts of the new Parliament was to pass a law forbidding the English monarch from being, or marrying, a Catholic – a law that is still on the statute books today.

The Persian technique of making sorbets and water ices was known in Florence by the 1660s, although the exact process was a well-guarded secret. A visiting Frenchman, one L. Audiger, then somehow took it to Paris in about 1665. He became *limonadier* to Louis XIV, having presented the king with some out-of-season peas by way of an introduction. How the technology came to England, and how it developed into 'ice cream' by the time of Charles II's great feast for the Order of the Garter in 1671, is not known, nor is the name of the confectioner who, according to the written menu, served 'One plate of white strawberries and one plate of ice cream' to the king's table alone. However, the name Demirco has long been anecdotally ascribed to the man who decided not to allow ice creams to remain a royal privilege. Some accounts have him working for Charles I, but as there are no records of him in the royal household at that time, and since ice cream had not been invented by then, it seems likely that over the centuries the two Charleses simply got mixed up.

In the decades following Charles II's death the knowledge of how to make ice cream slowly spread across Europe. One of the first books of recipes was an anonymous eighty-four-page manu-script entitled *The Art of Making Ices* which, through watermarks in the paper, has been dated to the period shortly before 1700. It includes recipes for violet, rose, chocolate, and caramel ice creams – flavours that would have seemed as extraordinary at the time as anything devised by molecular gastronomists today. In 1718 a woman called Mary Eales, who claimed to have been a confectioner at the English court, published a recipe 'for icing cream . . . either plain or sweetened, or with fruit in it'. There is also an ice cream recipe in *The Art of Cookery made Plain and Easy* by the Englishwoman Hannah Glasse in 1751, which is admirably simple: 'To make Ice Cream . . . set it into the larger Bason. Fill it with Ice, and a Handful of Salt.'

In the meantime, Quakers and other non-conformists had taken ice cream making to America. The earliest record in that country comes from Pennsylvania in 1744: 'Among the rarities . . . was some fine ice cream, which, with the strawberries and milk, eat most deliciously.' Both George Washington and Thomas Jefferson were known to have served it at state functions.

Madame Henrietta d'Angleterre, sister of Charles II, did indeed die after drinking a glass of iced chicory water. Although poison was suspected at the time, it is now thought her death was the result of peritonitis caused by a perforated ulcer. The secret Treaty of Dover which she had worked so hard for, and which was signed two weeks before her death, was known to no more than a dozen people in England, including Louise de Keroualle. It included the clause, 'The King of England will make a public profession of the Catholic faith, and will receive the sum of two million crowns to aid him in this project from the Most Christian King, in the course of the next six months. The date of this declaration is left absolutely to his own pleasure.' It is perhaps not surprising that Charles flatly denied the existence of this treaty to Parliament, when he was questioned about it in 1675: 'There is no other treaty with France, either before or since, not already printed, which shall not be made known.' A copy of the treaty was finally found and published in 1830.

Records kept by the French ambassador in London show that the French spent many millions of crowns bribing English politicians and ministers during this time. It seems likely, although it has never been proved, that France's ultimate aim was to swallow up the Netherlands and then invade England, possibly using the pretext of rescuing a Catholic Charles II from his own Parliament. This would have left Germany isolated as the last remaining major Protestant country in Europe.

The Royal Society, otherwise known as the Royal Society of London for the Improvement of Natural Knowledge, was established by Charles II in 1660. It numbered among its early members and guests Robert Boyle, Isaac Newton, Christopher Wren, Samuel Pepys, John Hooke, Gottfried Leibniz, Nicholas

Mercator, John Locke and Edmond Halley, to name just a few. Boyle was particularly interested in freezing, and his essay 'Observations touching Cold' was one of the first texts to investigate artificial freezing methods scientifically. He may have been influenced by the fact that, at the time, Europe was undergoing 'the little ice age', which led to frost fairs being held on the River Thames. Other members' interests ranged from how to make champagne bottles to the laws of light and motion. They are generally credited with being the first thinkers of the Enlightenment.

Reading Group Questions for
The Empress of Ice Cream

1. The Editor's Note says that the two stories, Louise's and Carlo's, might seem 'odd companions'. Did you find that to be the case? How did their narratives differ?
2. Were you surprised to discover that ice cream was invented in England? Did you find the historical background more or less interesting than other historical novels you have read?
3. Louise has to choose between the honourable marriage her parents brought her up to believe in, and becoming the king's mistress in order to achieve her political aims. Do you think she made the right choice?
4. Cold – and its opposite, warmth – are recurrent themes in the book. Who are the coldest characters, and who did you warm to?
5. Which characters changed most over the course of the novel? What made them change?
6. Were Carlo's relationships with the women in his life fair and equal?
7. What drove Louise to make the decisions she did?
8. How do Louise's views on status and success compare to those of Hannah?
9. What disruptions to class relations have taken place in post-civil war England, and how do Carlo's ideas about who should be allowed to eat ice cream reflect these changes?
10. How strongly does food influence events in the novel?
11. *The Empress of Ice Cream* moves from Italy to France and then to England. How does the change in setting reflect in the changes in the characters' lives?
12. Is Louise a character you can easily empathise with?
13. Did *The Empress of Ice Cream* end the way you expected it to?
14. How did you think the epigraph from Wallace Stevens related to the story?
15. Do you think Carlo will end up finding happiness?

Acknowledgements

I am, once again, deeply indebted to my readers at AP Watt: Caradoc King, Elinor Cooper and Louise Lamont, and my editors Rebecca Saunders, at Little, Brown, and Louise Davies, all of whom who helped me turn a book into a story.

Those who want to make the ice creams I describe should get *Ices: the Definitive Guide* by Caroline Liddell and Robin Weir (also published as *Frozen Desserts* and *The Ice Cream Book*), which includes many recipes from old cookbooks. Traditional recipes are also available at www.historicfood.com. My greatest debt, however, is to the book which first gave me the idea for this novel: Elizabeth David's *Harvest of the Cold Months*, a history of ice cream and ices.

Louise de Keroualle's biography was first written by Henri Forneron under the title *The Court of Charles II*. It is not a particularly sympathetic account. 'For fifteen years Louise de Keroualle held Great Britain in her delicate little hand, and manipulated its king and statesmen . . . as she might have done her fan,' is a fairly typical comment. The letters I use in Part Three between Colbert, Louvois and Louis XIV are taken directly from his translations.

Nell Gwyn's descendant Charles Beauclerk has written a fascinating biography of his ancestor which describes the rivalry between the royal mistresses. My description of the game of Questions and Commands, at which Louise contrived to lose the clothes of herself and her ladies-in-waiting in order to induce Charles to prorogue Parliament, is taken from that book, although I moved the date by a year.

While many of the events in *The Empress of Ice Cream* took place as I describe, Louise de Keroualle's ice palace is based on the one ordered by Empress Anna Ivanovna of Russia in 1740, described by Ivan Lazhechnkov in his book *The Ice Palace*.